On Wandering Planet

JEAN HARRISON

Published by Cinnamon Press
Meirion House
Tanygrisiau
Blaenau Ffestiniog
Gwynedd LL41 3SU
www.cinnamonpress.com

The right of Jean Harrison to be identified as author of this work has been asserted by her in accordance with the Copyright, Designs and Patent Act, 1988. © 2015 Jean Harrison.
ISBN 978-1-909077-70-6
British Library Cataloguing in Publication Data. A CIP record for this book can be obtained from the British Library.
All rights reserved. No part of this publication may be reproduced, stored in a retrieval system, or transmitted in any form or by any means, electronic, mechanical, photocopying, recording or otherwise without the prior written permission of the publishers. This book may not be lent, hired out, resold or otherwise disposed of by way of trade in any form of binding or cover other than that in which it is published, without the prior consent of the publishers.
Designed and typeset in Garamond by Cinnamon Press. Cover design by Adam Craig © Adam Craig.
Cinnamon Press is represented by Inpress and by the Welsh Books Council in Wales.
Printed in Poland

Acknowledgements

I should like to thank the following people for their time, patience and attention to changing versions of this book and for criticisms they have made: Anne McInnes for long attention to the first version, Elizabeth Burns for a meticulous examination of the text, Gillian Walton, Freda Beveridge for reading and commenting, Jan Fortune for quantities of encouragement – and of course to Barbara Bowman for listening time after time. Also to Debbie Clegg for relieving me of housework so that I had time to write.

ON A WANDERING PLANET

Part 1

Pock, pock, pock. I can hear it now.

The woman I'm telling you about – and she was a real woman – hadn't been generated by a computer though she often felt like it – but sometimes she checked and it was obvious she breathed, slept, ate, digested, produced a normal quantity of urine and shit requiring visits to the methy at what seemed to be standard intervals – blood too, of course: it was only that she felt unreal – though what she was doing just then – heating a mug of green protein soup – was real enough. She'd've been wearing her blue vansuit most likely – there's a feeling of ease and the blue was always more comfortable – the brown would have been spread over the table to dry – it was difficult in the life she'd got herself into to get things washed and ironed. And then she heard it, *pock, pock, pock*, approaching roughly from the south. Wembley, the old name leapt into her mind before she could stop it.

From the Freedom Centre. That should be OK. A routine journey. *Pock pock* passed directly overhead, continued in a straight line, faded. The book would have been lying beside the sink. She reached out and touched it, picked it up, carried it and the mug to the table under the window at the back of the van. Seated with crossed legs, turned sideways so she could see out if she lifted her head – kind of habit, hoping to see a sparrow or something – she sank into Jane Austen's world. That was the sort of unreal thing she used to do, unreal in her situation I mean – though the book had been Elizabeth's. Just then she wasn't thinking of her, simply escaping to a place where young ladies could walk in fields even if they did get their hems muddy.

Pock, pock. It was circling back. Her fingers tightened on the book. Hardback. Solid covers. A weight in the hand.

Real. Not virtual. The pock was real too. The branches of the oak that leant out overhead were beginning to toss, the van shook. Wind from the blades. A machine she still couldn't see was poising itself for the descent – that symbol of perfection, the spotless 'cherub'. Inside it a Freeguard was gazing down. He'd have spotted the white roof through the sheltering leaves.

She closed the book. It was obvious they'd find her one day. This was simply that day. She stood up still holding the book, re-opened it for a quick glance – possibly her finger touched words written inside the front cover. 'With love from Elizabeth', a date before the New Dawn. She certainly snapped it shut, pushed it down between the seat and the side of the van, pulled a cushion over, reached for her mask, clipped on her see-can, checked the angle of the mike, tugged on roll-shoes, opened the door, stepped down onto bare ground. Waited.

Air from the cherub's blades blew the legs of her vansuit against her calves. She watched dust eddy as the wheels scraped to a stop. Earth flying loose, tiny fragments of stone catching the sun, glinting and falling. Almost alive. The door slid back. A man in uniform got out. She made the shoes carry her a short way towards him and stood again, firming her knees, trying to relax her shoulders. Once or twice recently she'd gone outside in van-shoes, testing the way her soles sensed the ground, her toes spread to grip it. If you wanted not to stay rooted you had to flex your ankle, put a spring in your step. Back on wheels now she stiffened, as if mechanical motion transformed her into a robot.

The Free didn't bother with roll-shoes. They weren't compulsory and any way worked better on tarmac than these loose stones. The grey uniform fitted rather too tightly over a plump body. He wasn't wearing a mask – perhaps because of his spectacular glasses. Those up-curved wings above his eyebrows – How long since they'd been fashionable? His cheeks were pudgy, his chin slightly bristly. Much her age, she judged.

He read the number on her mask's forehead and checked it against the van. '24AV 2111/301?'

'Yes.'

He fed it into his computer and waited. 'Female M. T. Just you alone?'

'Had a trav but she died.'

'I'm sorry,' he said slowly as if he actually felt something. 'That was Female E. A.?'

'Yes.'

'And now we seem to have lost you from our records.'

'Light's gone out.' She watched visible lips move, the whole stretch of them, a chin, the whole stubby curve of it, a pinkish pimple. She looked away, over his shoulder at the sky and trees, conventionally shocked by a bare face – or threatened? Shouldn't have let her eyes rest on the trees and the sky either.

'Could have phoned in.'

'Phone went off at the same time.'

'You didn't disable it, I suppose?'

She spread her arms. 'Do I look as if I'd know how?' She was forced to look at him now.

His glance ran over her from head to foot. 'Probably not.' No way of telling whether he was amused or slightly derisive. 'I'll have to come and take a look.'

She stood aside as he swung himself up more lithely than she'd expected. He extracted some sort of little gadget from a pocket, kind of mini-computer with an eye, pointed it at the corner of the ceiling where the red connection light had gone dark, took a reading. 'Pass me that chair.'

She shoved it at him and watched as he climbed on, moved his machine slowly and delicately all round the fixture, slid it back in his pocket and ran his fingers along a groove, unscrewed something, felt into the space behind it, bare human fingers probing delicately, still used, even then, to test an object.

He climbed down. 'The fault's at our end. Someone probably just flicked the wrong switch.'

'The human element?'

'Eh?' The eyes behind those thick lenses were probably blue.

'Just a memory. Before the New Dawn, you know? Boss I worked under, whenever someone didn't hand in the statistics on time, would always mutter, 'The human element,' meaning there was something even his system couldn't control.'

'See-can.'

She activated the camera beside the mike, watched it flash while a Free miles away went through the formality of reading the number on her mask, checking it for the second time against the van.

At last he smiled. 'Not everything changes.'

But his gaze swung up over her shoulder, his mouth fell open, the lines of his face hardened. He pushed her aside, strode down the van to the end window, put his nose almost to the glass.

It had to come. The moment she'd removed that strand of barbed wire blocking the almost defunct track that led in here, she'd known it couldn't last, the moment she'd fished out that bean from a crack beside the bed she'd known she ought to throw it away. With disgust. Wiping her fingers. Instead, she'd stood there an age holding a wizened leftover, rubbing its blotched skin, remembering things he'd think she ought to have put aside for ever. Might have indulged forbidden thoughts.

So what? You do what you do, don't you?

She'd planted it and now he'd seen the leaves.

'D'you mind if I take a look outside?'

As he reached the ground he threw his head back. She came down and stood beside him. No need to look up. She knew what he could see – over the white curve of the roof, against the sky, red buds just opening, petals like wings. She followed him round, hardly aware she was pulling her arms into her sides to prevent them flying out to grab him and pull him back. Part of her, even then inside the robot she thought she'd become, wanted to scream, throw herself onto the ground, to rush at him and pummel him, do all she could to protect what seemed to be her children. Another part stood back, said it didn't care. Nothing was worth it now.

He was staring at the ground as if transfixed. She knew how it was. His mind would run off picturing long white worms wriggling down into the dirt – roots – tying a plant to one place, and the seed from which they'd grown, that hard little nugget, yet a womb to tendrils that could grow up and strangle you. Any proper person felt sick at the thought. And he was a Freeguard, a guardian of the people's freedom.

His eyes followed the stem up over the white paint, took in how support had been provided, rested again on the flowers. 'Well,' he said, 'a scarlet runner.'

Her eyes widened at the sound of the name. His mouth twisted. 'These too,' he said harshly, gesturing towards the row of pansies. '

She shrugged.

He turned slowly towards her. There was black hair growing out of his ears. 'My dad had a vegetable patch.'

She stared over his shoulder.

His voice came more firmly. 'We did it for their sake, remember?'

'These were never wild plants.'

'You know what I mean. You and I – sorry to make assumptions about your age. Don't mind, do you? Both of us were old enough to understand what we were doing. All other forms of life, we said. We'd separate ourselves from them for their sake? Humans couldn't be trusted to look after them. We'd live our lives and let them have theirs. That was it, wasn't it?'

'Yes,' she said, lowering her eyes, the only things that betrayed you, peering out through holes in a mask, 'yes, it was.'

'You can't tie yourself down like this. You must move on.' He leant forward, his words came in earnest gasps. 'There's nothing in this sort of thing. Understand? Nothing. Death lies this way, tied down, not moving on.'

She gazed at the ground. What was death? Just a great calm, perhaps?

'Look now, don't get upset. If these weren't here tomorrow –'

She went on looking down, bowing her head, submitting.

He took out a little notebook and made a note. 'Tomorrow then. Around 16.00 hours. If they're all gone I'll give you a clearance certificate. Get you back on the road. OK?' He snapped a band round the notebook. 'OK?'

She raised her eyes. He was being decent. 'OK.'

Instead of rushing back to the cherub, he lingered, looking round, clearing his throat. 'You'll be glad in the end. To be free, you know.' Then, when she still didn't smile he stroked the van. 'Vanacar. Good make this.' He walked slowly along the side caressing the paint as he went. 'Still in beautiful nick,' sweeping his arm out in a great circle and bending as he came to the rear so he could take in the curves of the mudguards. 'Such elegance. Don't make them like that nowadays, do they? Road-holding still good? May be difficult to get tyres. D'you find that?'

She watched, dumb as a pile of worn tyres. Trying to lift the ends of her mouth. Hearing the gentleness in his voice.

Those absurd spectacles flashed as he turned towards her. 'Don't mind me saying it? You're too much alone. Should join a Fem-tog.'

She nodded, forced a smile into her voice, 'You're probably right. Thanks.'

'Off now. See you tomorrow.'

'OK.'

He raised his hand in a gesture of old-fashioned courtesy. 'Joyful travelling, driver.'

' ... travelling.'

After he'd gone she sat a long time.

A blue tit tapped a twig. A chaffinch sang. A pair of sparrows had an argument.

She watched. A robin perched splay-legged and leant towards her, turning one eye as if it still expected a human to get going with a spade and throw it a worm.

If that hedge hadn't been there – and it shouldn't have been – she wouldn't have come through a gap left by careless slobs supposed to be fixing parking slots the other side. End of the day probably. Perhaps thought they'd come back. That's why they left the opening to the old track with only a few strands of barbed wire and a pile of old planks to bar it. They'd meant to come back next day, tar this section of the overnight, put in security screens, get it all up to standard and then had been called off to something else, or decided they'd get paypoints for it any way if they logged it as that day's work. No need actually to do it. No-one would come to inspect.

So this ancient privet hedge had been spared. And the oak whose thick leaves had so far prevented any Free nosing around in a cherub from spotting the van. Could this one must have been sent specially?

Both privet and oak perhaps had once been someone's garden. Someone had pruned and trimmed, two or three times each summer. Hard work, privet but a good, dense cover. When you kept it tidy it never flowered – so could be they hadn't enjoyed the same richness of scent she'd stumbled into. Or the buzz of busy insects. Sitting here she'd seen creatures she hadn't caught sight of for years, hoverflies, bumble-bees, and in the evenings, pale moths flapping in the gathering dark. As soon as she'd drawn up here that first evening – of course she hadn't done anything as furtive as to glance up and down along the line of locked screens to make sure nobody was looking – nosed her way in, put back the wire and the planks exactly as they had been, parked under the oak, she'd jumped out, run – simply couldn't stop herself – buried her face in those bunches of soft white flowers, revelled in that cloying scent. When she raised her face her cheeks had been smeared with tiny flowers. She'd given in to something that had felt like tears.

As things were now the workmen would return. Their robots would hack down the hedge, tear it out of the ground, take the trash off to burn, fell the oak, extract the stump. Nothing would be left.

So what?

Disgust was a good protection, the shame at the idea of roots and seeds, of clinging plants or soft-eyed mammals. It had been necessary to take it in, absorb it, make it absolutely part of you and then you could separate yourself from nature, refuse to do it any further damage. She and Elizabeth had gone into the question time after time watching and listening in the months after the New Dawn and always come to the same conclusion.

A wood pigeon took off from the oak with a clap of its wings. She pictured its plump body extended in flight and then those absurd spectacles the Freeguard had been wearing. Just before the New Dawn it had been wings with everything.

How had he managed to hold onto them all that time? His eyes surely must have changed? Eyes always did as you got older.

That year she'd bought a pair of boots, tight round the calves, opening at the top in a pair of wings that looked as if they sprang from the knees. She'd pranced into the sitting-room, put one foot on the seat of a chair, 'Look, Elizabeth.' And Elizabeth had been doubled up.

That was what she was like, you know, even then when disease was already thinning her down.

Why bother to go on? She could refuse to move her plants. Let the authorities tear them up if they must. She wouldn't put her hand to it. Would arm herself to stand by and watch them. Perhaps that was why she'd done it – to provoke them? Whoever knew why they did things? All sorts of strange reasons. Prepare to be locked away. An underground cell in the dark would be quiet and still.

But the darkness? She wasn't the stuff of which heroes are made.

She pulled herself to her feet. She'd go up the shopping centre, come back with a bottle, sozzle herself to sleep.

As soon as she passed the barbed wire she was in the grey world of security screens. Long rows of parking slots stretched right and left to the far perimeters of the overnight, each with its own iron door with a number painted on it. She stood at the junction reading 2501 – 2750 to the right, 2751- 3000 to the left. Those that were occupied were already locked shut. A light wind sent an empty Splatt bottle scudding across the tarmac and made the long metal walls shake and rattle. She remembered how the first night behind the hedge she'd been aware of the sudden absence of scrape and squeak.

The ground underfoot seemed unusually hard and looking down she realised she was still wearing her van-shoes. She swung out her legs, began to feel better. The main road and cycle-track to the shopping centre stretched straight ahead. The motorway itself must still be at least a kilometre off.

A Volta Airborne approached rather to fast over the calmers. Its lamps caught the sun as it suddenly swung right almost over her toes. She stared at them, unprotected in red lycra. Two more cars approached. All the slots near the centre must be taken by now. She caught the eyes of their drivers, glaring downwards toward her feet.

Go back, she thought, go back instantly and put on your roll-shoes. They were only a convention, just something to show you were a driver. No law that said you had to be always on wheels, only a belief that pedestrians were scum. She wanted to walk. Obstinate? Pig-headed? She wanted to walk. Which took a lot longer than skating.

After a quarter of an hour she realised the centre was much further away than she had imagined. Her calves were already beginning to ache. If she went on tiring herself at that rate – she saw herself slumped on the piazza steps, exhausted. The dark would be coming down. At the hooter, anyone who hadn't already done so would lock their screen. Without roll-shoes no-one could give her a tow.

A body struck her from behind, then another. She staggered forward, arms flailing, into the road. Two bicycles shot past. Heavier wheels ground on the tarmac. A horn blasted. She scrabbled back to the edge, caught a driver glaring.

On the far side of the road two small figures had come to a halt, fingers to the noses of their masks. She didn't need to hear what they were yelling, 'Yah seedy poltic, out the way you git.'

She turned instantly, walking as long as they could see her, then running, throwing herself awkwardly into this unaccustomed motion, tore open the barricade over the gap in the hedge, heaved it back into place, panted up to the van, struggled with the key, climbed in. Collapsed. The familiar walls folded around her. Sweat washed her ribs.

It was that heat. It bounced off the screens, radiated from the ground. The only shade was hard-edged. Even in light shoes your feet thudded on the tarmac. The ground didn't sway like the van floor but hit back through your soles, hard, totally ungiving.

Gradually she began to shiver, wrapped her arms round her. Why had she gone out? No point going out just to realise you were alone. And now it dawned on her the hedge didn't cut out all the sound. It still got to you, a distant, incessant itch.

She heaved herself up, dragged slowly to the front of the van, bent to the bottom drawer of her workstation, hesitated, drew out a notebook. Her thumb rubbed shiny blue plastic, rested on a rising sun embossed in the centre.

She turned to the second page. There was blue ink, Elizabeth's formal italic. *We left 96, Sydenham Road for our free life at 5.27 pm, Thursday, Day 1 of the New Dawn,*

Signed: Elizabeth Armley.

Underneath it her own scrawl, *Miranda Talbot.*

In the right hand bottom corner, cut to a neat circle, Elizabeth had stuck a photo of Soccie looking smugly over the edge of his basket on the top step of the van.

She stared, pushed the book back into the drawer, clipped on her roll-shoes.

She struck the wheels down hard onto the tarmac, remembered how you could make sparks that way. She drifted to a standstill watching Elizabeth, herself, Ed perhaps, a group of friends in the early days of the New Dawn circling and circling, stamping, sparks flying up. Adults behaving like kids. She could see them laughing, falling into each other's arms. So if today she stamped and made sparks? If she struck out fast, rhythmical? The stench of burning tyres drifted across from one of the crash yards, thinned by distance but still bitter.

Lights flashed off the roofs of bubble cars to her left. They were darting about like boiled sweets on the bub-course, twisting, swinging, leaping from low hillocks. In one corner was formation driving, lines passing at speed between each other, re-forming, plaiting a complicated, risky pattern. A junior would be grinning at the wheel of each. Who could be sour about such joy?

Yet she didn't feel it.

She came to a halt at the foot of the Piazza steps, kicked each foot forward in turn, felt the wheels click back into their slots. She set herself to climb the ribbed concrete.

Years ago – so far back she could remember flounces bouncing on her calves – and that must have been ages – before Safety banned all flounces, fringes, flowing scarves, trains etc – too easily caught in van-steps – there'd been some nasty accidents – somewhere way back in that early period she and Elizabeth had climbed an artificial mountain like this. It came back so clearly. Elizabeth had been wearing green as usual – that long dress embroidered with poppies – bronze scarf thrown round her shoulders – long dark tresses shining against it. She'd run her eyes slowly over the construction, following the ramps that curved up both sides of the steps and then, taking to the air, twisted like rams-horns before attaching themselves to balconies on the second floor. Above rose them two more storeys, a mansard roof, fluted gables in black and white concrete, corner turrets, brass balls on jets of water on the roof between them, tossed up and down. 'I love it,' she'd said, 'I absolutely love it. This absurd, exuberant theme park feel. There's never been anything like it before.'

That was how they'd all felt then. A brave new world.

The robot who sold her a purple Vit C smiled gently, 'Fine day, driver.'

She nodded, swallowed, wondered if she should have asked for pink, found herself studying his? – its? face. How did you think about a robot? They looked human but only a machine could endure life attached to one place. They watched over you, attended to your needs, smiled, laughed even – if something triggered that as the appropriate reaction. Some drivers alleged – and there was no proof –

she wasn't sure you really could do this – but the story went – these things weren't made in factories. A rumour existed that these were criminals who'd undergone brain surgery. This creature who'd smiled so nicely at her could once have been a murderer or a rapist. She pulled her arms into her to hold down the shudder, then thought, maybe it is better for him. Perhaps he's happy now. Perhaps that what's needed for happiness to last – to become a machine?

'I'll have a whisky.' She downed it, asked for another, began to feel warmer. On top of things now. Had really been letting herself go. Mustn't do that. No. Keep on top.
She slid off her stool, raised her hand to the barman, 'Gogo.' Always go nowadays, not come. You never arrived. Joke that was, idea of arriving.

'Gogo, he replied watching her. She felt there was a judgement in his eyes. How could you stand that – being judged by a robot? She swung off through the automatic doors that led to the news room.

It was cooler here and her head swam less. She wandered vaguely between banks of computers where intent drivers were leaning forward focussing on screens, eventually parked herself at an empty place, switched on, carefully typed in 'personal.' The little Freeguard had passed judgement. He had no right. Didn't know. Her life not his.

Read this all the same. Pass the time. Something to do. 'Drivers looking for 'Hitchmates' – Hunh. Why not 'travs'? Travs stayed too long, that's what, stood by you. No-one stood by anyone now. Shared adventure that had been the idea. Long term. Meant something. Now 'Male D' – driver that was – 'looking for male, Male D looking for female, female D looking for male, female looking for female.' All hitchmates. For a few months, couple of years. Then babies, bust ups. Usually the female kept the kids. Easier for her. Back to mother's van, travel with her. Perhaps sisters and their kids as well.

That kind of Fem-tog closed to her. No family..

Type it in all the same. Something wrong with this machine. Three shots to get spelling and that – little line up in the air – right. Interesting names these drivers had. Unrelated females, who drove together in small flocks, carrying on some kind of trade or business usually. Their children all put together, one family. They'd all have separate vans, might take a joint parking slot for the night. She'd heard them sometimes, laughing and talking the other side of screens. There'd been the scrape of chair and table legs on hard ground, the clink of glasses, the smell of rich proteins, children running about.

Didn't need that sort of closeness. Better to be loose, not to be one to one with anyone.

She began to scroll through the list. And stopped. 'The Jongleurs.' Really good name that.

Samantha, Carole, Emma, Beth, Marlie and Phenna. Six of them. Good number. Not too many. Enough for each to have own space. They wanted 'another woman, part-time business manager, part-time tutor for their children.' Extra to the Dawn-treaders' curriculum but the tutor 'would need to be familiar with it.' No problem. Taught it every day – what a joke – how could you teach students who switched off their screens soon as they realised teacher was at the other end? As for the business side, knew how to reckon pay-points, save, accumulate, format – yeah – format records – could do that. As for the business – what was it? Acrobats – oh! Performed on wheels on high wires. Lots of overnights would hire them a display ground. Never actually come across them – but they'd be good. Sure of that. That sort of entertainment interesting. Way the wheels flashed along the wires, how the performers' jumps and turns struck out showers of multi-coloured stars, the way your heart was in your mouth, you trembled, terrified someone would miss and come crashing to the ground. And the artists balanced on one foot, spread their arms, stepped past each other, spines straight, heads back, swinging their legs sideways, smiling, They flew as acrobats always had, swung from bars, arched their backs, stretched their whole body forward, landed on slender ramps, glided up then down.

She'd get to see that every day. Not do it. Not the stuff performers made of. But to watch. From a table at the door, clicking in pay-points. Could manage that. Negotiate rents with overnight managers. Other sources of funding. Course she'd find them. Authorities adored this kind of troupe. Drivers out of one another's hair.

What about the kids? Could be a pain, though this bunch didn't look like it. Seven of them. Jo, 16, Mil, 15 – full drivers – so what could she teach them? Never mind, find something. Axel, 13, Tyrella, 10 – juniors, something possible there; then twins, Bolt and Nut aged 9 – still unlies, avid probably to get their first licenses – and Wheeleeera, 4 – Wheee the document said they called her for short. Wh-h-h-heee, the whisper of well-inflated tyres on a smooth surface, the sound a parent makes, picking up a small child, holding her overhead or swinging her round,   'W h - h - h - heee. The child laughing.

Long brown curls, hugging herself. Enormous smile. Wheeleeera.

So long since she'd been with real kids in a classroom. Not always bliss but still. Only seven of this lot. Perhaps mostly only three. Looking at her. Or away. Answering, shouting out, excited. Or dreaming. Entering their own worlds.

Supplement the curriculum? No problem. Her mouse hovered over the button.

She couldn't do it. Not yet. Too much effort. If it kept her out of trouble? Did she care if she were in trouble?

Tomorrow. Evening.

*

Her waking next morning was a sudden crumpling under a heavy weight. She lay with her eyes closed longing to slip back into unfeeling. Eventually she dragged herself out.

From that moment she moved fast. What had to be done had to be done. She tried to make herself think about the twins, Nut and Bolt, little Whee, the Jongleurs pirouetting along their wires. They seemed very pale and far off. She couldn't believe this morning they'd ever accept a driver who'd apparently tried to undermine the New Dawn. They'd think she must have given in to unhealthy thoughts. Want to protect the children from her.

She didn't care, that was all. She picked up a pair of scissors and the old spoon she'd used before, went round to the back of the van. The scarlet runner was the hardest task. She couldn't transplant it. The only solution was to cut it right down to the ground. A waste of time even to leave the roots in hiding. Soon as she was gone they'd send in a workforce to tarmac the whole area. She cut, tugged, dragged the trailing stems across to the hedge on the far side, pushed them underneath. At least they would fulfil their natural function of making compost.

She dug out the pansies, keeping large rootballs of soft earth put them in a kitchen bowl, carried it without spilling to the gap she'd wriggled through before.

It was harder to find now the bushes were in full leaf but she was able to push aside swinging branches and come to the ruined walls. The ground round them was covered with cow parsley and bluebells. The scent of wild garlic rose round her feet. Outcrops of crumbling and broken yellow brick suggested that Watford – or perhaps this had been Kings Langley – they'd both been somewhere round here – had not been scraped away as completely as it should at the New Dawn. Not surprising. Such a whole-scale enterprise, to demolish every single house. People, even drivers, could always be careless. There must be many other hidden ruins sinking back into nature.

She'd found the pansies growing in the warmth close to the bricks, seen those markings as faces. To express it unvarnished she'd been a sentimental poltic.

Several clumps were still growing undisturbed. As she watched a bumble-bee sail in. White tailed. She stood quietly till it had taken all it wanted and buzzed off. Then she knelt and inserted her spoon into the earth.

It dug in dividing the granules cleanly. She enlarged the hole with her bare hands, pulled the sides apart, made a little hump at the bottom over which the roots would spread, poured in water, gently lowered the first plant, firmed the soil round it, watered again. Damp leaf mould and fragments of soil clung to her fingers.

The sun was warm on her back so, as was natural, she lingered over her work, easing and patting, not, of course, imagining the flowers were smiling up and thanking her for her care, or suppressing the knowledge she was playing with dirt, that these thoughts were slimy, that plants were a different order of being, not surrogate humans.

Suddenly she stiffened, sat back on her heels, swung round into a line of light pointed at her neck. At the far end a black crescent – a filthy thumbnail – a grimy hand, beyond it a torn sleeve half showing a thin arm, above that again, a small shoulder, draggly black hair, pointed ears, horned head, great gash of red lips, Devil Driver mask, child's. 'Keep still, you seedy poltic.'

Her lips were stiff. She went on staring. A junior. About ten years probably.

'You needn't think I wouldn't do it.' The voice was light for a ten year old but that was the size he seemed. 'Needn't think I'd miss. Show you, shall I?'

Her eyes were fixed. He slowly transferred the knife to his left hand watching her all the time, drew out a smaller blade from a sheath attached to his belt, bent his arm so his hand was level with his shoulder. 'See that bird?'

A blackbird, unaccustomed to humans, too bold, turning and tossing leaves. A sharp flash. The bird fell on its side. Blood trickled over a heap of quivering feathers.
'Got it?'

He was calm, ummoved by what he'd done so easily, so accurately. She nodded.

'Won't move, will you.' Not a question. She shook her head and watched as he walked sideways, knife always towards her, reached down to the body, pulled out the blade he'd thrown, wiped it on the leg of his vansuit, slid it back in its sheath, came back and stood so close the point of the knife was almost touching her neck. 'Get up.'

She got.

'Walk.'

She drew herself to her full height, stared down into his face, met his indifferent gaze, turned and walked the direction his gesture indicated. Though she towered over him, she had to walk. This was ridiculous.

He drove her like a sheep though the swinging branches, across the black, dusty ground to the steps of the van.

'Open it.'

She scrabbled in her pockets as if searching for a key.

'Not playing games. Saw you, didn't I? Know what sort you are. Didn't lock it, did you?'

She stumbled up, swung the door open and he followed.

'Now get the key and give it me.'

She took it from its hook and handed it over. He locked the door, dropped the key in his pocket.

Her knees were shaking. 'Mind if I sit?'

'Who d'you think you're talking to?'

She hesitated. 'Don't know.'

'Boss, that's me. You call me Boss.'

'Yes.'

The knife nicked the skin of her throat. 'Yes, Boss.'

'Yes, Boss.'

'Better. Now make me tea.'

'Yes, Boss.'

'And nosh. Good and sweet. Quick.' He flung himself back on a seat, spread his legs.

'Yes, Boss.' The Freeguard would come this afternoon. She quickly boiled water, filled a mug, opened a tin. She didn't normally keep biscuits or cake but recently she'd been indulging. Comfort eating, she now suspected. She handed over the food and sat down herself. He didn't seem to be objecting.

What skin of his she could see was grey, worn, his hair fell in rat-tails over his ears, a bruise stained the back of his hand. But no, this wasn't an undergrown youth. The curves of wrist-bones under the strained flesh were gentle. The mask wasn't. Or the sprawled body. It looked deadly tired, undernourished and yet relaxed. The kind of relaxation that came from not caring. He didn't care what happened to her. Or even to him. For the moment he was comfortable. That was all that mattered. Well, the Freeguard would come.

'When you expecting him?'

'Who?'

He snapped upright. 'What I tell you to call me?'

'Boss.'

'Don't pretend you don't understand. I been watching, know everything, see? That's how I know the sort you are. In trouble aren't you,' he said softly, 'big trouble?'

'Yes. In a way – Boss. Getting it sorted.'

He relaxed back. Tapped the flat of the blade up and down on his knee. 'Needn't think you're going to hand me over.'

'No, Boss.'

'So when's he coming?'

'Didn't say, Boss. Afternoon sometime.'

The leer of that mask was bloodcurdling. 'I'll be waiting.'

'OK, Boss.' She looked at his wiry frame. Heaven only knew what he'd do or where he'd try to hide but if he said he'd do something he would.

'I'll hear every word. If you try anything on I'll get you – and then – curtains. The pair of you, got it?'

'Yes Boss.' This conversation was becoming boring. But not unreal. Just repetitive, over-emphatic. Though not that. He meant it. Not melodramatic either. It was the flatness in his voice. The flatness of someone who didn't relate.

That made two of them – though something flickered inside her, not as definite as anger – something that said this situation was ridiculous. How had she got into it? Indeed how had she? She'd had no idea there was any risk.

By wandering off. He'd seen her brush side that undergrowth, known she shouldn't be there, latched onto her weakness.

She had years of experience. Surely she could cope?

He leant back, his eyes closed. The fingers of her right hand clenched. He wasn't far off. One quick dart and she'd have it. The knife in her grip. She tensed.

His eyelids flashed open. She sank back. Wait. With that weight of tiredness he'd drop off. Deeply. Soon.

A screen door clanged the other side of the hedge. A bee bumbled in at the side window and began buzzing against the glass. She watched him breathing. Pushed her hand against the back of the seat. Immediately he stirred. His eyes opened.

The bee was still banging its head against the glass, flying up, dropping to the sill, running along, climbing again, never finding the way it had come in. Her knees tautened for the leap. His eyes opened. Where had he learnt to be like that, never fully relaxed, never apparently finding deep sleep?

Grimy fingers rested on the thighs of a torn vansuit, skin showed palely through the hole. She wondered what soft curves were hidden under that leather. Where had he been? Had he had anyone to look after him? What kind of person?

The number across his mask's forehead had been roughly scraped off, not entirely erased. It might be possible with an effort to reconstruct it. What had he used? A large stone, a flint maybe? She imagined that grubby hand backwards and forwards as a child bent over his task, tongue protruding maybe, the way it often did when they wrote, using a Stone Age tool, leaving traces someone later might decipher.

By now he'd have gone feral. If so, there could be others. Would he go and fetch a pack? What did he want? The van? Did he plan to kill her and take it? Were his mates waiting? A gang of them, ready to swarm in? The Freeguard was coming. They rounded up feral children.

She longed to turn on a warm shower, hand him a soft cloth, soap, a towel, say, 'Here you are. Get on with it,' see him emerge, wet hair smoothed over his forehead, brighter eyed. Whatever had happened couldn't have been his fault. Someone had given up, not cared, thrown him out maybe. Left him behind. Moved on. Or died.

That didn't make him, as he was now, less dangerous. Too young to understand fully the consequences of what he chose to do. Not seeing a choice of actions. In his despair he'd go for the most obvious, the most violent. The Freeguard would know what to do.

The twins Bolt and Nut. In the photo standing with their legs apart, grinning shyly. They'd be ace on skateboards. Lovely, solid kids. Wheeleera, eyeing the world through her curls, head tilted sideways. Could be a madam, no doubt. You'd bite your tongue and love her.

Couldn't care that much. Not now.

The bee swung back from the window, circled up, blundered out into the open air. She rested back against the cushions. This evening she'd reply to that advert. All that was needed was patience. Where did this 'Boss' imagine he was going to hide?

What did the Frees do with feral children? She'd never seen or heard of a Home.

There'd be something.

The gap through the broken palisades into bushes that hid the ruined walls was the other side of hundreds of square yards of bare earth. He couldn't have heard from there. Perhaps he'd just watched and come to his own conclusions? He was probably no fool.

Or – could he have sprinted across when she wasn't looking, shinned up the oak, been right overhead when she was talking to the Freeguard? Had he been there spying while she planted and watered? Made a habit of it? Sussed her out.

He'd be relying on the tree today. From its branches he could see straight down both sides of the van. She considered closely. There was just one place near the steps where she could whisper something or slip a note.

So that was OK.

Silence curdled round her. The brown afternoon dragged on. The roar of distant motorways seemed almost soothing.

The red ceiling light flashed on. *Pock. Pock.* Still distant. She tensed and his head jerked up. He grasped the knife, stood up, came across, rested the point on her chest, bent forward, whispered into her face, 'Needn't think you can grass. Soon as you try, I'll get you.'

She gazed through the mask, the first time in years she'd looked into eyes. 'Boss, give me that knife. You're boss without it. I won't tell, I promise.'

Sharp steel pressed harder.

'Give it me, Boss.'

'Think I'm silly?' It was amazing, the sneer he could get into his voice.

'Boss, this is sense. This is what a man would do. He'd see what the sensible thing was to do. He'd hand it over and be proud. A real man isn't a thug.'

'Show you, shall I, what a man did to me?' He pulled open the top of his vansuit. A white D of scar-tissue, standing on his chest. 'Want my mark, do you?'

'No, Boss,' she whispered, 'no.'

He straightened. 'Remember then.'

'Yes, Boss.' And he was gone.

She was glad the number printed on her mask drew attention to the van, not her. Vans had no expressions. She clipped it over her face, came down the steps, firmed her body, held her knees tight against each other and waited while the cherub came to rest. The shadow of the oak tree stretched a third of the way toward it.

The door opened very slowly. The Freeguard swung himself down. A small man really. Perhaps a little taller than she was. Sandy eyebrows? Was that what she remembered? Yes – puffy cheeks and those pale blue eyes. He was walking, not gliding on wheels, his legs swinging in a way she hadn't seen for years. She'd grown up walking. Everyone used to walk. Puffs of black dust flew round his feet.

He was carrying a small, flat, black bag. Not hurrying. It was important to remember he had black hairs in his ears. He looked her over and smiled. 'Ready?'

She pulled herself even tighter together, nodded, left the shelter of the van, felt a small patch of sunlight flick her cheek, sharp as a knife blade through a gap in the branches. She entered the deep shadow behind the van and stood very still, staring at the ground.

'Excellent. Excellent. You've done a grand job.' A good carrying voice.

The loosened soil was obvious. However. She looked up with a pale smile.

He opened his bag and drew out a tiny laptop. 'Easier to use this on a table. Let me inside, will you? I'll do you a certificate.'

She drew in a sharp breath. The air seemed warmer. They could talk in there.

But the risk was enormous. Didn't the going in make a flying knife inevitable on the going out? The Free was staring at her. She gestured towards the steps.

Immediately inside he nodded towards the light, 'Nice to see that working.' His fingers ran rapidly across the keys, gave a final tap, paper began to roll from the printer. Her lips tensed. Now was the moment.

He held out the paper. 'There you are.' His voice was soft, almost enticing, as if he were befriending a shy animal.

She looked at him and read slowly

Vanacar Ensuite; 24AV 2111/301
Driver Female M. T.
Inspected 28th March, 15ND.
Vehicle: Roadworthy;
Driver grade: Satisfactory
Signature: Some sort of scrawl.

'Thank you.'

There was no reason to doubt or hesitate. Unthinkingly she began rolling it into a tube. It seemed firmer like that, something to hold onto. 'Thank you very much.'

He peered, leaning forward a little, 'Anything else you wanted to say?'

She took a deep breath and shook her head, turning away in case he should look through her mask into her eyes.

'Sure?' A little harder, more urgent.

'Sorry – it's, it's just you've been so kind.'

He gave her another sharp glance. Part of his job not to believe. Then smiled. 'We're not that bad, you know.'

He stepped out and stood on the ground leaning on the side of the door to rest his hand. The back was covered in pale hairs. 'Now you find a nice fem-tog and hitch yourself onto it.'

Nut and Bolt. Little Whee. She nodded. What a joke.

'I'll get the office to book you a slot for tonight.'

Boss was back long before the signal came to move. He was exultant. 'Knew you wouldn't dare. Couldn't do a thing, could you?'

She'd shrugged, 'OK, Boss,' and wondered why she hadn't spoken to the Freeguard. It hadn't felt like fear – at least, not of Boss – just something she didn't do.

Half an hour later she watched him lock the screen door and pocket the key. Herself and that junior in slot 3462, shut up together inside corrugated iron walls.

Ting, ting, ting.

A driver in the next slot was hammering, perhaps trying to straighten bent wheels on roll-shoes or roller blades.

The tings drove into her like nails but she had to keep still. She didn't dare shift a leg in case – and those legs and her hips and her shoulders weighed so much. Her head ached. She longed to relax, to fall asleep, but if she did, what would he do? Would he let her wake up to hear tomorrow's clatter?

Part 2

I'll never forget that awful drag.

This woman – that day she would have been wearing terylene/cotton trousers and a long-sleeved blouse – the blue one most likely – plain, tough clothes suitable for an inner city schoolroom – and a wide-brimmed hat too large to grip her head comfortably – had reached the far end of Elm Grove when a car bumped off the pavement. Awkward spot under the bobbles of a plane, bare branches harsh against the night sky.

Friday night. Aching all over. Same every week. By the time she picked up her order from the clerk at the collection point, she'd be past feeling. Neither of them ever smiled. Blank faces, it was all blank faces. His mind, she supposed, would be on his home journey while she was going to crawl from junction to junction, lights to lights, for three hours across North London. And when at last she made it, Sydenham Avenue double parked, the entire length, abandoned vehicles in the middle of the road. She'd grit her teeth. Camel Street parked up. Ditto Far End Lane, Eltwhistle Place, Cardew Gardens. She'd try cruising that car park that had replaced 2 – 4 Saviour Walk. Waste of time.

She grabbed her chance under the tree – neat bit of work – Daihatsu Elf would turn on one of those tiny coins we had then – 5p was it? Heave out folding trolley, wipe sweat off face, load shopping and school bags, set off trying to guide the damn thing – wheels veered at random, now right now left, dragged you down slopes you'd no idea existed. Struggle down Elm Grove, left into Camel Street, right into Eltwhistle Place, right again into Sydenham Street. At intervals she had to stand and gasp, actually came to a standstill on the corner of Sydenham Avenue. That terrible heat. In November. Every few minutes stopped to flop over the handles, wondering what was the matter. Seemed absurd to have so little strength.

Only another hundred yards, she'd mutter.

For many weeks a poster was pinned to a telegraph pole outside no 96. Man's head framed against a rising sun. She'd pause and look – ordinary little man – narrow rimmed glasses – bushy eyebrows. Just an excuse to take a breath, of course.

Unload, hump the whole lot upstairs. When they'd taken the flat, it had seemed a brilliant idea to live on the top floor. She told them all at school, day after day in the staffroom – took the bitter edge off that coffee – chattering on a bit but who wouldn't? It was the way they listened – set her off, didn't it? she'd explain to Elizabeth's questioning eye-brows.

And then she couldn't stop – good sized rooms lovely view rooftops amazing what a variety London not uniform starlings, pigeons, clouds – wonderful cloudscapes Hampstead Heath and beyond. Other people's heat helping to keep you warm, fancy gables not insulated.

That door had a nice click, good and firm behind her. She'd unclip the speakie that had been murmuring into her ear all day, throw it on the chair in the hall, relax into the job of sorting tins, packets, jars, fresh veg, fresh fruit, put them slowly away.

There was a rhythm to it. Bend into the bag, stretch on tiptoes to a top shelf, double forward into a low cupboard, extend fingers so the tips pushed a tin right to the back. Version of Tai Chi?

Ease off those four hours grinding home. In her bag 43 versions of 'A letter to the council complaining the wheelie bins haven't been emptied.' Such a trifling matter considering the state of the planet. Part of the traditional grind towards exams.

10C probably – hmmn, that won't mean anything to anyone else – group Chayne Potts was in. Good god, haven't thought of him for ages. Never forget, do you? Not that kind.

Shove the bag into a corner, collapse into chair. No drink till Elizabeth arrived, another hour or so. She'd switch on the TV. Temperature in London in the mid-eighties. Mid November. York was flooded. The usual weekend jams on the motorways. Five mile tailback on the M11, eight miles on the M4. Avoid the M1, the M2 and their parallels until midnight. Through traffic for Scotland diverted to the M654 through the Lake District. The M25 and all its parallels might be unclogged by Saturday mid-day.

Unlikely. People seemed to have their social lives in cars on motorways.

A key'd click just before ten. She'd leap up. 'Wherever you been?' Couldn't help herself. She'd listen for the rustle of Elizabeth's sun-coat as she hung it up, her voice from the hall, 'D'you need to ask?'

'Sherry? Gin? Tea? Coffee? Meal first and drinks later?'

She'd appear, muzzed somehow, drooping. 'Couldn't eat. Any of the others,' and slump into the other chair. They'd sit facing, glasses at their elbows.

Her friend would keep her eyes on the floor. You got up, drove to work, taught your classes. Did your marking, filled in reports, plan-sheets, drove home. Tried to park Didn't feel like eating. Had a drink instead. Went to bed. Over and over. 'If only we could get down to Hayle,' seemed an endless refrain, only occasionally voiced.

Elizabeth would put down her glass, stand so her skirt straightened in a cascade of dark and light green like leaves shaken by wind. Her eyes would be towards the kitchen. 'What is there to eat?' She'd touch her friend, a light hand on the shoulder. 'No use wrestling with the impossible. Forget Hayle.'

'Coleslaw, ham, couple of slices of quiche. Let me help. That what you tell your clients – give up?'

'When there's no sense in anything else.'

Week after week they expressed the same wish, dropped it and ate in silence. It's hard to date the evening when, in the middle of clearing the dishes, the woman found energy to suggest they could genuinely escape. 'We might make it to Hayle at my half-term. Any hope you could get the week off? Dad and Mum would love to see you.'

Elizabeth swilled a dish under the hot tap. 'Miranda, you know I'd love to – but we're snowed under – three dangerous drivings –

'Your clients found space to drive dangerously? Clever them.'

'Two involve "death by dangerous driving". Ted'll handle them but that simply means half his folio lands on my desk. Two of those fiends are eight years old. Poor little sods think they know it all and their eighteenth birthday is centuries away.'

'Much worse if you're forty and can't afford a car. I've told you why they gave up running buses in the area round the school. Understandable – you can't risk losing drivers. Give me that plate. I'll deal with it.' Take it gently from her hand, slip it into the washing-up machine, close the door. 'How can you hold down a job if you can't get there? Or get it in the first place?'

Elizabeth gave her a level look. 'Arrived on my desk today, malicious damage, four.'

'Head had her screen smashed yesterday. Somehow they got into the lock-ups.'

'We're defence lawyers for so many – motorway assault – you name it. D'you remember how all those pundits used to discuss its causes – until we got used to it? That's it, Mira. Come and sit down.'

Her friend crumpled into the chair. 'Mostly paperwork. What's the computer for? Fax it all in if they can't wait. Bloody hell, Elizabeth, when all this technology's available, why don't you use it? You can get so much more done in the quiet at home. I'd have thought even Silcock, Silcock and Withers could grasp the point.'

Somewhere beyond the curtains a motorbike roared, in Eltwhistle Place, maybe.

'What kind of life is this, Elizabeth?' She looked so pale, heavy marks under her eyes. 'I feel a prisoner. I am a prisoner. More or less. You're one too. How long did it take you to get home this evening?'

The bike screeched, went quiet, screeched again.

'Average for Friday. Why go on about it? I was late setting out.'

'Ealing to Hampstead, best part of four hours, I bet. It's ludicrous, Elizabeth, ludicrous. Can't you see? It's well after midnight and all we've done is drive home and have some supper. That's all. How many hours a day do you spend in your car?' The screech was fading. She leant forward and spoke softly, 'Might as well live in it?'

Elizabeth was silent.

'Come on, admit it.'

Elizabeth shrugged. Taut lines dug into her face. 'You know I'm not a fan of Gavin Claring.' The name rested in the air.

Miranda wouldn't let her off. 'Could be, you know. The only thing.'

'You'd take to it more easily than I would.'

'It's you who's ruthless. Odd, isn't it? I spend my days being hard on children for their own good, but it's you knows how to be ruthless.'

She wrapped thin arms round her chest. 'Let's go to bed.'

Later she lay with her back to her friend and when an arm slid over her waist, refused to turn round.

Not the only night that happened.

*

The leaves were just turning colour when Gavin began his series. Miranda turned from the window and drew the curtains. 7 p.m. September, the days drawing in.

Elizabeth had collapsed into her favourite chair, the one covered in chintz roses. Not quite either of their tastes but very comfortable. She'd inherited it. From her Aunt Jill, most like. She smiled and stretched, cradled her drink. 'Some things don't change. The quiet of Sunday evening.'

But much less energy. They both used to lie around all day.

'Think of all those thousands jammed up on the motorways. Though I bet a lot of them will manage to watch.' Illegal TVs. lowered over the driving mirror, seats tilted.

'Did I tell you? Ted has this client – police cycled up the hard shoulder and caught him watching. Really.'

'Do the police have the right to cycle on the motorway?'

'Ted's planning to argue since the car had been stationary for half an hour no offence had been committed. Police could follow the same line.'

'A draw?'

'In the other cars they were all reading.'

'Not drinking?'

'We-ell. Ted says he plays chess with his wife.'

'Who wins?'

'Doesn't let on. Got the remote?'

The channel slowly came to life. Urban motorway it was and then Jim Royal wearing one of the most flamboyant silk ties ever. 'And now for a Party Political on behalf of the New Dawn Party.'

'That man must have at least a hundred ties and not one's the right colour.' She slid her eyes sideways to catch Elizabeth pursing her mouth.

Could it have been a pose to hold back excitement? She must have been excited.

Tarmac and houses, then darkness, then hills edged with pale sunlight, a voice intoning, 'Ahead into the New Dawn.'

She hugged her knees.

Elizabeth stretched an elegant toe. She had such lovely feet. 'Do you suppose there's anyone in England doesn't already know what he's going to argue?'

'So why are we watching?'

They sank into listening. 'Gavin Claring takes a long, hard look at this country and tells us what he sees. But he doesn't stop there. He goes on to give us his vision of what might be.'

Two eyes expanding on a dark screen. The viewers moved slowly though them onto a motorway. All twelve lanes in both directions jam-packed. The camera panned across miles of tailback, then zoomed in. First thing – various sections of the Sundays propped on seatbacks or the wheel. People hidden behind them.

Bright young reporter waved his mike. Curly hair he had, round his ears. It bounced as he turned and bent. 'Let's pop the microphone through the window of this Airborne.' The camera panned over the passengers. 'Don't mind, do you?'

Enormous smiles.

Elizabeth sipped slowly. 'D'you remember years ago when Gavin did that series about badgers, how he had a camera inside the sett? Very revealing we thought then. Didn't ask them if they liked it.'

The reporter's bright face softened. He was a professional. 'Been here long?'

Those badgers had been wonderful. Parents and cubs revealed by ultra-violet cameras, curled in their sett, or in the woods bounding about with surprising agility. David Attenborough had done the same years before. No-one could match him in exploring those lives, till Gavin brought a new urgency. It was his voice – and the feeling you were looking through the eyes of someone who was enthralled but very afraid. 'Precarious,' he'd say.

*

'Not timing it, am I?' Voice muffled by a pollution mask. 'Feels like a century.'

She suddenly looked at Elizabeth. 'Why do they do it?'

'Addicted.'

They nibbled nuts and raisins, staring at the screen. The woman pondered –of course she wasn't drugged but all the same – 'I'd really love an Airborne,' she said slowly, 'Car, not the van. Fantastic acceleration.'

'Useful in the present state of the roads.' Elizabeth would cut her down in such a dry tone of voice.

And she would say things deliberately to provoke it.

They were waiting for Gavin Claring, relishing the knowledge there'd be no grand entrance, no gesturing arms, only a quiet little man in slacks and a plain shirt, sort you'd find yourself talking to in a queue.

He started by interviewing some police bigwig.

'I wonder now, Chief Inspector, if you could tell us the cause of this hold-up? Has there been some kind of special occurrence?'

'Nothing out of the ordinary.' The bloke had a rectangular face and a magnificent deadpan manner. 'The basic problem is the motorways aren't big enough to accommodate all the traffic that wants to use them.'

'Would you relate this to public spending cuts? As we all know the road building programme has had to be cut back while car ownership has continued to soar.'

'You should address that question to the politicians.'

'Hundreds of miles of new road have been built. But even private funding doesn't seem to meet the need.'

'He led the protest over Hollinger Wood, remember?' she murmured, feeling Elizabeth warm beside her. 'In those days the media made jokes about his eye-brows – *bushy as the blackthorn he was trying to save.* Changed their tone, haven't they? And the Windermere motorway. He objected to that.'

Elizabeth murmured, 'It was losing that set him off. Doesn't like losing.'

'Set him onto something much more exciting.' She couldn't take her eyes off those images.

'He's not the only one thinking – and he has to be in the lead.'

Those luminous eyes were fixed on her, straight out of the screen. They turned away and became the ones she saw with, as she'd done night after night – Mum and Dad shouldn't have let her have her own telly – she'd give up on homework, go through his eyes into the woods. Badgers, foxes, owls, millipedes, bees –

At that age you long to worship.

She was with him now as he turned that gaze on the Chief Inspector. 'So, what do you think now about the conservation lobby?'

All credit to him – that bloke's face didn't flicker. 'Of course, we all want to conserve our countryside. It's what this country stands for.' An honest looking man with a more acute gaze than you might expect. 'However, to support the life and commerce of the present day we require the ability to keep the traffic moving.'

'Would you say the answer is public transport?'

The inspector's lip curled. 'Tried that, didn't they? Years back now. Several initiatives. Never worked.' He squared his shoulders. 'When it comes to the crunch you've got to face facts. No-one wants to go by public transport when they can have their own car.'

'It never caught on, did it, that slogan,' Gavin smiled slightly derisively, 'Roam the roads of your dreams by bus'?'

'No-one could afford the fares.' He faded away.

More scenes from the motorways. Home in on Muslim family saying their prayers, prostrated under the turn-off sign for Bolton, then on a Red Volta Airborne with Granny knitting in the passenger seat. Eager young reporter leaning in. 'Excuse me, what kind of garment is that? Long skirt? Could you hold it up for viewers to see? That young lady your grand-daughter? Party wear for her – or for you?' Laughter. 'Can you tell us when you started it? On the way out? You hope to finish before you get in?'

Gavin's voice over, 'What sort of freedom is this?'

Switch to a motorist with a blood pouring over his face. 'How'd you get that?'

'Bugger in the next car. Wouldn't move up. I've took his number.'

'More work for Silcock, Silcock and Withers.' Her turn to be dry. Elizabeth winced.

Now an aerial view of North London, the camera feeling its way down through dense yellow-grey cloud. Coughs. Gavin Claring's even voice. 'It catches you in the throat. Even through a pollution mask.'

The view changed to an outline map. Broad blue strands radiated and curved away from a central blotch labelled 'City' through shopping centres, residential areas, industrial estates. No playing fields now, no parks. The blue lines split then reassembled in curling figures-of-eight at the junctions with the North and South Circular. Both of these with eight lanes. A flick to a camera revealed traffic crawling in both directions. Back to the map, the camera zooming out to take in the M25 and its parallel, out again to the Outer Orbital linking Bedford to Reading, Chelmsford to Maidstone. It was fringed in places with green but mostly was lined with houses, industrial estates and service stations.

Gavin's cool was magnificent, 'What happened to the Green Belt? How long before the rest of the country goes the same way?' Pause. 'I shall consider this further next week and end today with a visit to Inner London. What is life like in one of these houses huddled under the motorway?' Zoom in on red brick boxes. 'Lee and Charleen live almost directly under the North Circular.'

'Mum calls that area "suburbs". Lived round there for a time. Years ago.'

The pair of them on their front step in wide-brimmed hats, him with his arm round her. Red curls tumbled over her shoulders. Oversize glasses framed in psychedlic blues and greens, the kind that were sold to cut out ultra-violet, hid her eyes. Lee's hair hung limp. He looked as if he was clinging onto her. The camera rested on them to a background hiss of air brakes.

'Can you describe the impact of traffic on your lives?'

Charleen removed her mask.

'Put it on specially for the occasion,' Elizabeth murmured.

'Just terrible, really horrific. Never stops 24/7.'

'You have to wear that mask all the time?'

'Never dare take it off. Worst in this heat. Specially when there's no wind.. Catches you all the time in the throat. And the kids. You listen to them coughing and you think, my god, what's going to happen? How can you know what's in the air?'

'You've had the house fume-proofed?' Camera panning over pebble dash and curved bay windows.

'What good's that? Comes in any way, every time you open the door. Got to go in and out, you know. '

'Of course.'

'It's the stop-start does the damage. Every time they open up those engines. Gets on your nerves. Wouldn't be so bad if they kept moving.'

'Apart from the coughing – and god knows, that's bad enough – what other effects are there on the health of the community round here?'

Charleen's face twisted.

'A lot of people – get cancer?'

'No-one does anything,' she burst out. 'There's kids dying and no-one does a thing to stop it. Fumes get trapped between the houses. No-one lifts a bloody finger.'

'Thank you.'

Her face faded and Gavin Claring resumed his discourse. 'Today as many of you will know it's not really petrol fumes that are the hidden menace. That's one area we have tackled. However –' he paused, looking out beyond the audience he couldn't see, 'the hole in the ozone layer is still there. I could have taken you round the wards of the local hospital. I could have concentrated on success stories and cures.' He lowered his eyes and raised them, confiding, 'I don't want to pretend all is light and hope. And the professionals are reluctant to allow in the cameras. They tell me a view of some wards would be too harrowing. A child's death isn't something you go into easily. It's not something to stand and watch.' He broke off and remained silent, then the eyes filled screen again. 'Let's move on – to something that may at first seem lighter.'

Lee and Charleen re-appeared.

'What about parking round here? Where do you put your car, Lee?'

The camera moved up and down the neighbouring roads.

'Oh, Mira, look, they've cut down the flowering cherries. D'you remember those great blowsy masses? They made North London.'

Solid lines of cars, parked on concreted front gardens, in driveways, on pavements and verges, barely room for other vehicles to wriggle past.

'Got a permit for Brent Street.' When Lee stood straight he turned out to have hollow cheeks and a tough jaw.

'That's the one where they knocked down the houses?'

'Not enough room round here. Made sense, didn't it?'

'And Charleen? What does she do with hers?'

'Room for it in the garden. But the kids each have a powered buggy. Lucky Winston's only ten. When he's old enough to drive – things tense enough round here as it is.'

'There's been trouble?'

Charleen suddenly looked older. 'People coming to blows. That's how bad it is. Blokes coming to blows. Women too. Can't help it, some of them. Wouldn't want to be like that. But when you're pushed –' Her gaze swung into Gavin's eyes. 'When there's a shortage of space and everyone has to have it –'

Miranda looked at Elizabeth. 'Won't be long before it's like that round here. I like her, she's honest. You seen that yellow notice?'

'Not so's to say so.'

'Number 16. They want to demolish and open a way into the gardens behind to make a car park.'

'All of them?'

'Whole way along.'

'Would we all be allocated spaces?'

'Who knows?'

Gavin Claring was gazing down through a helicopter window. 'Already houses are being demolished to make room for cars, most in the city centre – but what about the suburbs? Or is it now a question of where suburbs begin? The city's spread past Bromley and Watford. Perhaps we should count Chelmsford and Basingstoke as suburbs? If you think I'm exaggerating, look at this map. My grandfather grew up in Dartford. It was a small town then. He said his father talked about playing in fields in Middlesex. D'you see? A few generations.' He paused. 'Now look at this.' The chopper tilted and cruised. 'New housing estates all round. Isn't this the natural consequence of increased mobility? Isn't it natural for people to seek a quieter, less polluted, healthier atmosphere in which to bring up their children? But is that what they find? They can't see ultra-violet rays so they think it doesn't matter if they cut down the trees. Just one, that's how it goes, just one to keep dead leaves off the path, prevent roots forcing up the tarmac, stop branches falling on the garage, open up the view from the sitting-room. Only one. And one. And one.

'Look at the congestion. Look at these tower blocks. Just two of them. Not much, you'd think. Space round them. Now look again. How many multi-storey car-parks? Four streets had to be demolished just to make space for them. So where has the excess population gone? Not all of them into the tower blocks. Here is where you will find them – Derbyshire, Northampton, Suffolk, Sussex. And further. Look at the Midland conurbation.

'Good luck to them you might say. Why grudge them a better life?' He let his eyes expand, questioning, 'Is it better? Really, genuinely better? What about those unseen rays?'

He paused, then began again in a brisker tone. 'I shall deal with those questions next time. Meanwhile I'm going to leave a few images with you, a few views from old photographs: – this wood was felled to make room for housing; these hedgerows were grubbed, all the birds and insects dispersed. Some won't have found places elsewhere. I leave you with questions –' Black eyebrows bristled – 'Is this what we want? Is there no way we can preserve our countryside? Does wildlife have no value? Aren't we ourselves part of nature, our needs linked to theirs?

'I'd like to leave you with one last question. Can we ever again be free to roam where sunlight is safe? Think about it. Next week I shall bring you doctors who regularly treat victims of various kinds of cancer. But for now one final image.'

The screen filled with a country lane some time in the nineteen twenties, sun filtering onto the bonnet of a Ford Model T, roof rolled back, driver's elbow propped on the edge of the window. 'When Henry Ford left the family farm for Chicago, he took the first step on a road that lead to the inception of a dream – a car within the pocket of every man. And equally now of every woman. Motoring for the masses. I ask you to sit back and consider. Is this a dream of the past, a kind of pastoral idyll? Is there no way in which the vision may be restored? No way in which every person may own a car, the countryside be preserved, that hole mended? I am convinced there is. Even now it is not too late.'

They sat in silence for a long time. At last Miranda heaved herself up. 'You finished with that glass?'

She carried the glasses to the kitchen, placed them in the bowl, ran the tap till the water came hot, rested her hands in it, accepted the warmth, stared out of the window. Four miles away – Danny. He'd habitually played outside. Where else could he? Running about in the hot spaces between buildings without a hat or any protective gel. 8C had sent him a card.

She squeezed out drops of blue-green washing-up liquid, swilled each glass in turn, held it to the tap, rinsed it in pure water, put it to dry, leant forward and opened the window.

His card passed from table to table. Signatures and messages. 'Love you.' 'Look after yourself, fathead.' 'All the best.' 'Looking forward to having you back.'

Brad read that one, his lip curled, he waved the card in the air, snorted. 'Won't be back, will he?'

A heavy silence, all of them looking up, waiting to see what she'd say.

Except Lou. Shoulders curved over her narrow chest, one finger rubbing the tabletop, eyes lowered. Always the one who took most things most to heart. You weren't allowed to take her into your arms; had had to find something to say. She took out a clean towel, dried the glasses slowly, holding the base in the left hand, with the thumb of the right inside the bowl, the fingers outside, rubbing thin glass. The truth. As gently as you could. Something to help them bear it.

She'd taken time off commas and full stops to talk about the dangers of playing outdoors, the need for barrier creams. Emphatically, over and over. Their parents didn't believe in the danger of something they couldn't see.

'Come and sit down, Mira. Worrying about something? School, is it?'

'Just the normal teacher's Sunday evening blues. First thing Monday – 8C. With luck that early they won't be awake yet. Clara, Cal, Chay. Not one of them can sit still or shut up. And it sets off the others. The teaching assistants are excellent but even so. Friday Period 2, Jill was working with Cal, Vanda asked something, she turned to answer, Chay shouted a word and Cal was across the room murdering him.'

'It's the tension.'

'Their parents absorbed lead in the days before hydrogen cars. How can hyperactive parents produce calm children? Know how I got on top of them? Decided to freeze their blood, didn't I? Told them if they went on drawing I'd tell them a story. Well, actually I bribed them, with sweets. And said they could draw the gory bits when I'd finished. Have to compete, don't you? Nothing I was going to say was half as horrific as the stuff they watch on-line.'

'So what was this inoffensive tale?'

'Just part of the National Curriculum. We have to do Ancient History.'

'No guarantee of nice behaviour.'

'Described Pompeii to them. How the people and the town had been buried. Mushroom cloud and all that. Ash beginning to fall. Sort of tsunami building up in the harbour. People refusing to leave until the waves were so huge they couldn't. Piled it on a bit. That got them. Sat with their ears flapping. I told them how ash had been falling like heavy rain, people rushed into the streets with cushions over their heads but ash still clogged their lungs, streams of molten lava were already creeping into the houses. That's why, I said, archaeologists were able to dig up the town exactly as it was. Meals on the tables. Corpses in the streets. I left their imaginations to work.'

'Sadist.'

'Necessary. Clara put her hand up. Why had the people been so stupid? They could have got out before things got really rough and come back later to dig their things out.

Naturally Chay had to shout she was a wally – bright girls set him off – and by the time I'd got him quiet she'd lost interest. It was a good question.'

'You got something across.'

The woman laid her hands on the arms of the chair, tugged herself up, went to stand behind her friend, stroked shining hair, 'Come on, tomorrow's another day.'

That ordinary little man knew how to get millions dreaming. News came in too. All over the world water levels were rising. One week the News showed the Maldives people filing onto boats, the next large areas of the Philippines were being evacuated, and nearer home, cliffs falling into the sea. November's heat-wave crashed out in thunderstorms and floods.

Gavin mocked the way the government wrung its hands while the opposition sat back and sneered. Ride it out, they advised. Changes in weather patterns were nothing new.

Thousands swarmed into the streets. The school closed for action. After protracted, anxious discussions backwards and forwards across the staff-room, the teachers had reached the conclusion they couldn't stand back.

But the crowd jamming the playground that morning wasn't just teachers. Half the kids were there plus parents, all waving banners. 'Action on Climate change.' 'Free up the roads.' And more simply – that was Chayne Potts and his dad – 'Wanna live.'

After half an hour or so milling about under the eyes of a posse of sardonic police the school got itself in order and set out for the Rye. The organisers were continually on their speakies keeping in touch with the leaders of crowds assembling in Hyde Park, on the steps of St. Paul's, on the Chelsea embankment. Plan was they'd all converge on Westminster by different routes.

Then the Knights appeared. Normal people had never taken them seriously – cardboard armour and studded gauntlets – and the way they posed, manly hands resting on hips, smirking. That day they kept appearing, more and more of them, closing in on both sides, silent at first, sneering. Then, all together, they broke into a chanting that had no distinguishable words but seemed to be repeating something you'd better take in but might be too stupid to understand, over and over again until you got it. Or else.

Some demonstrators raised a Freedom song and punched the air. She saw the Head of their school among the organisers going backwards and forwards trying to hold the ranks in formation. The police seemed to have melted away. They marched on past estate agents, chippies, newsagents, betting shops into what was considered a 'more salubrious area', luxury apartments. They were hung with banners 'Our homes are our castles. The balconies were filled with more Knights, silent this time, stock-still.

The crowd hated their silence and sang louder. The figures above them looked down.

Up there one arm moved. A young man in the front row of the demonstrators fell. For a moment the crowd stood still. A woman screamed. Bodies swayed and wavered. Chayne's dad, rushed forward towards the entrance to the flats, waving his fist.

And bullets rained down. She grabbed Chayne's shoulders and pushed him back the way they'd come. 'Run, run.'

She tried to turn back to see what she could do for his Mum but she herself was leaning forward, stumbling – a great weight pressing down on her from behind – saw if she fell she'd never get up, ran, kept running till she landed up, shaking, in a side-street.

Crept back to the corner and peered round. The Knights were swaggering up and down the street, stopping occasionally to kick a recumbent body.

She didn't stay. Later she did her best to forget that fact but it came back. Time after time.

What could she have done? What was possible? In those circumstances what could anyone have done?

Never saw Chayne again. No-one could tell her what had happened to his family.

The school didn't function properly from then. Half the staff left. Many of the kids didn't come in. There seemed no point chasing them.

South London's wasn't the only violence that day. The government still didn't act. Only 'troublemakers' asked where the guns had come from – smuggled in from America obviously but who dared stop them? The Prime Minister announced a Public Enquiry and spent the next six months arguing about its scope.

After a February when trampled snow turned London pavements into ice-rinks and Swiss grass stayed bare, March came in with daffodils and baking sunshine.

'We'll get to Hayle for Easter if it kills us.'

'Roads were bad last weekend.'

'They've discovered how to cure that.'

'Oh? Clever them.'

On the News. 'In view of the distress caused to drivers last week –'

'ie they all sat jammed for twenty-four hours, slip roads and main roads off too crowded to allow anyone to move, freezing cold, people just sitting there in their cars, no food, nothing –'

'Should have gone prepared.'

'Police going bonkers – not even able to get along the hard shoulders –'

'They've found the solution.'

'Which is?'

'Easy. Close the motorways from mid-afternoon Friday till the same time Saturday. Solves the problem.

'I see the logic.'

'So we set out late Saturday. Might be a few day-trippers taking it on earlier.'

A hot wind blew through the window against their cheeks.

'You'd think this would blow the pollution away.'

'It will, Mira, it will. And then you'll complain you're cold.'

'Better than all this heat.' High up, opening above the roofs, the sky seemed to promise a place where breath was easy, where she could indulge a dream.

Later she smiled as the car picked its way down a parked up street, another, another, cross-roads, traffic lights, junction, filter, main road, traffic lights, traffic lights, traffic lights, roundabout, more complicated roundabout and at last emerged onto a carriageway, miraculously empty.

She flicked her eyes up, enough to activate the v-cam strapped to her forehead to project the road miles ahead into the air in front of the windscreen. Several more miles with hardly any traffic. 'You're right, Elizabeth, pays to get away late.'

'You're ignoring the jam on the opposite carriageway – could just as well be this – and the power of luck.'

'Typical lawyer – who else considers the other side? Is luck a power?'

'Only one you can hope for – if you're dreaming of space on the roads.'

Soon the motorway, curving up into the North Downs, gave a clear view of bends higher up. Something was moving ahead, she gently pressed down with her right foot. The car responded. In front was something red, probably a Ford Flyer and in front of that, something slimmer, potentially more powerful, cruising along, almost dawdling. She swung into the middle lane, saw from the corner of her eye red paint slip behind, curved gently back, and now, a minute later, came up with the BMW Pilot. Check mirror, swing out again, see the other fall back, ease in. It was a dance. A smooth and stately dance.

She took her foot off the accelerator on the crest of the first hill, let the car have ease, steadied it for the descent. This was a partnership, like a rider must have with a horse. The car was alive, moving, responding to her and she to it.

Houses still flowed past though they were beginning to thin. An occasional field appeared. She remembered the Downs she'd known as a kid, open grasslands. Below was a valley where red roofs glowed through bare chestnut branches. And now the summit. Salisbury visible in the distance, Elizabeth silent at her side, she let the speed fall.

'Wish it could always be like this.'

Perhaps Elizabeth smiled.

A little later her friend remarked. 'This is great.' It was the way woods fitted into the hillsides. 'Odd isn't it, he started by protecting a wood from a new road.'

'And now he's all for roads.'

The other stiffened. 'Part of the same thing.'

'Of course.' Dry as ever.

A mile or so later they entered a cutting.

'You've got to admit, he's changed his song,' Elizabeth murmured.

Her friend other gazed at steep banks flowing past, let the speed drop.

'Cowslips here last year, d'you remember? And those kestrels, one after another? No shortage of rabbits.' Hawthorns showed tiny tips of green. 'He hasn't changed, you know, he's just setting about it another way.'

Elizabeth said nothing.

'Come on, you know these motorway fringes have become pathways for wildlife. All he's doing is expanding that idea – increasing the areas where humans aren't allowed.'

'Fairly drastic remedy.'

'Obvious really. Roads are the lesser evil. Do definitely take up less space than houses. If one or the other has to go – it's the realistic solution'

'Very neat.' She gave her friend a quick glance. 'And you can keep your car.'

'That's what's so clever, can't you see it? He knew he couldn't win against the car and came up with another solution. That man's a genius, you know.'

'Maybe.'

They were quiet for a while. Then they started dropping down with housing estates on both sides of the road. She knew they'd come to countryside again the other side. 'It's the urge to keep moving. You've heard him say it's built in. That makes sense to me. Can't bear being shut in a city. Some people seem to love it – but a city's a trap. This is much more natural – to be out here – and if we were camping – sort of – all the time – we'd be in among the trees and the wildlife where we belong.' She paused. 'You know, the Americans are so lucky.'

'That so?'

'So much space. Nomadic life-style already under way there. Crowds of them living in vans all the time.'

'As you say, there's plenty of room.'

'They're showing us the way.'

'You can't pull down New York.'

'Who says? If they were inspired –' she felt a cool in the air. 'Well – maybe – no, all of them probably won't come the whole way. Too many who don't believe in the environment. Swollen heads.'

'Don't abuse the opposing counsel. Gets you nowhere.'

'Shut up, Liza.'

'We have to live in the same world.'

Then it was road-works. Frost and snow followed by floods had riddled the tarmac.

'You know – about the States, Elizabeth?' She paused for a response and getting none, 'Mum sent this brochure. Thought I showed you.' Still no response. 'New apartments, beside Lake Ohio. She'd marked one – and underlined at the end – pledge from the President – all refugees from global warming welcome in the States.'

'Thought Martinez favoured the New Dawn?'

'Never get it through Congress, will he?'

It was almost dark when the sign for Frelland loomed up.

'The new road's open. Thank God.'

Two days later the weather had cooled and they were already coughing less.

'Pollution masks are an affectation.' Elizabeth's sun-jacket swung open as she pushed her hands deeper into the pockets. It was a day of brilliance between showers of hail.

'They do a different job from what most people think.' Her friend threw her head back. 'Isn't this just wonderful? Fresh air on your face and enough cloud to risk going out without barrier cream.' She gazed all round. Her heart wasn't leaping the way it should have been. 'Isn't that incredible?'

'I'm just about believing it.'

'Look how the daffs have been battered. And already they're picking up.' She felt heavy all over. 'How do they do it, Elizabeth? '

'But pollution masks, Mira. Is there any car now with that degree of emissions? There used to be a risk from carbon monoxide. Not now.'

'D'you have to go on about it? It's the ultra-violet.'

'Still offends me to go round looking like a TV surgeon. Not what life's for.'

'Give up, can't you? You never wear one anyway.'

'Tired of people going on about dangers that have passed, indulging their sick imaginations.'

Her friend turned away then back to survey deep-brimmed hat, swathes of dark hair framing a pale face, a green silk jacket, a straight blouse swinging over narrow hips, a slender skirt. Such a townie, even here in the country. This wasn't someone she could reach out to, who could share what she felt. She went on standing, heavy limbed, gazing. That body almost a needle. Those shoulders rounded forward. 'We could get down to Trenchard's Bridge and back before dinner.'

'Your mother won't like it if we're late.'

'No way I'm going to hurry.'

Elizabeth looked calm. 'OK. Fine. Bring your speakie?'

Her friend shook her head. 'No-one in this house goes round clipped to one.'

'How ever do they keep up with life?'

They laughed and brushed each other's hips.

'Oh Mira.'

'Oh Elizabeth.'

Thing's felt still better once they'd passed the gate onto the river path. That had been the way she'd always gone to the village. Brought friends back that way. They'd swing on branches over the water. When she was alone she had a special perch on the bank where she'd curled and read.

It was comforting now to have to force a way through under overhanging branches, then when space opened, come to a halt and watch the river swirling down dead wood, lumps of grass and teasel, handfuls of straw. It stuck them onto the banks, tore them off, carried them away, clots of black on foaming brown water.

'Such a tame river usually, but now, just look.' Her feet were slipping on pebbles half hidden under a thin coating of mud. She planted her legs firmly apart, turned to watch Elizabeth. Kingcups gleamed on the far bank, a yew made a still darkness behind them. 'To think we might be shut up in London.' A chaffinch trilled on top of a hawthorn. It would have been natural to sing back. Instead she gazed heavily all round wondering what was missing.

She took Elizabeth's wrist. 'This is the place for the kingfisher.'

They waited, side by side.

Bit later she shrugged. 'Did hope. Just for luck. To bring us luck.' Then, after a minute, 'Gone, you know. Won't come back.'

'Mira,' Elizabeth said softly, 'you accepted that years ago.'

'More fool me.'

A right-angled turn in the shadow of Jim Parker's creosoted shed brought them into the sun. The planks on the bridge were slimier than ever. In places they'd rotted and broken. They made it across, holding the rails, listening to the hollow thumps of their feet mix with the rush of water underneath, and at the same time slowly becoming aware of a thud, thud ahead the other side of the hedge. When they reached the gate they took in that orange monster.

Melodramatic? O.K. What else could you call it, when it was there in front of you tearing up the soil, trundling a hundred yards, opening its mouth, vomiting the contents onto a spoil-heap, the field changing from green to grey, dust flying from a surface already parched by unseasonable heat? She had a vision of worms diving desperately down, trying to find a place to go.

To look was unbearable. She turned her head away. The lower branches of an alder overhanging the river were festooned with dead vegetation. 'Next time we come, if we ever do make it –'

'Mira, please –'

'Perhaps, maybe, the water'll be all placid and peaceful. We'll see pebbles on the bottom.' She heard her voice sharpening. 'The storms will have done the trick – you imagine?'

'May be dried out. You remember, we came last summer and there was no water?'

'It was the drought.'

'It was the pumping station.'

'Both. The river was dead, Elizabeth, I couldn't bear to look. And now at least it's running again.'

Didn't look at her either. Elizabeth always had that piercing honesty – and after all the snow and storms –

Last year dry stones had peeped through cracked mud like the tips of bones. There'd been a dead fish belly up stranded at the heart of a swarm of flies. 'Dad said it didn't run for weeks. Could one minnow have survived? D'you think? I keep imaging this place – got the right, haven't I – as it used to be, when I was a kid.' She swung on her heel and started to stride off. Rows of houses, concrete foundations deep into the earth, tarred drives, access roads winding round. The earth underneath turning sour. Pipes with water for washing machines and baths supplying nothing for roots – which couldn't have grown any-way – no nutrients from dead plants leaching down. No sunlight getting through the tarmac. Perhaps a few snails might linger on, some tenacious mites. Bacteria maybe. No leather-jackets for rooks to probe after. No moles. 'OK, OK don't keep looking like that. I know – people need houses – they do, I admit – so no more buttercups.' Why specify them specially?

There'd been a day when her mother held one under her chin, 'Your chin's turned gold, Mira.' Another when she'd watched a bee take off from a shining bowl, thighs loaded with pollen. 'While we're at it, let the kingfisher go too. But – don't they have any rights? Why should we accept it?' Her mouth was a lid wobbling on a boiling kettle. 'Or do people? Really need houses?'

'Please – not today, Mira.'

The final assertion came through stiff lips. 'Better stay in London all the time. Won't see what's going on.'

Elizabeth laid a hand on her shoulder. 'We've planted your mother's lilies out for her. We'll have to come back to see them flowering.'

Her friend felt calmer, all the same pulled away back onto the bridge and laid her arms on the rail. Her shoulders wanted to roll forward and let her head drop onto those arms – and then she'd cry and never stop. She gazed upstream across a tussocky meadow towards the house and the elegant blue-green canopy of the cedar on the front lawn. There was nothing to say. She pushed back, 'Time's moving. Come on.'

Such old-fashioned meals her parents had – cold lamb, boiled potatoes, casseroled leeks. They still grew their own vegetables.

She cleared the last scraps on her plate and took time laying the knife and fork neatly across it. 'What's going on in Trenchard's Field? We were down there this morning and there was some kind of mechanical digger churning it up.'

Her mother formed a ball of mashed potato, lodged on her fork, paused holding it in the air. 'Housing estate. You knew that.'

'Forgotten. How big?'

She took time before swallowing. 'Herald could have said a thousand.' She turned to her husband. 'Have I got it right, Dan? Or was it that other one?' And as he paused,

'That one at the end of Farm Close Estate – or is it an extension to Farm Close? Not a whole new one, you know. Fair size. They're all that. They say we have to have them. Quite nice little houses, some of them. Once they get the gardens going.'

'Trenchard's field. You said you'd object.'

'Your father did.'

'You know how diplomatically he does it. No-one would ever know he'd said anything. You could have put in an objection on your own. You'd be entitled.'

'We act as one. Elizabeth, some more potato?'

'How could anyone think that number was viable?' Perhaps he'd understand that argument. 'The aquifers are drying up and everyone needs water.'

Her father laid down his fork. 'This is getting boring, Miranda.'

She glared. 'You wrote a letter and sat back. I'd have staged a sit-in.'

Her mother's smile was stiff. 'Don't spoil things, Mira. You're not here so often.'

On a chair later under the cedar, listening to two blackbirds, trying to make out whether the cries were love or war, she said, 'They've got their heads in the sand – more houses – at this stage. Can't they see? The planet's being destroyed and they're letting it happen. Why?'

Elizabeth allowed her right arm to trail over the edge of the chair, then began making shapes in the dust with one finger. Round and round, idly. As if not thinking.

'Liza, please, it matters.'

A murmur. 'I don't answer to Liza'

'You wouldn't answer if I said anything else.'

Elizabeth examined a dusty maze. 'You actually know the way you're wanting to go, don't you? Whether Gavin's right is another matter.' She glanced up sideways through her hair. 'You'll never be satisfied till you've had the guts to test his submission from all sides.'

'Don't agree with it, do you?'

'I can see the attractions. I'm a lawyer, Mira. In the habit of suspecting worthy arguments. Sceptical mind, you know. Not nice.'

When afternoon walks were called off because of rain, a semi-robot who could still be plumped up by a feeling of extreme virtue, got on with the job of preparing lessons, sitting in her room at the same desk where years before she'd mugged up A-level biology and maths. She rested her chin on her hand. A wonderful, hot summer. A cuckoo had sat apparently just outside the window – a flock of them to judge from the racket – but cuckoos fly solo – it was just the sheer persistence, cuckoo, cuckoo, cuckoo on and on though even in those days the call was becoming rarer, you were supposed to be glad to hear it.

Not 'sat'. A cuckoo calls as it flies. The sound had faded towards Trenchard's Bridge. That year it had been the impossibility of graphs that had wound her up.

Today it was the full stop – or rather the chore of making it a fun thing for 7C. Waste of time when half of them didn't come in any more. And those who were left? Hyperactive, streetwise kids. Little sods, you said in the staffroom. Entirely inappropriate to throw your arms round them, offer them the love life seemed to be denying. For a teacher, 'love' meant hammering away at the full stop.

Cuckoo, cuckoo. The repetition had knocked its way in like a woodpecker's beak. She'd put up with it once. No cuckoo now. So bear the sight of houses, clustering like aphids, sucking the life out of the countryside?

She designed statements that made nonsense without a full stop. 'People have to have houses without trees the air is dead.' The orange monster would be raising and lowering its neck, gulping down Trenchard's Field. Next week she'd be back in London. The field would be flayed.

She couldn't make out what was eating her. In London she was absolutely clear how to save the planet. What was shaking her here at home, making her slip and slide?

Trenchard's Field was only a hectare or so of grass where there used to be cows, Friesians, then later Charollais. She'd wait at the gate and they'd gather towards her, lowering their heads, sniffing, slobbering over her sleeve, raising blue eyes to stare under curling lashes. Huge, inquisitive ninnies.

Just ordinary. Not the Lake District or the Cairngorms. So why not allow families with kids like Chay to move here and enjoy the countryside? The river was running again.

Because of storms followed by unprecedented snow.

Gavin's answer was radical.

That evening her father rested his hands on the arms of his chair. 'Well, Elizabeth, what are you and Miranda planning for your holiday this year?' He could keep lids on boiling kettles. That's why they made him principal. She watched him let his back slide down into the upholstery, stretch his legs, lift his elbows onto the arms, clasp his hands over his stomach, regard Elizabeth with level brown eyes.

She co-operated. 'We'd thought of Norway – or Iceland.'

Had they? Well perhaps – and given up the idea.

She concentrated on him. Brown jacket, brown shoes, brown hair. Designed not to be noticed while he got his own way. Fancy tie to make the students think he was cool.

Elizabeth sat up and went on graciously, 'I've never seen a glacier.'

Her profile was so calm it seemed distant, shining palely the other side of double-glazing where she'd left her friend outside, watching, strangely able to hear everything – and yet all was incredibly remote.

She couldn't shout out that the glaciers had melted long ago, there was nothing left except cliffs and rock. The room was cut off. Armchairs she'd known all her life, and always, it seemed, covered in the same flowered somewhat shabby chintz, the off-white Chinese rug, the Copenhagen mermaid on the side table all looked as if they were nothing to do with her. In a strange way, finished.

Even her father's voice seemed remote. 'I remember, Elizabeth, when Emma and I were first hitched we had a week up near the Jostalbree. Quite amazing, very remote in those days. Don't know what it's like now, of course. Have you thought of that area?'

One of his gifts, always to know something that would suit you better than what you'd thought of for yourself. Indignation kicked her back through the screen to a place she'd rather not have been, ranting on. 'Just to look at empty hillsides? What d'you imagine there is to see now? You know the glaciers have melted? Or you didn't take it in? Or perhaps you'd like to stand there and indulge some kind of sadness that won't interfere too much with your holiday. Might even spice it up, who knows?' She heard the harshness in her voice; let it leap on because the subject justified it. 'Come on, admit it. You'll go somewhere this summer 'just to get away from it all' won't pay attention to what's in front of you – because your little life's so important everything else seems miles away.'

Her father gave her one of his patient looks. 'At the end of a long summer term, what would anyone do?'

'God, Dad, you're so flabby over things that matter – though I bet the governors wince at that tie.'

He sharpened. 'They don't give me instructions about my ties – or my holidays either if you're imagining that.'

She was still wrestling with that orange monster, to defend Hayle – and somehow at the same time stand up for Chay and Danny and Julie, helpless, blasted by rays that people who lived in nice places discounted in favour of economic development. The words jerked out, 'Why didn't you stop the council giving permission for Trenchard's Field? You say you get what you want from the governors. Or is that just a story?'

'Time for the news.' Her mother always swallowed before coming up with that soft voice, 'Your father isn't God, dear.'

He looked at his watch. 'Wouldn't mind the headlines.' He reached for the remote, half rising from his chair, showing the curve in his back that was becoming more pronounced, more difficult to straighten. Years back, a cheeky thirteen year old, she'd let him see she thought a stoop was funny. One of those growing up things when you try to be big about something you don't really find funny at all. 'Serve you right,' she'd said, 'for spending your time looking down on other people.'

Cruel, hitting back at him for something time was doing to him, understanding just enough to suspect he was powerless – but he should have power, your father, shouldn't he?

Even at that age she'd expected a cold answer. 'In case you hadn't noticed, Miranda, my students are all grown up.'

That day she was battling with him again, trying to pull out all his resources. Maybe that was the only way she knew to cling on to him. Certainly wasn't watching TV with any interest.

'An explosion has occurred in the Solomon Islands. At 10 a.m. Greenwich Mean Time, the power station blew up.'

He leant forward, straining his fingers together, listening to the expert whose warnings had been ignored.

'An American aircraft carrier is standing by to take off survivors.'

Long lines bit into his face. She thought he must be tired. College would sap his energy as school did hers. Students, lecturers, maintenance officers, barging in with irreconcilable demands. The lecturers apparently the most difficult. Easier than thirty-eight hyperactive fourteen year olds.

And the college campus leafy.

'Manchester United have lost to Accra Great Olympics.'

He pointed the remote at a sandy stadium, the picture vanished.

He'd sit in his office, offer a chair, lean back and listen – or pretend to. He'd developed this canny, non-confrontational approach, trusting the reasonableness of adults. Or was if fear? Was he afraid to stand up to them?

Fear was powerless in the face of global warming, pollution, the endless snaking of roads.

But roads were OK.

'Perhaps Elizabeth would like to see some of our pictures.' Mum suggested. It wasn't the time for one of her diversionary tactics. It was a moment to come to grips.

Emma glanced sideways at her husband and smiled at Elizabeth. 'Just before we went, Dan's uncle gave him this splendid camera. Cost the earth, I imagine. He had a wonderful time playing with all those menus all the time we were there. Kept scrolling through and each time he found a new facility he came running to show it. Wasted on me. I don't understand these things as I should but he loved it. Fantastic what you can do. Quite fantastic.'

This chatter was terrible. 'Mum there's no way you can expect people to be reasonable all the time.'

Elizabeth and Emma exchanged glances.

Her father blinked, 'Relevance please?' Frowned, nodded. 'Ah, but that expert had no nous. In my experience people respond well when explanations are presented the right way.'

Wrong end of the stick as usual. The Solomon Islands were the other side of the world, symptomatic, of course, of the way no-one was coming to grips. But distant. The true pain burst out. 'The devastation. Hayle's had it. You haven't done a thing to stop it.'

'I wrote a strong letter.'

Her mother's voice leapt across trying to stitch edges together. 'This is the hotel we stayed in. That window's our bedroom. At least, I think so. The garden went right down to the fiord. Dan, d'you remember how we used to take the boat out from the boathouse behind those firs? Every morning, Elizabeth, we were out on that water. Reflections, the mountains, soft sun. It really was a dream.'

'Frelland had it years ago.' The words set on her daughter's lips like a concrete road-sign. The three of them were turning away form her, bending their heads, huddled over that photo. But a stream of grey lava had been creeping over the village ever since she'd been ten. First the Church Commissioners had sold off the vicarage and the Glebe Meadow. When she was little she'd lain in bed listening to the strange cries of the tawny owls. It was then they'd stopped. Five houses had been built on the old station, thirteen more along the line of the railway. Not that she'd ever known trains, but they'd walked there, she and her mother and Aunty Jan. Cow parsley, Herb Robert, white campion, muddy streak on the bank where the badgers had clambered down, corner where a fox cub had stared before whishing off into the grass. Her first school had gone, the lime trees in the playground – in spite of a preservation order. Huxtables Farm, Longfield Farm, the wood at the bottom of Hadlow Hill replaced by chi-chi brick and gardens with space for three cars and begonias. 'Two thousand houses,' people said,' – can you believe it?'

'If Frelland goes, Hayle does too –' The garden would be tarmacked, the house left staring at a row of garages.

'Is that a photo of the cold table?' Elizabeth asked. 'What did you think of the food?'

Another expert at diversionary tactics. 'As long as people need houses they'll go on building them.' Her friend was still hoping to bring them round but her mother flinched and that made her see, not exactly red, more like deep purple. It was them she was afraid for, both of them, that they would be trapped under the creeping stream of concrete. That was the immediate danger. Beside and beyond that was the power of ultra-violet rays.

Elizabeth was beside her on the sofa. Her side was warm, her face turned away. Experience said that when she spoke her words would be aimed into the air – 'Can't fight your father all your life.'

If reason was required, her partner would summon it up from that place deep inside her where it seemed to lie buried. And present it. Logically, irresistibly. As she did. 'We've got to make a choice.' She was sure her voice was, if not totally calm, at least quiet enough for no-one to notice the tremble. Like her hands would be if she could lay them on his shoulders to hold him till he saw sense. 'Basically there are three things – cars, houses, the ecological system.' She shook three fingers at him in turn, checking them off. 'We can't have all three. Perhaps your generation could when you were young – things weren't so clear then – they've moved on now – we've all got to choose. The time's come.'

He looked at her. 'Gavin Claring?' He looked sideways, enrolling his wife as he always did so that his daughter was on her own.. 'That man's got a lot to pay for. Very plausible, of course, good manner on the box, academic credentials – what are they worth nowadays? But his substance –'

'Bilge I suppose?' She longed to rip off those heavy brown spectacles.

They were impenetrable, reflecting the window.

'Did I say so?' He contemplated his fingers and looked up. 'The man wouldn't have the following he has if everything he said was totally 'bilge' as you call it. It's not complete nonsense, Miranda, simply, in my opinion, against human nature.' He leant back again, touching his fingertips together.

'But education? Don't you believe in education – and reason?'

'In something as fundamental as this? Are you hoping to change human nature?' He gave his daughter a long, cold stare. 'How much difference d'you think you make to your pupils, in fundamentals that is?'

Skills, she'd often said, and tools. That's all you could realistically hope to give them.

'I've heard you often enough, going on about *giving them a vision*.' How fatuous it had seemed, but now – 'That's it. What we need is a vision – sort of – more a decision based on reason. The facts are all round us, anyone can see. The riversdrying up. I was down this morning beside the Amond. It's better than it was – and we've had rain – but another new development – what then? And you haven't seen London. Round our way, they've knocked down the corner houses in Saviour Walk and opened a road in so people can park on the back gardens. They're doing the same in our street. All the houses are flatted. Four flats in each house. Probably at least two people getting to work, everyone over eighteen with a car. Work out how many that means.'

Elizabeth laid a hand on her arm

'Why not get rid of the cars?' It was the level tone of someone introducing a seminar.

'Whoever'd want to give up their car? You can't go back, Dad, you can't go back.'

'Sounds to me as if the way back is the way forward.' The windows reflected in his glasses were streaked with oily, iridescent greens and purples, opaque, disturbing, not seeming to relate to trees or flowers outside. 'Have you considered how compact cities would be if we weren't addicted to cars?'

'You and Mum have one each. And the Airborne for special. Be honest. You'd never give them up. And if you did, you'd always have had them. You'd be one of those who'd enjoyed them. What about those who've never had one? Who've watched other people swanning round while they struggled with public transport, couldn't take jobs because they couldn't get there? Who've hoped and hoped, a better life one day and now you come breezing along and say they can do without. How heartless can you get?'

'Occasionally,' the glasses were obviously made of one-way glass, 'groups of students feel they have to make personal attacks in order to get their own way.'

'I'm trying to talk on level terms.'

'Have you imagined the world that man wants – the demolishers moving in on this house?'

'It wouldn't happen.'

'D'you see your mother and me spending our old age in a caravan?'

The monster was half a mile away, at work gulping Frelland down.

'Gavin's not in the grip of money. Developers are.'

'You seem to know him well.'

Mum was fidgetting. 'Can't think what I've done with my speakie. I was using it this afternoon, in the kitchen, wasn't it, Mira?'

She stared blankly. 'No idea, Mum.' Was she some kind of lost property expert? She struggled to get back to a clear line of thought. 'The idea's not to knock down absolutely everything. Suburbs, yes, the whole soggy mass. Tower blocks, estates, ribbon developments, cram-jammed terraces, all those pimply bungalows – and good riddance. 'Hayle's heritage. Different.'

'Your mother and I would be kept on as caretakers?'

'If that's what you want. Gavin says there'll be homes for the disabled and the really old. He knows not everyone can cope.' Her father looked more tired than ever. 'I'm sure they'd be glad for the owners to take care of them. You could see to it that everything stayed as lovely as ever.' Her arms tensed, she shot upright. 'Please Dad, please, don't talk as if you were both toddling into your graves. Come off it – you're only middle-aged. It's not too late. Does all change have to be bad?' She could feel sweat in her armpits and prickling down her sides.

He spoke harshly. 'Don't be fooled. You're not going to uproot a whole population.'

'But to let them die, trapped in the inner city, burnt by ultra-violet light? Kids dying of cancer? And it's not just this country you know.'

'I'm aware there are voices overseas repeating the same mantras.'

'The States, Russia, China – all over the globe and you still think you know better?'

'Be a love, please Miranda, do get my speakie.'

Her father's stare was colder than ever. 'That man doesn't have a solution. He's not a great brain.' She opened her mouth but he bore down. 'Wonderful what TV can do.'

'Sorry –' her mother's voice was frantic, 'I could get it myself but I'm really tired – been a long day somehow – don't know what I did with it but it's gone on and on. Days do that nowadays. Promised your Uncle Arthur I'd ring.'

When she came back with it, Dad had taken himself off to his study. She scowled at the empty chair.

'It's been a difficult term. Your Dad's tired.' Her mother folded her hands onto the lap of her shabby dress. 'Sit down, Mira. Tell me a bit more about it.'

'You know already. Been on TV.'

'I'm afraid I don't always pay enough attention.'

'This is really important.'

'Mira,' Elizabeth said gently, 'just tell her, will you?'

She sat still. Then she spoke slowly. 'The idea is to try to reduce emissions to an extent that will reduce the hole in the ozone layer. Cars of course produce some, but houses are responsible for more. No government has ever come to terms with this – not more than to come up with a little fiddle-faddling on the subject of solar panels – Gavin

Claring's come up with the answer 'Get rid of houses, totally.' Well – not all – but most. Then divide out the country so that there are large areas reserved for wildlife where people don't go. These will be mostly in the uplands and along estuaries. But they will be big. Think of it, Mum, if wild creatures can flourish the balance of nature will be restored. Think of it, round here, this garden, the river, Trenchard's field – wouldn't it be wonderful, the kingfisher, the owls, fritillaries? Like there used to be? You and Dad could keep bees –'

'Yes,' her mother said thoughtfully, 'that's what I thought.'

'Thought? What did you think?

'That that was what he was saying.' She glanced at her daughter. 'Just wanted to be sure. And if Hayle's demolished?'

'We have a choice what to do with the rest of the country but it seems an enormous opportunity – like no-one's had for centuries – to be free to move where we like. It looks like a tough choice – cars or houses but, when you think it all out, which do you value more?'

'And if we need both?'

'Can't you see that's become impossible?' She was close to tears.

Elizabeth turned and placed both hands round her shoulders. She'd never before been as open as this in front of others. 'Mira, Mira,' she was rubbing her back, 'this is where we are. In this impossible situation.'

Next morning after she'd made her bed and walked in the garden she tracked Elizabeth to the sitting-room absorbed in a book. The sound of Elgar floated down the stairs. Her mother would be up there in whatever room that was playing. The guest bedroom, as it turned out.

She was standing on a chair taking down the curtains. Her shoes had been placed neatly side by side under the wall to one side of the chair. Her daughter watched as her arms strained up lifting the clips out of the holders, then gradually filled with a mass of heavy material that pushed her body away from the wall and threatened to over-balance her. It came to her how drawn Mother's face had looked last night.

She reached her arms up. 'Give me those.'

The weight came down, it filled her arms, covered her face. Her mother lifted one end off her. They drew apart and folded it between them. Then they took all the rest down, folded them, piled them on a chair.

'What are you going to do with them, Mum?'

'Wash and iron.' She drew the back of her hand across her face. They both stood listening to Elgar till the older woman said, 'Let's sit for a moment.'

They sank onto the bed and sat, side by side.

'Your father and I had a holiday once in Malvern. That's exactly the Worcestershire countryside he's describing in that music, isn't it?'

She nodded. A river bubbled past, wind blew through grass.

It finished. The room filled with quiet. Then Emma – the name came suddenly to her daughter, looking into her mother's face, seeing her suddenly as a person with her own life to sort out – laid her hand on her daughter's lap. 'Your Dad's more upset than you realise.'

The younger woman looked down at the hand that lay across her knee a little plump, the back covered in freckles, old-fashioned ring sunk into the folds of soft flesh.

'I'm not blaming you, Mira, just saying.' Emma drew herself together and threw back her shoulders. 'He'd been looking forward to his retirement. Didn't tell you, did we, he was planning to go back to his own college as a student?'

'To learn what?'

'Bricklaying. He wanted to repair the old wall round the orchard. You know what he's like about getting everything exactly right. He may never have been to university, Miranda, but he knows what knowledge is.'

She brooded over a career her mother had so often described – ten years teaching in Secondary Modern schools, then the move into Further Education, his rise to Principal, a progress she'd often told her friends about, trying not to boast of course, just saying, while she stored up inside her the knowledge it was ordinary kids she wanted to teach.

'It surprised me, Mira, when we bought this house how keen he was on DIY. He's put so much into it.'

'Yeah – when I was a kid. He was fitting the banisters. The way he touched them.'

'It's very hard for him to have to leave.'

'You're really going?' She'd known for ages. Now she began to believe it.

'Whatever happens, Hayle won't be the same. And as for what could happen if that man gets in –'

'But Mum –'

'Your Dad has his convictions.'

There was nothing to say.

The curtains were amethyst with a pattern of deep blue geraniums and almost purple petunias. She'd often wished she could have them for her room.

'Are you taking these with you?' She knew perfectly well they were the wrong size for a van.

'We don't know yet how much we'll be able to take.' Emma took a deep breath. 'Mira dear, why don't you come with us? Both of you?'

Her daughter screwed the images of flowers tight between her fingers. A house with a view of a lake. Room to breathe. So different from here. Another world.

'I'm sorry, Mum, really, really sorry, I can't.' She paused, looked at her words. That was the truth, perhaps the first time she'd ever reached down into herself at that depth.

If she'd known universes could fly so far apart, would she have made the same choice? There was no way to know.

Two days later she and Elizabeth left for London. The last time she saw them.

A brand new Vanacar was gleaming outside number 96. She studied its roof from the flat window. Another hour. And then? She turned sharply back. 'Shall I take the box down? Is it to go for clearance?'

Arms full of bulging cardboard, chins holding down raised lids, neither of them able to see over, the stairs were a nightmare. Made it to the outside and plonked it all down beside quantities of other stuff.

She wiped her cheek. 'OK, Elizabeth? Heaviest job over.'

No reply.

She moved forward and touched sun-warmed metal.

'This white. Thought it might be too austere but it's just right.'

'Glad you let us have it sober.'

'Sucker for jazzy designs, aren't I? But you're right. Better to keep things simple.' She pointed two vans down. 'Just look at that. Whose is it?'

'Only ones it could be – Bensons – top flat in 94. You might say they've gone overboard in their choice of colours.'

'Don't laugh. Most of us wouldn't dare – wow what a sight – Op Art in yellow and black – the whole thing.

Makes me feel like jumping around hugging myself.'

'Try growing up.'

'Be the first off too. You'll see.' The family were already on board, grinning out through the windows. She went on looking. 'Or just in too much of a hurry? But I've got to love them, Elizabeth, for simply daring.'

'To try out the harmonies of the New Dawn?' Her voice was dry.

Her friend stirred. 'They are harmonies.'

'Of a kind.' Elizabeth gazed down the line of vans drawn up at the pavement two deep, blocking the road. Red, blue, orange and green, plain orange, blue again, yellow and blue, pink and blue with a gold sun on the roof. 'Gipsy Life', 'Fancy Free', 'Wanderlust', 'Queen of the Road', Tramp's Delight.' Her face was calm as usual, almost deliberately expressionless.

'Don't you feel the excitement? At all?'

People ran up and down the steps, their arms full of groceries, family tee shirts, piles of sheets, boxes of crockery, TV sets. They dodged round, stepped over, swore at the clobber on the pavement; clambered into vans, stuck their heads out, yelled for children.

The speakie beside Miranda's ear brought in voices from Bristol, Nottingham, Market Dereham reporting on all that was happening there.

Elizabeth went on looking.

Two doors down a pair of teenagers were resting their bottoms against a garden wall. The finger of the nearest was twiddling the knobs of some machine slung round his neck. Strands of pink roses hung over the wall. Their heads were haloed by brick dust rising from a house on the corner. It spurted fifty, maybe sixty feet into the air and swooshed down in a hazy waterfall. Fragments of brick clattered like small bombs. The boys' faces were dreamy.

'Only the old –' Elizabeth said softly.

'They won't stay here.'

'No, even here they've got to move. Hard to lose your home like this – at their age.' She seemed rooted to the pavement. 'You said last night you'd got yourself sorted out about Hayle?'

'It'll still be there. Different, but good. Don't look at me like that. I don't need sympathy. I can imagine all those old people living there. They'll really enjoy it.'

'I hope so. Your parents seem happy.'

'Will be when they get their visas for the States.' What had to be, had to be. Mum's herb garden, the dirty mark on the wall by the back door where Dad rested his hand when he pulled off his wellies, the bare patch under the cedar where they put out chairs on hot days. 'Harder for Mum. She was brought up there.'

Elizabeth reached out to touch her. 'We'll call in and see them before they go. You'd like that, wouldn't you? For myself, I feel I'd like to, if you don't mind.'

Of course, it didn't happen.

'Why should I? They like you. Better than me sometimes, I think.'

'Easier when you're not related. Your Dad and I are on same wavelength.' She pressed her hand down on her friend's shoulder. 'He does love you, you know. Just not very good at showing it.'

She tossed it off. 'Maybe. Too late now. They're going.'

'They respect your decision.'

'Our decision.'

Elizabeth's lips firmed. 'Our decision. Come upstairs and I'll show you something.'

She laid the album on the kitchen worktop. 'We'll sign it later, shall we, once we're ready to go?'

Her friend stroked the soft leather, ran her fingertip along lines and curls of gold tooling. 'When did you get this?'

'Other day.'

'Didn't tell me.'

'Need something to help us remember.'

Her partner turned to smile at her over her shoulder, laid the book softly on the table, bent and emptied the pedal bin.

When they got downstairs again she saw a small crowd had gathered on the pavement at the far end of Sydenham Avenue. She grabbed Elizabeth's hand and towed her down there.

The front and side walls had been bashed off numbers 2 and 4. They could see walls in different rooms, papered plain in one, a mass of sprawling climbers in another, neat rosebuds in a third, a horrific pattern of broad red and black stripes in a fourth, slanting lines of white marble heads. And the people who'd chosen those papers had lived side by side. It was a revelation.

Washbasins clung at crazy angles, carpets dangled over edges, floorboards ends stuck out, plaster swung in webs. A jagged fragment broke from a ceiling and came planing down.

A small boy, eight years old maybe, bounced on the step of the Op-Art caravan. 'Where's my Blackberry?'

His mother's voice shrilled from inside. 'Packed. I told you.' A flowered dress swung into the doorway. 'Can't have it till we reach camp.' The eyes were green, the mouth pinched. 'Won't be long now, Matt. Off soon.' She shot a glance over his shoulder. 'He's so excited.'

Miranda smiled up. 'Who isn't?'

The woman's glance passed beyond. 'Don, put that chair on the pavement. Not there, the other side, dumbo.' Her glance shifted to the cloud of brick dust, she stared at them. 'Strange, isn't it, you spend years collecting all these things, and then, when the crunch comes, you let them go. To old people's homes, junk piles, whatever. Absolutely no problem. All of a sudden you can do without.' With one eye on her family, she murmured a report on goings on in West Hampstead to anyone who might be listening in the rest of England.

All round, both sides of the road, pavements were stacked with chairs, tables, beds, bedside lockers, cookers and washing machines, commodes, the odd chest of drawers, a battered wooden cupboard.

Elizabeth murmured, 'Everyone clings till the last moment.'

'Need a bed to sleep on. And the Council's swamped. Be hours before the lorries can get round to pick it all up.'

'What'll they do with it?'

'Homes for the severely disabled. The rest – somewhere. They said they would.'

Bins had been placed at convenient intervals to receive redundant crockery, rugs, flower vases, garden tools, mops, newspaper racks, excess saucepans, floor polish.

'Perhaps they'll export them.'

Matt's mother came down the steps. 'You know, when we first started listening to Gavin, this one wasn't born. His sister was just, I think. Or maybe not. In those days Gavin sounded utterly barmy. It was only – the idea wouldn't go away.'

'Now we're doing it.'

And it's wonderful,' but her eyes were still anxious. 'Never had such a sense of daring. And freedom. From everything. We'll all be free.' The green eyes wavered. 'Don, the washing machine's labelled for the launderette in the Swindon camp. They're collecting it at three. By the gate post. That's right. That's what's so wonderful about Gavin. Shows you the way, doesn't he? Why did we ever want our own private washing machines?'

'Well,' Elizabeth said slowly, 'with the quantity going now they'll be able to keep the camps stocked for years. It is an economy certainly.'

The woman swung her hand in a vague gesture. 'Surely our lives have been far too complicated – haven't they?'

Two doors further down a man lifted a dining-room chair at the full height of his arms up over the steps of a blue van. A woman reached down to grab it.

Elizabeth watched with soft eyes. 'We've found our things useful enough.'

'And now we're free.' 'Enough for what?' A simultaneous outburst from two women who looked at each other, broke off.

Elizabeth gave them a cool look, then broke into a laugh. 'At least we shan't have to pay household insurance any more.'

A man in designer jeans dashed past clutching three cartons of milk.

'Have you seen any of these people before, Elizabeth? Astonishing – they've all been our neighbours – could have been for years – now we're standing in the street and talking.'

'Final supplies,' the man said coming to a standstill, clapping his hand against the cartons. 'Last cows' milk they had.' He studied their faces. 'Didn't you know? All soya from now on.'

'You're ready for off?'

'In the next half hour.' He suddenly swung back his head. They did the same. Their end of the three-storey redbrick terrace was shaking – solid walls quivering like the branches of a weeping willow in high wind. She tracked the cause, a ball swinging half way down.

'Lumbering the earth,' he said, 'pompous Edwardian monstrosities. Not sorry to see them go.' He brought his gaze down from the upheaval and shot them a sideways glance. 'Don't know what you think – unfriendly place this. North London. Definitely unfriendly. Notorious for it. Be better, d'you think, when we can't shut ourselves away?'

His smile was a chink opening.

'We'll look out for you at the first camp.'

He raised his hand in a gesture that wasn't quite 'see you', not quite 'good-bye.'

Elizabeth was watching that wall. Her hand shot to her mouth. 'We've left Soccie. Council should have sent someone to warn us. Don't need the key. Nothing left to lock in.'

She ran up the steps. Her friend hesitated, decided to trust her.

'See – gone – roof gone?' A boy jumped down from the orange and black van and pointed. 'Sky.'

She shot towards the steps. They met half way up. Soccie's fur was crushed against the bars of his carrying basket. He was wailing like a lost vampire. She grabbed him in one hand, Elizabeth's arm with the other; they spilled out into the open air.

'Two and four, gone.' A woman on the pavement flung her arm up, pointing. 'Stand back, stand back,' and the whole block came thudding down in a cloud of dust.

A laburnum left in a front garden seemed to have shot up, king of all it surveyed. Solitary now, it hung over the row of caravans, the people milling backwards and forwards, outer branches still swaying from the blast. Outlined against blue.

'When the rubble settles, nature will take over. You see, Elizabeth? That was a nice beginning – that man talking. Gives me hope.'

'Are you imagining cuckoos here – or dandelions?'

'Everything. They'll all come.'

Elizabeth gave her friend a twisted, little smile and she did nothing to comfort her.

The woman beside them on the pavement had taken her mind off her speakie and was listening in. 'D'you hear that, Jim? In a few years this place will be full of birds.'

Jim rubbed his head. 'Meanwhile, Meg – what about shifting this junk from the pavement?'

'Council are supposed to be taking it. Come out of that van, Matt. I told you to wait here. Where've Sally and Gemma gone? OK go and fetch them at once.' Her eyes roved up and down the street, then fixed on the pavement. 'All this junk.' She stared as if seeing it for the first time.

'Why don't we burn it? ' She turned, fired with inspiration. 'Now the houses are coming down – space for a bonfire. Mother said they were wonderful – when she was little – she'd sit in our kitchen and tell me – but now? This once? All this dust flying any way.'

'What, the whole lot?'

Meg pushed strands of reddish, greasy hair off her face with the heel of her palm. 'Ours any-way. Save anyone else having to do it. Others can bring theirs if they want. Hey,' she cried turning, waving to everybody up and down the road, 'we're going to burn this rubbish. Any of you can bring yours.'

Jim rubbed his hands. 'That's my girl. Nothing if not masterful.'

She stuck her tongue out at him, waved to Matt and two small girls in red trousers bouncing on the van steps, shouted, 'Come on all of you.'

The woman watched, amazed how one decision had let loose an energy that gave her authority.

'Each carry what you can. When I've checked with the workmen.'

Figures hung round murmuring and gawping till she returned. 'They're going to Elm Grove next. Behind number two's safe. If you look where you're going.' Her voice became softer. 'Right Matt, you carry that chair, Sal and Gemma, take the table between you. Jim, you help me with the bed. Watch where you put your feet, girls. Matt's found the best way. Sorry, didn't mean to bump into you. Just taking things we don't want to burn them. On space behind number two. Open now, see? Why don't you bring yours? Most hygienic thing, burning. Waste of time waiting for the council. Anything you like to bring. Good, Matt, back already? Careful how you lift that one. Do watch out, Jay.'

People began to drift along the pavement and peer through the space where a terrace had been only ten minutes earlier. Megan and her family picked their way under the shadow of the laburnum, clambered over the ruins, descended through the rubble onto the lawn. The demolition crane had come to a standstill ready to start on Elm Grove while the driver, perched high up there in his cab with his hand on a lever, twisted his head back over his shoulder, had a good look down.

An old man on the pavement gave a chair a sly, sideways glance, suddenly swept it by a leg high into the air above his head. Blue veins and sinews stood up on the back of his hand. He had a mole on his wrist. He leant back waving it, seemed to be measuring the distance, let his arm drop. The chair hung like a dead rabbit. 'Not much use now?' he said coaxingly.

No-one said anything. With a sudden grimace he stepped off the pavement and began to stumble through the rubble. Dust flew up round him and plastered his jacket. He rubbed his eyes with his free hand.

On the pavement a young man clapped the shoulder of a girl at his side. 'Hey, Sam, isn't this just crazy? Let's give them your mother's drinks cabinet, shall we?'

She giggled and clutched his arm. 'We'll add that ghastly holograph you got last time we were in Washington.'

'Never thought I'd see these Brits let themselves go like this. Aren't you glad we've stayed?'

'Can always go home if it doesn't work.'

He looked at her oddly. 'How come you haven't taken on board it's the same there?'

'Not a piddling little place like Europe. There's space.'

'Not enough,' he said, unclipping his speakie, reaching out towards her. 'Listen to this.'

She shoved it away. 'Keep it.'

He shrugged and re-attached it to his ear.

In number two's back garden Megan stuffed rolled-up newspaper against the legs of a small table, threw her arm out. 'Kindling. Quick. Matt, Gemma, pull some of those stalks. Over there, yes. Dead flowers.' She back sat on her heels and wiped her cheek. 'Seems almost instinctive.'

The children ran backwards and forwards leaping over the bricks. The crowd watched from the pavement.

'Quick, quick, here. Come on.' She crouched, poking dry twigs under the table, held out a match. A flame leapt. She jerked her hand back. The flame flickered and became two. She stood up, wiping her hands over her hips. 'Anyone got anything to add?' Black streaks over her cheeks and down her trousers, a frame of smoke and a dust cloud rising from Elm Grove, made her look like a Gothic princess. 'OK, Matt, that'll do. Anyone got anything to add?'

The woman was being swept into the garden in a surge of bodies, with a unknown coffee table in her hands. The leaders were already leaping from lump to lump of rubble.

A dark haired boy of about fifteen, hurtled forward, scrambling with flailing arms and legs from brick to brick, brandishing a large, floppy paperback in his right hand. She thought it was that textbook she'd often seen lying round in classrooms and staffrooms. 'Comprehensible Mathematics –' something of that sort. No way of telling which of five grades this volume was. A few yards from the fire he threw his arm back and hurled the book, up towards the sky. It flew up and up, curved in a tight parabola down into the flames.

'Adrian,' – a woman's voice, sharp with anxiety – 'Adrian, what do you think you're doing?'

He tossed back his black hair. 'Shan't need it, shall I?'

His teeth gleamed.

His mother bit her lips.

Elizabeth touched her partner's arm. 'There's one got the wrong end of the stick.'

'Just the excitement. That's all.' Voices chattered from the speakie in her ear, reporting houses coming down in Wolverhampton, city gates being demolished in Carlisle, families loading vans in Norwich, releasing a cat into the wild in Rye. 'Can't you feel it? We're all in it together – one mass movement.'

People thrust past their arms crammed with pictures, chairs, a folding bed, cushions, flower vases.

Elizabeth thrust her hands into the pockets of her loose coat. 'What makes them imagine all that's going to burn?'

'Does it matter? It's the gesture. Today demands a grand gesture.'

The heap already towered above them all. Legs of tables and chairs stuck out and crossed one another in a jagged geometry, creating a weird scaffolding through which orange and blue flames surged crackling. Blue suddenly puffed up out of some bottle or can high in the stack and mounted like an Olympic torch. A bitter smell swept down over the crowd.

Elizabeth's hand leapt to her mouth. 'If that heap's got plastic in it –'

'Can't you see how beautiful it is?'

A cloud of smoke hid the sky.

A white-haired woman leant forward and prodded the flames with a garden rake, pushing it further and further till the handle blackened. And still she didn't let go. A girl in tight yellow trousers grasped a young man's arm, pulling him down as she came to crouch, pointing, till their noses were almost into the flames. 'I've always hated that chair, hated it, d'you understand?'

An elderly man pushed her aside. His arms were stiff above his head supporting a bookcase. His forehead and cheeks shone with sweat. He stood for a moment, arms stretched high like an ancient statue brought to life. She felt like skipping. 'D'you remember, Elizabeth, Zeus with his arm thrown back holding a thunderbolt, the Cloud-gatherer?'

The arms strained back, the bookcase tilted, skimmed forward, crashed into the centre of the fire.

People twisted towards the noise. Mouths pulled downwards, lines fanning from the corners of eyes, their faces seemed etched against a surface of brilliant light. Flames gasped under the bookcase and it went black. A pink tongue curled up and licked along a shelf.

The whole mass of people fell silent. The tongue flickered, died, came again. Two more licked up, then the whole shelf was aflame.

A sigh trembled. 'Aaaah.'

Somewhere at the back a man's voice exploded. 'Ga – vin'. The sound shot like a missile over the massed heads and through the flames to be answered from the opposite side. 'Ga – vin. New – Dawn. A moment's silence then the first voice roared again, 'Gaa – vinn.'

A new voice rose from deeper in among the bodies, 'Freeee – dom. New – Dawn.' The chant swelled, 'Freee – dom, New – Dawn, Gaa – vin.'

The name came each time like a drum roll.

She forgot Elizabeth at her side, saw Meg and Jay with eyes rolled upwards, lips expanding and closing with words that were lost in the din. She watched their throat muscles rise and fall against a sky streaked by leaping flames, bright, dark, bright, dark, a visual Morse that de-coded inside her. Far over to the right someone stamped, the rhythm swept through the mass in time with the chanting. Her mouth opened by itself.

Elizabeth grabbed her wrist. 'Let's go.'

She shook it off. 'Freedom,' she chanted. Her voice sounded thin among the rest. She filled her chest. 'Freee-dom. Freeee-dom.' Never again would they endure weekends in a stuffy flat. Never hear again this or that species was becoming extinct. They'd go wherever they liked, work wherever they came to rest – and time, there'd be time for things that mattered, lovers together, friends continually meeting, space for wildlife to breathe in, room to know another human being. Everyone felt it.. Eyes shone like headlamps. The shouting and stamping rolled in, swept her along, wrapped her in warmth.

The Dawn was breaking.

She reached out, met Jay's pudgy fingers and took them. They hesitated then squeezed hers and held on.

'Freeee –dom, freeee – dom.'

Now the crowd was holding hands, swinging them in time with the chant. The flames parted; there was a glimpse of the demolisher's crane. A dark ball was swaying, back, forward, a pendulum whose momentum increased with every swing.

People stood further apart to give room for linked hands to swing to shoulder height. It became harder for those who were shorter to keep in rhythm, sockets being jerked as people swung and stamped, stamped and swung. The centre of the fire fell in. All heads strained back, one last roar thundered out. In the silence that followed the ball thudded.

The crowd dropped hands, balanced, hesitant and uneasy, exchanged shy glances. A buzz crept through.

'Time to go,'

She turned. Elizabeth wasn't there.

She found her standing beside the van, shoulders hunched, studying the pavement.

As her friend came near she pulled in her arms as if gathering a cloak round her, spoke sideways, 'Sorry. Couldn't stand any more.'

'Could've told me you were going.'

'Would you have heard?'

The man who had been carrying cartons of milk brushed past and stopped. 'Still here?'

She gazed at him. 'And you?

He too seemed interested in the pavement. Shot a little glance. 'Had to stay, didn't you?'

She nodded. Elizabeth straightened.

'Needed something like that,' he said, ' – sort of?'

'It was a release, I suppose,' Elizabeth said slowly. 'Do you feel better for it?'

He drew into himself, waited. 'Could say I feel ten years younger – but something's gone. Feels like for ever.'

She smiled. 'Perhaps we need the weight of possessions.'

Her friend fidgeted. 'Don't be silly. We've been into all that.'

He shook himself. 'Won't keep you. Meet again sometime maybe.'

'Maybe. Travsure,' she said, trying out the new word, not as final as good-bye. It tasted good.

'Tomorrow, next week, who knows?' he paused. 'Travsure.' He hurried off.

A voice shrilled from the speakie in her ear. 'Post Office Tower's gone.'

She spoke clearly into her mike. 'West London, 3.27 pm, last house gone.' No way of knowing who heard. All part of the buzz.

She checked the tyres while wind swirled acrid smoke down the street. Made her cough.

Elizabeth fumbled in her bag, pulled out her camera, put Soccie's basket on the top step, focussed her lens.

They signed the album that night, looking at each other in a new place.

Part 3

The woman sat facing him in the darkness. A repeated tic jerked her right leg.

The New Dawn had been the right thing. She was still committed to it. Absolutely. Not absolutely maybe, more maturely perhaps, with greater understanding, which would include doubts – which had to be faced. At that time, think back to it, what else could anyone have done? If she hadn't realised a gap was opening, universes sliding apart, so what?

Cracks must have made themselves felt.

Had anyone realised? Mum perhaps? Looking back now at some of the things she'd said? Gavin Claring himself – so-called *Dawn Prophet* – had he understood then when every screen, noticeboard, lamppost even had been plastered with his portrait?

So-called? Wasn't prophet what he was? Shouldn't a prophet have known?

But think back. Think. Didn't every bit of daily life make it obvious something had to give?

It had to be houses. They were responsible for more emissions than cars. And larger. They took up more space. They trapped foul air. Politicians half-heartedly urging insulation, rising fuel costs –

The radical solution was the only one possible.

Hadn't seen then how radical. That so many people would refuse it. That Mum and Dad would refuse it.

Radical was right, right.

'Getting it, are you?'

Dark figure framed in light from the passageway pointing the knife straight at her stomach.

The woman gasped, flinched back, searched into the contorted mask.

Sunlight was slanting in touching the corner beside the back seat. Mid-morning. How long had he been standing there?

'Taken over. Don't you forget.'

Glancing sideways, she saw the top of a green van backing out of the next slot. Yell? She turned back to him.

'Taken over. Got it?' His stink wafted across.

Her legs were wet. 'What do you want me to do, Boss?

'Drive I said, didn't I?'

'Yes, Boss. Of course.' She looked him up and down. Had he something in mind, a robbery, someone – he wanted to catch up with –? She sat up. 'You want me to drive you? Where?'

'Where I want.'

'Kind of chauffeur?'

The smell came closer. 'Drive,' I said.

'A chauffeur's a posh kind of driver.'

'Posh, yeah.' He drew back, twisting the knife over and over in circles between thumb and first finger. Light flashed and died, flashed and died. He caught the handle and all was still. 'Good that. Yeah, I tell you where to go.'

'I'll have to get up.'

He almost spat, 'Think I didn't know that?' He stood watch while she made her way to the sink and splashed water on her face; backed before her into the sitting area.

'D'you think I could sit down, Boss?' She eased her hip gently sideways onto a bench. 'Where will you want to go?'

'Somewhere different.'

'Think I can manage that. Tomorrow, eh?' She sank against the padded back.

The devil driver dropped the hand with the knife. 'Needn't think I'm going to put this away.' He dropped onto the bench on the other side of the centre aisle and sat drumming a heel against the locker underneath. 'Today. Today, today.' His voice rose like a shrieking choirboy's.

'We'll need to eat first.'

'Won't.' He drummed harder, chewing the lips of the mask. At last, 'Said you was going to get me Crunchies.' She rose and strolled elaborately to the kitchen. Every time she moved his hand rose.

After they'd eaten he told her to sit quiet. 'Gonna search the seeding van.'

Her eyes opened, then, slowly, she nodded.

He started with the overhead lockers, balancing on tiptoe on the seat backs, swept his hand into far corners, tugged out duvets, hurled them onto the floor. Next he tore open the cupboard under the sink, twisted the lid off a bottle of cleaning liquid – 'How come you let the place get filthy like this?' and poured undiluted slime over the carpet, slammed the door shut. The van shook. He pulled out the kitchen drawers. Cutlery crashed onto the floor.

She hugged her arms round her.

He jerked open the drawers under the workstation.

She stiffened. 'Nothing but paper there, Boss.'

He slowly turned the top one upside down, let the papers cascade onto the floor, whisked into her bedroom. Bangs. Shoes? Thrown onto the floor?

Try explaining to the Frees – he had a knife – a knife, I tell you?

'Forgotten how to use the emergency button, have we? Like some other little things we've forgotten?' She shivered.

Crash. Not just contents but the drawers themselves tossed onto the floor?

Giggles bubbled up, took over, made her feel like a quivering blanket, better at least then tears. She was so tired. Listen to him, she thought, just listen to him.

Frenetic. Ought to be locked up.

Like a feral cat she'd been told about in the old days. Captured and brought into 'a good home,' went frantic, hissed, backed into a corner, spat, ran up the curtains. They had to let it go in the end. What drove it frantic? Was it the people watching? Or walls all round? Cats had domesticated themselves, archaeologists said. Could they lose that taste for warmth and comfort?

He appeared in the doorway, flapping something small, brown. Dead bird?

How'd he get it?

'What's this?'

'Bring it here, Boss.'

'You can see.'

It was a book.

He opened it, stared, took the two covers one in each hand, turned it over, let go one of them, shook, ran his fingers through the fanned leaves, tugged one, found it firm, swung the book shut, scratched the cover with his first finger.

'Don't do that.'

The hideous mask swung up. He raised the book to his nose and sniffed it.

She recognised Elizabeth's copy of *The Odyssey*. She'd knelt by the bookcase in the flat. Her hand had gone straight for it. 'Just right for travellers don't you think?' She'd been wearing a slinky green skirt and creamy blouse.

'Boss,' she said quickly. 'Bring it here. Before we had videos we had these. You've seen fax paper? In the old days people used to put all their documents on pieces of paper rather like that. They fastened them together to keep them safe.'

'Those squiggles not words.'

'They are, in another language.'

The smell as he came close took her back to other kids, Chay, Danny, Clara. What had happened to them now? Parents themselves by this time maybe. When they came near you tried not to flinch. She flinched away now from the memory.

The waistcoat he wore over his vansuit flapped open. She saw the sheath where he kept his knives.

'It's a long and very famous story. About a man trying to get home.'

'Why did he leave his van?'

'He went to a war and got lost on the way back.'

'Should've taken the van with him.'

He threw himself onto a seat curling down as if suddenly exhausted. His eyes closed. As soon as she moved they opened.

'Boss, d'you think I could tidy the van?'

'Told you to get on with it, didn't I?'

She tightened her lips, swallowed, started the job of restoring order.

When she'd finished he was still curled in the same place. His eyes were shut.

She crept forward and stood over him, looking down. Dark hair creeping out under the edge of the mask curled on his neck. She tried to imagine the soft contours of childhood. Whiteish drops oozed from the red mark on his hand.

Her hand reached out. Instantly he was awake.

She drew back and sat as far away as space allowed.

Early dark drew in. Rain tapped the window. The screens began to creak, the child stirred, and as the wind rose, a shudder ran along the metal panels making them moan. Something crashed and crashed again.
Perhaps one had come loose.

She looked through the darkness to a form she could barely see. She thought he'd sat up now, imagined she could see the whites of his eyes shining out of the mask.

'Won't last long,' she said.

'Don't care.' There was a long silence then a voice came. 'Reckon you're scared.'

'Just wanting to go to bed.'

'Don says only poltics are scared.'

The wind shook the screens till they screeched.

'No-one here's scared.' She said softly. 'Who's Don?'

'Driver.'

She wanted to sleep. The van rocked. His fingers began to drum.

'Please, Boss, don't do that.'

In some slot over to the right a woman's voice rose in a yell. The fingers hesitated then continued. How long would the storm last?

The two of them were divided by half the length of the van but the dark drew them together like a blanket. Two little creatures, she thought, cowering side by side till it was all over.

Gradually the rain eased and the wind dropped. She realised the fingers were quiet. Her eyes ached; her stomach was heavy.

'D'you think, Boss, I could get to bed?'

'Do what you like.'

As she came to next morning, her stomach sank. She lay with her eyes closed, head pushed down into the pillow, tried to cut out the rattle of security screens.

A voice spoke beside her ear. Blue-green, slimy, yet precise, like an ancient recording of Lord Haw-Haw. 'You were afraid.' She stiffened. There was no-one there. The words could only have come from inside her. She repeated them silently to herself. 'You were afraid.' Listening, trying to steel herself against them. It hadn't felt like fear. Just a reaction to events. A natural way to respond.

And she was doing right. A sacrifice had to be made for the sake of nature. This life was something she could endure for the sake of nature.

'You were afraid.' How come she'd heard these words? Actually heard? Words that had to be hers because no-one was in the room to say them? Welling up from the subconscious, telling her what she was ashamed to admit? Or perhaps she was right to be afraid? She considered this slowly and found herself looking into the depths of fear.

She was locked in – with a child – ridiculous to be frightened of a child – but a child who killed a sparrow just to prove his point, pulled out the blade and wiped it on his vansuit, whose eyes, as far as they could be seen in the depths of that mask, remained dull while he did it? Too young perhaps to really understand? Child soldiers? Hardened to killing? A feral child?

What did he want? The van? Could he drive it? Surely. Could he get past the Frees, a driver his size? Did he imagine he could? What would he do with her? Why hadn't she spoken, yesterday, to the Free? She could have done it. Kidded herself she could do something great, redeem him or something? Swollen head. You great enormous seedy poltic.

Turn him in today?

Tell a Free, 'I have this certificate. *Temporary breakdown of communication equipment.*' Point out a signature, show the problem was solved.

He'd give it a careful look. 'This boy, how did he find you? Exactly where were you parked?' It was, in its way, a false document – Free who signed it – nice little driver. Would someone else see through it, accuse her of forgery? In any case it was obvious she'd been where she shouldn't, committed 'obscene acts'.

She'd landed herself right in it. And she was afraid.

She sat up slowly and hugged her knees, considered the fact that she was feeling an emotion, not one she wanted to feel, still something that rooted her into this place and time, made them abound all round her.

In its way that was good. The warmth that came with it a dawning of self-respect – for admitting it? Yes – in a way.

Possibly she was brighter than him? Never safe to assume. You found out gradually, observing how quickly they understood. Some kids would go far beyond you one day. Some already. This one? Too soon to say but at least she was older than him, had had more time to learn. She'd need every little bit of knowledge and experience she'd ever acquired to get out of here in one piece. Maybe he'd take off one day, sudden as he arrived.

When she came into the main part of the van he'd already tidied away the fold-up bed. She searched all round, came upon a small figure sitting tense and upright staring out at the screens. His right hand rested beside his belt. The pose seemed habitual.

He jerked round. 'Where you been? Ages I been waiting.'

She regarded him carefully. 'Sorry,'

'Sorry, Boss,' and when she went on standing and looking, 'Say it, Sorry, Boss.'

'Sorry, Boss,' gritting her teeth. She laid bread on the table, which he was already shovelling down in the seconds before she put out the jam. She lowered herself onto the opposite seat and watched slices disappear between the swollen lips of the mask. She suspected he hadn't take it off all night.

Those dreadful eyebrows and monstrous nose. She tried to speak evenly.

'You don't have to wear that indoors.'

'Boss. Don't you forget it.'

Something made her persist. 'So why keep it on – Boss?'

He shrugged. 'Like it, I suppose.'

Wouldn't do to ask why.

She felt his eyes on her as she cleared the table and washed up, put the cutlery back in its drawers, the crockery back in the cupboard.

'Get on with it. Not going to wait much longer.'

She returned and sat opposite again. Tried not to let him see she was keeping a distance. What was a safe distance? 'The Frees'll want us to move on this morning, Boss. I'll book a place on the hook.'

'Hook's boring.'

She almost sighed. 'They won't let us go any other way, Boss. Not after yesterday.' You bet they wouldn't, she thought. And it would be peaceful, cruising along in a queue held at safe intervals apart by the electronic hook. Talking was easier sometimes when both parties were staring ahead. So important – a bond with the highjacker.

He grunted. 'I'll listen in.'

No flies on you, driver. 'I won't tell. Promise.'

'Promises, nothing but air, innit?'

The knifepoint escorted her into the driver's cab, it pricked her ribs as she switched on.

'Boss, I'd drive better if that weren't quite so close,' she said softly and when it didn't move. 'Don't you understand, driver – Boss, I can't grass you up, not after yesterday. Understand?'

He paused. 'You're a criminal.' His voice brooded over the word. 'Yeah, cri-mi-nal.' He rolled the syllables round his mouth, turned sideways towards her. 'Got you, haven't I? Criminal. Yeah. I got you.'

The green light on the dashboard began to flash. 'Time for off. That's the signal.'

She eased the van forward onto the slip-road, picked up a little speed, not too much, saw a gap open in the stream of traffic, felt the hook take hold, the van edging out without effort on her part into the second and then the third stream, settling down there with other vehicles equidistant all round. The authorities weren't taking any risks. In a middle lane she'd have to stay where she was. She took her hands off the wheel and made herself breathe deeply. Relax. She glanced down sideways into the gap between him and her. No gleam of metal. Though the knife wouldn't be far away

The road sped past. Vans rolled on either side, the stream to her right moving that little bit faster, the one on her left slower. Always that slight change of colour, red then blue going ahead one side, green then red stripes on grey sliding back. Her hands rested on her lap. The child next to her was silent and still, not stiff as he had been that morning but curled back against the seat. He seemed smaller. And he stank.

All the same it was good to be sitting here letting the van carry them as it had carried first her and Elizabeth, then her on her own for so many years. This soothing glide day after day. It seemed to take him the same way. Her backbone softened against the upholstery. She closed her eyes.

Half an hour later she opened them. The traffic was still moving at the same even speed. He was still silent, more relaxed than she'd seen him so far.

'Boss,' she murmured, 'you awake?'

'Never sleep, do I?'

She didn't notice herself smiling. 'Like travelling?'

'Boss. How often I got to say it? Don't ask silly questions.'

Well, yes, that hadn't been one of her best. She searched for a topic.

'We're booked in at Thamesdown, Boss. D'you like it?'

'Why you want to know?'

'No special reason, Boss. Just talking.'

'Well don't.'

His tone was out of keeping with his size, as if he were echoing someone, and not she thought, someone related. This wasn't the tone of a father or uncle, nothing personal in its harshness. It was more that of a commanding officer or sergeant-major. The second probably, a bully. She could believe he'd lived under a bully.

An hour later the hook detached them for Thamesdown.

'I'll book a slot for the night first, Boss, OK?'

'Yeah, get you locked in.'

Suddenly she shuddered. Her hand stuck to the gear lever.

'Scared, aren't you? That's good.'

She dared not turn him in.

A row of half-inflated balloons hung over the kiosk where they checked in. 'Boss, I'm not supposed to have a passenger. Think you can hide, duck down or something?'

Instantly he slipped off the seat and wriggled into some dark corner of the cab. She kept her head up and got her lips to move the lips of the mask in a smile at the Free.

He allocated a slot where, as he'd threatened, Boss left her locked in.

In the quiet after he'd gone, she sat picturing his style. He'd stood facing her, tossed the key up and caught it, snapped his hand shut, stamped down the steps, swaggered across to the gate, opened it, rested his hand on the side, looked back and leered, shut it behind him. In a former life she'd have wanted to slap him but now it all seemed such a great act. And it was good to be alone.

She had more or less finished the course of lessons she was preparing when the gate rattled.

She looked up as he climbed in. 'That you, Boss?'

His shoulders drooped. He looked shrivelled. The swagger was more pronounced.

'Need paypoints.'

'Just been earning them,' and as his hand jerked, 'Boss.'

'You better.'

'Want some tea?'

He nodded.

She let him sit and drink till his shoulders relaxed. Then she said carefully,

'We need food, Boss. We'll have to go shopping. OK with you?'

The mask didn't turn. He appeared to be staring at something she couldn't see.

'Boss?'

He didn't answer.

'Another tea?' She re-filled his mug and waited. It began to grow dark.

'If we're to have anything to eat tonight we'll have to go shopping.'

He shot to his feet. 'What's this, shop, shop, shop? Leave me alone, can't you?' He clenched his fists and waved his arms above his head, stamped up and down the aisle between the seats. She waited.

'Go alone, shall I?'

At last he looked at her. 'Not seeding likely.'

'OK then, Boss. Let's go.'

It was lights visible from a distance over the screen that drew them to the bub-course. Boss turned from the direct route to the Centre towards the roar. They came closer and saw a moving jigsaw of bubble cars dashing over roads and spaces, their glass roofs sparkling in the beams of lamps that hung from a network of iron scaffolding through the gaps of which no stars cold be seen. Miniature headlamps flashed, disappeared, flashed again as they twisted and turned. In one section of the course they circled and overtook, in another they crested ramps and flew, further off spread over the rise of a small hill, formation driving was taking place, three lines with twenty or so in each passing through each other in an elaborate plaiting.

They came to a standstill gazing over the fence. She laid both hands on top tracing the lights as they moved. She couldn't take much of the nearest, flashing suddenly and randomly into her face. This was chaos but she could lift her head and look over them to the hill. Here there was pattern and order, continually moving, so you had to follow, fascinated, as the lines unfolded and changed place, the same formation shifting left, then right. It looked inevitable each car would pass through the appropriate gap. But she knew each contained a kid between ten and fourteen years old, concentrating, sucking up the risk.

She watched brooding. How come she'd never seen this before? Or had she never looked? There'd been nothing to draw her. But now with Boss at her side she was transfixed. She could feel his tension, both feet thrust against the ground, his body an upright wire. The same kid who'd recently been sneering and sulking. He's focussed at last, she thought; this is him coming through.

'Driven one of these, Boss?'

'Hundreds of times.' The hideous mask swung towards her. 'You think I couldn't? Been driving for years, I have. Long before they let me, I was driving. Can drive better than these poltics. Rubbish most of these.'

'OK, Boss, I'm sure you're good.'

'Not good, brilliant.'

'Yes, Boss, you're brilliant.' If he'd been adult, she wouldn't have agreed. This was a child. 'I need to add some paypoints to my phone. Then you can have a go.'

He drew a long breath, 'Just saying it.'

'No. I mean it.'

He stood absolutely still, then shrugged. 'Not worth it. Don't bother.'

'But – Boss –'

'Shut up,' he screamed, 'shut up. You seedy digger, shut up.'

On the course headlamps flashed, disappeared, flashed again.

She clashed the wheels of her skates into the ground, spun away, heard his wheels grinding behind her. It wasn't till she reached the steps of the centre she thought of his pack of throwing knives.

But he hadn't.

I'm more valuable to him alive, she thought. He's no fool.

At the foot of the Centre steps she flipped back the wheels and waited for him to do the same. He shook his foot in the standard way, nothing happened, he swore, shook again harder, bent down, tugged at the strap. At the moment he kicked again it came away in his hand, the shoe flew out of his hand and crashed onto the concrete. She saw a wheel had come off and she tensed herself for the outburst.

He took off the other shoe, threw it on the ground, said nothing. She suspected his face was expressionless and suddenly all her fear came flooding back. Roll-shoes were special. Because they moved, you had this illusion they were alive, under your feet, touching your body, close to you, like a pet. She'd thought it was her loneliness after Elizabeth died that gave her this feeling but she'd seen other drivers – on sunny mornings when drivers felt relaxed and left the screens open – sitting unmasked on the bottom step oiling their roll-shoes, rubbing each wheel till it shone, holding a shoe up and shaking to see the parts moved freely, placing them back down, running them across the ground, smiling. Singing sometimes. Clean metal flashed in the sunlight. Almost safe to call out, 'Go-go, driver' and get an answer.

He behaved as if nothing was the matter.

She could imagine a feral child talking to his roll-shoes at night, but this? She stood further off. 'I'll get you a new pair.'

'You better.' A statement of fact.

She did some desultory shopping with him always beside her, sly on his feet as a cat.

'D'you want wings on your shoes?' Winged heels, like Mercury.

He shrugged but came closer.

She picked up a pair striped navy and white with white wings, held them out, let her hand drop as she followed his gaze to the wonders arrayed along the back of the display.

'Which ones?'

They were emerald with sapphire wings. Not a boy's choice she'd have thought but you mustn't stereotype. Maybe he was even younger than she'd thought.

There was a pleasant buzz in the café, families collecting food, choosing tables, talking. The air was warm and smelt good. She turned to face him.

'How about eating out, Boss?'

He twice swore at people who came too close in the queue. She turned her back, thankful for masks, aware of him freezing as they approached the counter. Now he was the one to turn away.

'What would you like, Boss?'

'Whatever.'

She surveyed the display, noting as she always did the treacherous way her mind, translating the names, sween-vit – sweet green Vit C – apples, regrund-vit, carrots, whigrund-vit – potatoes, was happy with 'meat.' In this world nowadays that was OK because there was a long way between a live animal and dead meat; your mind stayed in the shop.

The robot that was serving smiled at her. She hoped desperately it was a machine, not a driver who'd once had a mind like hers.

Still, she was being punished enough as it was, helpless in the grip of an evil child.

He showed no interest in food though she suspected he was very hungry. She piled his plate with colours and strong tastes.

At the table he regarded it coldly. 'No Aussie balls.'

Should have known steak was the only food he'd think worthy of a man. 'Sorry, Boss. They're out of them.'

She waited for him to throw the plate. Instead he bent forward till his nose was almost touching the food, lifted his head, gave her what seemed even through the mask to be a sly glance, plunged in his left hand, raised a lump of curry-covered rice dripping to his mouth, shoved it in, slurped it down, all the time looking at her, radiating complacency. She ate her own food, gazing out of the window, secretly watching the way his plate was being polished.

'More, Boss?'

She brought a second helping together with the largest, most foamy, vari-coloured available ice-cream. He demolished them both and sat back licking the last traces off his lips and when he became aware of her watching, wriggling his shoulders, giving her slimy, sideways looks

Part of her wanted to slap him, another to hold those shoulders, slide her hands round onto his back and pat it. A third shouted silently this didn't seem natural, she didn't understand, didn't know where he'd come from or what he'd been through, didn't want to know, didn't want to spend another night locked in a small van with him.

No other option appeared.

After the meal they spent some time wandering round the Centre inspecting the entertainments, most of which Boss appeared to despise. They came out at a side door.

'Which way, Boss?' She had this instinct he'd know.

He set off past a row of brightly coloured wooden cells, about the size telephone boxes had been before the New Dawn, placed with their backs to the wall of the centre, 'Spook Bins', miniature cinemas for one driver at a time to indulge in horror movies, great test of manhood. She'd often overheard drivers boasting. 'Three hours last night in the Spook Bin. Three pile-ups – or four – forget which. All went up in these awesome fires. Not to mention drivers chained to their seats, windscreens shattering into daggers. Cool as an ice-lolly all the way through, I was.' She didn't believe them but thousands were addicted.

Boss stopped outside the last to clip on his new roll-shoes. They seemed to please him.

*

The first day set a pattern for those that followed. She'd get up to find the van already tidy, him sitting staring out. They'd eat, get the van on the road. They still allocated her to middle lanes. She didn't mind. Once the hook was on things flowed peacefully. Boss seemed to feel that too.

The rest of the time he was unpredictable. At one time he'd flare up for no reason she could grasp, at another refuse to speak, turn savage if she spoke or made a noise, at another give his full attention to hunting flies. He'd fence one in with the back of his widest knife against the window, and when it ran jump the blade to block its escape, then get it flying backwards and forwards in the confined space, not trying to catch it apparently, just watching it knock its head onto the glass. When it fell exhausted onto the sill he'd tip it onto its back and watch it frantically waving its legs, suddenly lose interest, crush it with the flat of the blade. He did all this with precise, dainty movements.

She'd watch, imagining ways to get those knives off him. Or the key. He allowed her the driving key. Always pocketed the one that closed the security screen. It seemed to her he'd been well trained. Or observed thoughtfully.

She began to change her estimate of his age. Ten was far too young. She'd been deceived by the childish mask. Must be an undersize adolescent. Was it possible – could he be – actually fifteen? But those fine wrists? She didn't feel that could be the right answer.

She began to be glad of times when he went out and left her locked in. She knew he'd come in silent and savage, wondered if he was addicted to Spook Bins, took refuge in her work.

She was glad of time to log up paypoints. She'd never before been short, wasn't really now but the boy's requirements were beginning to eat into her income. Not that she was desperate – was in credit, being paid a teacher's supplement in addition to the basic salary everyone received simply for not using up world resources.

That side of things was taken care of so well now. Most of the vans ran on hydrogen, no-one owned a private washing machine, the use of public ones was rationed, vans, being compact, needed little energy to heat. That bottle standing beside the sink – how many times had its glass been re-cycled? It was the end-product of a closed system in which the same materials were shaped into something, used, re-cycled, manufacture imitating the way nature worked with living things.

She'd switch on Educ-Prof. She had already prepared careful lesson plans for Lauda – a girl, she'd been amused to discover – and McClaren and Singer. Whether she would get to talk to them through the screen was another question. Probably not McClaren. She'd have a leisurely chat about the weather or the present position of roadworks with his mother or her hitchmate in the course of which she'd remark it was a pity McClaren wasn't there to be taught and whoever it was would say it was a shame but he'd gone out roller-jumping so what could you do? She'd record this as 'positive interaction with the responsible adult'. It would have been pleasant after all. A distant computer would log up time spent and award double pay. Triple pay if she got to speak to the student. Lauda and Singer often seemed pleased to have someone different to talk to, going on about their feats, leaping in bubs, sweeping down roller-skating slaloms, complaining a wheel had been ripped off a roll-shoe by the edge of a pavement. At some stage she'd try to drop in a word on the topic they were supposed to be studying and do her best to extract a reply. She'd record this afterwards. 'I was impressed by Lauda's interest in/understanding of/feeling for,' at least two of these and one item of criticism, 'I suggested she should consider, it would be better if.' And the success of the lesson as a whole 'We discussed –' She'd get paid for all those. She'd learnt years ago to hold down any tendency to feel ashamed. The Dawn Servants must know she was playing the system. All teachers must be doing it. How in the name of the New Dawn could anyone hope to do better?

Unless of course they had a student like Chang. She had the impression he devoted his life to the Web. He'd found and read obscure sites full of esoteric information. He'd send in long assignments describing the behaviour of ultimate particles, the insubstantiality of matter, the customs of extinct tribes, the nine ranks of angels. She felt she earned the triple pay she received for marking – though all she could do was try to estimate how much of this was plagiarised and let him know she'd spotted it. Whether he'd copied correctly she couldn't judge. Better hope he hadn't hacked into somewhere sensitive and implicated her in the process.

As for the others – if one of them sent in the odd assignment, she'd mark it but presumed they never read her comments. Why should they? No exams now. They'd dominated schools before the New Dawn. That had been going to issue in an age of disinterested study. But in a world where most people only worked at most a few months a year, the subject the young really wanted to study was each other. And there, she thought, she had sometimes been useful. When a student's voice changed, telling her he was old enough to take off with a mate he fancied, why should anyone stop him? Or her mum had wanted to kill her – you could tell from the voice when this wasn't metaphorical – or she'd wanted to kill her mum's hitchmate. Issues had become more intense in the confined living spaces.

When he came in that morning she took her hands off the keyboard. 'Boss, d'you think you could possibly take that mask off?' she asked and gasped at the risk she was taking.

'No,' he said gently.

She stared, realising suddenly it was good to have a real kid in front of her again, she was tired of faces coming and going on a screen.

Even if he was dangerous?

She'd been in a room before with kids who carried knives. Not cooped up like this. That classroom hadn't been locked. Other teachers walked past. Those kids hadn't stolen the key or concealed their faces. She shouldn't fool herself. Here she was alone. But perhaps that was why it meant so much to hear a real voice at close quarters.

She glanced at him carefully. The ends of hair that straggled out under the mask were wet. There was no smell. That was it. Must have washed.

'What you staring at?'

'Thought you looked nice.'

He twisted his head and wriggled his hips, slid into a few dance steps, turned the mask full on her so she could see down into his eyes. Green. Glinting. Elfin. She chased the absurd word out of her mind a soon as it arrived. Fiendish more like. That look was calculated; and in some other way she couldn't define, strange, even if he were older than she'd imagined.

'Come and sit down, Boss. We need to decide where we're going today.'

He slid onto the seat opposite. 'Boring.'

'What's boring?'

'Middle lanes. No speed.'

'That's what they give us.'

'You don't ask.'

True enough. She'd felt it wise to keep her head down. One finger of the hand that lay on the table began rubbing the wood. By now perhaps they'd have forgotten her van was trouble. Someone else would've done something. The record would always be there but for the moment – 'What do you want, Boss?'

'Go fast.'

She stiffened. 'Speed lane?'

'What you think?'

She never had, except once immediately after Elizabeth died.

'Get on with it.'

'I wasn't brought up on a bub-course.'

Then he tilted his head. 'Come on, you'll love it.'

She started at the change of tone. 'Don't want to kill us both.'

'You couldn't.' She didn't know whether the wheedling was sincere or a disguised way of expressing contempt, felt more at home when he sat up straight. 'You know I'll make you. Fact.'

His hand rested on his belt.

She remembered the red D carved on his chest.

Half an hour later they were drawn up at the entrance to the speed lanes.

The Free signalled, she nosed forward onto the slip road, picked up speed. Seventy. She pressed her foot down.

As soon as they were out of sight of the Free he put his hand to his belt and drew out a knife, brandished it overhead.

'Please Boss, put that thing away.'

It swooped under her nose.

'You want me to go fast?'

'Said so, didn't I?'

She'd reached eighty, the minimum permitted. 'Can't concentrate with you waving that thing.'

The blade flashed past her eye.

She wasn't allowed to slow. 'Boss, please.'

He raised it in a rude gesture at a passing driver.

She concentrated on the road.

The hand dropped. 'Faster.'

The needle crept up. She glanced at the speedometer. For once she needed to. A hundred. Warmth began to creep through her. She was in charge. She was free to choose her speed. She could judge what was best. Had to pay, of course, for the freedom. A deposit they said. They hadn't lost her record.

Wouldn't repay.

'Faster, he repeated. He leant forward.

From the corner of her eye she saw a pink tongue creep out and lick the lips of the mask.

'You scared or don't you know how?'

A hundred and five, ten, fifteen.

The van swung a little. Her hands firmed on the wheel.

Other vehicles were sweeping past.

'Haven't caught that artic yet. Don never does under one-fifty. Five seeding minutes and you not overtaken a thing.'

Her foot gently pressed the accelerator. Mad. She was mad. She firmed her back against the seat, deliberately relaxed her arms. If these were her last moments she'd enjoy them. The van edged forward. She didn't know it had it in it. Wasn't an Airborne. Even so it knew how to move. Tarmac rushed backwards. She raised her eyes. Look ahead, ahead. Air seethed past. The engine sounded happy. She pressed her toe down again.

Boss had apparently forgotten his wish to impress. He'd put away the knife and was slumped down in the passenger seat, hands clasped on the curve of his stomach. He yawned elaborately. Perhaps the storm last night had kept him awake and he was really tired

She'd be the one to shake him now. She jabbed her foot down, swung out behind a blue van overtaking an artic, indicated again, moved into the third lane, swept past it. A line of artics filled the lane ahead. Again she swung out and surged past. Everything she asked, the van did. She checked the mirror, brought it back into the third lane. Control. She was in control.

One-sixty. Above the limit. You swept along like a destroying angel.

A weird keening rose from the seat beside her. A thin childish voice, not very tuneful, pouring out a cry like a flying witch.

Something swooshed past. How dare it? She put her foot down. The engine began to thud.

Boss stopped singing and thrust his nose against the windscreen. 'Vibro-Rocket.' The van swayed in the slipstream. 'Devil-fiend driver,' he whispered.

She clung to the wheel and pressed. The needle didn't move.

Boss shook his head. 'You'll never catch it.'

She pressed hard. The van shuddered. No, she thought, no, I mustn't. Her foot relaxed and immediately the van fell back. A horn blasted. She gave a frantic glance at the mirror, indicated, saw an artic fall back, moved cautiously over, relaxed.

Boss was crooning again.

Her knees, wasn't sure of her knees. Must keep going. How long to the next exit?

'Crappy van.' He pushed his fingers through the distorted lips and began to chew the nails. 'You can drive a bit.'

More than a bit, she thought. You could put it all down to adrenalin but it wasn't that. Something had come back so that, even now it was all over, her blood seemed to be flowing more freely; she knew she'd felt a joy she hadn't known since the early days of the New Dawn. In her depths she wasn't the dull creature she thought she'd become.

When she woke next morning rain was pattering and the window framed a close-up view of corrugated metal. Must have fallen into bed without drawing the curtains.

That kid. Had he slept? She was sure if she went in to the main part of the van she'd find him sitting. She'd offered to do get down the folding bed but he'd snarled. Could have been up all night, watching her door.

Yesterday had been a high. Reality was this grey through the window. She dressed slowly.

He was silent all through breakfast, apparently labouring under the same sullen cloud that closed her in. The weather, perhaps? They'd be better to get moving.

'Slow lane today, Boss? What d'you think?'

A time would come perhaps when they'd spend days in the same overnight, sample all its entertainments. Not yet.

An hour later the lock slotted them into their place in the traffic. Lane after lane of traffic to their right. To the left hoardings advertised a new kind of subdued headlamp.

Boss slumped in his seat, spread his legs, began to slurp rhythmically through his teeth, a sound half-way between a chew and a suck.

Crash repair-shops flowed past, a mile or so of battered notice-boards, 'Lev's Lovelies', 'Greg's Gorgeous Guzzlers,' lurid depictions of second-hand vehicles. You couldn't see the verge or scenery. Though she knew there wasn't much to see, just service roads to industrial estates where they re-charged, straightened, re-trod, re-sprayed. She'd heard drivers talking in overnight cafés. 'Good it was, peaceful. Get into yourself, you know, working on a car. Wouldn't mind work-service all year round.' Cruising past she'd sometimes pictured their fingers delicately testing surfaces. The Dawn Servants kept careful records of work allocations. Never more than three months, she'd heard. Didn't want to risk anyone getting stuck.

Though by all accounts some managed it. She watched out for glimpses of low concrete buildings. Roads between them. Great hiding places – so it was alleged – for drivers everyone would like the Frees to catch up with, the kind whose impact on other drivers' windscreens, chassis, bonnets, tyres was only too obvious but always, so the story went, had always 'Gone travelling, driver,' when the cherub pocked in. The Frees no doubt examined permits to deal, repair, spray to their hearts' content. Never found one that was dicey.

The countryside was hidden behind all this mess.

A silver Shadow glided past. 'Bullet-proof windows. Know that? Gun-rack behind the driving-seat.'

'Oh.'

'Never applied for a gun licence?'

'No.'

'Wish you had?'

'No.'

'No, Boss. Wouldn't, would you?' He chuckled. 'Better safe than sorry, Don said.'

'This Don – he the one who said don't believe promises? His own or other people's?'

The Devil Driver mask gave nothing away. At last a voice came. 'Air. All air, he said. Never believe a promise. Said if I ever make a promise you needn't believe a seeding word.'

'Did he ever?'

He was watching light run up and down the blade of his knife as he moved it around. 'Kill you. Now. With this one. That's a promise. Both of us together. Wouldn't care, wouldn't seeding care – long as I weren't the only one.'

'Need I believe that?'

'Your business.'

'Look for Aussieballs, shall we, when we get there?'

'If you want.'

Their destination was an hour of this away. Then, coming round a bend, she saw the green road-sign, 'Historic monument. Viewing point one mile. If desired press, 'Peel left.'

'Free-wire Junction. They say it's great. All over TV when it was new. Look, shall we, Boss? See if they got it right?'

She took his silence for agreement.

The side-road to the viewing platform snaked up between gigantic pillars. Above them the main courses twisted and turned, high up, incredibly slender. Shafts of sunlight occasionally ran over the van. In other places they looked almost solid against the concrete.

The side-road drew out to one side. She pressed the knob a second time and slowed as the sat-nav directed. A wall ahead tilted to make a ramp leading into a platform posed on top of a slender stalk. As she drove across a picture came to her from year before – a waiter balancing a tray above his head on this flattened palm. That had seemed precarious. It had obviously been a normal strategy, nothing to worry about. .

Boss leant from the window and sucked. 'Way up, aren't we?'

She didn't answer till they'd come to a halt on the platform. 'It is said to be high.'

He didn't bother with roll-shoes, threw open the door, ran to the balustrade.

She stretched cramped legs and followed towards the railing that allowed a view of the roads. The platform was a little to the side of the junction and, though hundreds of metres above ground level compelled her to look up still further to a sky where the highest roads flowed in slender parabolas, shapes similar to the tendrils of her scarlet runner. But these were firm, the product of specially manufactured reinforced concrete. And yet so graceful. 'The outcome of precise mathematics,' Elizabeth had murmured, gazing at a different junction, one that at the time had seemed a great advance on Spaghetti Junction.

That had been low beside this. This wasn't just a junction but an artwork. With no appointments to meet there was time now for drivers to sit back and enjoy themselves. The roads could be extravagant. There could be loops to test their skill. And all this was nothing so she'd heard beside the cross-channel Riddle-me-ree.

Boss stood close beside her as she followed the soaring lines of graduated pillars, the way they marched across the land. So pure and so audacious. Cars moved along them. Windscreens sparkled. What more could anyone want? She could only praise a system that had produced this.

Far beyond she thought she could make out trees.

She glanced at knuckles grasping the rail beside hers. He spat over the edge. White foam shot down and faded out. She felt dizzy watching.

'Long time now they've stood here, Boss.'

'My dad been here. Concrete dentist. Full of holes them pillars.'

She glanced rapidly at him. The crumpled features of the mask hid what lay below. She imagined the curve of a cheek, the sweet, upwards tilt of a half-formed nose. The fanged grin on the back of his waistcoat was creased in two.

Eventually she turned away. 'OK, Boss. You seen enough?'

Suddenly he was off, running, hauling himself up on his stomach with his legs flailing behind him onto the balustrade near the ramp where the rails gave way to a solid wall. Standing on it. Holding his arms out level with his shoulders.

Her mouth opened. She closed it.

She watched him walk, lower his arms and go further. Head up.

Not so long ago she'd been thinking of joining a troop of acrobats. That Fem-tog and their children. Knut, Bolt, Whee. Those kids had been brought up to it.

Boss didn't look as relaxed as they might be. There was a metal edge to his pose, a way of not looking sideways or down. She walked slowly towards him and held out her hand. 'You're doing well.' She didn't know where the words had come from. They echoed madly in her head.

He took a few more steps and jumped down. On the right side. Well away from her.

All the way to the overnight she was chewing it over. Why hadn't she rushed? Afraid a harsh noise might make him fall? Or hoping he would? It would be wonderful to be free. Could have left the body at the foot of the pillars and upped. He wasn't registered to her, had forced himself upon her, hadn't said one pleasant word in all the days he'd been with her.

In fact, apparently, she'd admired him. What a poltic.

That evening he stood at the end of the table in the van. 'What you called?'

Nice if he'd asked that long ago.

All the same she hesitated, letting the word form silently, getting used to the feel of it after so long, M soft on the lips i lifting back to roll r across the tongue and down to the soft n at the back, the whole mouth wide open before she allowed it come out fully voiced, 'Miranda.' She wanted to say it again and again but this wasn't the moment. And to hear it spoken back.

'That a name? Never heard of it.'

What had she expected? She looked him calmly in the mask. 'Well, it's mine.'

He seemed to be studying her.

Then he slid onto the seat where she was sitting and edged closer. She stiffened, then relaxed. He rested his wrists on the edge of the table-top and stared ahead. They sat in silence side by side. Eventually she reached out a hand.

He threw himself sideways away, stamped, clenched his fists, waved them. 'Don't never do that,' rushed to the back of the van, hammered on the window, turned, drew his knife, rushed back, leant over the table, pointed it into her face. 'Don't you never dare.' His yells sounded shrill as a girl's.

They had an edge of tears.

A sensible person would try to grab his wrists.

He quietened. She looked up at him. 'Sorry, Boss. I didn't mean anything.'

'Better hadn't.'

'Yes, Boss.'

She was so tired, so very tired.

The following days were up and down. She tried changing the routine to see what would suit him. He remained unpredictable, one minute almost friendly, the next in a fury or sitting, staring out in a silence she interpreted as angry. She was encouraged he'd mentioned a father. Couldn't get any more out of him. Every day he'd lock her in and go out, come back shrunk.

She spent hours on the computer, preparing lessons – good for paypoints – idly trawling just to pass the time.

On one of these searches she came across a site for 'Educational Visits.' Could be just the thing to take his mind off whatever it was he brooded over, experiences of 'significant adults' who'd upped, or worse, she suspected.

There had to be some reason for her imprisonment.

But the visits – the Morris/Austin Museum, road design laboratories, one or two castles (carefully preserved for the sake of Heritage) and, tucked away at the bottom of the last page, a farm. 'Come and see where your food comes from.'

She read the details carefully several times. It didn't seem to be a joke. This place existed, somewhere on the edge of East Anglia apparently. You could go and see. How much would be permitted? Would they really reveal all? As she revolved the question she realised that for days she'd been holding onto an after-image of those trees she'd glimpsed from the viewing platform at Free-wire Junction, too far off to make out if they were ashes or oaks, certainly not conifers. It hadn't been a vague picture in her mind. They seemed to stand in the air in front of her, their canopies gently swaying against each other, their trunks shining.

The farm would be all very hygienic no doubt; they'd have to put on special gloves and boots, but there would be fields with things growing: upright, close-packed wheat, flowing lines of barley, dancing oats, the dense, undulating foliage of potatoes, sea-green distances of cabbage. Might even be able to handle a leaf, at least under proper supervision. But it would be enough just to look.

Laughter burst through from the next slot. She jerked to her feet, opened the door. She could hear people, almost smell them. All she could see was grey corrugated metal. Last night, as they rolled back from shopping, starlings had been ransacking the litter bins. She'd almost stopped to observe their energy as they jumped down and in, seized scraps of plastic and paper in their beaks, shook them, threw them over the edge. Wild creatures not bothered by drivers. A couple of black-headed gulls had found the remains of a sandwich. She'd watched avidly from the corner of her eye, looked round to see no-one had noticed.

But why? How had this absurd, this idiotic, this empty world, come to pass?

This wasn't what they'd wanted when they gave up their houses. All they'd wanted was to save the environment.

At the New Dawn that had been easy. Campsites were fringed with grass and scrub. People used to go wandering off, picnic in clearings or beside streams.

You talked to strangers. You sat and laughed. In the winter you jumped on iced-up puddles to feel them crack under you. Snowballing at Thamesdown.

Everyone joined in. Must have been first winter.

"Campsites", "caravanserais" – became "overnights". How? When did we start saying "Gogo" – don't notice, do you?

When the Dawn Servants said we'd all got to keep moving, stays limited to – fortnight was it? Seems incredible now, so long.

Some people drove vans off-road, lit fires, cut down trees. Really was nothing for it but to fence off the countryside. You stood and watched those palisades going up, knew that was the right thing. It was, it was – but also – a puritan gladness, an ache like a nagging tooth. You stopped talking. It was the shame. Started hiding your face. Hating other people. All 'drivers' now. Car number stamped on mask. That's what everyone looks for. All anyone wants to know.

Sign of health this – someone suggesting 'farm visit?' How do you get a permit?'

Be good for that kid. Get him in group for a bit with something different to look at. Weight off her shoulders?

Might even manage to dump him. Up and go while he's in the methy. Sure to be one there. Help feed –' green protein' and 'Vit Cs'.

The real names were precise designations.

Three hours later they were in a queue, short, stationary – waiting at a locked iron gate. Boss was fidgeting.

A guard in a green uniform appeared in the lane beyond the gate. He stooped, unlocked it, came through, closed it behind him, waved his arm with the palm flat. Drivers slowly started their engines and moved onto a tarmac bay to the left of the entrance. He turned back, locked the gate behind him.

Sun beat on the vans. Gradually drivers and passengers began to get out of their cabs and wander about, mostly family groups, a few lone adults like herself in charge of juniors. Most of the kids had newer masks than Boss's. If only he'd remove that one she'd buy him something brighter – more, more – aspirational.

A mask nodded to her. She tried to nod back. She noticed others doing the same. Their stiffness made you wonder why they did it. A memory perhaps, of an ancient system of manners? A few began to coagulate in uneasy clots. She peered at high fences. All that showed over them was sky.

Drivers who appeared to know each other. Pairs mostly, small family groupings, began to murmur to each other, not quite glancing over their shoulders. They'd all have permits of course.

Two guards appeared and swung the gates wide open. Behind them a golden tractor came into view. It chugged towards the entrance and when it reached it swung round and parked. Everyone stared at the float it was dragging, an island of raised empty seats.

Immediately a coach purred in from the opposite direction. The upper parts were pale blue. The rays of the rising sun reached up into and through them. The wheel guards were dark navy. It was almost the height of a double-decker though it was clear there was only one raised deck. Strange masked faces peered down from it.

It stopped. A door slid back. People – not drivers – these were clearly people – of a sort – began to emerge. They were all wearing bright yellow vansuits made of some shiny material and puffed over shoulders and hips, tapering to wrists and ankles. The women had ice-blue cummerbunds, the men pink. Their heads were crowned with spiky tiaras of differing sizes. Their masks were a soft material that moulded itself to their features and shone angelically. Each carried a black canvas bag slung over one shoulder and held their arms folded over each other, clasping a laptop size container close to their chest.

'Dawn Servants.' The whisper was so close it seemed to come through her back.

The officials paired up and set out like choirboys at the end of a service – or infants in the kind of crocodile she remembered her grandmother describing. Those with the smallest tiaras went first. They walked across the tarmac not quite in time, putting their feet down delicately, like the bees whose broad-shoulders and tapering abdomen they seemed so oddly to have put on.

'What they doing here?' Voice somewhere to her right.

No-one answered till the last golden suit had climbed to its seat on the float and the whole contraption had disappeared towards the farmyard. Presuming there were any such place. She was beginning to doubt it. She was beginning to doubt everything.

'Conference?'

'Why here?'

'Nice and private perhaps?' The voice had a sly turn. The speaker's white hair straggled onto his neck. He nudged the female standing next to him. She seemed no chicken either. 'Carrying out an inspection? Seeing what they're getting up to here with all those you-know-whats?'

'Peas,' someone suggested. Cackles from the crowd. 'Beans,' Words spread and guffaws. 'Carrots.' They were doubled up.

Miranda heard her mother's voice. 'There's nothing funny about bad language.'

Boss was staring, and all the children, and teenagers too, gazes fixed on their elders. Rounded eyes, she thought, they can't make it out. They'll never have heard some of these words. Too many of them. The vocabulary of a foul-mouth had expanded so much. 'Spinach,' she thought, 'oh goodness keep my mind open clean, 'spinach', don't let me corrupt – dark green leaves' Some of those kids would be rolling their eyes up under the masks. No time to try to spot them at it. A man's voice came loud and clear, 'Artichokes,' and even though the voice had an undertone of aggression – or perhaps because of it – laughter ripped through her. It was too much, artichokes, artichokes. Such a ridiculous word but wonderful. They were wonderful things, artichokes. It was wonderful to laugh.

Suddenly all went quiet. The guard had appeared again. He opened the gates. The golden tractor was coming back.

It advanced into the car park, swung round and came to a stop. She turned to look for Boss and at that moment there was a crash of roll-shoes and hurtling bodies as children and teenagers threw themselves onto the float, scrambled to the top platform and danced along it. Boss was leader. She could see him now, poised at the far end, hand resting on one thrust out hip, head thrown back. He saw her and waved, as to one far below. Can't catch me – eh?

Well, let him. She waved back and felt a stiffening in the bodies of those drivers standing closest to her.

The guards shouted, the youngsters, even Boss she was thankful to see, calmed down. The older people climbed aboard and sat tight-packed on the steps that made benches.

'So we get to park our bums in the same place as the Dawns?'

'But not at the same time.'

They'd both spoken looking forward, not turning their heads, uncomfortable at the touch of a stranger's side. Must be years since any of them had shared any sort of public transport. Strangely too, masks that usually kept them apart, today made it easier to relate. Perhaps no-one needed to know who anyone else was, only that they were sharing this slightly shady activity. Anonymous, irresponsible remarks drew them together.

She liked sitting sideways to the tractor watching hedges go past. Hawthorn, six foot high, shaped and trimmed so the edges were almost right angles, fresh young leaves 'bread and cheese they used to call them in Frelland when she was a kid. Picked them off and chewed them. Some large bird was circling against the clouds. Could be a buzzard. Stop it, stop those words. She drew herself in tight.

An elbow dug into her ribs. 'Get the other side of those, eh?'

'The biological defences you observe on either side enclose growing spaces.' A rotund, canned voice expressed no emotion whatever. 'Experiments have been conducted to regulate the size and aspect of spaces to suit the requirements of varieties of Vit-C organisms. The varying climatic patterns – if you can call them patterns – of these islands make the attempt difficult. Endeavours will continue to be made until the problem is overcome.'

Her neighbour's hip shifted against hers.

'Now we are approaching the centre of operations.'

There was a general shuffle of feet. Though the wheels on their roll-shoes were retracted they made a metallic hum.

They were in a yard enclosed by buildings. On two sides they were pieced together from white-painted corrugated iron. Barns presumably. The others appeared to have three storeys and were solidly constructed from white concrete. There didn't seem to be a single straw or drop of shit anywhere.

'You will remark on the perfect hygiene. All surfaces are kept meticulously clean.' Two rails of white garments slid out of the nearest door. Someone must have pressed a button. 'Please take a white overall and put it on.'

They queued and picked one. No point fussing about the fit.

She stood breathing in the sunshine. Boss must be among the children milling around the other rail. If only he'd agree, just once, to have a go on the bub-course. Or the skate-board park. Or the acrobatic roll. The mere suggestion of any of them threw him into a frenzy. Now, just for a minute, he wasn't keeping guard close beside her.

Soon a figure in white wellies summoned them into the nearer barn. She accustomed her eyes to the gloom and heard something growling.

The figure gestured. 'Over here if you please.'

He really was a man, not a robot. You could tell from his eyes. Not that they were particularly lively but they moved as he swept them over the group, inspecting them, assessing – their intelligence, perhaps, or their mood? He looked trim, severe, brisk, and yet relaxed – very carefully relaxed – she saw him breathe and lower his shoulders – the right type to handle dicey topics. Perhaps working here could be seen more as reward than as punishment?

She looked round. The growl came from a huge rectangular box with its end towards them. Its plain lines looked very solid against a network of metal rafters. Metal tubes ran from both ends and disappeared through holes in the walls. Those leading to what she thought must be the inner wall were slimmer than the ones she supposed came in from 'growing spaces.' The growl seemed to be caused by vibrations inside the metal box.

The guide turned the flat of his palm towards it. 'We'll start at the beginning.' He studied their masks in silence, flicked fluff off his sleeve, announced, 'Today we're processing green protein.'

A field of scarlet runners.

Protein. Stick to that word. What fun to say, 'Artichoke, artichoke.' Now, 'Scarlet runners.' She wriggled, glanced round from behind her mask.

'You see that pipe? It's attached to a cutter that moves up and down rows of growing material and cuts nine centimetres from the soil. It then passes the severed tissue to a feeler which separates the capsules.'

'Pods'?

'These are sucked up by a hose that feeds them to this machine which strips off the outer integuments. The sound you hear is a knife – kindly control those juniors. They must stand back at least a metre. Behind that line if you please.'

Boss among the offenders? Of course. She glared between the heads. He stood his ground for a moment then allowed himself to be drawn back in the swirl of small bodies.

After a long silence the guide turned his eyes back to his audience. 'The entire process is under the command of one man. If you'd like to meet him, follow me.'

He opened a small side door. Their shoes scraped as he led them up a flight of circular steps to a room with a view down onto the barn and approached an operative seated at a screen. 'Here you are, Jamie. You take over.' He stepped aside and waved the group forward. 'Jamie's doing his work module here. He thinks it's a great privilege, don't you Jamie?'

It was, she supposed, one way of earning paypoints.

Boss seemed reasonably calm among the other kids. If only he'd join in with them at the overnights.

'Show them how you do it, Jamie.'

Jamie grinned. 'See this display? Mind if I stop the operation a minute, Hal?'

'Go ahead. You're in charge, Jamie.'

Some robots were much brighter than him.

'First click this icon. That's what makes it start. Brings up this menu. I clicks 'cut.'

She watched, let the words run through her head and away. A mountain she thought, you had to be calm as a mountain.

The explanation went on. Feet began to scuffle. The guide's shoulders relaxed even more elaborately as he ran his eyes over the crowd. Fifty drivers at most, strangers obliged to share one another's tension in the middle of an alien space, felt like a crowd. Heads turned in all directions. With Boss in the lead, the juniors edged towards the window that looked down on the barn, along past it towards the door.

'When you arrived it was the stripper in action –'

The children had vanished.

Other drivers' glances were straying. The guide went on talking. Boss would be OK with his own age group, wouldn't he? As long as no-one provoked him?

'Now we proceed to the next section. I must ask you to take care on the walkway.'

They passed through a door to the left of Jamie and found themselves on a metal bridge crossing what must be the interior of the second barn. Below them were three rows of shining vats connected by a complicated system of tubes.

He indicated with chops of his hand. 'Potassium, nitrates, phosphates. Each of these rows specialises in one nutrient, at a different strength in each vat. The required mixture is sucked out and spread over the growing space by the system underneath the dial on the end wall. New supplies are fed in over there from the yard.'

Something flashed across the corner of the open door.

He guided them to the far end of the bridge, unlocked a small door, stood aside while they filed through, gestured them up steps with views of the sky. At the top was a wide white corridor lit by generous windows. She had a feeling the blinds that covered them had been lowered specially for their party. He showed them into a large room and spoke in a lowered voice. 'This is one of the laboratories.'

White clad figures were sitting there absorbed, gazing at screens and down microscopes. Rapt almost. She felt they must be discovering secrets. These would be wonderful. She feared very much how they would be used.

The group had drawn close. She could smell her neighbours' breath. It made her think of wolves, a thought which was off-limits in here.

The calm voice lectured on. 'You are all familiar with GM and the great possibilities it has opened up in agriculture. Without it we would not have been able to dedicate so much of the countryside to conservation. It would have been needed to grow food – and, of course, for us to enjoy the wonderful freedom we have to travel.'

'Joyful travelling?' she thought. Never said now. Except by that little Freeguard.

'These researchers are working at the cutting edge of our knowledge, studying how to reduce even further the land required for agriculture. They are investigating stem cells to try to produce proteins, vitamins, carbohydrates, all the components of our food, without any use of vegetational resources.' The bodies next to hers drew back into their own space as if the repetition of dull words had soothed them. This distance, she thought, always this cold distance – and when we come close it's as if we had spikes sticking out all over. 'When we reach the limits of botany, we can give over all these acres of growing space to other uses, thus increasing our freedom and that of wildlife.'

It was a splendid vision. In its way, it was. And it made allowance for an expanding population.

Apples, she thought, crumbling in your mouth, plums, warm flesh and sweet juice, the way you wiped your mouth afterwards, how you sat pulling an artichoke apart, cooked sepals still a little stiff, chewed the soft ends, deposited them on the edge of the plate and lifted a forkful of stamens. Mildly bitter. She glanced round again, thankful for her mask.

'On your way out please take time to visit the farm shop. There is an excellent range of jams and soups.'

The guide drew out another key. He seemed to be counting heads. 'I had stated junior drivers should be kept under control.'

Every mask swung towards him.

'We had no chance to say.' A male voice, difficult to say whose in that faceless crowd.

'It would be better if we all returned to Reception.'

The crowd stiffened, retracted wheels ground on a concrete floor. Boss, she thought, she must get to him. The others must have had similar thoughts because the whole crowd turned and trooped back downstairs.

Five of the youngest children were playing roll-shoe hopscotch in the yard. The wheels flashed in the sun, crashing against the paving as the kids jumped, balanced with outspread arms, came staggering off the shapes they'd chalked.

The guide stood over them. 'The others?'

'Went off that way.' Mickey Mouse pointed to the barn.

The guide strode across followed by a crowd of anxious parents. The woman was afraid but still pushed forward. The 'juniors' were 'children' now, walking along the pipes. They swung round, she saw a row of masks, among them Wondermouse, Giggly Giant, Posh the Panda, the Angel Gabriel; feet thudded onto the floor.

She twisted her head up towards figures swinging along the higher tubes, Gingerbread Albie, The Sheriff of Wandering Noose, the Runcible Pieman, no Devil Driver.

'Get down at once.'

They went on swinging, looking down, sticking their tongues out through masked lips.

A male in the group threw his head back. 'Do what you're told, you seedy little poltics.'

'Leave them.' A mother surged forward. 'What harm are they doing?' The group closed in behind her. The guide tensed. A child laughed. The guide drew out a phone and began to speak.

The woman felt sick. Someone would knock it out of his hand. Always on the overnights, this sense of suppressed violence.

The kids began to let go, swinging with arched backs, landing on tiptoe. Thanks to arm-ache, she guessed.

'Would all drivers kindly collect their own juniors?' He waited while people shuffled forward. 'The visit is now terminated. Please make your way to the office. It will be necessary to complete an incident report before anyone leaves.'

She watched while families were checked against permits, described where they'd come from, where they were going next recorded, one by one trickled out of the office into the sunlit yard, found seats on the trailer behind the golden tractor and she was left, standing beside the counter.

'Permit?'

He checked it against the number stamped on her mask.

'One passenger? Junior male?'

'Yes.'

'Where is he?'

'I thought he was with the others.'

'Sit there till he turns up.' He indicated a bench.

'What if he doesn't?'

He looked at her calmly. 'Bound to show up on one of the cameras.'

She nodded and drank, taking in a bank of screens, an array of flashing lights over the door.

He re-activated the computer and sank into a heavy gaze.

She leant back and closed her eyes. The tubes ran from the vats to the outside. There must be some way through for humans. He'd be out in the fields now, feasting on strawberries no doubt. This was her chance to up. Her fingers tightened on her handbag.

'Excuse me –'

He took no notice so she'd tried again, louder.

He looked round, 'Wait a minute, will you, driver.'

'When's the next time the tractor goes to the gate?'

'Won't be back just yet. Then whenever I ask it.'

He sounded as if nothing would disturb or even interest him.

Sweat was gathering on the fold of his fat neck, trickling down under the collar of his uniform. She was sweating too, but more secretly. She resigned herself, sank back and the words crept into her mind with pictures of the things themselves. Boss sitting among the beans, touching them, absorbing their scent. This was what you did to a loved being, and why not? She could still, very faintly, recall the scent of Elizabeth's hair, her neck, her body. Was that wrong? Was it wrong to love living things? Wasn't the New Dawn all about loving? And weren't plants innocent? Why smear things that were innocent?

It was very strange, she thought. Today these words weren't euphemisms for testicles. The things they denoted were the taboo items themselves, being brought into the open and named, the way naughty boys had once mouthed, 'Penis'. No-one could stand the names. They had to bring them down in case they got too powerful.

What if, to be loyal to the New Dawn, you had to be loyal to the plants, seeing them as clean?

What if Boss had got himself entangled in machinery? How could he? With those covers. But he was an ingenious little bean. She didn't want him with his 'integuments' stripped off, didn't know any more what to hope, that he'd get clean away or they'd bring him back.

The official took his fingers off the keyboard and wiped them on a tissue

'Invasion of ferals – week or so ago – rounded up the lot in the end.'

When they got him she'd tell them to keep him. By this time her record would be too old for them to trace it. Not that they couldn't. Just too many movements since them for it to show up quickly.

She relaxed, crossed her legs the other way, looked round to see the golden tractor passing the window.

'The Dawns – very impressive. What a lot of them.'

'Doing an audit.' He leant back in his chair and held up his hand. 'You're right it's impressive. Not a thing they don't look at,' checking them off one by one on his fingers, 'hygiene, finance, quality – you name it. Go right through the labs, assess progress, take samples from all the growing spaces, measure the products.'

'Measure them?'

'All have to be same size.'

'So how long does it take?'

'Be at it till late afternoon. Then there's a reception in the banqueting room.'

'Oh – I see.' Her thoughts trailed away.

The sun slowly moved round the office. He closed down his programme.

She asked slowly, 'Those ferals – what happened to them?'

'Frees rounded them up.'

'What did they do with them?'

He screwed up a piece of waste paper and threw it in the bin. 'Took them off and shot them.' He went out and left her. Came back half an hour later. 'Still haven't got him.'

Later still she didn't know what made her look round and catch the devil driver mask sidling in. 'Where the hell've you been?'

'I'll deal with this.' The official swung his chair round and stretched out his legs. 'Now, junior, what you got to say?'

'Nothing.'

He shrugged. 'You can wait.' He rotated the chair back and switched on his computer. 'I'll get your mother to help me fill in the details.'

'I'm not his mother.'

'Date, time. Reason for visit?'

'Education. I'm a teacher.'

'Not his mother?'

'She asked me to look after him.'

'And why was that?'

'His dad upped and then she got another hitchmate. Hitchmate didn't like kids.' Boss had frozen in the doorway.

'Father's name?'

'Don – Danny – something like that. Never knew him. Upped before I met her.'

'Her name?'

'Mara.'

'Mara what?'

'Scott,' she said quickly and watched him enter it.

'Junior's name?'

'Boss.' The man's fingers paused over the keyboard. 'Short for 'Embossed'

His Dad had his initials embossed on the van door. Quite something, I can tell you.'

'Must have been. Now junior – that mask's a mess. Can't read the number.'

The woman gulped. 'Sorry – we came out in a hurry. Didn't notice he'd taken the old one.'

'Old enough to know better, aren't you junior?'

She jumped in quickly. 'He came back of his own accord.' She leant forward.

'He's not normally like this. Must have been confused. This is quite a place, you know.' She gazed up into the official mask. 'And he wasn't the only one.'

He hesitated.

'I think they all found what the guide was saying a little long. Aimed more at full drivers. And you know what juniors are – and this one can't keep his eyes off machinery. Longing for the day he's old enough to learn crash repairs.'

He hesitated, sighed and shrugged, turned the chair back into the room.. 'There's ways and ways of learning. Promise me you'll deal with him.'

'Yes indeed. Indeed yes.'

The tractor took the two of them back in solitary state.

The gate shut behind them. They climbed into the van and collapsed either side of the table.

'You didn't grass.'
'No.'
'Could've.'
'Can't think why I didn't.' She leant toward him. 'Now listen to me, junior. You want to go places, yeah? Can't do it without me. Right? And I'm not taking you while you have those knives.'

He tautened.

'This van won't budge an inch as long as you've got them.' She folded her hands in her lap and sat back.

'Not fair.'

It wasn't the wail she'd expected. She held out her hand.

His head sank forward.

'Hurry up.'

He unbuckled the sheath, very slowly handed it over.

She took it, opened the door and threw, watched as it arced over the farm fence, disappeared.

When they'd parked and locked themselves in, he put his arms on the table and grinned, 'Hi, Ranna.'

She stood by the sink taking in the sound of her name. To hear even that deformed version was like when you became tired walking on the hills, felt in your pocket for a healthy booster which wasn't there, so you searched deeper and found this object in a grimy wrapper, saw the sweet attached to the paper by sugar that stretched into thinner and thinner hairs under the tension. Finally you swallowed the thing because there was nothing else. It still tasted good.

Part 4

When she woke next morning Ed's name swam up. At least that was how it seemed. Though his eyes came first, before his name, so large they seemed to split his face, green streaked with brown, calm, thoughtful. A voice too – rather light – or not exactly a voice, nothing to hear, more the memory of a voice, chatting on and on, emerging from dark, expressive lips; clear skin that gave the impression it had been polished, white round the nostrils, almost transparent over the cheeks where red glowed through, browned by the sun on forehead and high cheekbones, olive in shadows round the eyes and under the floppy hair. Years since she'd seen him. Amazing he'd made so much impression.

She sat on the edge of the bunk and looked at herself in the mirror, female driver, pale with untidy grey hair. Elizabeth had said, 'You want to beware.'

Of what?

Of what had come back just now – 'Those El Greco good looks.'

She opened the cupboard, lifted out a spare duvet, two pillows, two green duvet covers – why on earth was she keeping all this clobber? She felt under Elizabeth's bras and blouses and drew out the album.

Yes, that was them – Elizabeth, resting on her hand with her legs turned sideways and that cool, slightly sceptical look; Ed leaning back on both hands, head raised with one leg stretched straight out the other bent up, those enormous feet.

'Badly co-ordinated', she'd said to Elizabeth. 'Feet the size of breadboards.'

Must have been her who said that. Too blunt for Elizabeth.

Who were those other boys? Must have been travs of Ed's. Someone called Matt, was there?

How young they all looked. Pink faced, bright haired. Sprawling on grass.

Yes, grass. Yes, then, in the first flush of the New Dawn you parked often on grass. Sun dappling – must have been warm – but the leaves yellow, littering the grass. Late September perhaps.

That first autumn when you didn't have to move on, if you liked the site, you stayed, wandered off down paths, picked blackberries, paddled, splashed each other, mucked about.

The other day – those kids mucking about on the pipes at the farm – they'd come across something no driver had shown them. Taken full advantage – very naughty – but – a bare moment of freedom?

These kids were free. They had climbing walls, swimming and paddling pools, bubcourses, rollerblading. Why hanker after a world where they were allowed to take risks? If some activities had been banned there were good reasons – motor-cycle polo, for instance – would anyone in their right mind find that a good idea?

But that first summer – were we all playing Peter Pan? Eternal holiday, did we think?

We had jobs. I was trav-teaching, Elizabeth had clients – no shortage even then of accidents and rows.

The overnights were still being thrown up. You could lie on the grass, gaze at fantastic white domes and turrets while over to the side concrete blocks were still being hoisted to make walls for cafés and sports halls. Must have been years before we used indoor methies instead of chemical toilets. There used to be grocery stalls all over the steps Then they weren't there any more.

At the beginning all that was part of the fun. In the afternoons, pale inner city people without pollution masks, picnicking, basking. And the buzz from the speakie in the ear.

It wasn't all fun, far from it.

'Why ever aren't they replying?' she'd ask time after time and Elizabeth had no answer. 'They can't be out – not every time.' And she'd use her V-cam to view Hayle, every room, the garage, the whole garden – chairs, tables, carpets, saucepans, even soap on the side of the bath – never wet – the windows – ones she'd helped her mother strip – still had no curtains – the others did – but them, her father and mother?

'They can't have gone to America leaving it like that.'

Elizabeth would hold her shoulders. 'I don't know, I don't know.'

It was Ed pointed the way, asking, 'What happened to the Knights?'

'The Knights?' They were sitting cross-legged on the grass.

'Defended their castles – remember? Have you seen them – or anyone like them – anywhere here?'

'They don't belong here.'

'Exactly,' he said, 'they're in another universe.'

Her mouth flopped, her eyes went out of focus, she leant forward over her legs.

He sat observing. Then 'Been thinking,' he said slowly, quietly as he always did. 'They said they'd never let their houses be demolished. They'd fight to the end. And they would have, I'm sure. Have you heard any report of fighting? It all seems to have gone through so smoothly. So where are the Knights?'

'Perhaps they took off their armour and mixed,' Elizabeth suggested. 'Without it they'd look much the same as anyone else.'

He nodded. 'And yet, I think, one would notice. To put it bluntly, they wouldn't look happy.' He clasped his huge hands together, sitting on the grass, gazing down. Finally he raised his head, 'So what did happen? Why have so many people disappeared?'

Miranda raised her head and gazed full at him.

'Your father and mother,' he said, 'my brother. People Elizabeth knows perhaps?'

'Don't have many relatives,' she said. 'Most of the people I know are colleagues. Haven't tried to keep up with them in all this.'

At last Miranda's lips worked. 'So what are you saying?'

He considered his fingers again and again looked up, straight at her. 'We all have to live with our decisions – and there are some that determine where you stand. There's no going back, I'm afraid, Miranda,' he said softly. 'we're where we are and they're where they are.'

She wrinkled her face and said nothing.

'It seems a fact that every moment we make a decision there's a separation of ways. Both things happen in different universes. We live with that fact all the time without noticing. What's happened this time is different, because, I think, of the numbers involved. Millions of people faced the same fundamental choice at the same time and made opposite decisions. The result has to be that the two groups separated completely. Their minds were in such opposite worlds, they wanted to live in such different ways – it was impossible – they couldn't hold together any more.'

She saw a universe slowly cut itself into two cells which reached one side out urgently into new territory while their longing to be together stretched the other to its limit, till finally the last tips lost hold and they floated off into separate existences. 'Is that possible?'

His warmth reached her across a gap she so much liked him for keeping between them. 'I'm sorry – I think so.'

She was silent, pulling at the grass. Then, 'Never?'

He studied her carefully. 'Probably not.'

She sat, then suddenly pushed herself to her feet. 'I'll go for a walk.'

That was the last time she found comfort under trees. Until, of course, she took herself off where she shouldn't have.

At that early stage it was the continual murmur in the ear that kept her on course, all those voices coming in reporting new interchanges and overnights, fantastic buildings. Any time you liked you could jump in your van and rush off and see them.

Though on the whole she didn't. Elizabeth, Ed and his travs took their speakies from their ears and seemed to want nothing more than to spend their time watching. They didn't say much. Then they'd put back their machines, listen, take them out and view. Still not say much.

She was glad to have time to wander off and gaze at the intricate pattern of branches and leaves against the sky, listen to wood pigeons, a chiff-chaff, a wary pheasant. At the same time she contemplated mud where grass had been trampled by thousands of exploring feet and wheels. Tracks were stretching deeper and deeper into the countryside.

'It's hopeless,' she said to Elizabeth, 'if anything's to survive, we'll have to be banned.'

'That what they're saying in your ear?'

'What I think.'

'Mira, that's the message all the time coming over the speakies.'

'So what? Right, isn't it?'

Elizabeth sighed. 'May be — but —'

'But what?'

'Ask Ed.'

She plonked herself down beside him. 'Elizabeth's uptight about the idea of fences to stop the countryside being trampled.'

He smiled. Then, 'Common sense, you think?'

She ran her eyes slowly over him. 'Of course.'

'It does seem like that. Yes. So why is she bothered? Why am I?'

She examined olive shadows either side of his nose, veins winding across lids that had fallen to hide his eyes.

At last he looked up. 'What I'm thinking doesn't entirely make sense. Maybe I'm suffering from paranoia. The idea has a lot going for it – but I'm uncomfortable – with the way it's being promoted.'

'Is it?'

'It seems so obviously right to you, Miranda, but yes, it is. It's being pushed. If you listen to the speakies –'

'I don't bother with them.'

'They've got to you all the same. Pip after pip and mostly in the same words. That's what bothers me. They all seem to come from the same source.'

'Not all.'

'Enough to worry me. There's someone behind it.'

'So what if there is? If it's a good idea?'

'The New Dawn was the brainchild of Gavin Claring. We all knew that. We could see him on telly. He went about, addressed rallies, got supporters and they had names and faces. We could look them up. But this – it's coming from nowhere, not a soul you can put a face to –'

She looked at him sharply. Her eyes shone. 'But if it's the voice of the swarm?'

He pondered. 'Bees would all use the same code, I suppose.' He leant back, pulling his knuckles. 'But humans, you know, we're capable of greater variation.' He spoke more firmly now. 'And that's what's lacking. There's one mind behind this – the mind, I mean of one person.'

'Or a committee?'

'Maybe.' He looked directly into her face. 'But who elected them, Miranda? Who gave them the right?'

'The government – the New Dawn Party.'

'I'd like to see their faces,' he said obstinately.

She shrugged.

Not long after that the V-cams went blank – though not completely. She thought it was just a glitch, kept trying to view Hayle, failing over and over. She could watch motorways and overnights, nothing else.

About this time lorries brought teams who unloaded metal stakes and erected twenty-foot palisades round the edges of the overnight. Excited voices in her speakie revealed this was going on all over the country. This was 'a great, a wonderful, an epoch-making event, a masterpiece of forethought, a triumph of human wisdom'. She wriggled, didn't say anything to Ed, watched birds flying over, tried to rest her thoughts on safe nests, plentiful seeds, humming insects in places free from human interference. Her V-cam refused to bring up their pictures.

'I suppose,' she said to Elizabeth, 'they want us to forget.'

'Very likely.'

Elizabeth would be sitting side by side with Ed, discussing. Actually he did most of the talking, slowly, with gaps she didn't break into and she'd be listening with her head turned towards him. Miranda would sit a little apart, watching.

One evening Elizabeth turned to her in the van. 'What would really suit you would be to become a Green Settler.' Or did she say 'ought'?

'One of those dreamies?'

'You won't be able to bear being cut off from nature. You love it too much.'

'That's exactly why we had to have the New Dawn.' She took a deep breath. 'No other option.'

If it had come earlier Elizabeth might be here now.

Ed did have a problem. Difficult period to be a vet. He played with Soccie. Miranda caught him twirling a grassblade. He stopped instantly when he saw she was looking. She wouldn't have minded. Liked it.

Shielding himself, perhaps?

Did she let on she thought he was soft?

Probably.

Yes, obviously. Elizabeth wouldn't have been on at her otherwise.

Though he was asking her opinion. So she told him. He wanted to know.

Not that she would ever have called him soft. Not in so many words. Only in general terms, expressing what she thought about people who wanted to settle.

It was this great sacrifice they were making to save the planet.

She wouldn't have missed adding it was natural for humans to be nomads – partly at least because she so loved the way Gavin made his point. He said 'planet' in Greek meant 'wanderer' and the Greeks gave that name to these particular heavenly bodies because they didn't stay in fixed positions but moved to different parts of the sky. Later astronomers named them after gods. You remembered that. Then he went on, it seemed apt that the most intelligent creatures on a wandering heavenly body should themselves be wanderers. Not cause and result, of course, though a sign of intelligence. Our earliest ancestors had been hunter/gatherers wandering along the coast out of Africa into Asia and as a result restlessness was in our genes. If anyone dug back into their family history they'd be surprised – even the most stable families had histories of moving, perhaps only to the next village, or the next county, to the other side of a river. But not fixed for hundreds of years. Think of the arrival of Normans, Anglo-Saxons, Celts. Where had they come from? All those centuries of human flow. So it seemed natural that anyone who didn't want to take to the road was dim.

Already she was shying away from hankerings, learning not to refer to 'roots.'

Ed wasn't dim. She hadn't grasped his situation. He'd spent the previous summer putting down unwanted pets. Had to if he was asked. And when you think of it – Great Bernard in a campervan? Pair of collies? He must have been besieged by owners claiming it was the kindest thing. Buying memorial photos.

Soccie hadn't run away then. She began to understand, to see it that night calling and calling – March, probably next year – he didn't come then nor next morning and the Frees wouldn't let them stay.

Not a good life for animals, in vans, he'd said.

She wriggled, refused to listen. He played with Soccie, said he was afraid of dogs and cats gone wild, roaming the countryside. What good would they do to wildlife?

She told him animals in vans would need vets.

'So they will,' he said, 'so they will.'

He said his skills were transferable. That sounded like a cop-out. Old people weren't animals.

'I'll get training,' he said.

'These places,' she said, 'are for people too old – "decrepit" was trembling on her lips – to travel. You're young. Let the old look after the old.' Sounded good.

A job for the thick – did she think – or imply – that?

Elizabeth was right. It was amazing he was still speaking to her afterwards.

She may have been on at him more than once. He said he'd already started training as a nurse and she was convinced that was wrong for him. It was the awkward way he moved his hands and that shambling walk. He'd be totally in the wrong place.

Anyway they all knew, after the New Dawn there wouldn't be a nurse or doctor on hand whenever they needed one. All drivers had to go on courses. Didn't anyone take on board a person might some day need more than First Aid?

When she got Elizabeth finally to the head of the queue at the Sandown Overnight – one of the few with more advanced medical facilities – life after the New Dawn would be so natural and healthy – leukaemia, induced by exposure to air-borne chemicals and ultra-violet light, exacerbated by stress – had too firm a grip.

That was later. At that time, what was it finally brought out that dangerous El Greco look, rapturous rather than dreamy? Was it when she suggested even if he did train he might go settled in the end? Rolling stones, people used to say, are softer on the environment. That was her vision.

He responded with a different one.

She'd have attacked. 'You'd give up your freedom?'

'Miranda, some people can't have that freedom.'

An exchange like that wells up now as if it happened.

'A few, I suppose.'

'Those too handicapped to travel, people in pain.'

'Not so many of them.' She hadn't heard then, night after night, coughing from other vans.

When she met him again fifteen – seventeen – maybe only twelve – years later – since the New Dawn time went round from day to day without any effective marking out by weeks, without times for work and times to relax, shopping hours and hours when you could buy nothing – only dark and light, warmer seasons and colder ones – though in a van parked on concrete they didn't affect you much – memories persisted, unplaced but indelible –

So all that time later she asked if he'd been upset by what she said. He said he'd no idea they'd ever talked like that. She felt really put down. She'd come as near as anyone could to quarrelling with Elizabeth over him – that cool lawyer was so clever at dodging hard words. 'Freak' had been one step too much even for her.

It was because she'd watched them together – openly, on the grass. Elizabeth said something, he started humming, she picked it up, they looked at each other.

After that Miranda said he was weird.

He did take her from her in the end. But not the way she'd feared then. Later she fought for permission to drive her to his place and hand her over, trusting his skills.

She should have reckoned with the sight of him on those old-fashioned roller skates that suddenly appeared in the shops alongside skate-boards and roller skates. It was a craze – everyone wanted to be on skates, crashed round flailing their arms, screaming women, great fat men overbalancing on top of passers-by, tumbling about, laughing.

She and Ed and Ed's travs bought roller skates. 'Still got each foot separate,' she said, stamping left, then right, experimenting with the rhythm, then leaning forward from the hips, swinging out. 'Legs can still do it.' Which seemed strange, stranger still that all five of them who'd grown up in an age of skateboards had, even as children, discovered roller skates and preferred them now. Looking at them took her back to a dull brown cupboard in the tack-room at the back of the stable-block where she'd found a rusty pair. She'd carried them off to show Dad. He'd taken them from her, gazed at them, smiled, cleaned and oiled them for her.

Now Ed leapt into the air, twiddled round, landed on bent knees, struck down with all his force, sparks flew and he sprang up again, crossing and uncrossing his legs like a ballet dancer. How on earth did that great angular gowk manage it? But he did and she did too, curving her arms above her head, gazing at him, his travs circling them, then as they landed grabbing their hands, towing them round and in the background, Elizabeth watching. She was wearing red then, in the new style, the first step to vansuits, slim jacket that hung over her thighs, slim trousers pulled into her ankles and above them her straight black hair and pale face. She was laughing, her eyes shining.

Miranda glided towards her holding out her hands. 'Do come and try, Elizabeth. It's such fun.'

She shook her head. 'I'm sorry. Just don't have the energy. But I love watching, really do.' And then looking into her eyes. 'Don't worry, Mira. I'll be OK.'

Miranda went back to the boys and they started again, but this time the dance was slower, the wheeling wider. The circles took each dancer further from the others, enticed them into their own lonely swoops. She felt the ground rolling under her. This movement was something that caught you, made you feel things could come right, that you could go places and get somewhere. At last they all turned back, held hands, circled. That was what life seemed to be about, this continuous movement. Apart and together, together and apart.

Can't have been many days later his name came over the intercom. They were eating greengages. Sitting on the grass as usual – still was some and they scorned picnic tables. The Medical Training Unit had left Birmingham Caravanserai. The 'Dawn Servants' wanted him on the admin steps in twenty minutes.

They said good-bye with juice all over their chins.

Ed's travs soon drifted off, and that was the last they saw of them. There seemed nothing to hold them together.

The overnight shops were packed people trying to get hold of the most recent gadgets – tin-openers that worked from a distance, self-sweeping floor-mats –' Great fun to live with' a poster announced, 'as well as supremely useful'.

Miranda shoved paypoints at the salesman.

'Thanks, driver,' he said and she paused, gazing into his face, taking in the new greeting. It sounded good.

Then she rushed back to the van, spread this wonder on the floor, collected shovelfuls of dust and pebbles from the parking lot and dropped them on it. They sat side by side, watching it shuffle towards the door in successive loops like a very wide caterpillar and rear up with just that droop at the top edge that made them feel it was begging. Miranda opened the door, it shook itself like a Labrador and all the dust flew out.

'What if it feels moved to act when we're out?' Elizabeth asked.

They put up a frieze of magnetic tiles round the front half of the van just under the ceiling, a toning set across the balcony tucked against it. They hadn't taken to raising the roof so that someone could sleep up there. All they wanted was to make their sitting-space look cosy.

The cab could do with tiles as well, and dangly things, not obscuring views of course but if you were going to spend hours in there – though there were fascinations –

'Goggly lights – over there, third down in the outside lane, d'you see?' Miranda pointed through the jam. 'What's that on the roof? Horizontal angel – or what?'

'No end to people's invention.'

'Love those triangles on top of squares on top of circles, kind of maze – over there, see, on that Dreamtime? Such fun tracing ways through.'

'Plenty of time to do it.'

Miranda sank against the seat. 'It's odd, you know, but I feel happy sitting here in this jam. I'm not up-tight.'

'No pressure. Nowhere real to go.'

'Not alone. All those vans are company, aren't they?'

'In a way.'

The sun shone in through the windscreen. Miranda laid her hand on Elizabeth's lap. 'Cheer up, not so bad, is it?' She turned to look at her, reached out and touched her friend's nose. 'You're peeling. Why don't you use a barrier cream?'

'Can't find one fit for the job.'

Miranda drew back and dropped her hand. 'No. They say emissions are reducing.'

'Where'd you learn that?'

'Endlessly through the speakie. You turned yours off again?'

'That incessant chatter in my ears.'

'Can be useful. What day of the week is it?'

'No idea. Why?'

'Realised I didn't know. Adds to the sense of leisure, I suppose.' She gazed round over vans jamming six carriageways. 'Peaceful.'

'My clients don't find it that way.'

'Oh? What do they get up to?'

Elizabeth pulled into herself. 'Don't want to go into it.'

'OK.' Then more eagerly, 'Think the angel's moving. Be us soon.'

Later they put on their skates and joined the crowd hurrying up to the shops in the overnight centre.

Miranda gazed through the first window. 'What about getting ourselves masks, Elizabeth?' She laid her hand on her shoulder, 'These aren't surgical style. Much smarter.'

They considered ways in which pale plastic moulded itself to the contours of a face, openings for eyes and lips, some following natural lines, others exaggerated and coloured, imitating lipstick and kohl. 'Everyone's wearing them now.'

They giggled trying them on.

It was some time – probably a couple of summers had passed, one winter maybe – a cool day anyway, cloud, breeze you could enjoy on your cheeks when a Free posted half-way up the steps to the Centre summoned her with a wave of his arm, 'Hey you, driver, come here.'

She stopped.

'I said, come here.'

She couldn't take him in, towering over her from the steps, a Free, speaking like that, assured in every line of his body.

'You going to do as you're told?'

She stood in front of him.

'Why aren't you masked?'

Her eyes opened. 'But –'

'Ought to be masked.'

'What?' Her head was level with his knees.

His pose was casual, his feet seemed to go down into the earth, his boots reflected the sun. 'You arguing?'

She shook her head.

'Know the law, don't you?'

'What? – Sorry – probably heard something over the speakie. Didn't take in – this was a law. Who made it?' she mumbled.

'All did, didn't we?' He looked her slowly up and down, then over her shoulder and round, as if comparing her with other drivers. At last he spoke less roughly, 'Get yourself back to your van fast as you can. Don't ever come out again exposed like that. Understand?'

It was the difference in tone did it. She lowered her eyes, drew into herself, shrank, didn't dare look round in case someone was watching this grub creep home, but angry too that he'd cut the ground away under her like this, made her so small, so deformed.

It took her a long time to tell Elizabeth, 'Seems we're to wear masks all the time now out of doors.' Then she took herself off to the back seat of the van and listened to voices over the speakie.

Many were innocuous greetings: 'Hiya, Tom, Mandy, just keeping in touch,' 'See you soon, Bill.' and as she listened in a way she'd never done, she began to recognise an admixture of continental voices, 'Bonjour, tous les autres.' 'Bom dia.'

Others were part of a general sparrow chatter: 'We're just coming up to Thamesdown,' 'Sitting in a jam eating chocolates,' 'Think I'll take a break for a shower.'

Excited voices got her transfixed.

'Just printing my van number on my mask,'

'Hi, I, I, that's fan-tast-ic,'

'What font you using? How you get it into the printer?'

'Thinking of doing ours.'

And from a couple apparently walking around an overnight, publishing their conversation for the planet to hear, 'Say, Marta, see that driver with a radiator stamped all over his face?' 'Mask, silly.' 'Hey, but what an idea.'

But the angry voices were the most common.

'What's that driver think he's doing?'

'God, Ali, when's this jam going to move?'

'Would I like a coffee? Would I like one? Use your common-sense, driver. I'm sitting strapped in this seat all these hours and you ask, would I like a coffee? Hey you out there,' he roared into the speakie, 'Serve her right, wouldn't it, if I belted this poltic?'

Miranda's hand rose to unclip the set but the next voice made her pause. 'Nothing's changed, we're still sitting in jams. Hour after hour. This wasn't what we voted for.'

'Betrayal of the New Dawn,' someone else shrieked, 'Intolerable.'

'Not what we expected,' she said to herself sternly. 'We have to accept it. Best for the environment.'

By this time huge screens dominated the halls of overnight centres. 'Emissions down 5%.'

Discussions of jams swelled over the airwaves for weeks and then solutions began to emerge – more strands on the motorways, staggered departure times.

'Bit of order, that's what we want.'

'Das Ordnung haben wir gern.' Naturally, she thought, Germans would like order and, staring out at a sea of many-coloured vans, took in the New Dawn wasn't confined to one country, they had a right to a say. Obviously the movement had to be global. Of course.

'Dawn Servants could easily organise it.'

'Have a signal in the van. Then we sit comfortably till we're called.'

That last was repeated by different voices at intervals for days. 'Give the Frees power of enforcement.'

'Seems to be a tide of opinion –' Miranda said casually to Elizabeth, leaning her elbows on the table, cradling a mug, 'in favour of linking the vans to the Freecentre so they can organise our movements.'

'Can see the sense of it,' she replied palely.

Miranda went on warming her hands on her mug. She turned her head and watched rain trickle down the window.

'Long time since Ed left.'

'Six months.'

'Thought you'd lost count of time?'

Elizabeth shook her head. 'Not for things that matter.'

'Yes, he mattered.' She went on watching the rain. 'Know what he said?'

'He said such a lot.'

Miranda put her mug on the table. 'He wasn't sure about all that stuff that comes over the speakies. Implied there was someone behind it. And that Free – one who told me off for not wearing a mask – said it was a law we'd all made. How did we do that, Elizabeth?'

'No idea.'

Miranda gritted her teeth, glanced sharply across.

'I'm sorry, Mira. I don't have the energy to wonder.'

'No.' She watched the window again. Somewhere behind the vans parked to the left drivers were shouting. Any minute now they'd be at each other's throats – if they weren't already. Raindrops meandered down the pane, bumped into each other, merged, each one apparently at random but still part of a steady, relentless process. 'Didn't mean to get at you, Elizabeth.'

'I know.' She stretched across the table and took her friend's hand, 'We'll cope.'

Miranda forced a smile, 'Of course.'

They were looking for a seat in the café at Heart's Home – it had been Thamesdown but what with the continual movement and the rise of palisades you gave up wondering where you were in the country. They approached table after table with vacant chairs; masks turned towards them, eyes inspected them through holes, hands indicated strangers wouldn't be welcome.

There was one left with two drivers already seated, one with a tumble of black curls – dyed, Miranda thought instantly – bouncing round a bright-cheeked mask, the other with a cap of pale yellow hair that took on a violet sheen as a pale plastic face turned towards them. The angle of the heads was encouraging. Miranda approached cautiously. 'May we?'

'Of course.' The voice that emerged through the lips of the pale mask had a smile in it. Its owner pulled out a chair and patted the seat.

That's how they met Lucie and May. Travelled with them for what might have been several months. It was still difficult to tell one day from another.

In her mind Miranda compared them with Elizabeth and herself. May, the one with the tumbling hair, was all over the place, like herself, Lucie restrained like Elizabeth. In other ways of course they were completely different. Younger, for one thing, with less feeling of torn roots.

That word was already becoming dicey. More than dicey. Voices over the speakies went out of their way to avoid it.

'Things hidden underground,' they said, 'holding on, gripping. Disgusting to grip like that. Be mature. Move on. Enjoy your freedom.' These underground things were pale, secretive; they embodied longings grown people didn't indulge in. She felt herself sucked into the shuddering.

So quickly – within a year of the New Dawn? Two maybe? People changed so fast once their lips began to refuse the names of plants and animals.

Roots and bones became something she dwelt on at night. Her mind wouldn't leave them alone. On their way up to the café a workman had been spraying dandelions. Two days later the leaves were bent and shrivelled. The image of those plants' suffering recurred night after night. Which was absurd. She'd zapped plenty in her time.

Lucie and May were good laughers. Good party-makers. They hung their van with streamers – it was a very good summer that year, the first year of the parking slots, which were larger then – when you put two together it was almost like having a garden – except that there were no flowers. The streamers made up for them with exuberant colours and a variety of shapes. The four of them would open a couple of bottles and sit outside until it was dark, sometimes longer, while May told stories about things she alleged she'd seen or had happened to her – more likely to some friend she couldn't exactly remember who but it had definitely occurred – it was mad of course – you weren't going to believe her – all the same the person had landed up with the nose of his car over a cliff and been pushed back by a sheep stranded on a ledge that had found this way of extricating itself – someone else at a wedding whose winged hat had blown off and landed on the head of a great-aunt –

It was the way she told it, while Lucie smiled and the evenings went quickly.

They were going to travel to the ends of the world. No problem now with the Channel. The main lines of what later became the Riddle-me-Ree were open. 'We'll go down through the west side of France. There's a magnificent new motorway. Ten strands, they say, into Spain, maybe a detour into Portugal, they've bridged the straits of Gibraltar, there's another motorway under construction down the west coast of the Sahara and all round Africa, down to where Cape Town used to be then back up the East side, cross the Suez Canal – another bridge – then you've got the whole of Asia before you – and, we hope, by the time we get there, they'll have bridged the Bering Straits. Once we're in America – well – where can't we go? It's so exciting, I'm simply dying –'

Miranda sat back as this bubbling poured out. She gazed at the sky, took another sip of wine, looked over the edge of her glass and saw Lucie's face. They would go. There was no doubt.

She hesitated. 'Is it all like this country?' Suppose you could get to The States and – 'I mean – well – palisades, overnights, everywhere?'

'All in it together, aren't we, in this universe?' She sounded surprised, superior, almost.

Miranda sank into herself.

In the quiet of their own van she asked, 'What did you think, Elizabeth? Apparently they think it's worth going. But would you se much over the top of the palisades – and the whole idea's not to see over – the climates at least would be different.'

'Brighter light –'

'Yes.' Miranda fiddled about, took a couple of mugs off their hooks, arranged them beside the kettle, turned to study her friend's pale face. 'Not encouraging.'

'No.'

'We'd never planned to go.'

So when their friends took off, they waved, let them go.

Before then Miranda had an evening alone with them in their van.

'I haven't the energy, you go on your own, Mira.'

The two were hospitable as ever but somehow the conversation didn't flow.

After a period of silence, Miranda raised her head. 'Stupendous curry, this May. We shall miss you.' She paused with her fork in the air. She had no idea then how much like her mother she looked, making a searching question sound casual. 'Any idea who these – "Dawn Servants" – are?'

Lucie stared up sharply. 'Organisers, I suppose. Sort of government.'

'Who elected them?'

'Does it matter? Long as things get done. Need to have someone.'

'Yes – you really don't know?'

May intervened. 'Know what I imagine?'

'You're always imagining things,' Lucie said softly.

'How'd we ever get anywhere if I didn't? Anyway, this is what I think. There's this huge computer, everything anyone says on their speakie's fed into it and it sorts it all out, finds what the majority want. The Dawn Servants are the humans who look after it and do what it says. That's why they're servants, see? They carry out what it tells them we want.'

'I see.' Miranda turned it over. Was that what Ed meant – saying they'd all made the law?

Lucie was smiling now. 'Thanks, May, sounds likely.'

Elizabeth was in bed when she got back so she didn't ask her what she thought of the theory. Nor the next day. She was always so tired.

Meanwhile Miranda drove, parked, shopped a little, cooked a little, occasionally sat on the steps of an overnight or the van, watched little creatures scuttling about their business, wondered how much of their lives they understood.

Part 5

If she'd hoped Boss would have taken off that mask, she was wrong. He was slumped in his usual corner out of range of the morning sun, legs stretched out, staring at his feet.

What mattered now was breakfast. 'Sweetie Pops?'

He shrugged. Five minutes later a plastic leer rose to face her. 'You can give them me now.'

'Come here then.'

Leaning both elbows on the table, cradling a warm mug, gazing out at the screens while her body sank lower and lower into the seat, she watched him gather the sweet mass in both hands and cram it through lurid, swollen lips. Eventually she said, 'We won't move on today.'

He didn't look up.

Later she laid both hands on the table, looked across, sank back, stared again at that sneer, forced herself up, collected the dirty things, carried them to the sink, washed them. Lay on her bed.

After that he was standing over her, shouting, waving his arms.

She tensed, flopped back. He pulled out a drawer and tipped her underclothes over the floor.

She sat up. 'What the hell d'you think you're doing?'

The fixed grimace came close. 'Getting you up.'

'Van's not on fire.'

When he came for her she seized his wrists. They were so thin and when she leaned towards him her weight pushed him back. She slid onto her feet with him still in her grasp, drew him to her till her eyes were glaring in through the eyeholes. 'You don't do that, understand?'

She thrust her arms down straight-elbowed, pushed him away, held him in hands that seemed to become more clumsy the longer she led on.

The yells died down. She weakened her grip, felt him slip away out of her grasp like a tiny fish and stood, listening to her breath, looking at the mess on the floor, then out of the window at a tiny patch of sky. 'We both need a warm drink. Go and sit down.'

She slowly picked up her clothes, boiled a kettle.

Later she put her elbows on the table for the second time that day. 'Don wasn't your Dad?'

'What d'you want to know that for?'

'Interested that's all.'

'Don't care about him.'

'Or what he did to you?'

'Didn't do nothing that bothers me. Leave it alone.'

She sipped her tea. 'OK, Boss.' She ran her eyes over him. 'How about if I bought you a new vansuit?'

'What's wrong with this one?'

'Bit torn, I thought.' And then, eyeing tightness over the chest, 'You're beginning to grow out of it.'

He looked down and examined himself. Vain, she thought.

'Yeah, that's right. Growing, aren't I?' There was wonder in his voice.

'Soon be as tall as I am.'

It had surprised her that she could hold him. 'Well, if you want this vansuit, shall we go up the Centre?'

He pranced in and out of changing rooms, displaying himself, one hand on projecting hip, head tilted; arch, almost, settled on a pattern of red and yellow flames on a blue background.

'Celebrate with Aussieballs?'

While they ate she tried again. 'Don was your Mum's hitchmate?'

'Kind of. You got most of it right. How you know?'

'"Got it right?" – when?'

'To that poltic at the farm.'

'Oh him. Guessed that's all. That sort of thing – happens a lot. To all sorts of people.'

Green eyes stared at her though the mask and quickly dropped.

Later, up in the Centre, he gestured at an overhead screen. 'This month's reduction in emissions 5%'

'Don says that's crap.'

She hesitated, frowning a little. 'He wouldn't understand the scientific reason why that statement's rubbish.'

'Shut your gob.'

She glanced at him quickly, felt a need to defend her tone. 'If the amount's exactly the same every month, they haven't been measuring carefully.'

'Obvious.'

She glanced again, remembering plenty who wouldn't have grasped as quickly.

Then he held out his stick for her to put paypoints onto it.

'What you going to buy?'

'None of your business.'

Perhaps it wasn't.

She spent the rest of the afternoon wondering what he was doing.

Three days later the lock released them onto the Westminster slip road.

It was hard to stop herself searching for the Houses of Parliament, Big Ben or to stop herself re-running that debate – demolish or not demolish? Months and months of reading blogs, thinking, not able to get on with the New Dawn. That was Direct Democracy – the mind of the swarm slowly turning over, blog after blog building up to a referendum.

The discussion had been like that when they discussed the palisades – Elizabeth sceptical as ever. 'Asking for trouble, Mira, shutting people in like that.'

'Tough but no other option.' To protect the countryside. Protect. Protect.

Feral cats sang in the overnights.

She and Boss had supper on a terrace overlooking the Thames. Setting sun on the water, palisade on the far bank. This must have been the Members' Terrace, she thought. How many deals had been done here, how many plots hatched? Today there were only tables and chairs, a view of water the other side of a wall. There were no swans. She wondered if a branch of the Frees existed to keep them out. As they glided back to their parking slot the ghost of Big Ben was chiming.

She came to grips with facts next morning. 'This used to be a very famous place.'

'Uhhh.'

'We'll see what they've got in the Visitor Centre.'

He shovelled down Posties.

'I'm going anyway.' It seemed a due that had to be paid, like visiting a family grave. 'You come if you like.'

"Parliament in Action" filled a suite of darkened rooms. Boss ran past election manifestoes, explanations, photographs, slowed to look vaguely at excerpts from contemporary films. Miranda came and stood beside him. Her grandmother had talked about Maggie Thatcher and there she was on the wall to the right with that prissy voice and disciplined hair, and again, older and greyer. There on the left with the wavy hair – that must be Tony Blair – the one Gran helped to put in office the first time she was old enough to vote, then right, David Cameron, left, Ken Livingstone, followed by Arish Patel, then where the wall was painted green, Gemma O'Brien, Melissa Cohen, Gavin Claring –

'You seem to know them all.' All of them – except Gavin who'd never actually bothered with the House, always spoken on TV, 'directly to the people' – were leaning an elbow on the dispatch box, gesturing against a background of roars. 'Some kind of match, is it?'

'Sort of – just trying to put their points across. You know how it is when other people don't listen.'

'Look like poltics to me.'

'That word, Boss, the one you've just used – comes from 'politician'. That was what they called these people.'

'Always rubbish, then?'

She would have liked time to think. 'Not always. No, they weren't rubbish but the system didn't work. That's why we had to have the New Dawn.'

'That what we got now?'

She stared at him. 'Yes.'

It was the teacher in her she supposed made her try to explain better on the terrace again eating ice-creams among the coming and going of long-dead politicians – talking, laughing, slapping each other on the back, wheeling and dealing, sorting out world affairs. Or not.

'The old way didn't work.' She watched a breeze rippling the Thames. 'We were destroying the planet. The trouble was, with all our machinery we could do so much to make our lives better and the machines did that, but we always put humans first. We didn't think about our environment or wildlife. We took over their space and let them die.'

He scraped up the last traces of ice-cream. 'Another.'

She lit up. 'Bad for you – but yes.'

But the topic wasn't exhausted. 'We wanted something new. You see, if we destroy the planet there's nowhere else to go. Insects, birds, animals, they've all got a right to life.' She ran her eyes over the contours of the mask that hid his cheeks, tried to reach his eyes through the slits. 'It really was the start of something new – people – drivers – would take up so much less space – everything else would have room to live too – and at the same time we'd have direct democracy; no politicians playing party games and taking their cut, just ordinary drivers sitting in their vans thinking and voting directly.' Now he was looking away across the water. She leant across the table. 'You'll be old enough to blog in your bit in a few years.'

'All dead aren't they?'

'Who?'

'Politics we saw.'

'Yes.' She saw more clearly now they had been surrounded by the gesturing dead.

'Spook bins are much better.'

'Have you been in them often?' Non-stop diet of accidents, rapes, murders, torture available for a low price in 3D + smells.

He shrugged. 'Few times, yeah.'

'Since I've known you?'

He glanced at her sideways. 'Go somewhere else now?'

The third morning he went off by himself. An hour later he stood at the bottom of the van steps. 'Ranna.'

She clicked the third layer of Edu-trav.

'Ranna.' And again, 'Ranna, you listening? I want you, Ranna.'

She turned slowly. 'Miranda,' she murmured. 'What is it?'

'Come and see what I found.' The Devil Drover grinned above printed flames dancing on his vansuit as he bounced up and down. His voice was eager, human.

She turned off the computer and stood up.

He led her through lanes that branched into smaller and smaller alleys. Soon they were pushing their way between rows of security screens with the roar of the motorways gradually fading away. Eventually they came up short at a palisade. The slots either side were fastened with rusty padlocks.

'Look.' He shook the barrier, a stake fell sideways, she saw they were all loose.

'Been through.'

Naturally. She studied him carefully. 'You needn't think I'm coming.'

'Come on, Ranna. Know you. You're not scared.'

'What is there through there?'

'Big wall.'

'How big?'

'Huge.'

Remains of an office block?

He measured air with his hands. 'Thick. Not normal. Huge stones.'

'Stones?' Westminster to the City how far? 'When I was your age –' But how old was he? 'there were still bits left of the ancient wall of the City of London.' Something so old still standing in all this desolation? Go through and touch it?

Massive stones, a flight of broken steps that led up to the remains of a small room – guard-post?

'Can see down the other side.'

'What's there?'

'Drivers in funny clothes.'

'Can't be part of the overnight.' She stood at the bottom and stroked warm stone. The steps had been worn by feet.

She followed him up. He'd found a place to look without being seen. There was room for the two of them squashed together in the wide mouth of an arrow slit.

A three-storey terrace. Long narrow London gardens. As she watched, a woman came out of French windows carrying a bowl of fruit on a tray. She was wearing a narrow skirt and high heels. Her hair was piled elegantly on top of her head. Two girls in floppy blouses were batting a shuttlecock to each other across a lawn. A dog was sitting on its haunches. A black and white cat was curled on garden chair. Two men in white trousers were lounging in the shade of an ornamental plum, fingering wineglasses. Peonies and delphiniums were flowering in long borders. The walls were soft with clematis and roses.

Miranda drew in a sharp breath. Her face hardened.

'What are they?'

'Not sure.'

They were both whispering.

The shuttlecock went backwards and forwards. The men chatted. The woman fetched a music player. Mozart floated across the grass. One of the children ran inside and appeared a minute or two later, shouting from an upstairs window, 'The blue one', reappeared carrying two sweaters. She gave one to her sister. The dog made off with the shuttlecock. The girls chased it laughing.

Miranda slowly assembled her thoughts. 'Dawns, I think, got to be. Let's get down, Boss. Not good for us to be here.'

She waited for him at the bottom but he was slow, standing on the top step, waggling his hips. Almost seeing a floppy blouse lift to the movement she had to laugh, covering her mouth, careful not to be heard. How much he'd grown, much taller now, slender as a girl. She waved to him fiercely to come down.

He descended in his own time, pointing his toes.

She didn't answer his questions until he'd locked the screens behind them and they'd climbed into the van.

'What was it then?'

'Things we shouldn't have seen.'

'Was them we saw at the farm.'

'Yes, I think so.' Her gaze travelled round inside the van, the frieze of decorative tiles, curtains in abstract patterns, floor mats, all past their best, you might say. She was surprised how coldly she'd spoken. 'Quite a performance, wasn't it the other day, in their nice clean uniforms pretending to be the New Dawn?'

The mats seized her attention. None of them was self-cleaning. That one had stopped working about the time Elizabeth died. And now her shoulders sank forward, the shame came swinging up. She'd said good bye to Ed, switched on, driven to the nearest overnight, calm, almost cheerful even, carried on her ordinary life, moved on and parked as normal. Then one morning she'd seen the mat was thick in dust. She'd prodded, shaken it a little, talked gently, shouted. Nothing she could do would make it curl up and shuffle towards the door. Then she'd collapsed onto a seat and howled for that silly little machine in a way she never had for Elizabeth.

She pulled herself together. That was ancient history and Boss was waiting.

She glanced sideways at him, and again, then, 'What did you think?'

'Putting it on, weren't they?'

'You could say that, yes.'

'Rubbish,' he said, 'they got to be rubbish.' Then with sudden change of voice, 'Where are their vans, Ranna?'

'They live in the houses.' Then seeing his blank expression, poor little toad. 'Those buildings behind them were houses. We all used to live in them once. There's parts, aren't there, to this van – kitchen end, sitting end, bathroom, bedroom? A house has more rooms and is much bigger.'

It felt very silly explaining all this.

He sat still, then, 'Bigger than a double-decker trailer?'

'Much bigger. You saw.' She leant forward, warming to the task. 'Probably each of those girls has a bedroom to herself.'

'You lived in something like that?'

She nodded.

'Don't look like it could move.'

'They stay in one place.'

'Boring.'

'It wasn't,' she looked at her words, swallowed, 'though we were right to choose to live in vans.'

He looked at her sharply. 'Which is it, Ranna?'

She stood up quickly. 'I'll get tea.'

A mocking voice followed her. 'Which one, Ranna?'

He went out later and returned after dark, tense and morose as always.

Each morning he'd grab a Reddiroll, slump into a corner, tear off a piece, cram it into his mouth, refuse to look up. It was her life he was chewing.

When he took himself off she sat at her computer, as she had ever since the New Dawn, but how long since the last time. It had been a daily routine – but now? It was good, she said to herself, sliding onto the seat, settling her bottom, reaching out to the keyboard, to get back to routine.

First the egghead, Chang. She read his latest assignment. 'Excellent selection of material,' (abstruse, some of it) 'you should take care always to acknowledge your sources.'

Then she set to, chasing up Col, Rog, Tiro. Drew the expected blank. Clicked Admin at Edu-trav. Milla's plump face appeared – she claimed a face on a screen was only an avatar so she could work maskless. Her fingers rested as usual on her keyboard, her eyes smiled over well-rounded cheeks.

'How's things, Miranda?'

'So so. How they with you?'

'Great.' Milla stretched back. 'Tell you shall, I?'

'Go ahead.'

'Dil and I got in with these drivers. Know how it is don't you? Can't stop drivers talking to you in queues. Turned out he was a games designer like Dil. Different style but same line. She designs vansuits. Any way we got talking, ended up booking a double slot, pulled back the interior screens, had drinks. Then Baz – that's the gamesman – trotted off into their van and came out with these ancient playing cards. Said he'd no idea how they came to have them but why not play? So we sat all evening in the open air between the vans playing old-fashioned Bridge. More to it than you'd expect.

They're such fun, you know, Baz and Jee, such a lovely couple. We decided to travel together and now one or two more have come in on it.'

'So glad. Lovely to have company.'

Milla shot a glance. Her broad lips warmed into a smile. 'So, what can I do for you, Miranda?'

'Chang. You got his notes, XW235N/Q699?' She watched fingers tapping a keyboard. 'This is my fourth time of asking – sorry, Milla, just pass it up the line – but when is Edu-Trav going to turn up a tutor who knows something about astronomy?. Chang's knowledge is light-years ahead of me. I've been explaining his need for I don't know how long.'

'Two years.' Words of an avatar in whose world time still counted.

'So what about it then?'

'The system's been activated.'

Miranda let a laugh slide into her voice. 'Non-system more like.'

'You have to live with the tangles to understand.' The shrug ran the length of her arms. 'We'll come up with someone. Not next week. Six months, maybe.'

'OK. Still can't contact Tiro.'

'You reported this – yes, couple of months back. Number's dead.'

'Mum may have upped? Part of a Fem-tog, wasn't she?'

'Can't trace him. Sorry, Miranda, we'll go on trying, honest, we do genuinely try.' She leant forward as if trying to reach through the screen. 'From where I'm sitting your shoulders look very tired.'

'Maybe they are.'

Milla gazed down at her keyboard, then raised her eyes. 'Look after yourself, Miranda. It's a nasty world we live in. Female driver needs all the support she can get. You look as if you could do with a holiday. Put in for one. Who knows, by the time you manage both to book it and have it, we'll have found Tiro.'

Day after day Boss would return in the afternoon and they'd move on. He'd sit beside her in the passenger seat and croon. She thought that was perhaps what he came back for, to find her still there, daring to build an expectation. He never demanded a speed lane and she never suggested it.

One evening she lost her temper. They were parked in a cul-de-sac of an exceptionally dreary overnight, at the end of a motorway that led nowhere, somewhere near where Southend had been, she thought. "Paradise Port" in gold letters dancing over the entrance.

He hadn't spoken all day except in grunts. She was tired.

'You're not going out tonight.'

'Can't stop me.'

'I've a right to sleep.' She heard her voice rise.

He shoved the nose of the mask toward her, 'Don't care, do I?'

He swung on the handrail of the top step. 'Bye, bye.'

She ran to the door. 'Don't bother coming back.' I'll up, she thought. At last I'll up. She grabbed the key out of his hand. His fist swung up as if to attack her, then he stuck up two fingers, turned and ran. Wait for him to get past the end of the row, she thought, then up.

A few minutes later she opened the screen, climbed into the driving seat, turned the key. The van lumbered down the empty road. She drew up at a cross-road, looked in the mirror, saw a small figure emerge from a side-road, saw him stand, catch sight of the van, saw even at that distance his shoulders drop, that he stood there drooping, didn't coming skating in pursuit.

She moved on slowly towards the exit.

When she reached it there was a queue. How long, she thought, how long? When would she get her supper? She turned the van round, drove slowly toward the Centre.

She found him standing outside the Spook Bins. 'Have you been in one?'

'You was going to up.'

'Is that why you came here – to visit a Spook Bin?'

'Best place to come.'

'I'm sorry, Boss. I was angry.'

He tensed. 'Why you saying that?'

'I'm very tired.'

'Shut up, you poltic. Shut up, shut up, up, up. Talk sense.' Then flailing clenched fists. 'What you said makes no sense.'

Words surged out from somewhere. 'It makes no sense to you but it does to me.' She stood still, hearing the words in her head; not what she'd expected to say.

He drew back, staring. A long time passed.

'Let's get back to the van.'

He came quietly.

As they moved on from overnight to overnight she kept putting off the question of the Spook Bins, preferring to search for holidays.

'Beach? Country?' The website enquired. 'Hills. Further details.'

Could you really? Really for one whole day sit on a beach? She'd heard theoretically it could be done – but really, actually sit and watch the waves come in?

It could indeed.

She shut her eyes, listened to a distant crash and shuffle. But if it rained? She clicked 'Country.'

'Two hours? Half day? Day?'

A whole day in the country?

Wouldn't be Hayle.

She pictured the front of the house the last time she'd seen it, the day she took Elizabeth there and prepared to leave her, the day they'd sat in the car under the cedar reluctant to get out.

'You know, Mira, I hope in their universe, they got to the States.'

'Perhaps they did.'

'Let's hope so.'

She'd laid her hand on Elizabeth's wrist. 'It's kind of you to think of them now.'

'They're so much part of this place.'

'There must be another Hayle, in another universe.'

She'd helped her out and supported her across the gravel. Ed met them in the front porch, older, greying a little, still the same enormous feet – new assurance in his tread – same flush in the cheeks, same dreamy eyes.

Upstairs, propped against pillows, Elizabeth said, 'You were attracted by him once, weren't you? Do you remember, Mira?'

Blue flowers on the duvet. Not bluebells, one of those made-up flowers, with parts like several plants, not really anything. An Omni-tech had been hammering not far away. An old-fashioned, comfortable sound.

'It was you – you were always talking to him.'

'We were on the same wavelength, he and I. I understood what he wanted.' She'd smiled so quietly. 'All the same, Mira –'

'But Elizabeth,' she'd blurted out then laid her hand on hers on the sheet. 'It was the way he used to lean towards you, the way he looked – those big eyes and hollow cheeks – I was scared.' She squared her shoulders, frowning. 'It was the way he made what he wanted sound noble when it wasn't. We were the ones going the right way.'

'Nothing happened, did it?' Her eyes closed. Then she opened them again. 'You understood too – about the rest of what he was saying – but didn't want to know. You were fighting him.'

Elizabeth didn't often get things wrong. That was why you remembered when she did. Didn't discuss much after that. Sat beside her while the sun slowly shifted its angle.

Hayle was out of the question. Anyway, wouldn't appear in any holiday list.

Paradise Port was over-run by feral cats whose war-songs or love-songs – she couldn't make out which – rose and fell like sirens. Towards midnight they hushed. It was then the speedvan whined down the avenue, screeched round the corner, came to a standstill – how many slots away? She held her breath.

She leaned toward the window, lifted a corner of the curtain, an out of date reaction. All she could see – the corrugated screen. Someone would call the Frees. Not her.

A moment's silence then a pale flash above the screens. They had a laser saw. It would cut metal in a couple of seconds. There was a crash, someone screamed. The screen in front of her shook. They would be shaking all down the street.

Her fingers whitened on the sill. There was a hiss like the sigh of hydraulic brakes. She was kneeling up now, head pressed against the glass. She gritted her teeth, heard the speedvan's engine surge, a rattling which died almost instantly. That was all.

Speedvans relied on laser saws to open the screens plus electronic siphons that sucked out the target van. No brakes were proof against them. No-one ever heard the saws, only the screen collapsing, the long breath of the suck. Then they were gone. Tomorrow omni-techs would be repairing the entrance gates. She crouched a long time by the window. Drivers must have been sleeping in that van. When she got up her feet were ice-blocks. Boss seemed to have slept through it all.

'Heard them, did you?' he remarked next morning. 'Good wasn't it?'

'Good? Good? What d'you suppose happened to those drivers?

'Threw them out on the motorway. What you think?'

She let water run slowly into the kettle. 'I'm afraid to think.'

'You're too innocent, Ranna.'

She turned sharply. 'I suppose you're going to tell me that's what Don used to do?'

'Best way to get rid of them,' he said.'

'Don lived in the Breakers' Yards?'

'No need for you to know.'

Was that why he hadn't come to watch? The whole incident too ordinary for him?

'Want some paypoints for the bubcourse?'

He shrugged and took them.

She called up Milla. 'Still no tutor for Chang?'

'Why you asking? You only asked last week.' The dark eyes sharpened. 'You OK, Miranda?'

'Bit shaken. Speedvan last night. Took a van from two slots down.'

'That's horrible. Oh Miranda, I'm so sorry.'

'Nothing you can do, is there?'

'Better move on. Where are you?'

'Paradise Port.'

'Seedy dump. Was there once, that was enough. Dangerous too, on the edge like that. Better get back somewhere central.'

'Speedvan won't come two nights running. I'll be OK. It's just thinking about those drivers.'

'Don't. There's nothing you can do. Look, Dil and I are at Temple Park. Why not come here?'

'Temple of the Car?'

'Wouldn't bother with that place but you could park near us.'

Her hands folded together. 'Thanks a million. I'd love to, really love to – but – I don't know – somehow I'm not ready. Can cope, that's it. Understand?'

'Not really. But if it's what you want – keep in touch.'

'Thanks and thanks again.'

'It's nothing, Miranda – and actually, though you wouldn't believe it, I've got some good news for you. Guess what?'

She opened her mouth. 'Tracked down Tiro?'

'Nothing as definite as that. Thought his Mum was going to come clean at last. Instead she hid behind a piece of scrawl she held up to show me. I copied it. Want to see?'

'Show me.'

'It's in reply to our query of last November.'

A simple message appeared. 'Tiro can reed tuter not needed, sined, glad brewer'

'Depends what you mean by reading. Do we know where Glad was then?'

'Where she is now that counts.'

'Apparently both still alive. This is a seedy job, isn't it?'

'Sometimes.' She paused. 'Miranda, after what happened – anyone would feel sick – imagining those poor drivers. Don't let it get to you. Take a day out.'

'Might just do that. Thanks, Milla.'

It didn't seem time yet to shut down.

Milla's jaw tightened. 'They need to clean up the Breakers' Yards.'

'You suppose the Frees dare go down there?'

Milla's fingers moved. 'Bye, Miranda, look after yourself.' Her face faded.

Miranda sank back against the seat, struggling to clear her mind of a vision of rows of grey concrete sheds behind barbed wire fences. Or perhaps she needed to look closer, to understand? It wasn't the sheds themselves – all drivers needed new tyres and, from time to time unfortunately, to have dents beaten out – it was what lay behind them, an expanse that grew as she looked at it, monstrous in its unplanned sprawl. Metal gates that opened on one side to the motorways would give entry to a labyrinth on the other, lanes through which she saw tentacles reaching out from hideouts well back from the motorways.

Boss, apparently, had lived in that country. At the very least, was familiar with its goings on.

They parked next night at Celebration Corner, which was larger, cleaner and brighter, in a slot as close to the Centre as the office could allocate.

They both woke up late next morning. Boss went out. Miranda did some desultory reading, picked at a small lunch, went and lay on her bed.

When she woke she needed the bathroom. She opened the door.

A white figure swung to face her, green eyes large in a narrow face with high cheekbones, below it budding breasts, a hint of hips beginning to swell, scar on the chest bleeding. She stood blank.

'Get out.'

She drew back, shut the door, stood in the space outside, went to sit at the table, stared at nothing. After a while she went to her bedroom, pulled out a drawer, found bandaging, knocked on the bathroom door. 'Sorry, didn't know you were there. I really had no idea. Got something for you.'

'Keep your creepy eyes to yourself. Who you think you are? Dirty minded spy.'

She retreated and sat again staring out at corrugations. At last a slim figure appeared. The devil driver mask was back in place.

'Tea?'

Shrug.

'Cake?'

Shrug.

When placed on the table both appeared consumable.

'I'm really sorry. Heard you go out and fell asleep. Thought you were still out.'

'What's this – "sorry"? Just wanted to know, didn't you?'

Miranda looked at the statement carefully. Had she? Secretly? 'I didn't know there was anything to know – look, Boss – Boss, I can't call you that –'

'Why not? Perfectly good. Don –'

'Men throwing their weight round. We don't relate that way.'

'We? Who's we?'

'Women.'

'No difference is there, men and women?'

'Big question that. Come on – take that mask off. Seen you now haven't I? I'm not wearing one, am I? You know who I am – fair's fair.'

There was a long silence, then a coy glance. 'This one too young for me? What you think?'

'Agree one hundred per cent.'

'Get me a better one?'

Miranda drew away. 'You'll need one to go out in.'

Small fingers crept round to the back of the head, pulled off one side then the other, green eyes rolled toward her.

'Like me?'

'Don't talk like that. Couldn't care less what you look like. Could have a green face with purple spots all over it for all I care. Just so's we can talk naturally.' The small body tensed. 'And don't throw a tantrum. I've had as much as I can take. No, I didn't actually say you'd got a green face so don't try saying so.' I'm ranting, she thought. 'Just want to talk like human beings.' Humans, not "drivers". 'And while we're at it you can tell me your real name.'

'No-one talks to me like that.'

'That's what Don said, isn't it?'

'What I say.' A wild cat cornered.

'Look. It's OK. OK I tell you. Look, girl, in all the time you've been in this van, have I hurt you?'

'Had a knife.'

'Not all the time.'

Thin fingers pulled the lips of the mask to full length and let them bounce back.

'Never had a name.'

'What did your Mum call you?'

'Tammy.'

Would have been nice, she thought three days later in another overnight, if all this had made any difference. Though it seemed to in one way. In others things were just the same, if not worse, as if Tammy felt she'd made enough concessions and was going to make clear her right to go in and out, behave just as she pleased. Only sitting in the passenger seat seemed to soothe whatever devils were driving her. There she'd curl up, crooning to herself.

They did achieve a calm afternoon buying a new mask. Aggressively feminine with long blonde curls and purple lips, it seemed to express some sort of dream. Tammy gazed deep into the mirror, then let her eyes slide over her shoulder to watch the woman watching.

Miranda turned away quickly. To let her go out in it? Alone? That kid knew how to look after herself. But a girl? Why did you worry more about a girl than a boy?

How to stop her? Drive all night?

Perhaps this parody of womanhood might be a first step towards truth? But to let her go out in it?

'We'll get that one if you like – on condition you have another as well.'

'Don't want another.'

Miranda eyed the dangling row of female masks – Snow White, doe-eyed Bambi, Saint Teresa, Little Miss Muppet, Madame Curie with green lights in her hair, Florence

Nightingale. The New Dawn didn't seem to have done much for women.

'I like the plain ones,' she said at last, 'that don't give away you're female.'

Silence.

Then, 'See what you mean.' A longer silence, then. 'Yeah, slip through them. You'd be free.'

'Yes.'

They came away with one.

Tammy went out in it, demanded paypoints, screamed if she didn't get them, sank into silences when she'd curl in a corner, refuse to look up, barely even to eat. They could last days.

Miranda sank back into robot mode and talked to Milla. The trace of Tiro had faded into the aether. It was far too early to hope for a tutor for Chang.

Milla's private life was swimming along. 'Guess what, Miranda?'

She gave the required answer. 'What?'

'Dil and I are getting married.'

'Wonderful.' She stirred, tried to relax into it, 'Congratulations –' and floundering along, registering life still going on, ' – but – must be able to if you're doing it - but can you still? Thought as long as you registered the kids nothing else mattered.'

'Private ceremony. No reason why not.' Milla lowered her eyes and raised them. 'Fact is, I was trawling, the way you do, you know, and came on this document, opened it and in it were these old words. I yelled for Dil and said Read this. Don't you think these words are just "us"? He thought so too, so it's going to be the two of us, and friends. All you need, isn't it? Don't need any official.' Her eyes fell. Not like Milla to look shy. 'They're so beautiful, Miranda. Dil and I see, hitched along years now, thought we'd like something a bit more, show we'd achieved something.'

'You certainly have. How long, actually?'

'We tried to count it up – fifteen years? Sixteen? Never had kids to reckon it by.'

'Could be a record. You've done well, Milla.'

'We're making a real slap-up do of it... now we're absolutely sure... once in a lifetime, after all. Dil's having a lamé jacket. And you should see his pants.'

Miranda tried to picture them. 'And you?'

'Oh – that's a secret. Not quite finished, any way. Just wait. You'll be bowled over.' Her eyes went serious. 'Miranda, I'd love you to come – but it's space. We didn't want to hire one of those rooms in a Centre – too much risk of gatecrashers – so we've booked a block of slots at The Hoard of Gold. Still doesn't give enough room – we've a whole tribe of friends – can't think where they all come from – all of them so wonderful – like you, Miranda, we've never met but we've talked so much.' She paused for breath. 'So we're going live. You'll click in, won't you? Here's our private site.' Her fingers ran quickly over the key board. 'You'll get a perfect view – and we'll talk – a little at least, exchange greetings, you know what I mean – but even in the old days bride and groom, didn't have much time for guests, did they? Not with the cake and the speeches and the dancing and the going away and being hyped up for the occasion. According to my mum, any rate. You and I can talk again afterwards – and you can get to know all our friends. Thursday 20[th.] Don't you dare forget.'

'Impossible, Milla. I'm so glad.'

'OK. Bye for now. Look after yourself – I mean it. Get yourself a break.' The bright face faded.

Must be lovely to fit so easily – and not to be lumbered with this girl she'd caught this morning washing a bloodstained tee-shirt.

'What you done to yourself, Tammy?'

'Nothing.'

'We could have taken it to the washeteria.'

Fierce eyes. 'How many you think I got?'

She'd had a point. But. And now she was out again. What was she doing?

She pulled out Elizabeth's *Odyssey*. It would take her mind to a world where the things that brought trouble were gods or forces of nature. There were recognised techniques for dealing or putting up with them.

Tammy came in long after dark, refused to take off her mask, curled into a corner.

A cold shape that sat watching at the other end of the van eventually remarked, 'What you see in the Spook Bins is sensational stories some idiot made up.'

Not a flicker of response.

'You shouldn't go there. They do you no good.'

Sly eyes glinted. 'You don't know a thing.'

'I know you come in upset.'

Tammy jerked upright. 'Can take anything. You who's soft.'

'Why do you want to be hard?'

'Sensible. What's that you got?'

'Book. The one you found and asked me about.'

'Belonged to your hitchmate?'

'That's right.'

'It was hers and you've kept it.'

'Of course.'

'You're peculiar, aren't you, Ranna?'

'Am I?'

'You let yourself care. My Mum said never care. If someone ups, don't mind; if Don's a seedy corm, don't mind. So I don't.'

'The Spook Bins help you not to care?'

'Show what you got to do to win.'

Tense, narrow face, wiry arms and legs, hair still full of tangles. Not a child. Undernourished teenager more like. With all the wrong experience.

'I think it's better to care.' She looked at the words with some surprise. Presumably she'd meant them. She rose to her feet. 'Bedtime now, if you think you can sleep. Shall I help you get down the bunk?'

Next morning she mentioned a day out. 'Want to help me book it?'

Tammy threw herself onto the seat beside her.

Sea? Hills? Country?

'There's a special place I went with my hitchmate. OK?'

'Really special?'

Miranda nodded and clicked Hills. Scotland. Borders. She felt the warmth of Tammy pushing close to see, smiled to herself. 'I'll need an assistant.'

The young female who came up on the screen was wearing a red velvet forehead band, which made her mask look more human. All the same, if masks it was – better reply in kind.

The lips that showed under the mask were the same red as the band. 'Borders, whole day?'

'How soon?'

'Tomorrow?'

'Not much available at that notice. Melrose Abbey? Let's see. Fully booked.' She was obviously scrolling down the screen. 'Nothing in that range. Very difficult at this notice.' She smiled. 'Sorry, but you are in a rush. Love a change sometimes, wouldn't you? So'd I, to tell the truth.'

'You're on a work placement? Summer shift?'

'May to November. Hardly be worse, could it? Now for your problem. Can't get anything of any real interest. So many spaces allocated to Dawn Servants. Be for it if I let them go before the very last minute. That's tomorrow – and not first thing, I can tell you.'

Miranda let a smile into her voice. 'Never mind the big places. There was one, small site. I remember it from years back. Might not be listed – but – if it did happen to be –'

'Name?'

'Hermitage Castle.'

The wait seemed endless.

'Not much there. No shop, displays, models. Available though. Shouldn't think many people want it. Not very exciting.'

Miranda shrugged. 'At this notice –'

'Right then. Book you in.' The e-mail slot opened. 'Report at the entrance gate 10 am, leave 7.30. Don't suppose they'd make a fuss if you turned up at eight. Book in again for tomorrow night somewhere you can get back to easily. That should keep them happy. How's that then?'

'Fine.' Half choked. 'Thank you, thank you very much. We've got it solo?'

The clerk nodded.

Miranda bent over the keyboard. 'We'll need to get a move-on today, Tammy, to be in reach of that gate tomorrow.'

An hour later the crooning in the passenger seat was more like song.

The next morning the Free slowly read every word on her pass. 'Nothing to see. Can't think why you want to go there.'

'Only thing available.'

'Wouldn't come here myself.'

'No?'

'Don't suppose any driver would who could help it. Know how many have reached this gate since I've been posted? You're the third. Six seeding months and three drivers.' He spat and watched the spittle dissolve into the ground. 'Some who trained same time as I did get sent to the Riddle-me-re. You must have heard of it. Can see the race-tracks from the toll-booths. Above the Channel, you know? They say when the cars are taking some of the nearer bends you're looking directly up underneath. No problem passing the time there. But here? Count the seeding sparrows. Noisy little SJs. Did you know? Always quarrelling, sparrows.'

'Had forgotten. Interesting.'

She kept him talking while he checked the details against the record on his screen, did a stolid inspection of the interior of the van, failed to notice the bathroom door behind her when he emerged from investigating her bedroom. Then he checked the red light was working, undid the padlock, stood as if he still wasn't convinced, swung the gate open and waved them through.

The river was still there, the turn onto the bridge just as awkward. The little town beyond it, ruins in a wood. Grass roughened the centre of the road; bindweed and brambles smothered the gardens.

She opened the window and drove slowly. The air was full of birdsong. Fox cubs playing beside the road looked up with puzzled expressions.

She turned onto a rough track and pulled off onto open ground at the top of the pass, relaxed in the driving seat, took off her mask.

Tammy had already leapt out and was standing with her back to the van one hip slightly raised, her body curved, looking down into the valley. Her hair flickered round her shoulders. Miranda wondered how she could ever have imagined she was a boy.

She climbed out and went to stand beside her. 'Beautiful, isn't it?'

'All stones.' She sounded distressed.

'Well – yes.' Boulders half hidden in the bracken, a cliff on the far side of the deep valley, a river cascading over rock, heather growing through pebbles.

'Why not?'

'Can't see what they're for. All over the place.'

'Not for anything.' Explain millennia in a few words? 'It's the wind and rain that have done it.'

Tammy was silent. Then, 'When I was living wild it was rain that was worst.'

Miranda waited.

'No drivers here. Somewhere like this – nobody could live there.'

'People did used to. It was a hard life.' The sun was warm on her back though the breeze was fresh. 'Maybe a few still do. A settlement of Dreamies. Come on, let's get down to the castle. I want to show you where Elizabeth and I picnicked.'

'That the name of your hitchmate?'

It was later, when they'd parked outside the locked gate to the enclosure surrounding the castle and were sitting with their feet in the burn, Tammy said, 'You oughta forget her.' For a moment she sounded the older of the two.

Miranda stiffened. 'I can't ever forget.'

Harebells were growing along the top of a ruined wall. 'They call them "bluebells" in Scotland,' Elizabeth had murmured raising a small bell with the tip of a finger, bending towards it, intent, loving. How could you want to forget?

'I've forgot everyone.'

A blue flash passed along the burn. Miranda followed the bird to its perch. 'Kingfisher, look.' She pictured Hayle, felt tears coming. 'Let's have our sandwiches.'

They ate, then climbed the gate into the castle enclosure. Grey walls stood square on their mound. They wandered across towards them, increasingly aware of height. So little left – the keep; a couple of square, high-walled enclosures open to the sky; niches where floor-beams might have rested.

'What's it for, Ranna?'

Border wars – how to describe them? She coped as briefly as possible. They came round to smooth sward at the back. Rabbits looked up from grazing, turning a flock of single, serious eyes, went back to it.

Miranda held Tammy. 'Keep still.' she whispered. 'This is amazing.' They stood silently. The rabbits went on feeding. Now and then one shuffled and hunched itself forward, the closest came almost to their feet. Then suddenly a quiver ran through all of them simultaneously; scuts up, heads down they vanished.

Tammy cried, 'Why they do that?'

Miranda twisted her head up and pointed. 'That bird – with the big wings circling – buzzard. They eat rabbits.' She felt a need to explain more. 'Drop from the sky, just like that. Grab one in their claws. Carry it off.'

'Speedvan.'

'I suppose – like that, yes.'

'How they eat it?'

Miranda hesitated. 'With their beaks. Tear it apart.'

Tammy nodded. 'Would, yeah.'

It was better, wandering again beside the burn. More harebells, Grass of Parnassus, Bog Asphodel. Warm sun, the sound of running water.

'Gavin was right, Tammy.'

'Gavin?'

'Dawn Prophet. Think that's what they call him now.'

'Oh him.'

'He was right. He said shut people out and let nature take over. It's worked. Look it's worked. Oh Tammy, it's all worth it.' She gazed round, taking in dappled shadow under birch and hazel, the way alders leant over the water. 'Under that bank, d'you see? Grey wagtail. Must have a nest there. Let's wait and see it come out.'

When it appeared and flew off Tammy said it was a nice-looking bird. 'Better than sparrows. Used to feed them sometimes when Don was out.'

They wandered on.

'Going a bit far, aren't we?' Tammy remarked. 'Bet you don't mind though.'

Miranda wriggled. 'We haven't gone off the road.' She watched a bumble-bee zoom in on the stamens of a burnet rose. 'But yes, there should have been a driver on duty at the castle to keep us in.' She looked at her watch. 'My see-can's not out of range of the van. Can risk a bit further, probably.'

Without rollshoes she staggered on rough ground. A sailor coming home, she thought. Tammy seemed to be coping.

A wooden barrier appeared directly ahead, shutting off the faint traces of a path that ran straight ahead beside the burn and disappeared round a rocky spur. To their left a scrub of birch, hawthorn and bramble blocked further progress. She remembered a road through that valley and was glad. It was impossible for humans to go that way now.

Tammy ducked under the barrier and stood with narrowed shoulders, staring.

Miranda followed. 'What is it?'

'So much of it, all round'.

She went and stood beside her. 'Open country.'

The shoulders softened. 'Yeah.'

'Let's go and look.' This was pushing things – if a Free saw a sputter in the report her see-can was giving – this was where the device really worked, this tie to the van –

The grass was soft beneath their vanshoes. The burn tumbled from fall to fall. She breathed in the honey scent of heather and for a moment, felt not heavy, weighing down the ground but properly there, balanced, alive.

Years ago, she'd have thought the line she was picking out between bracken and rock was a sheep-track. Maybe now it was the nighttime route of a fox or a badger. It steepened; she began to pant. It curved and brought them face to face with a heap of boulders at the foot of a rock wall. She glanced back. Both road and castle were invisible.

Gaunt hills jagged the skyline. Wind and rain on their own couldn't have been enough to hone those edges. It had taken ice, grinding over resistant rock for thousands of years.

Her eyes swung away and she saw there was a way to the left of the crags down towards the burn. Could that lighter trace worn over the surface of dried mud and pebbles be the work of humans? Could it have lasted thirty years since the New Dawn? Who could have been here recently to make it in this lonely spot? And this little summit she and Tammy had reached was tucked into a fold that, she suddenly realised, must hide the true shape of the terrain. If that line ahead was a path it must rise towards the source of the burn. Not far beyond the burn on a patch of level ground under the hillside a more solid heap of boulders shaped itself up.

She saw white water dashing against black rock, cloud moving in over the shoulder of the hill, drew her elbows into her sides, gave herself a little shake, realised Tammy was no longer beside her.

She looked all round. Not on the path. Not down ahead beside the burn. She swung round and saw her, well over towards the right, spread-eagled against rock. The girl who'd seemed threatened by this landscape was assaulting it, climbing far too fast, reaching too randomly, not sufficiently testing her footholds. What on earth had possessed her? She had no training, no experience, had no idea what she was up against. Her only assets lightness and wiry limbs.

No fear? Recently she had been afraid. Now she seemed to have thrown it aside — or swallowed it down.

She stood frozen. Skilled climbers went up smoothly. Tammy would throw a hand out, scrabble with a foot, heave. Why risk it? She gave the impression of being far from stupid.

At last she reached the top, hauled herself onto her stomach, stood up, posed on what looked like exactly the edge, gazed vaguely at the ground beside her, the sky, towards the way they'd come, gave a long, almost longing, look down onto the boulders.

The watcher decided to move on slowly. As if indifferent? Calm at least, on the outside.

Her tactic paid off. Tammy began prancing towards the top of the path. She arrived there first, stopped jiggling, waited. There was a stillness in the look with which she met Miranda's opening mouth that made it close again.

They continued in silence and came down beside the burn. She looked across and saw that what had appeared from a distance to be boulders was the walls of a ruined cottage.

She strode down to the ford and took off her vanshoes.

'You going to walk in that?'

She tied the laces together and hung the shoes round her neck. 'Yes, why not?' She stepped forward. Icy water cut her shins. Slithery pebbles knocked her toes. She was across.

She could see clearly now. A dead apple tree stretched a bare branch over the missing roof. A few blackened rafters reached over the hole. Brambles, nettles, rosebay willowherb were growing up through. She walked bare-footed over grass that was warm all way to the cottage. As she reached it, the sun went in.

'What's this?'

'A cottage. Someone's home once. See that iron hook – at the end there in front of that black wall? There'd be a fire there. They used the hook to hang a cooking pot.'

'Where they now?'

'Gone years ago. Long before the New Dawn maybe.'

'Why?'

'Too hard.' She remembered pictures she'd seen – a woman in a black skirt carrying water in an iron bucket, sheets stretched to dry on gorse bushes, a man with a special spade standing beside a cart loaded with peat, his heavy boots and patched jacket. 'They wanted a better life.'

A drop of rain stung the back of her neck. She started on up the track.

'We going on in this?'

'Won't be much.' You hope, she thought, and crouched down pointing. 'Look at these, Tammy.' Like no wheel marks she'd ever seen those long, smooth grooves still had to be from wheels. Nothing else could have made them.

'They're quite recent. Made in this universe,' she said softly, rubbing the hardened earth. 'I think it was carts made them. Never seen a cart, have you?' She stood up. 'To tell the truth, I haven't either, not at work any way.'

The path left the burn and rose towards the shoulder of a spur. Already she could see beyond it to the upper slopes of a hillside covered in dark woods. She paused to give herself time. Cloud colours – Prussian blue, almost black, rolling over grey, patches of greenish blue sky in between; the circling song of a lark. How many decades? She swallowed down tears.

Tammy was standing on the summit, one foot placed on a rock, leaning on the bent leg, peering.

'What's there, Tammy?'

'Things. What you call houses. Could be.'

Miranda stood beside her. In the valley a clump of black walls of different heights and roofs. In good condition.

'Yes, they're houses.'

'Whose?'

Miranda paused. 'Got to be Dreamies, I think. Fields with stone walls. See? Sheep.'

'What's that?'

'Animals we get red protein from.' Perhaps the Dreamies use wool? 'And cattle – the ones with horns over there.' Best to explain through things the girl would know. 'Your aussieballs are made from them.'

Tammy looked blank.

Those black shapes on the roofs could be solar panels. One of the things they went in for. 'That tall shining thing on the mound over there – must be a radio mast. We shouldn't be here.'

Tammy said nothing, then shrugged. 'These Dreamies – how come they're here?'

'Got special exemption – time of the New Dawn. Hopeless cases. Just couldn't take to vans.' This harsh voice – whose was it? 'Mustn't stay here.'

'Afraid of being caught?'

'The Dreamies wouldn't tell the Frees.' She looked at the sky and her watch. 'Going to rain. We've a deadline to meet.'

'What's it like, Ranna, living in a house?'

She paused, half turned. Her whole body was sinking into the ground. 'You feel you belong in a place.'

A rising breeze blew her vansuit against her legs. She glanced at the sky. 'We need to run.' Something stung her bare arms. Tammy was pounding downhill way ahead. Hail hissed down, pounded on the rocks, leapt back into the air. She ran downhill behind Tammy, reckless, uncontrolled, leaping over rocks, heather, tussocks of grass.

The following days the authorities kept them on the move. Never more than one's night's parking available. 'That'll teach you?' she wondered. Maybe just chance, the way things panned out?

The first two nights she tried to keep Tammy in, to go on talking. In Scotland she'd seemed to be beginning to open up but since they were back in what had to be considered the real world, silence had sunk down over her. Each night she came back more huddled in.

Miranda thought of glass spheres inside which Father Christmas – or some other figure – struggled with snowstorms.

The third she locked the screen gate as soon as they came in and pocketed the key.

Half an hour later Tammy slipped down the van steps. The screens rattled and crashed. Apparently she was kicking them. How wonderful she could find the energy. They rattled again. The rattling stopped, the only sound was voices in the next slot, raucous music, a van cornering too fast, the distant motorways.

Then when Tammy didn't come in, Miranda went out to look. The girl wasn't standing at the gate. Not hiding under the van or slumped in a sulk in a corner. The slot was empty.

Miranda clenched her fists. She would have loved to hammer and hammer on the screens. Or to stand and scream up at that restricted patch of sky. She felt in her pocket, opened the gate, stared up and down the road. And if Tammy had been in sight what could have been done about it? Chase after and grab her, drag her back – come on, Miranda, when it comes down to it, which of you is stronger? If she can climb that gate? Have a fight in the middle of the road? She closed the padlock, climbed back into the van, cursed, sat down, got up and made herself a warm drink, sat down again.

Later she fetched Elizabeth's book, opened the front cover, rubbed a finger-tip over that signature – you should forget her – turned over – Greek text one side, translation the other – Odysseus' companions had been turned into pigs. Serve them right, they'd been stupid. Hermes gave him a magic plant to strike them with and turn them back into humans. Lucky Odysseus.

She stretched her arms across the table and laid her head on them. The posture soon stopped feeling comfortable. She raised her head and gazed slowly round the van, remembered another heaviness, that last night before Tammy took over, when she'd felt the only thing was to drink herself silly, to join in the business of degrading herself, become the disgusting object life seemed to designate. She pushed herself to sit straight-backed. There was no way she'd do that tonight even if a teenager – not much more than a child – had defied and outwitted her, thrown back in her face all attempts she'd made to smile, feed her, clothe her, give her a decent life. OK grudging enough at first and why not? Didn't you have the right? Could have handed her over any time.

But now the little toad had become a harsh, faint scent that changed the nature of the van. That was her mask lying on the seat under the window. She'd gone out without a mask. Asking for trouble. Inviting it?

Miranda fastened on her own.

The Piazza spires were dancing with fairy lights. Drivers were coming and going under them, twos and threes carrying bags of tins and bottles or making their way to cafés or restaurants. Soft music was playing. She went from space to space, was relieved not to find Tammy sitting with a stranger at any of those tables.

From a distance the Spook Bins looked peaceful under the shadow of the side roof. As she came closer she saw flickering lights round the edges of the doors. A variety of canned screeches and screams reached her in turn as she passed along the line. How to guess which one held the girl she was looking for? Couldn't really go along the line and open each door in turn,

'Sorree, sorree,' She decided to wait.

One by one doors opened, the wrong person came out. Other people went in. Eventually there was only one left unopened. She approached slowly, laid her hand on the handle. How to invade this privacy?

At that moment the flickering stopped. She stepped back. After a minute or two the door slowly opened, Tammy appeared.

Miranda reached towards her. 'I've brought your mask.'

Almost automatically the girl put it on.

It was like having a robot rolling beside you all way to the van.

'Now sit. We're going to talk.'

The robot complied.

'Tammy, why do you do it?'

She waited, then repeated the question. 'Don't enjoy it, do you?'

'Enjoy?' Word muttered towards the table.

'Does it make you feel happy?'

'Passes the time, don' it?'

'There are other ways of passing the time.' A teacher heard herself lecturing. She leant across the table. 'Tammy, there really are other things to do – really – that you'd like better. But why? Why do you go there?'

'Told you before, didn't I?'

'Tell me again.'

'Show you how you win.'

'I see.' Her companion looked at her narrowly. 'How did you learn this?'

'Don, He got me started.'

'How?'

'Took me with him, didn't he? Loves them, see. Wanted me along with him.'

'You sat beside him while he watched?'

'On his knee sometimes.'

'I see.' Miranda slowly digested the information. She gazed at the hair falling over a face that was turned down toward the table and reached out a hand. 'It's OK, Tammy, together we'll cope. It'll be all right.'

Green eyes met hers for the first time. 'You're too innocent, Ranna. Leave it alone, can't you?'

The front of the vansuit swung open. Miranda saw blood on the front of the t-shirt. A big stain.

'What's that?'

Tammy tugged the sides of the vansuit together. 'Nothing.'

'Nonsense. You're covered in blood.'

'Been scratching probably. Itches sometimes.'

'What does? That scar – is that it – itches sometimes. And you scratch it.'

Nod.

'Looks a lot of blood.'

'So?'

'Let me look at it.'

'What for?'

'See what needs doing.'

'Don't nothing need doing.'

'It'll need a bandage at least. Tammy, you shouldn't do that to yourself.'

'Leave me alone.'

Miranda fetched bandages and laid it on the table. 'Here you are. Take it into the bathroom. If you need help, call.'

She lay awake a long time that night, tossing and turning.

The Free at the entrance to the Westminster overnight checked the number on his hand-held computer and waved them to one side. They waited. It wasn't a particularly fascinating gate. After an interval he returned. 'What you doing here?'

'You told us to wait.'

'Did I?' He unhitched his computer from his belt, checked the number again.

'Oh yeah, I did. They want you.'

He fumbled with his belt, humming the Song of Speed.

'Who do? Why?'

He looked up. 'This clasp's lost its shape. Something or other. Going to endorse the van, I think.'

'What?'

He tugged the computer to make sure the clip was holding. 'Rubbish this modern equipment. My Dad was a Free – one of the first – all his stuff really worked.' He started to move off. The humming started again.

'What do they want to endorse me for?'

He turned back sharply. 'How should I know?'

'I'm in the clear. Got a certificate.'

'Oh – that'll be it.'

'What?'

'Be the signature. Someone's being investigated.'

'Investigated for what?'

'Done something – or someone's got a knife into him. Happens.'

'My van's to be endorsed because someone's got their knife into the Free who signed the certificate?'

He shrugged. 'Natural, innit? Everything he signed comes under suspicion.'

'But –'

'Only five years. After that you can apply to have it removed.'

Her voice rose, 'Five years?'

'Calm down, can't you? Wait there till I find you a slot.'

'This isn't a regular slot, is it?' Tammy's voice rose as she asked. 'Why we innit?'

'You heard. They're going to endorse the van.'

The girl's shoulders relaxed. 'Course. Serves you right, doesn't it?'

'It's only that they're investigating that Free. Nothing to do with me.'

'You were up to something, weren't you? And since then? See-can always in range of the van, was it?'

'For goodness sake, leave it alone, Tammy.'

'They were always wanting to mark Don. He weren't ever there.'

'Cleverer than me. Where'd he go?'

'Breakers' yards.'

Of course. 'What did they want him for?'

'Things.'

Of course.

Tammy went and sat on the step with her back to the van.

Miranda fidgeted at the sink, finished, came back and joined her. 'You need to get out of view of the omni-techs.'

'Won't come today. Like to keep you waiting.'

Sitting up in bed next morning, peering out, Miranda was surprised to see so much space, gradually realised the van had spent a night in a kind of open – beside the entry gate, of course, under the eye of a Free – if he was awake –

The view might be only an acre or so of tarmac backed by a line of standard screens – but even so –

She rested her fingers on the narrow sill and gazed at a so much bigger allowance of sky than she'd enjoyed for years. She could see clouds moving across a great blue expanse. Might their progress help to pass time that would have to be spent waiting?

She dressed slowly and went into the main part of the van. The folding bed was still down with Tammy curled in it. Miranda suspected from the super-stillness of the body that its owner was lying awake pretending. She made her own breakfast, rattling crockery, banging the kettle on the worktop. The body never budged.

She resigned herself to the only space available, sat at her workstation, slowly ploughed her way through protein mush and tea, was about to wash up when she remembered Milla's wedding.

She swung the chair round. 'Tammy, come on wake up. Guess what's happening today.'

The body lay dumb.

Miranda studied blurred lines. 'It'll need dressing up for.'

A mumble from the sheets. 'Eh?'

'I think I've got an old dress that will do.' She didn't dare reach out and touch that small body, curled on its side. 'Look, please, Tammy. Be kind to me. Just today.'

A long silence, then a resigned grunt, 'What you want?'

'A friend of mine's getting married.'

'You haven't got any friends.'

'I talk to her over the web. We'll both watch. She's lovely, Tammy. She wants us at her party.'

'Don't want to go to no party.'

'Have you ever been to one?' Miranda asked softly.

'Wouldn't want to.'

Enough of talking to a concealed back. She stood up. 'I'm going to change.'

When she came back Tammy was sitting up. The expected rude comment on Miranda's skirt failed to come.

'Think you can get dressed? You feeling well?'

'Yeah.' The tone indicated both questions were pointless.

Sitting and watching the drag of hands and leg, the sag of the back, Miranda frowned. It was a long time before the bed was put away, the girl accepted a mug of tea.

When she was sure she'd drunk it all, a woman who was beginning to think almost routinely of herself again as 'Miranda' rummaged in a deep drawer, found a square scarf of Elizabeth's, swirls of green, amethyst and coral, handed it to her. 'Put this round your shoulders. We're going to be guests at a wedding today.'

Tammy ran the tips of her fingers over the silk, rubbed it between them, held it to her nose.

'You'll look good with it on. May I?' Miranda took the glowing fabric out of uncertain hands and spread it over the hunched shoulders. 'Now go and look.'

Tammy slumped off and came back, stood in the doorway. She'd tied the scarf round her waist so that the points hung to one side. Elizabeth had never worn it that way. She leant one hand on the post, tilted a hip.

Miranda's mind ran to Don. She tensed. 'No need to say anything. Just come and sit. We'll switch on.'

Tammy's face showed nothing.

*

Space had been created for the wedding by pushing the vans close to the outer screens. People in bright vansuits were lounging in it with glasses in their hands. Others were sitting on plastic chairs. Quite a lot of them seemed to know each other. No-one was wearing a mask.

'That beer they're drinking?'

'Mostly wine, I think.'

'Don give me beer.'

'Can't go down the Piazza today. But there's some red Vit C juice in the fridge. Party colour. Fancy some?'

She poured. 'We'll enjoy this now and another when come to the toasts.'

A driver in a lurex waistcoat slid through the milling bodies and began talking to a couple near the front of the crowd.

'Must be Dil,' Miranda said quickly.

'Who?'

'Milla's hitchmate. The one she's marrying.'

'What's this – marrying?'

Dil was holding up his hand. Everyone turned towards him.

'There's Milla.' Miranda watched as her friend made her way through the mass of guests and came to stand beside Dil. She was wearing a flowing gown made of different coloured strips of some shiny material. They were coiled tightly round the upper body, outlining the shape of bust, waist and the swell onto the hips. From there they flowed to the ground in gently swaying stripes   Miranda realised she'd never seen the whole person before. Or her face unmasked. Milla smiled at the crowd, her eyes gravitating towards Dil.

He lowered his hand and took hers. 'Thank you all for being here this morning – those of you who are with us here at Hoard of Gold and those who are watching at a distance.' He turned full face towards the screen. 'So many of you out there. I can't see you all at this moment but during the day I'll call you in one after another. Meanwhile, be assured, though invisible much of the time, you're still with us, a cloud of unseen witnesses. We couldn't do without you.'

'Quite a flowery turn of speech,' Miranda murmured. 'But lovely, lovely to hear that kind of thing again.'

He turned back to the guests, raised both his hands and one of Milla's. 'Now please, if you'll all be silent, my – almost ex-hitchmate and I will make our vows.'

The pair turned towards each other and held both hands.

'What they doing?'

'They're going to promise to stay together,' Miranda whispered. 'Shh. I want to hear.'

Those old words her parents had used, that resonated back through centuries.

'I Dil Markson take you Millicinda –'

'What they going on about?'

Miranda let the flow of rich words end – 'till death do us part' – before she explained. She was glad to see Tammy was watching closely.

'Those rings?'

'Didn't your mum wear a ring?'

'Not little things like that.'

'People who have them think they're important.'

'Shouldn't think many drivers have them.'

'Probably not. Not now.'

Everyone on the screen was clapping. People were scattering to tables.

Women appeared carrying plates.

Miranda jumped up. 'There's something nice for us in the fridge.'

Later Dil made a speech and everyone laughed. Then Milla spoke and they laughed even more.

After the speeches Milla called in her screen friends and spoke to them one by one. The guests present waved and they waved back. When it was their turn Miranda introduced Tammy – 'My co-vanner.'

Milla surveyed her with soft eyes. 'Lovely to meet you.'

Tammy lowered her gaze and shuffled. Looked up at the end, managed an awkward little wave.

Later that day Miranda asked, 'When your Mum upped – Don ever get a new hitchmate?'

'Said women were only trouble.'

'But he kept you?'

'Long as I looked after van. He was a corm, Ranna. Leave it.'

The omni-techs pocked in next morning. Miranda slipped on her mask and stood outside where they could see her.

The shadow of wings passed across her face, the cherub landed in a swirl of dust, a pair of uniformed arms swung out a blue plastic crate. She craned and saw it held several paint-pots and a handful of brushes. She watched as two officials climbed down and came towards her. Sun glinted on their metal masks.

'Trav, drivers,' she faltered.

They ignored her, checking the details in their see-can.

'That's the one.'

The shorter one went back and returned with pair of steps, which he set up beside the passenger door. His mate picked up a paint-pot. He took off the lid. She saw a shiny black surface. He mounted the steps, dipped a brush into the black, leant sideways and swept it across the front of the van above the windscreen. The metal backs of his gauntlets flashed in the sun.

The other stood in front of the bonnet. 'Not perfect. I'll pass the straight-edge.'

'How's that then?'

'Better.'

They moved the steps round to the driver's door. The painter leant again, swept his brush. His mate kept check.

They painted black lines along both sides. Stood back and inspected their work.

'That'll do.' For the first time they looked in her direction.

'Finish the job?'

The taller selected a small brush, ran the fine tip over the back of his hand, nodded. He approached her. She took a step back.

The official addressed his mate. 'Hold her will you.'

She smelt the sickliness of paint. The smaller man pressed his side into hers, reached across her, forced up her chin. She had to look straight at his mask and through it into unresponsive eyes. The metal backs of his gloves scraped her skin. Male bodies pressed against hers back and front. She shrank as thin as she could make herself between them. Her fingers curled

The brush stroked, almost caressed, the forehead of her mask. And again. A third time. The painter stepped back. 'Now she won't hide what sort of thing she is.' Sneered in her face.

The fingers released their grip. 'Excellent job.'

'How long we been?'

The fingers swept back a cuff. 'From base, twenty minutes.'

'Better stand over her till it's dry. Tell them another quarter of an hour.' His hand reached towards her. 'Paycard.'

She handed it over.

They picked up their equipment and retreated to the cherub where they sat side by side legs apart on the step. They drew out wads of gum and began to chew.

She turned to enter the van.

'Stand still. Face toward the sun.'

She was still standing there praying after they'd returned the card – twenty points deducted – and the cherub disappeared over the screens.

Tammy sneered when she saw the mask. 'Don wouldn't have let them do that.'

Miranda exploded. 'Get out. Out.'

A pale face stared.

Miranda waved. 'Get out I tell you.'

'But – '

'Out.'

'If you're going to be like that –' The girl heaved herself to her feet and pushed roughly past.

'Stay there till I tell you to come back.'

The woman took off her mask and gazed at the black line across it. The van's numbers somehow shone through it in red. It was very strange. What kind of paint could do that?

She lowered herself onto a seat at the table, leant her head on her hands and gave way to silent tears.

Some time later, she stood up and called from the door. 'You'd better come in now.'

Tammy heaved herself from a seat on the ground with her back to the door and climbed in. She didn't look at the woman.

They ate in silence. The woman went to lie on her bed.

When she got up the van was empty; so was the slot. So that girl had climbed out again and there was her mask again on the table?

An afternoon's peace. Good.

She went to the bathroom. The door wouldn't open. She pushed and shook, remembered she'd meant to get it fixed. This catching was a sign the van was getting old. She shook again, rattled. Locked on the inside. Oh hell, oh hell. How long's the girl going to be?

She waited. Knocked. 'Tammy, I need it urgently.'

No sound. She knocked harder. 'Tammy, I've got to.'

No voice told her to do it where she was – and in that mood –

'Tammy —' She shook the door with all her strength. Dropped her arms, stood in the narrow corridor, reached into the kitchen, pulled out her largest kitchen knife, inserted the tip in the crack, worked at it. The door shifted. She inserted the whole blade and the catch gave. She saw Tammy, slumped on the loo seat, chest raised covered in blood, arms dropped sideways, staring up. Alive.

Miranda moved forward slowly, trying to make out where the blood was coming from. Thank goodness all those years ago at the beginning of the New Dawn they'd had to study First aid. Not spurting – so not from an artery. Very wet. The stains slowly growing. She gently pulled the edges of the vansuit apart. Blood was oozing through slashes in the t-shirt. She enlarged the holes and saw the cuts from and through the scar. It seemed to have had its ridges cut off. How could anyone have borne to do this? Miranda reached down and lifted a hand. There were deep cuts at the wrist, not in the vital places. Blood was still gathering on the skin.

'Don't move, Tammy.'

It was a slow business washing and bandaging the body of someone who seemed totally uninterested. The blood clotted. 'Stand up now.'

Miranda supported her to the main room and got down the folding bed.

'Get in and rest.'

Tammy shut her eyes. 'I'm not worth bothering with, Ranna.'

'Don't talk nonsense. Rest now. And behave yourself, young lady. I shan't be far away.'

The sound of her own voice surprised her. This sensible, almost automatic response seemed to be programmed in. It came up through the turmoil on top, because there was something to do perhaps. You had to do something and when you finished – what next?

The thought of Ed didn't come till 3.00 am.

Part 6

Next morning she spoke briskly, 'Tammy, there's something I can't do, but you could.' She saw the girl's eyes widen and paused. 'You know so much I don't.'

They'd taken off the first bandages this morning. The wound was healing nicely.

'Stop trying to get round me, Ranna. What you want?' This girl stood straighter.

Miranda considered her carefully. 'How old are you, Tammy?'

Green eyes flickered. 'Eighteen – if it matters to you.'

'Your Mum tell you your age?'

'What you think?'

'Sorry – it's just you acted the part so well – Boss, you know.'

'Men's always kids.'

She pressed her lips. 'Now look, do you know how to disable the intercom?'

'Might do.' A sly look. 'You up to things again?'

A robot who'd earned her living as a teacher pushed her hands down her sides, clenched her fists, turned away to stare out at corrugated iron. In a little while she spoke over her shoulder. 'Don't see any other option.'

A hand touched her arm. 'No problem. I'll see to it.'

Tammy climbed onto a seat, inserted the tip of the screwdriver into the overhead groove, stood on tiptoe, pushed with full weight. The screw moved. She reached fingertips up to the cap, turned it very slowly, let it drop into her palm, handed it down.

'Small screwdriver.' With it she pushed a wire very gently out of position. 'When I tells you, switch off – get on with it, see – they could know. One second that's all.'

The robot knelt at the cupboard.

'OK. Now.'

She switched off, watched Tammy's slim, confident fingers as she swiftly disconnected something.

'Now switch on.'

The light came back on, but weaker.

'But – ?'

Tammy jumped down. 'Loose now, see? When we're out the gate, on the sliproad, see, you stalls the engine, hard. Shakes the whole thing loose. Then you starts up again, you're on the motorway, see and they're after someone else by that time. Not interested in you. "Where'd you go?" they think. Don't know much, do they?'

'Apparently not.'

The road they used to get in to Hayle was more than unofficial but at last they made it, through a break in thick, dark cypress, onto the drive. She heard Elizabeth, 'A still centre away from the noise and sight of traffic. Ed did well planting this hedge. Thanks, Mira, for bringing me back.'

She drew up under the cedar, raised her hand to her mask, slowly pulled it off, let it swing, still warm from her face, between her fingers. 'We shan't need these here.' She saw Tammy's expression, 'No-one's "up to" anything here. They're just not part of things, that's all.'

She sat on letting the back of the seat support her spine while she blanked her mind against a dream that was demanding entrance, mad, unrealistic, time-wasting, an eater of energy. She mustn't remember Elizabeth or ask herself why she came here. She heaved herself out.

The heavy white door was open today as it had been then. Soon the porch would load her shoulders with darkness, there'd be a scent of flowers in the hall, her footsteps would echo across blue and white institutional vinyl, fall quiet on boards and quiet rugs, check at the right turn at the foot of the stairs, start forward again into the room that was still the lounge. Elizabeth would be sitting in one of Ed's chintzy armchairs facing the cedar and the river. She'd turn her head and smile. The robot woman would say, 'You're looking better today.' The terrible years would slide away.

'Funny colour this place is.'

'What?' That was the wrong voice. 'Sorry, but why's it funny? Looks very nice to me.'

'Red overnight?'

'Hayle's not an overnight.' Though for the two of them that day it would act as that. 'It's an old house. In this part of England they always used red brick.'

'Born in a house, wasn't you?'

'Come on, get that mask off.'

There was a pause. She refused to allow her foot to tap. Then, suddenly, the artificial face was swinging from the girl's hand.

Her cheeks shone in the fresh air as she stood and looked, frowning, a little tense, apparently in no hurry to find out what was inside this place. Miranda took it all in: white porch piled with yellow clematis, four windows downstairs, two for the sitting room one side, two on the other for their dining room, extended now with glass, conservatory, she'd guess; five upstairs – Dad and Mum's room, the landing, the guest room; her bedroom had been in the wing that ran back at right angles to the sitting-room, invisible from the front of the house.

The end window up there, on the left, had been the half of the strangely divided guest room where Elizabeth –

The roofline wasn't the same. A ridge outlining a triangle of new tiles, darker than the originals, was just visible beyond it, running back, indicating a rooms she'd never known that must be attached somehow to the back of the lounge and the landing above it. She couldn't picture where doors might have been cut.

She swung round, locked the van door. 'Can't stand here all day.'

She still had to look. The yew hedge Ed had planted to the right of the house was beginning to take on mass. More slowly than the cypress the other side. When she'd come before it had been low enough to see over. The view of the fields down to Trenchard's Bridge had still been visible. Now – how many years later? – the hedge was a green wall making the house an island. Stately homes, churchyards. It showed a kind of faith to plant yew.

Time had passed while she roamed the motorways in accordance with the whims of Frees directed vans from one overnight to the next as the flow of traffic suggested. She'd had no reason to mark its passing. Why cling onto birthdays? Calendars weren't published any more. The days were all the same. There were no deadlines. You lost count of weeks, months, years. Six to ten years did it take for yew to reach a good thickness? Was that how long it was since Elizabeth died? Or longer? There was still a gate to the river path.

Tammy was fidgeting. 'Get it over with, Ranna.'

'Get it over?'

'Go in.'

'Obviously. Just waiting for you to get used to it, that's all.' She smiled, put on the brisk tone again, 'You've been inside plenty of overnights – this isn't so different,' marched across the gravel and rang the bell.

The door was opened by a white uniformed woman with disciplined hair. Miranda took a deep breath, 'Can I see Ed?' In spite of all efforts to throw back her shoulders, her head sank towards the floor.

She knew the nurse must be looking them over. Then the body relaxed as if a smile had appeared, the kind suitable for over-anxious relatives. 'I'll go and fetch him.' Feet tip-tapped off down the hall.

Tammy, who had been rocking backwards and forwards on her toes, came to rest as the sounds died out. 'Dawn Servant, is he, living in this?'

'No. Just someone you'll like.' Miranda saw her expression, knew what it meant, fixed her eyes on a coir doormat. Good tough object. Useful. Abrasive. Her hearing reached out into the hall. Footsteps. Less resonant than she'd expected. A pair of black shoes came to a stop. She looked up.

He still stooped, a little more perhaps. The gap in the hair at the front of his head had spread. The legs of blue trousers he was wearing under his overall exposed ankles as bony as ever.

For a moment there was silence.

'It is, isn't it, Miranda, after all these years?'

She could only nod and swallow tears. He opened his arms.

He let her go and before she could say anything, smiled at Tammy. 'And you're?'

The girl stared from narrowed eyes.

'She's called Tammy. Co-vanner of mine,' Miranda said hastily.

'That makes her very welcome. Though she would be in her own right.'

Tammy glanced past him into the dark interior, inspected his white overall, thrust her hands into her pockets; looked straight into his eyes. 'Trav, driver.'

Ed considered her slowly. 'Trav, Tammy.'

Miranda watched, taking in his profile, waiting. 'Just passing by,' she murmured, 'thought we might drop in.'

His lips firmed. That corner of eye half-hidden under the heavy lid was the same green-brown mixture she remembered. A shade duller perhaps. Time could have worn him down.

'Impulsive as ever. Did you know,' he said to Tammy, 'your friend's a creature of impulse? Or likes to imagine she is.'

He didn't used to talk that way. He spoke directly to you, taking the Mickey maybe, but not like this, sideways.

Tammy's forehead wrinkled.

'She does things the minute she thinks of them.'

'Not this, she didn't.'

Ed let Miranda have his full face. They burst out laughing, years slid away. Tammy watched glowering.

Ed recovered first. 'I know,' he said to the air, 'she gives every impulse deep thought before she gives way to it.'

'Oh Ed, it's wonderful to see you.' Amazing how you could fall back into something. But she was afraid too. This banter had always stood between them, this sparring. With Elizabeth he'd been natural. At the early camp sites, and here, that day she'd helped her from the van, when her arm was round Elizabeth's waist, Elizabeth was leaning on her and he appeared from the back of the house, those two had looked at each other. Something passed between them. So when at last he took in Miranda was there too, all she could manage had been, 'So you called it 'Travellers' Rest'? You corny S.J.'

Today he was leading them in through a hall that seemed not as dark as it had been – something was missing – and the floor – there was something about the floor – and now he was waving a long arm towards a door. 'The lounge's empty at the moment. Shall we have coffee?'

'Thanks.' She stopped in the doorway. This room wasn't the lounge she'd sat in when Elizabeth was here, nor the sitting room she'd grown up in. Moved forward again. Didn't matter. Why should anything matter?

Tammy gazed at the grouped armchairs, the long curtains, the shelves of discs. She rubbed the toe of her van-shoe in the pile of the carpet. Miranda glanced at Ed.

The girl turned her head, wide-eyed, tense, then still, like a pointer indicating a rabbit, transfixed apparently by a bowl of roses, suddenly a child.

Ed's arm waving towards a choice of chairs had a professional courtesy, as did his gentle tone. 'D'you remember, last time you were here, we were discussing how this room looked in your parents' time?'

She'd fought her father in this room. He'd been sitting almost where Ed was standing now.

'You alleged the wallpaper had been pale blue.'

'Did I?' Her mind was a lump of sour dough.

Mum, Dad, sitting in this room in their habitual armchairs, facing each other, Mum speaking while Dad brought his finger-tips together and nodded, the pair of them united in the story about rooms they'd looked over on a hillside outside Chicago, how they'd gazed out at a view through pine trees to Lake Michigan.

She could hear voices now, but not in the room – no – reaching in from the hall, two residents pausing for a chat.

She firmed her shoulders. Those last years must have made Mum and Dad, wherever they were, happy. That's what she had to believe.

To tell the truth, she didn't really care, not today, not in this alien room.

Two universes had drifted side by side for a time, almost clinging, before each slid away in its own direction. It was after that she'd thought she heard her mother asking her to join them. She hadn't been able. Genuinely hadn't.

She brought her head up smartly. Somehow she'd arrived in a chair. 'Nonsense, Ed. Mum always hated blue.' Once more she listened to that efficient briskness. She was doing well. 'She'd never have had blue wallpaper.'

If she hadn't bought the Vanacar – she'd been the one who went dancing off saying, isn't this fun – perhaps there'd have been time – before the separation – but they hadn't known – how could they – that differences of choice could cause this split between two universes so they would never touch again – could she and Elizabeth and Mum and Dad have lived together beside Lake Michigan?

Made no attempt to save the planet?

Elizabeth? Waste of time thinking about her.

Waste of time thinking. Waste. Everything. Wasted.

'That's exactly what you said was so surprising.' He was grinning, apparently laughing at her bad memory.

'Ed, please —'

He gave her one of his slow looks.

Her shoulders sank against the cushions. They were delightfully soft, one of the best features of this room which wasn't the room she remembered — though it had some of the same proportions — why not all of them? She half closed her eyes, could still see him watching.

'They'll soon be here with the coffee,' he said, 'I've told them to bring some of our special crispits. We have a very good cook at present. Six months' work service.'

She stirred her shoulders. 'Long allowance, isn't it?'

'Far too good to let go so I wangled an extra three months.' He stretched his legs, not clumsily as he had once, but slowly, luxuriously in a world he'd made for himself. 'Though I'm afraid we shan't be able to hold on to her longer.'

No point worrying about that. So large a room — even if it wasn't the right one — only three people, soft chairs, the scent of roses, trees outside the windows. In that quiet you felt your back resting against the chair, heard the notes a blackbird in the cedar was encompassing, all of them one by one, quiet voices in the distant depths of the house. The sounds weren't pressing on you, rubbing against you. Maybe this was what she'd come for. Not Ed himself — what would she want him for? This blank that was creeping over her was worth having. Peace? What most people might call it, she supposed. Not peace — whatever they meant when their voices softened and they breathed 'peace' — that couldn't be this emptiness.

Still fine. To be allowed to be nothing.

Maybe Tammy looked a fraction less sullen.

Ed was still there of course. He'd clasped his hands over his stomach and was apparently admiring an arrangement of dried flowers in the hearth. He'd have smiled at whoever did it. Like all those years ago when she'd bought a duster for his van. 'Got a cloth for the paintwork,' he'd said, smiling from a great height. 'Never thought of a separate one for the interior.' Hopeless, she'd thought, but he'd learnt.

The attendant who brought the coffee murmured a few words.

Ed stood up. 'I'm sorry – Marcia – one of our residents – is in pain again. It's hard to keep the dosage right. Please help yourselves. I may be away some time – so do feel free to wander out and enjoy the garden.' He glanced out, his eyes rested briefly on the van. Then he went.

The crispists were firm and buttery at the same time. Nothing like them in any 'Nomadic Market'. Tammy devoured three but, even before she'd swallowed the last crumb, she was on her feet, rocking onto her toes and down, next roaming the room, first hugging herself, then bending forward, poking her nose towards the furniture, speeding up with flailing arms. Miranda wondered if she would to fall, remembered the feral cat that had climbed the curtains, got to her feet. 'Let's go out.'

In the open air she turned her back on the house. 'Shall we look at the river?'

Tammy shrugged. At least it was a more fluent movement than that wild flailing.

Miranda had to lift the gate on its hinges and push till at last, reluctantly, the rusty bolt gave way.

There had been a path under the hazels, soft, brown, dotted with light. There it was, a line of firmer ground almost immediately disappearing under a mat of bramble. She picked her way ahead and peered down the bank. There it was too, that pool of sunlight under a willow. 'I think we could get through.'

She ducked under a branch of hazel, swung her legs gently through cow parsley, used her hands to push aside vivid spikes of rosebay willow herb. 'No-one can see us from the road.' She sank down to sit hugging her legs in a hidey-hole over-hung by weeping branches, carpeted with pale yellow leaves, the top layer dry, shining softly. She couldn't really hear the viaduct that now spanned the valley.

Tammy trampled behind her and dumped herself at her side. They watched flowing water.

Some minutes lately the girl muttered into her knees, 'When I'd upped from Don – found somewhere bit like this once.'

'Was it good?'

'Partly – yeah – but on your own –'

'Yes.'

The river was fuller than when she'd last seen it. Only the biggest stones were exposed. The hideout was too far back from the edge to see down to pebbles, which would be shining up, almost golden under streaming brown water. All she could see was surface, most of it dark, except where sunlight caught the ripples or lay still and dappled under the alders.

'What is this place, Ranna?'

Miranda sagged, then threw her shoulders back. 'Here? Oh, Hayle. That's its name, Hayle.'

'Yeah but – what is it?'

She tightened her lips. 'A place where sick people come to be happy before they die.'

'Not possible.'

'I've heard residents here laughing.'

The girl slid her eyes sideways. 'Not today you haven't.' There was a pause. 'Been here before, have you?'

Miranda leant her hand against the ground. 'Come on, let's go.'

'Hitchmate? That it?'

She took a deep breath. 'Co-vanner – yes.'

'What we doing here? Not going to die are you?'

Miranda had reached kneeling but now rested back down again. Compacted yellow leaves sank to fit her bottom. She gazed into a child's face. 'Not die, no.' Below them, a few yards forward from their refuge, the river was flowing through the shadows of overhanging trees, broken from time to time by sunlight. 'Otherwise – don't know.' There was no clarity, only shade and light followed by more shade and light. 'Sorry, Tammy, can't tell you. Talk to Ed, I suppose.'

'Like him, don't you?'

'He's a friend from way back.' She listened to herself, laughed harshly. 'Too long ago to count, really.'

'Not going to die, are you?' Tammy re-iterated.

'Definitely not.' Not far off tits were cheeping. She watched them as they flitted from one branch to the next, staying close, never synchronising their moves.

'So?'

'Leave it, Tammy. For God's sake, leave it.' She'd have liked to stretch out on the soft ground, close her eyes.

The girl was pulling grass to pieces. 'Wouldn't care if you did die.'

'Pull me up,' Miranda said wearily. 'We'll go and see the van's OK.'

'How they manage here without screens?'

Ed sent soup and sandwiches into the lounge. Tammy gobbled hers, continually glancing round. While she ate Miranda listened to voices from the dining room, smelt roast chicken.

Eventually there was a stir, feet, and wheels rolling through the hall, a disturbance in the doorway, a small girl peering in. Long red curls, green trousers, flowered top, no vansuit.

Then Ed towered. 'What you doing, Wheera?'

The child threw her head back, grinning. 'I show people round.'

He ruffled her hair. 'Yes, you do. That's your job, isn't it?'

The kid advanced into the room, looked them over in turns, grabbed Tammy's hand. 'Going to take you.'

Though she was twice her size, Tammy let the child tow her out of the room.

Ed sank into a chair, took in Miranda's expression, arranged his legs. 'Wheera loves showing people round. Seems to be her mission in life.'

'What's she doing here? I thought –'

'Her mum leaves her here.'

'That legal?'

'Not really. I just find a way.' He frowned at the floor for a minute then lifted his gaze. 'I think, Miranda, you had a reason for coming here.'

Her lips went stiff.

'Trouble?' he said gently.

She noticed the way his nose flowed like a tubular flower into his nostrils. White skin, slightly pitted, tinged with green shadows. There was a new, ugly mole on the back of his hand.

'I sent you cards,' he said suddenly. 'Did you get them?'

She examined the smooth fabric of his overall. 'What did you do that for?'

'Elizabeth's anniversaries. Each resident who dies – I try to keep in touch with a close friend or relative – just once a year – to let them know, you know. They don't always get through.'

He sounded complacent, sitting there, weighing more than he used to, in that room that wasn't what it should be. The real room had floated off into another universe.

'You could have faxed it.'

'You didn't leave a number.'

'But Ed – to do an old-fashioned thing like sending a card when there was no difficulty getting hold of a number.' Her voice was running along nicely now. 'Cards are hopeless. Unless you call in at the overnight they're addressed to you'll never get them. They don't display them for long. Talk about throwing your bread upon the waters – and wasting it. You must be insane. Do you behave like this with everyone?' It was easy to say all this, gazing at the walls, trying to trace where the bookshelves had been – but of course the marks would have been plastered out – not like Dad's expression – she was seeing it now – in those days you spoke face to face, looking –

'Quite often fax them a message to say where I've sent it. In case they don't want it. Gives them the option.'

She sat silent, hands clasped on her lap, glaring at the floor.

'You were so angry,' he said gently. 'Thought I'd better leave it to chance.'

'You did all you could do. I'm sure I did my best to thank you.'

'I'm not god.' He considered his clasped fingers and looked up. 'Miranda, the existence of this place depends on my keeping the rules – or not bending them so much that the bend becomes visible – so I can't put you up for more than a few days at most – but we could say you'd come for Elizabeth's anniversary –'

'Sounds a bit random'

'Didn't you know?' he asked gently.

For the first time she looked him fully in the face. 'Time, you know – when it's all the same – you lose count.'

'Your subconscious brought you almost on the dot. So – if you'd like?'

She suddenly bowed her head. If only she hadn't taken off her mask. 'Thanks, Ed.'

'First thing is to get that van out of sight. I'll show you where.'

He guided her round the new road to the back, opened the barn door. The squash court wasn't there.

He shifted some dusty objects. 'Take it right to the back. I'll arrange this junk to block the view.'

When the job was complete he stood her in the door to look back. 'It's not actually hidden, see. Just that the dark and all that clobber in front of it makes you really need to look. And if anyone did come looking I'd have a lot to talk about, wave my arms, you know; suggest they notice this and that in every other direction. Wonderful how I can flow along when necessary.' He wasn't waving his arms now. 'Still, on the whole, it would be better not.'

They returned to the lounge through a maze of passages. Perhaps she remembered some of them. A door appeared to lead to kitchens – to judge from the clatter the other side. She might have recognised some corners. This flight of stairs, for example, especially the turning under the window? The shadow that flicked round it, Tammy perhaps? A leg of her vansuit?

When they got back to it the big room looked so formal in its emptiness. 'Don't the residents ever come here?'

'This time of year they'd rather be in the conservatory.'

They found chairs and sat. She rested against the cushion and stared at flowers on the carpet. How did the purple splodges relate to the pink? What were they supposed to be – shadows? On roses? Peonies? Cherry blossom? Any way something blowsy – not that it mattered. Nor that the chairs were different shapes but all upholstered in chintz which meant more flowers, all different, though with these she could form some idea what they were meant to be – but kind of writhing, too pointy to be real. In those huge black shoes his feet were out of sync with this room. Who was he, anyway?

Ed. Of course. You poltic.

Ed was way back, before time faded out. How come she was sitting here looking at him? Sitting the easiest thing?

Why not? Sit, that was.

He broke the silence – though he may have made some other remarks – not anything that caught her attention. 'Just one thing Miranda. You were on the river path this morning.'

'Of course.'

'The way you always went to the village – naturally –' he eyed her seriously – 'reserved ground now.'

'Gate's still there.'

'Have to get through to trim the hedge. Otherwise, no. No-one goes there.'

'Of course,' she said, staring at her hands.

'Sorry,' he said, 'anxiety about this place – one of my problems. But I do have to take care.'

'OK, OK.'

A bell rang, he got to his feet. 'Back soon.'

He came back quarter of an hour later, smiling, subsided into a chair. She watched the tired way he stretched his legs. 'Everything OK?'

He nodded. She went on watching. Eventually he said, 'You didn't come to the placing of her stone.'

The question sharpened things. 'But you did? You left the hospice?'

'For an occasion like that. I missed you, Miranda.'

Oh heck, Oh yeah.

'Miranda, it wasn't your fault.'

'Who said it was?'

'You did.' He looked towards her face. She turned it away. 'Just listen. No, you never actually said it – but it was terrible to see – you were so full of anger. Which wasn't aimed at me, I knew that. You were sucking it into yourself – it sounds ridiculous –'

'It is.'

'I felt your fury was a sweet you were sucking to make you feel good.'

'You've no right.'

His fingers moved over his knuckles pulling them silently apart. 'None.' He changed to the other hand. 'I'm sorry. I think this must be something I've brooded over. Perhaps I feel I ought to have done more to comfort you.'

'Forget it.'

He nodded, still pulling at his knuckles, then looked up sharply, spread his lips into a smile. 'Now I've wrecked my chances of finding out why you're here.'

'You can bear the frustration.' A minute ago she'd been resting in the strange quiet. But it was uneasy as well. After all – this was Ed – perhaps if she tried? 'Tell me about Wheera. What's she doing here?' She raised her head with a sense of triumph. 'How'd you square that with the existence of this place?'

'Her Mum's in a fem-tog. Wheera finds that difficult.'

'Can't have her mum all to herself?'

'Something like that. And the work they do. Very hazardous performance. Scares the child out of her mind.'

'Thought you were scared for this place?'

'I've adopted her.' It was his turn to be brisk. 'Her mother comes as often as she can. The regulations just about allow this sort of thing – "in cases of real need" etc.' He smiled at her gently. 'Your go now. Tell me about Tammy. Not yours, I take it?'

'Course not. Nothing to do with me.' She clasped her fingers more tightly, glanced at the door, lowered her voice, listened – the house might have been empty for all she could hear–

'Wheera will keep her busy – one endless stream of chatter, that kid.'

Then she told him – where and when a little blurred – how she'd been taken over by a boy who – how helpless she'd felt but later she'd taken away his knives.

'What are those marks on her wrists?'

She stiffened. 'It's OK. I found it on the bathroom floor. It's out of the van now.'

'But not before – ?'

'Could have been just a gesture.'

'Got you worried.'

'What you expect?' She firmly unclasped her hands, breathed in the cool, slightly scented air of that formal room. 'The day in Scotland seemed to have done her good – she's stopped calling me a poltic every time she spoke – only every other time and – well – she can be quite sweet – you know.'

'When it suits her?'

'Helped me out today,' she said briskly, 'job I couldn't do and she did it, just like that.' One twiddle of slim fingers and the light wobbled. 'She was kind – it's true – she really was.' She nodded her head towards him. And again, watching his eyes. 'There was a genuine kindness there. I'm beginning to feel we can talk. Perhaps I should have given her more chances.'

'Maybe,' he said carefully.

He stood up. 'Perhaps it's time to round up those kids. I'll get someone to show you where you can sleep.'

It was the way the staff lit up when he spoke to them that told her this was his place.

The attendant's name was Hal. He had flat cheeks veined with pink. Odd how you noticed that sort of thing – and the way people offered you names.

He led them into that strangely light hall, through the dark passage – fragrant at that time of day with soup, tomato, she'd guess, light evening meal for the terminally ill – then out into the yard.

The brick paving had been re-pointed. Not a scrap of moss. Through the archway on the left she caught sight of vans parked in the space behind the barn. The great oak was still there.

Hal opened a door she recognised – though re-painted in a green her father would never have allowed. 'We were using these for storage last time you came.'

'You were here then?'

He paused in the entrance, turning to look back at her. 'We all thought Elizabeth was a splendid person. So of course we remember you too. We thought you were so brave – the way you hid your upset.'

She hadn't been capable of caring. 'Long time ago now.'

He smiled and swung open a door. 'This is the room Ed thought this young lady might like.'

A bed with a patchwork bedspread, rush-bottomed chair, patterned carpet. No space for much else.

'Ed says to leave it exactly like this in the daytime, as if nobody's there. Understand?'

'Tammy's great at clearing things away, aren't you? At night you can spread yourself in here – not like the van.'

She watched the girl's eyes measuring a huge space and turned to Hal. 'Where are you putting me?'

'Upstairs.'

She frowned.

'Immediately at the top.'

'Leave the door open,' she said quietly to Tammy. 'You can always call.'

That night one of those storms blew up. She lay in bed listening, picturing the oak's trunk unmoved while the crown tossed, the tips of the yew hedge dragged to full length, while low down the lee side stayed quiet.

Later rain swished on the windows, not a thunderous pounding on metal fences and roofs, just this steady drumming and through it all the house stood still. It was so small this dot on the landscape.

Next morning in spite of a cloud filling her head, making her limbs feel soggy so she wondered if she could be going down with a cold – but no, it wasn't that – it was a kind of tiredness that wouldn't let her rest. Sun lay across the foot of her bed. It curved up the opposite wall. The patchwork quilt shone.

She crept down, past Tammy's closed door. The bricks were damp, the air fresh. The open back door revealed that length of dark passageway. A trolley rattled somewhere far inside, pans banged in the kitchen.

A faint scent was drifting over the cool yard. She crossed slowly to the gate in the opposite wall, peered through, self-consciously laughing at a hesitation which could hardly be due, she thought, to purity of mind, a decent shrinking, a turning of the eyes away from growing plants – not in a person who'd sat among the brambles on the river bank yesterday. She strode through, into a walled garden that at first sight at least hadn't changed much.

Excellent crop of runners. A few flowers still blazed high up against the sky. Below them, only just distinguishable from the leaves by their shape, long pods hung in bunches. She found she'd reached out and touched one tough, stringy length. A leaf scraped her wrist.

She wouldn't behave like this, of course, once she was back on the road but here, in this secluded enclave, touching was no harm. Obviously. She let go and moved on.

Ed's yew hedge had replaced the end wall her father had always been going to get done up. The gravel was free of weeds.

The other two walls were still lined with espaliered fruit trees. She walked round and spoke to them one by one, Newton Wonder, Allington Pippin, Blenheim Orange.

The cold frame was still at the far end. She laid her hand on its edge. Clammy. The sun wouldn't touch it for some time yet. In the neighbouring beds water still clung to cabbage and cauliflower. It hung there, bluish, gleaming while the stiff leaves drank. She touched one and watched the drop slowly stretch, fall, sink into the dark earth. It was impossible to know where it had been.

Sun was already angling into the base of the hedge. She lowered her bottom onto soft ground and hugged her knees under the over-hanging branches.

With any luck Tammy would sleep late. It would give her a chance to relax. If she did wake and get going it was safe here. Nowhere for her to go, nothing she shouldn't to get up to.

She watched a chaffinch hop along the path pecking here and there. What did chaffinches eat? Not worms, seeds more like, tiny scraps of something. This was freedom, to sit in the sun, watch other creatures work.

The garden had always felt like the heart of the place – though it wasn't – tacked onto the side of the stable yard. But it had changed less. Even the range of vegetables – green beans, cabbages, onions, potatoes – was much the same – in spite of the climate change – sudden tempestuous storms – baking heat – late springs – all in spite of 'Emissions reduced 5% this month' proclaimed on overhead screens in all the overnights – it was always 5% – how come emissions weren't down to negative figures by now?

But the climate was better? Yes, the air was – modern masks weren't there to protect the nose or the mouth – only the skin.

They didn't wear them at Hayle.

So the New Dawn was having an effect?

Suddenly Ed was there, standing at the near end of the central path. It was those soft-soled shoes he always wore.

A diffident smile slid her way. 'Lovely morning.' Seedy bean-pole, all charm.

'Lovely morning, driver.'

'Obscene settler by your reckoning. Not so? That's a good spot you've got there. Mind if I join you?'

She shifted sideways and pulled her arms tighter round her knees. He doubled those long legs and lowered himself beside her. They sat in the warm sun.

'I really like the smell of yew,' he said softly.

'I'm glad you planted this – though how you got away with it – how did you?'

'Promised to put up a fence inside.'

'You haven't.'

'Never had time.' He gazed absently round while his fingers plucked at a blade of grass. 'Basically, it's good for the residents, thick, dark, that age-old feel. Brings out the quiet.' He dropped the grass and became still. At last he said, 'I think I was a bit rough with you yesterday. I was taken by surprise – not expecting you and you turning up with that van and Tammy – well – I didn't handle things the way I'd like.'

'I shouldn't have come.'

'I think you had to.'

'Why d'you say that?'

'You have so many associations with Hayle.'

'You think I came here for the sake of Elizabeth?'

'Partly – and of the place itself, perhaps? With you the roots run deep.'

She shuddered. 'No. Don't say that. No.'

'D'you remember all those years ago when we first met how we'd sit around in the evening? You were always the first who wanted to go walking. I'd see you fall out of the talk your eyes straying to the trees. I didn't know the names of all of them. You did. You knew which species of bat was flittering over us. You could tell us where to find sundew. D'you remember? I'd never seen it and there you were crouching with your fingers in a bog?'

'You were a vet.'

'Transferred quite happily to humans. As long as my skills are needed I'm OK. You're more specialised. You care for nature far more deeply than any of us.'

'What's that got to do with Hayle?'

'This is where you learned to care.'

'You're making accusations, Ed.'

He sighed, fiddling with yew needles. 'Just reflecting. Take it or leave it.' Green eyes swung sideways towards her, 'I knew this was where I would find you.'

She gave a brisk look at the familiar paths. 'The garden's looking well.'

'Our gardeners do their best.'

'Work service are they?'

He laughed. 'Beyond the pale for drivers. We take in those who can't drive – disabled – mentally or physically – just one or two and employ them. The authorities wanted to send robots but I said, no way. But if there were 'drivers who couldn't drive' –?' He let the question float for a moment. 'That formula was the key. Locks ground open. And our gardeners seem happy here. That's what I like to think, at least.'

'Making your own little paradise?'

'Why not?'

She shrugged, then gave him a sharp glance. 'Do they get paypoints?'

He smiled and slowly extended those long legs. 'No-one here gets paid, as such. But we are part of the system, so they reckon paypoints for each person here. Most of it we receive in kind. I do make shopping expeditions from time to time but they aren't eager to have us buzzing about out there – like us to keep ourselves apart – hearts not quite in the right place. We take in the wrecks of the system, not kosher.'

'What would they do with them – or the ones who don't get here?'

'That's something I don't let myself think about.'

'You must do sometimes.'

He sighed. 'When I need to buy something they don't supply – the staff and I talk it over, they give me ideas.

Occasionally I can get permission for one of them to come too but mostly they're not interested. Why did they choose to come here? When I have to, I profess to the authorities I have this yearning to see the great world out there, don't go unless there's a very good reason. Most of the time there's more than enough to get on with here.'

'Seems very selfish.'

His face was placid as a goldfish pond. 'No more than most humans.'

How about letting loose a hornet in this paradise of his? 'There's Tammy.'

He pushed his long body off the ground. 'Shouldn't be taking all this time out.'

She scowled as he swung off, watched him stop to talk to a slim figure in the gateway.

Then Tammy was eyeing her from a distance. She waved back, radiating care.

The girl came striding and threw herself down. 'Didn't tell me you was here.'

'Looked in but you were asleep.'

'Just pretending.'

'You do that well.'

'Making fun of me, are you?'

'Just stating facts. You have gifts that way.'

'What you mean?'

'I mean you're good at acting. Clever.'

There was a long pause. 'Don't talk rubbish.'

'Not rubbish.'

'What was you and him talking about?'

'This place mostly.'

'Why? Going to stay here, are we?'

'Would you like to?'

'Don't be a poltic. Can't.'

'No, we can't.'

'So why were you talking?'

'I was born here.'

'What's that to do with him?'

'Not much really.' She gazed round at sun resting on brick walls, fruit trees, sparkling cabbages. 'Did Wheera bring you here yesterday?'

'We was inside the house.'

'You said at supper. You met some residents.'

'They're all over that kid.'

'Glad to meet someone young. They'd be the same for you.'

'Those old horrors? Ought to hide their faces.'

'You can't say that Tammy.'

'Faces all wrong. Crumpled. Why don't they wear masks? And creeping around. This place is a Spook Bin.'

'No it's not. This is real life.' She leant on each word as it came. 'They're not horrors, Tammy, just people. Many of them old. Or ill. Suffering.'

'Don't care.'

Miranda eyed scars on thin wrists, could see no blood on the tee-shirt. 'You OK?'

'Course.'

The woman let the word hang, then, jerkily, 'I'd like something to eat. You coming?'

Later that morning when Wheera grabbed Tammy's arm. 'Got more things to show you,' the older girl didn't resist.

Miranda went up to rest on her bed in the stable block – but there was that view along the landing to a closed door. She thought of swallows, how she used to be alone with the swallows. Nine or ten years old, maybe – she'd gone on long after that – year after year she'd leant her elbows on that quiet window-sill – and now – furnished rooms in this block – her bedroom last night seemed somewhere else so she'd slept without remembering – but now she remembered – how a small girl crouched beside a window to watch swallows swoop across the yard, slip in and out of cups on the barn wall.

That room had always been empty.

Now there were boxes piled against the wall. How'd they got there? Last time she'd seen them they'd been in the spare bedroom. She'd helped pack them so why not look inside? She slid the clasps off the holders.

And waited, resting her fingertips on the lid, then lifted it, found the curtains, folds of bulky cloth. She heaved them out pair by pair and laid them on the floor – stylised blue flowers for the sitting-room, green for Mum and Dad's bedroom, roses for the guest bedroom, peacocks for hers. She spread these last fully out and sat a long time thinking about mornings before school, other holiday mornings, rooks cawing, circling but not settling in the cedar. They'd colonised the horse chestnut in the lower field.

Last of all, the yellow drapes Mum had insisted on calling golden. She'd come home triumphant, unwrapped the material like a revelation. 'Just what I've been looking for to light up the dining-room.'

She stroked them now. Strange how objects came over from one universe to another. There were duplicates of these perhaps with her mother now, perhaps, in another Hayle or beside Lake Michagan? She unfolded the layers, stroked them flat, lifted them to her nose, laid them down again. Sat a long time while the sun rested on dancing motes.

She was roused by feet, dashing in at the lower door, scrambling on the stairs. Tammy and Wheera pounding in. 'What you doing? The pair of them laughing, Wheera holding Tammy's hand.

'What's that?'

She wasn't sure which of them asked.

'Our old curtains.'

'What you going to do with them?' That was definitely Tammy.

'Hadn't thought. Just look, I suppose.'

Tammy snatched up the blue flowered cloth and flung it round her shoulders. She raised one hip, jiggled it, gave a sultry glance under her eye-lashes – how long they were, lifted slightly at the tips – gave in to a teenage itch to be moving, began to prance round the room, calling, 'Come on, Whee. You get one.'

Whee?

After some thought the child chose a green curtain. Auburn curls swung as she danced.

'Can we take them into the garden?' Wheera's enormous eyes were utterly confident.

Miranda hesitated. 'Go on. Why not?' She followed the girls downstairs and through the gate. A Red Admiral wobbled off a bed of thyme.

Wheera jumped onto the plank edge that bordered the onion bed, lifted both arms holding the ends of the green material, the top edge sagged, too long to sit on her shoulders. Without thinking Miranda leant forward, found the ends of the drawstrings, 'I'll tie these together.'

She drew back and saw Tammy's scowl as the child danced along, holding out her hands, putting her feet down exactly right. Wheera had the makings of a gymnast, the enchantment power of a six-year old. Tammy grabbed another curtain, leapt up beside her, almost knocked her off, and stood there swaying, veiling her body in peacocks, then swinging the folds open, flourishing them like wings, hiding again in their depths.

The children paused for breath. Someone clapped. Miranda swung round. Ed was there, watching.

Tammy jumped off the wall, threw the curtain on the ground, put up her hands as if holding a wheel, began to sway in the rhythm of the drivers' hornpipe. Swing right, corner, swing back for the next bend. Swing left.

Ed came to face her. Forward, reverse, forward, reverse, park, switch off – fingers flicked in the air – switch on, away, Tammy coy at first, then meeting a challenge in his eyes, flinging her head back, defiant. Miranda watched his huge feet imitating pressures, clutch, brake, accelerator, each movement precise, clear.

The dancers passed and re-passed, faced, backed, advanced took turns to do three point turns, overtake, the pace speeding up, till they were circling, racing, Ed's face tightening till at last Tammy gave up. He looked at Miranda. 'How about you?'

She shook her head.

He went on looking, inviting.

'Couldn't.' It was a time for sitting, watching maybe, not dancing or caring.

He held out a hand. 'Come on, Mira.'

She looked up sharply.

He said it again, 'Mira,' smiling at her, 'just try.'

She narrowed her eyes at him. 'You never called me that.'

'Trying to get round you, i'n he? Don't take notice.'

Miranda stood up. 'I'd be delighted.' She stood facing him, lifted heavy legs, felt her arms rise, felt the imaginary wheel under her hands – and then as she mirrored his actions, the rhythm came, familiar and sweet, her feet responded in remembered patterns. She turned and reversed as the dance required, becoming vaguely aware of fruit-trees, walls, the long line of the stable block, the red-tiled roof of the main house, not really seeing them but feeling their presence, her body moving the way it used to, everything coming back, things revealing themselves as OK, promising to be as they had been.

Wheera pulled at Tammy but the older girl stood staring.

At last their elders lowered their arms, laughing into each other's faces.

'That was really good, Ed. Didn't know you could do it.'

'Wonderful what I know. Now you two – you look absolutely splendid in those cloaks. Mavis and Frank are in the conservatory. Why don't you go and show them?'

Tammy glowered, but Wheera was tugging her hand.

Mirnada watched them go. 'That child's a great thing for Tammy,'

Ed smiled. 'They'll be back soon. Look, come to my office, Miranda. We can talk there undisturbed.'

She felt cold. 'Do we have to?'

'I think we do. Presumably you came here for something.'

He led her again past the kitchen and touched the wall. A door flush with it slid back and revealed a small room slightly larger than a confessional. She gazed round, gradually coming to terms with half of the old scullery. They'd never used it as that, of course, just as a base for the washing machine and somewhere to store wellies. It was another place now, behind closed shutters, lit only by artificial light, furnished with desk, office chair, bank of computers, board for a time planner, two soft chairs either side of a small table.

He waved her to one of them.

She sat up, looked across, 'Well?'

'I have a bigger office the Dawns can look into.' He stretched out his legs, clasped his hands across his stomach, gave them the ritual examination. His quiet filled the small space. Finally he raised his head. 'I don't want to pry, Miranda, but if we're to achieve anything in the time you can be here – couldn't help seeing the van – but if you don't want to tell me –'

The scent of some aromatic soap drifted across to her.

She shrugged. 'One of those things – irregular signature, that's all.'

He smiled. 'Not yours, of course?'

'A Free who was getting himself investigated.'

'Implicated you?'

She shrugged again. 'Happens, you know.'

'Just the fact he'd signed something that involved you?'

'How it goes.'

He let the quiet spread. 'You'll have to trust me a bit further.'

She inspected the bank of computers, firmed up her voice, 'I came here for Tammy's sake.'

'Yes.' He inspected his fingers again. They rested against each other without moving. 'What did you hope?'

She gazed round an inexpressive room – 'Somewhere quiet, I suppose. Get her in a quiet place. You know, relax her.'

'That child needs more than relaxation. Did you think I'd produce some kind of professional help?'

The walls gave little help. 'Well – I suppose – Ed – what I thought – you're quite good at sorting people out.'

'Not a magician. Tammy may be beyond me – but you, Miranda – d'you know what I think?'

'How could I?'

His smile had some mischief in it. 'I think, knowing you, I can guess what kind of activity the signature was supposed to cover.'

She hardened herself to stare him out, gradually realising she was finding the resources to look another person full-face in the eye.

'OK – that's your side of the problem.' His voice was calm but not indifferent. 'So what about Tammy? She can't be easy.'

'Varies.' She ran her eyes along the bank of computers. Each had a different design as screen saver, blues, pinks, reds curled together mixed like fibres in an uncombed fleece. 'That's the problem. She's so unpredictable. Can't make out what sets her off.'

'What's her history?'

'Told you how she took over. Before then she says she was with someone called Don. Ex-hitchmate of her mother's. Mother presumably got fed up and upped, dumped the kid on him.'

'Not his kid?'

'She's always talked as if he wasn't her father.'
'And not a good experience to live with?'
'She called him a 'seedy corm'. And quite right – if half of what she alleges is true. He abused her, Ed. There's a scar on her chest and that's only part of it. I don't know exactly what else got up to but he took her with him into the Spook Bins.' She lowered her eyes. 'I think he abused her there.'

They looked at the idea together in silence.

'Have you asked her?'

She stared into her lap. 'No. Could have done her good – I suppose – but when you're sharing a van – in that confined space – before I got the knives off her she used to go out and lock me in – I hadn't taken her on – been forced – all excuses, I know – but – just didn't.'

'You've done well to survive at all. Be gentle with yourself, Miranda.'

She wriggled, compared patterns on the computers, confused but somehow soothing.

After a time he asked, 'Where did she go?'

'What?'

'When she went out, where did she go?'

'Spook Bins mostly. That's a guess. Caught her in one once. She'd come in shuddering.' She looked up. 'What I don't understand – once she was free of Don why keep going back?'

'Got something out of it,' he said quietly.

'She said once "Shows you how to win".'

'Not happy, is it? But you see what she learnt? And from Don too? He'd be unlikely to have a mind above direct violence.'

'She has a scar from a wound he made,' she said slowly. 'I don't know of anything else. Though I guess, of course. Try not to let my mind run on it. The Spook Bins – I can't find words – so totally – disgusting, vile. Muck – and someone put their mind to dreaming it up.'

'I think she's still living with it. Miranda, you need to watch.'

'She's been quiet since I took her knives.'

'From what you've told me, could be she's turned the violence off you onto herself?'

This was a room without external windows. 'Maybe. Yes. I suppose so.'

'Obviously yes.' His look challenged her. 'How can you go on sharing your life with a girl in that state?'

'What do you suggest I do?' Even when they were still those screen-saving patterns swirled across the screen. She jolted onto her feet. 'Ed, I've just remembered – I left the curtains spread all over the garden.'

He tightened his lips, then smiled. 'OK, go and look after them.'

She gathered them slowly, smoothed and folded, carried them upstairs, not to the empty attic where she'd found them but to her bedroom.

A ginger cat curled on the bed opened one eye and closed it.

She put down the curtains and approached slowly. The animal raised its head. She reached out, touched the space between the ears, began to stroke. A luxurious paw extended over the cover. She went on rubbing velvety fur, feeling bone underneath. The cat started purring. She sat with it a long time.

A gong sounded somewhere in the depths of the main house. 'Bye, puss.'

Tammy's door was closed. She knocked, got no answer. Probably the girl was still romping around with Wheera – but that was a long time ago. She opened the door. Tammy was sitting on the bed glaring. Her breasts and the space between them were red.

Not again. Oh hell, not again, you blasted little sod. 'You'll need bandages.' No sign of a knife. So what had she used – her bare nails? 'At least in this house they're sure to have plenty of bandages.' She came closer. 'Come along, I'll take you.' And as she took her arm. 'Oh Tammy, why do you have to do this?'

'Take your hands off.' The girl wrenched sideways.

'But you need –'

'You don't care what I need. Just leave me.'

'Tammy, I do care.' She listened to herself, mouthing heavy words. 'Shall I ask Ed to come here?'

'Told you before, Ranna, I'm not worth bothering with.'

Why not run out of the door and leave her, she was only trouble? She placed a hand under her elbow. 'You're perfectly capable of walking.'

Ed surveyed the damage and called a nurse. 'Mandy, can you deal with this? When you've finished, put them both in the conservatory. I'll arrange for them to have their supper quietly in there.' He turned on his heel and went.

It was a glum meal.

A bat was flittering backwards and forwards in circles between the cedar and the house when he came back. 'Supper OK?'

She raised her face towards him. 'Excellent.'

He curled himself down into an armchair. 'There's a bed for you, Tammy, in the main house where the night staff can keep an eye on you.'

'Don't want nobody.'

'Look, Tammy,' he said gently, 'from time to time we have a resident who's got themself in a state. This is what we always do to help them. You need rest and looking after.' He smiled gently. 'I know you're not used to that.'

Tammy glared. 'Don't have to do what you say.'

'Miranda needs a rest too. While you're here it's my job to see you both get both. Mandy will come for you in a little while.'

The girl slumped into sullen silence, the way she'd done so often on the back seat of the van.

Miranda made no attempt to call her to.

'So, Miranda, this a good place to sit?'

She gazed out into the gathering dark. 'You know, Ed, not long ago we had a day's holiday. What I really missed was not being able to stay on into the evening. To sit and watch trees get dark.'

'There's something about that process, the calm, the sense of an ending – of something unknown beginning. The rest of the visit, was it good?'

'Wonderful. And peculiar. The castle was closed but we saw a settlement of Dreamies.'

'Some folks say, "The Wild Ones".'

Tammy suddenly broke out of her torpor. '"The Mob" – what they say in the Breakers' Yards.'

'Hardly rivals of theirs, I'd have thought.'

'Don' mean it. Just saying they're stupid gits. Like the pair of you.' She sank back and closed her eyes.

'"Golden Oldies",' Miranda murmured. This was a great game.

Ed grinned. '"Green Shysters".'

'"The latest version of Amish". Must have been Milla said that.'

'Who's Milla? Oh never mind. Your favourite title is "Dreamies"?'

'Seems to suit. "Tree-huggers".'

He slowly brought the tips of his fingers together. 'You might be surprised. They're very practical people.'

'How d'you know?'

'Even the healthiest life-style – which they have – can't protect you from all life's troubles. In other words, some of them sometimes need the help of this place and even the Dawns have enough heart to let them have it. Only in the most extreme circumstances, naturally, but that's what we're here to deal with.'

'What do you mean, practical?'

'How do you picture them – sandals and beards? Robes covered in stars? Wands?'

She gazed slowly, then smiled. 'Not wands, certainly.'

'But the rest.'

'When we looked down, you know, there was a mast. Radio, or something.'

'That's how they contact me.'

'They're supposed to keep out.'

'They do – except in emergencies. It was a struggle to establish they were entitled to help – but with persistence we won through.'

Her head turned towards the darkness outside. 'Something odd,' she said slowly, 'about the houses. The walls were black, couldn't be soot that did it –obviously, in that setting. Too high for peat, not stiff enough for wood.' Her eyes swung back. 'A sort of slight curve to them, up and down and along their length. How could I tell – at that distance? Distribution of shadows? Not harsh enough for metal.'

'They've developed some new materials.'

'Out in that wilderness? We saw cart tracks.'

He looked up. 'Hi, Mandy, ready now are you? Go along with her now, Tammy.'

Miranda stood up quickly. 'I'll come and see you settled.'

When she returned with tense shoulders, the ginger cat was on his lap; he looked up from running his fingers through its fur. 'This is Hermes.'

'Posh name. He was on my bed this evening.'

'To do with his role as a healer. He doesn't know it but he's here to make residents feel better. And they do. Get quite competitive sometimes, all of them trying to entice him to choose their lap. I seem to remember you and Elizabeth had a cat? Not sure of its name. Stockings was it?'

She laughed. 'Soccie.'

'I never understood why.'

'Short for Socrates.'

'Because of the wise look?'

She took her time over the answer. 'Because of his habit of asking awkward questions. Sounded like it, at least.'

He grinned and fell serious. 'How is she?'

'Finally agreed to take something Mandy gave her to make her sleep.'

'How did she do it this time?'

'Couldn't find a knife – one reason I was so long – went to look – but nothing. Her nails, I think. Tore off the scab. Damage doesn't seem to be deep.'

'Seeking attention?'

'Don't know.'

'Miranda, have you any idea why she picked on you in the first place?'

'Opportunity. Saw I was exposed.'

'You would be, of course.' He looked amused. 'Nothing to do with that endorsement, of course.'

She didn't answer.

'Listen,' he said softly, leaning forward, 'I think she'd been watching some time before she attacked you. Yes, she spotted you were vulnerable but I think she also liked you.'

'Funny way of showing it.'

'You realise she's jealous, hates my guts?' His eyes narrowed, relaxed; he spread his hands palms up. 'Let's not argue. Earlier you said something much more important.'

'Did I?'

'You referred to the Dreamies; I thought, yes, that's where I can see her. That bleak hassle on the motorways doesn't suit her. She ought to be out among living things. She could flourish there.'

'For goodness sake, Ed, don't be silly.' Tears were pressing, trying to force themselves out. 'Life's bad enough without you being silly.'

'Sorry. I know. Didn't mean to upset you.'

'You were needling me. You knew it.'

'Maybe that's what I'm like. Forget it, Miranda.'

*

Going to find Tammy next morning she paused at the foot of the back stairs. That turning under the tall window was where she'd seen Ed, one of those last days after Elizabeth died, the day before she'd left expecting never to return. She'd been coming from the back, from the old visitors' room in the stable block, peered up the stairs into gloom that always hung there framed in dark oak, saw him, white-coated, descending with a tray in his hand.

A long look had passed. 'Miranda, if you ever want to talk –'

Then she'd flung back her head, laughed. A tinny sound had echoed against the walls of the stairwell. 'Taking on the robes of an agony aunt?'

He'd looked like a depressed donkey. 'Even the best of us sometimes – you know?'

He could only have re-iterated what she already knew. The pain had been controlled. That was the best they'd expected, coming there. And a little time.

But just at that point, to accept those things as facts seemed callous. You couldn't just write off someone as marvellous as Elizabeth. So funny. So intelligent. So beautiful. At her side she'd had to be calm, cheerful, full of warmth. At night she'd lain in bed awake and cold.

Now she was slowly climbing these stairs again to deal with that girl. Ed at her again to talk. Seemed to see undermining as his mission in life. At that earlier time she'd needed to firm every fibre or she'd never have gone back to the roads.

Didn't seem much easier now – and he was telling her to turn her back on the New Dawn.

When she got to the room Tammy was dressed. A little sheepish possibly. Had no problems with breakfast. They sat on. Neither had anything to say. Miranda closed he fingers round a coffee cup. That Free had suggested a Fem-tog. Did you have to carry everything on your own? Why not share trouble – responsibility? Not that she had any, not really. Only a weird disinclination to ditch a stray teenager. Another woman – who'd perhaps had children of her own? – might understand. Might take her off her hands from time to time. The warmth and weight of the group – a kind of confinement – better than an isolated van?

Wheera came dancing in and threw her arms round Tammy's waist. The older girl suddenly bent down, rested her head on red curls and hugged her.

Miranda watched as the child slipped out of Tammy's grip demanding, 'Can we have those curtains again?'

'Let's take them into the walled garden.'

She sat on the edge of the cold frame and watched Wheera wrapping herself in flowered mystery, crouching, jumping up to catch Tammy, pulling her into a whirling dance, Tammy first allowing it to happen, then catching fire, launching into a Devil Driver performance with a mocking edge to it. It must be her age. A few weeks – days ago – she'd been laying herself out to prove she was exactly that. And now this parody. Only a teenager could swing like that from one mood to another.

The sun shone, the children ran along the tops of the planks bordering the paths, jumped down, spun each other round. Tammy lowered Wheera gently onto her feet. 'There you are, Whee.'

Miranda jerked upright – a face on a screen, a child with long curls. Who came from a Fem-tog. 'Some hazardous profession,' Ed had said. Acrobats, that was it. Little Whee.

The girls came to sit beside her on the edge of the frame. Tammy pulled a leaf, rubbed it between her fingers, raised it to her nose, shoved it at Miranda. 'Smell that.'

Mint. So she found thyme. 'Try this one.' They tried the garlic, the runner beans, the fennel, the roses in the yard. It was all so innocent. They watched a snail climbing a beanpole.

The children went back to the curtains.

Miranda suddenly asked, 'Which ones are your favourites?'

Tammy snatched up a yellow one, flourished it, threw it round her shoulders, posed.

'Would you like me to make you a dress?' She'd no idea how – but in this place they must have some sort of means of mending things – or might not have thrown away machines they'd once used. 'Like Milla's,' she said, 'remember? Or not quite as special as that – there isn't time – couldn't get it to fit so well –'

'What you waiting for, Ranna?'

She spread the material on the attic floor and sat back on her heels. 'Old gold,' Mum had called it. 'Egg yolk,' Dad said. She'd loved his down to earth tone. But it was rich, rich. It dazzled. No, it was more subtle. They were both right. She smoothed the last crease and picked up the scissors.

In spite of the long time they'd lain unused the blades ran crisply, the points snipped delicately. Her face relaxed.

She gathered the pieces and piled them on a trestle table she didn't recognise. Perhaps Ed, when he first moved in?

She laid edges together, pinned, tacked, threaded the machine, slid the material under the needle. Her hand circled with the wheel, the machine hummed, sunlight slowly changed angle. At last she gathered her work over her arm, descended to the yard and called.

A cloak for Wheera, with ties at the throat to hold it and lots of folds to throw out or wrap round her.

A dress for Tammy. 'Very primitive I'm afraid.' The shoulders held by seams that curved softly over the tops of the arms making short sleeves, round neck bound with strips cut on the cross, long under-arm seams. Calf length. A sash for the waist. 'Come here, I'll slip it on you.'

Her hair was swallowed up, then re-appeared, the ends trapped under the neckline. Miranda reached forward and gently tweaked them out.

'Want to see ourselves.' This time it was Tammy who plunged first downstairs, with Wheera tumbling behind her.

Miranda puffed in their wake through the dark kitchen passage into the hall, stood in the doorway to watch them pirouetting in front of the mirror, two golden girls prancing across the tiles, two golden girls in the cloudy depth of the glass. If only they could be sisters.

Long-lost relations belonged to fairy tales — but in a Fem-tog? It seemed to stabilise Tammy to have that child around. Wheera obviously liked her. If Tammy were there all the time, perhaps Wheera could live with her mother?

She felt the warmth of a body, turned and saw Ed standing beside her.

The girls darted into the lounge and leapt onto the sofa, bounced on an unofficial trampoline.

'Sorry,' she said. 'they're a bit high at the moment.'

'Within parameters considering —'

'Last night was a blip. Both girls will come fine.'

'In the right places.'

'Which isn't here. One more day.'

He touched her hand. 'Do take me seriously. I can help you contact the Dreamies.'

She tore her hand away. He could have fixed her a job in his hospice.

She cornered him going out of the dining room after supper. 'I've made up my mind. There's a Fem-tog I can join.' Even if they no longer needed an administrator or a teacher, Wheera was so delightful — if the adults were like that — and they had to be to produce that kid — surely they'd see her problem and take her in.

He nodded. 'Whatever you want.'

That night she lay awake hearing the screech of security screens. Next morning didn't feel like being anywhere. The lounge was a conventional arrangement of chintz, the walled garden a soulless rectangle containing vegetables, the river path horribly overgrown and harsh with the roar from the motorway. From time to time a thought about Tammy disturbed her. Ed had made things plain. 'Mandy kept an eye on her most of the night. I can't spare a member of staff during the day.' Each time she pushed it away. The girl would be OK with Wheera.

She gravitated back towards the house and was hanging about where she shouldn't have been near the front door when the motorbike arrived. She heard its screech as it braked to turn in to the drive; its bumps over potholes, then saw it slow and wheel into the space under the cedar. A figure slid off the seat and stood facing the house. A crash helmet was removed; long fair hair cascaded over dragon leathers. Scales gleamed over shoulders and hips, firmed in a neat waist; scaly arms tapered to wrists, scaly legs to ankles.

Miranda drew back, hesitated, was on the point of turning away when a small body brushed her side, Wheera rushing to throw herself into the arms of this monster, who bent down to greet her, heaved her off her feet and spun her round.

At last she put the child down. Wheera took her hand, chattering, pointing to Miranda.

The woman firmed up her body, straightened her shoulders, strode heavily across, held out her hand. 'I'm Angel.'

'Miranda'

'Hear you've been looking after this one?'

'She looks after us.'

Angel glanced past, her face light up.

'Weltrav, Angel,' Ed said. 'Good journey?'

'Great to be here. Wheera seems to be having a good time.'

'Come into the lounge. You too, Miranda. Angel, you should get Wheera to show you her golden cloak.'

Miranda sat quietly, watching this woman. If she asked – could she ask? – drop a hint? – hints no way to go about things – but to ask, directly, blatantly? – not the same thing as applying – no vacancy on offer – they'd got the number they wanted –   and this Angel – how'd she'd react – say she'd ask the rest of the fem-tog? – promise and go off, forget – say something now to fob off an unwanted request?

Angel and Ed were absorbed in an exchange of news. His eyes lit, gazing into hers.

Wheera danced in swirling her cloak, Tammy hovering in the doorway behind her.

Miranda smiled at Angel. 'She moves so well. You can tell she's an acrobat's daughter.'

'Acrobat?'

'But –' Miranda sank down.

Ed's lips were twitching. 'She's a stunt-rider. I think that's what you want to know, isn't it? The things she does on a motorbike –' He caught her eye again.

Of course, that outfit.

'Do you have nerves, Angel?'

She spread her hands and laughed. 'Practice, that's all. And the fun of it. It's just such fun.'

All the time she was watching her daughter. Her and Ed, both watching.

'The tastes people have – What d'you think, Miranda?'

'Can't say I've ever been tempted.' She was taking in the size of hands, which had been hidden in scaly gauntlets; hands which were now lifting a daughter onto a lap; the child resting her head against her mother. Ed watching.

Angel looked over Wheera's shoulder towards the door where Tammy had consolidated. 'So you're Wheera's friend? You look lovely in that golden dress. Miranda's been very clever.' She buried her face in her child's curls.

'On your way to the Riddle-me-re, are you? Festival time,' he added turning to me. 'Her Fem-tog go every year. They're notorious.'

'Famous,' she corrected him, shaking her curls and laughing.

'Whatever way you like it. I'm taking it you've never seen them, Miranda? Tell her about it, Angel.'

Miranda shook her head. 'I've heard of the Riddle-me-re. Probably seen pictures. Never got there. You think of things, don't you? Don't do them.'

Angel looked doubtful. 'If you've never seen it – Ed, you describe things so much better than I can – you tell her.'

'You've been there?' Miranda said more fiercely than she'd intended. 'Left this place and been there?'

'Don't look at me like that. It's well worth going.' He leant back and brought his fingertips together 'Art Addling's pièce de résistance'. Sorry – but faced with that amazing construction I really don't know what to say.' His face gathered in a frown. 'Basically it's very simple, just two bridges across the Channel. Each supports a four lane motorway, one taking traffic towards France, the other to England. That in itself is a feat of engineering and would have been totally impossible without the materials they were pioneering at the time of the New Dawn. Though it's not just the length of it but the height. It soars and it's so light, two curves resting on slender pillars. But that's not all. It's the slip roads, a whole system of them. They peel off one motorway, plunge almost to sea level and twist up to join the other. The whole thing gives the impression of a large openwork basket. First time I saw it – I really didn't know what to say. Your eye follows the lines, you begin to detect an underlying symmetry. I can only say you should see it.'

'It's not actually intended for getting to France.' That felt like a sensible remark.

'No. I was quoting a little while back. One of those on-line reviews. Do stick, don't they? 'Site of a multi-media extravaganza.' That's what Angel and her friends have been going for, goodness knows how many years.' His head swung towards her. 'Racing again this year?'

'Not this time. Engine problems. Next year probably.' She pushed a strand of hair behind her ear. 'Won't miss the orchestra. Not after last year. Billy the Blast-off conducted us in person – unbelievable. What a beat. Not coming this year but all the same –'

At last Ed was looking at Miranda. 'To quote my source again 'the pulsations of a thousand throbbing motor-bikes.'

'I see, she said slowly, 'I think I've heard of "drifting"?'

Angel's eyes shone. 'When they only let on a few at a time. You go really slow, down those slip roads and up, riding low above the sea, then cruising up to where you can see cliffs both sides of the channel and there's gulls and clouds and things.'

'You love the racing too.'

'Passionate. But it's more complicated. Don't know how to explain it.'

A furrow appeared between Ed's eyes. He sat apparently counting on his fingers. 'Right. There are three kinds of race: the ordinary circular one when they close off all the slip roads except two. That's pure speed. And two versions of 'Town Centre,' one scored by the time taken to complete the course which includes all the slip roads, the other by skill in using each of them only once. You're disqualified as soon as you enter one a second time. It's based on a computer game – they thought it would be more fun in real life – and that was based on what Granddad had said way back before the New Dawn. I've a feeling I've heard my parents going on about the topic.'

'What topic?'

'In those days when there were towns – you'll remember – some roads were a bit narrow and there was lots of traffic. So – all those complicated one-way systems. Easy to wonder off and when you found yourself passing the Town Hall for the third time you knew something had gone wrong. Satnavs put an end to that, of course, but seems some games designer found an inspiration.'

'So all these racers are charging round trying out roads at random?'

'It's a bit risky. We once had a resident –' He paused. 'People like Angel have turned the idea into a demonstration of formation riding – coming off slip roads into a stream on a main carriageway, both sets of riders maintaining exact intervals. Best watched at night when the lights show where everything is. Coloured strobes, music. I went once. Unforgettable.'

They sat quietly imagining. 'Is it the noise Wheera doesn't like?' Miranda asked.

'No, it's not that. It's the regular job. Can't bear to see her Mum jumping through fire. And no use putting her where she can't see. Knows what's going on, poor little mouse. Be better when she can learn for herself. See then there's nothing to it.'

Miranda watched her spread confident legs, relax. 'Right out of the way here. Chance to forget. And Ed loves her, don't you, Ed?'

'Gave her my name.' The words mingled with distant sounds, a zimmer, a wheelchair, a pair of brisk feet. 'And it's good having her. A lot of the residents love her. It's good for them to have a child to talk to – and play with. We found these antique board games, Miranda. Your family's?'

'Maybe.' Chess, draughts, snakes and ladders.

'Many of our residents don't have eyes good enough for computers and even the younger ones may be too ill to concentrate on a screen – but the real things, objects set out on a board – they seem to get on better. And it's more natural – two people on opposite sides of a table. I come in sometimes and this chatterbox has made someone forget the game listening to her. And they comfort her about her Mum.'

He and Angel launched into a discussion of the cost of new clothes for a growing child.

It was great to see someone so happy in her life, so well adapted to conditions, who didn't look back, or through holes in fences, a woman who existed in the place where she was and made it good. She showed what could be done.

Miranda sank back. Angel and Ed. Herself and Ed – What was this she'd been feeling? Or imagining she felt? After Elizabeth, could she want Ed? Did she have that in her?

She realised the doorway had emptied. She stood up. 'Mind if I go and look for Tammy? Lovely meeting you, Angel.'

Pans clattered in the kitchen. The dark passageway closed in with heaviness. Instead of searching she went through into the yard and the garden and sat under the yew hedge.

Ed had spoken of the beauty of the Riddle-me-re. An achievement of the New Dawn. Which had been a splendid thing. And still was.

The quiet of yew needles, the scent of yew bark. They were good and ages old, older than any human in the scale of evolution. Nature had looked after itself centuries before the first gardener emerged, was at its best looking after itself. Wildernesses and jungles had their own order. What gave humans the right to think they could dictate? Why should their ugly sprawl destroy the lives of other creatures? The arguments hadn't changed. The New Dawn was worth living out.

Her fingers began working through the mass of dead needles, dry on top, damp and decaying underneath. Time to get over Elizabeth's death. They'd both known it had to come.

Looking back – had she let it undermine her?

Admit it, yes. She'd let it hollow her out – become that thing huddled in the van – thinned down version of herself – natural something so pathetic should start looking to pansies for comfort – sort of spook.

If you've set yourself to do something you should do it. Look how Angel had succeeded. And Ed. Who didn't want her in the hospice. Though Ed made the wrong choice, settling. No, couldn't say that. Good job, this place.

All the same – she hadn't. She belonged to the New Dawn. Belonged. It was her core. Give upon that equalled give up on herself. If Angel wouldn't admit her, there were plenty of other Fem-togs.

She sat there in the sun, thinking, not much longer.

Just before supper she rushed towards screams, down from her room across the yard, into the passage to see a dark figure at the far end with its hands on another smaller one, leaning onto the child's shoulders, thumping her into the floor, kicking her.

She flew forward, pushed between, grabbed the child, pulled her back into her arms, gathered her up. Ed appeared at the other end of the passage.

Tammy staggering back saw where Miranda was looking, got herself onto her feet, whirled round to face him like a wild cat cornered.

'What's going on here?' Neither of them had heard that thunder from him before.

Tammy jumped sideways through the kitchen door, re-appeared waving a knife, its tip pointed directly at him.

'Get Wheera away, Miranda. So Tammy, what do you want?'

Miranda whisked the child into the sunny courtyard. 'It's all right, Wheera. Tammy didn't mean it.' But she did, she did. 'She's upset sometimes. It wasn't your fault.' Couldn't have been. An innocent child. That was the worst of it.

Wheera clung to her, crying. Miranda patted her head, her upper back until the wailing calmed to great gulping sobs, to sniffs, then quiet.

'Shall we go and find Mandy? She looks after you, doesn't she?'

There was no sign in the passage of either Ed or Tammy.

Ed found her later, grim-faced.

She glared. 'You locked her in.'

'What else could I do? Why aren't you with her? Who's looking after her?'

'She wouldn't have me and Mandy offered.'

'She's got plenty else to do. Let's go to my office.'

He led her through interminable mazes and opened the door.

'You'd no right. How could you make her a prisoner?'

He waved his hand. 'Let's sit shall we?' He tilted the head of a desk lamp so that it would shine onto the table between them and switched it on, sat a long time scrutinising clasped hands. His shoulders sagged.

'She was frantic, Ed.'

'Is she calm now?'

'Quiet at least.'

'Good. Look, Miranda, I had to. You'd vanished.'

'You'd taken the knife. She'd stopped being dangerous.'

'She was in a highly volatile state. I couldn't know she wouldn't rush out and try to throw herself into the river.'

'She's never done anything like that.'

'Never had access to a river. I'm sorry, Miranda, really.' His shoulders were folding down. 'It's not my style, not what I do – but –'

She dropped her gaze onto the pool of light. A little later she said, 'She locked me in. More than once. I was adult and calm but I hated her.'

'She won't like me. That's OK. She won't have to.' He fixed grave eyes on me. 'Why don't you get rid of her?'

For a moment her heart leapt. 'What?'

'Turn her in. Hand her over.'

'To who?' There was only one answer – unless, in his wangling way, he'd found another.

'The Frees, I suppose.'

Her body tautened. 'No.'

He regarded her. 'That leaves you in charge.'

They both studied that small pool of light.

He looked up. 'I had been going to say how sorry I am you're leaving.'

'But you're not now. Of course not. How could you be anything but glad? Look – Wheera's OK. She was very shaken – but basically fine. I handed her over to Hal.'

He smiled. 'I knew you'd done that. Thanks.' He considered his clasped fingers. 'Tammy's another question.'

'I can't understand why she did it. She's so fond of Wheera.'

'When I'd got the knife off her and after she'd stopped slagging me off all she could find to say was that Wheera "needed to learn".'

'She's had a tough life. You know that. Don was a prime shit. Sorry for the language – but – is there much else anyone could say about him? And she's seemed so much better these last few days – the garden, the quiet, playing with Wheera – you must have seen that – a normal kid.'

'She's not, is she?' He searched her face. 'I know you don't like it – but – you can't cope, can you? She's too much, isn't she?'

'What do you suggest I do?'

He leant forward. 'Stop fooling yourself. It takes experts to deal with a kid like that. Of course you want to help.

Who wouldn't? Candidly though, you haven't the expertise. This isn't for you.'

She looked at him coldly. 'In the world we live in where would I find anyone better?'

He didn't reply.

'I'm thinking of joining a fem-tog.'

His eyes swung up. 'Be realistic, Miranda. Do you think they'd have you? If there were other children? You'd have to tell them.'

'I told you.'

'There'd be more to say now.'

After a time a light flashed. He clicked "Transfer".'

'Hal can field that. You know – I've been thinking hard. There's only one way out. You arrived exhausted, that's the truth of the matter, isn't it? You are a little better now but could do with far more time – great expanses of it – which aren't available. The situation dictates, you can stay exactly one more day. That's balancing the needs of my residents and Tammy. I can't spare staff from the residents. They have to be washed, clothed, fed, medicated, to have their pain controlled, to be talked to, entertained. I want life here to be full of their happiness. You know that's possible, Miranda.'

'Yes.' But Tammy?

'There's also the question of inspectors. They make random visits.'

'Yes.'

'I know.' he said softly, 'I seem to be condemning you to a life in a small van cooped up with a traumatised girl who works out her past in violence. The confinement would make her worse.' His voice changed tone. 'You'd be cut off from resources that might enable you to cope.'

She looked up under her lashes. 'What resources?'

'The natural world we all evolved in. You need to be in that. Of course we all do but we're talking about you. You need plants and animals. There's this companionship. Look how you enjoyed the garden, and Hermes found your bed to lie on.'

She smiled. 'Hermes met Odysseus on his way to Circe and gave him a magic plant.'

He smiled back. 'You're an expert at dodging issues.'

'It would be wonderful though, a magic plant to turn pigs back into humans.'

'We don't have one. Though in a way, that is what I'm suggesting. Go to the Dreamies, Miranda, and become the human you are. They've got space. They live in nature – you'll be surprised what they mean by "living according to nature".'

It was like an axe falling.

She sat for a moment curled in, then looked up. 'How would we get there?'

'There's a labyrinth of back roads through the Breakers' Yards. Tammy will know how to cope. And – as I said, d'you remember? – I've taken in residents from there so I have contacts. I'll send a message. Extremely cryptic but they'll make something of it.'

He stood up, came round the desk and laid a hand on her shoulder. She knew that moment of professional intimacy was the best she could hope for.

'That's the best I can do,' he said.

'Yes, I know. Thanks. Couldn't diich Tammy, you know; it's too late.'

Part 7

It was a relief when Tammy began to stonewall. But that was next morning.

That night Miranda escorted her to their quarters in the old stable, closed the door, knew Hal – or someone – would come soon to lock them in. 'Can't take risks,' he'd said and she'd had no answer.

She sat on the chair in Tammy's room. 'Day after tomorrow, we got to leave.'

'Why?'

'Ed wants it.'

'Why?'

'Always said we couldn't stay long.'

'Not that is it?'

'No.'

'Not fair. Lets her stay.' Her hands twisted, she looked round wildly, snatched up a hairbrush. 'That Ed never liked me.'

'Wheera's a lot smaller than you.'

'Asked for it.'

'Put that down, Tammy. I can't see how. What did she do?'

'Stupid are you, you useless cow?' She flung back her head, stared her full in the face without meeting her eyes, turned and threw herself onto the bed, turned her back, curled tightly on her side.

Miranda sat till the curl relaxed, then murmured, 'Get into bed properly now.' She stayed with her till the girl's breath lengthened and she was asleep.

And then of course, Miranda couldn't. She got out of bed, wandered to the loo and coming back, noticed moonlight, filling the room where she'd found the curtains. She didn't know moonlight calls up ghosts.

She went in and crossed to the window to look out. It was night – she couldn't expect to see swallows – they'd gone by now, of course – early October and a harvester moon – a huge golden lamp so low anyone might think it was touching the earth. Owls were calling close by.

It was so like Hayle, what Hayle had always been – and she had to leave – for the third time – the Hayle of the first time was in another universe now – though if she turned she'd find her mother standing behind her –

Later Elizabeth leant on her arm, then lay in bed, almost too tired to raise a hand, smiled.

Her eyes probed the shadows of the yard, trying to trace out all those familiar windows and doors, the soft lines of brick and imprint them on her brain. This last leaving would be different.

Next morning when Tammy's worst was to put up a 'Don't care' to everything, she felt her elbows long to bend, her fingers to curl round the girl's throat, her tongue to threaten to up – 'If you don't mind where you are, just try staying here on your own.'

She despised herself for not doing any of these.

Instead she worked at it. 'I can't do this without you,' and, 'The only way's through the Breakers' Yards – you can handle that,' and, 'You remember that day at the castle, those houses we saw – that's where we're going.'

At last the little sod tossed the hair off her eyes. 'I'm Boss, see?'

Oh hell, Miranda thought, looking at her cautiously. 'OK.'

'First we paint out those lines.'

'The endorsement? We paint that out?'

'No Breakers puts up with that.'

'I see.'

'Take off the number plates.'

'You sure?'

'Want me to help you?'

'Yes, Boss. Can you deal with it?'

'No problem.'

She left the girl to it, confident she'd know how to lay hands on paint and tools, came back to find a pure white, unlabelled van.

'Very handsome. You've done a grand job, Tammy.'

Green eyes slid sideways. 'Boss.'

She hesitated. Then, 'Both. Boss at this moment, always Tammy.'

Ed watched them pack the van, asked for the return of the curtains. 'Keep Tammy's dress. Wheera would love to have her cloak – as for the rest – no use to you. Made for these windows.'

She left them to him with a lordly wave of the hand, let in the clutch, eased off into gathering darkness.

To Miranda the main gate to the Breakers' Yards had always been a place where you waited till someone rolled out the tyre you'd asked for. Now with orange light calling an unearthly gleam up from iron panels, it looked more solid than ever. And they had to get through.

Tammy held out her hand. 'Paypoint card.'

'You can't get in by paying.'

'You'll see.'

Light poured over her as she stood beside the gate, reaching up to the slot, not needing to stand on tiptoe. She'd grown, her body, though still far too skinny, was beginning to fill out, the wrists still bony, the fingers that were working so deftly slim, well-shaped. Miranda watched every move as, instead of the official token, she inserted the card back to front into the slot and performed what was clearly an experienced wiggle. The gate slid open.

'Well done, Tammy.'

'Get on. Keep driving. Speedsters can suck you.'

On the far side – no lights spaced at tidy intervals, defining roads, squares, roundabouts but all over the place, presumably marking something, a corner perhaps or a gate, a mast, a crumbly traffic island, front door, shed – something someone fancied having lit. Other places apparently better left obscure.

Vans storming round in all directions. Hadn't been long inside when one hurled itself straight at them. She stood on the brakes.

'What you do that for?'

'For heaven's sake – I've given way.' Her knees were shaking. 'Not my scene. Which way now?'

'There.'

'Sure that's north? Got the compass?'

'Obvious.' Tammy pointed up. High above beyond the huddled, one-storey workshops to their left a motorway sign shone in the darkness, 'Outer Web. Northern Stream.'

Ed's hand had been warm, pressing a compass into hers. 'Keep heading north.' He'd laid his hand on the lintel, let his fingers spread over fresh white paint, bent to look in. 'Look after her, Tammy. You'll make it.'

Miranda was the one who had answered through frozen lips, 'Thanks. Of course we will.'

She let in the clutch, turned away from the lights into a side-road lined by iron railings.

'Tammy, she said suddenly. 'You're a right devil. You put me up to things.'

'Actually, I think I did quite well. Blaming me are you?'

'Oh yeah?'

'Didn't you notice?' Miranda's voice sharpened, 'way I slipped out of the drive onto the motorway? Really neat, I thought, sort of thing no-one would notice.'

'Noticed the way you hung onto that van.'

Miranda giggled.

Grey expanses sped past in the darkness, concrete walls, broken at intervals by lines of metal stakes. Buildings flicked behind them, sharpened by glare from a motorway that was still not far off. Deeper into the maze, the walls gave way to fences enclosing derelict spaces where shadowy vans were parked, figures stood in groups, walked with some kind of purpose or bent over some job. Sometimes fires blazed, perhaps from braziers. Lights flickered in windows.

'Does nobody ever sleep here?'

'Daytime mostly.'

The van's wheels purred. From time to time a wave of raucous music pounded in and faded away behind them. All signs of the motorway had disappeared.

When colour began to streak the sky Tammy pointed to a side-road. 'Down there.'

'You know a place?'

'Something there that'll do.'

An open, rusty gate. Groundsel and dandelions growing through split tarmac. A gleaming puddle. A small hill of disused tyres.

'There. Behind them.'

They lay up for the day in the shelter of decaying rubber. Miranda stayed on her bunk trying to shut out the smell till late afternoon when Tammy, who she hadn't noticed going out, shook the van as she climbed back in, grinning, with a loaf under her arm.

Next night was the same sequence of random lights, massed outlines of hard-edged buildings, people bent over mysterious tasks. She gripped the wheel, cornered, braked, turned right and left as Tammy directed. The girl seemed to have an inbuilt sense of north and south.

Miranda guessed they were zig-zagging, north-east, north-west, the motorway lights sometimes so close they could look up at the gantries and read the signs but mostly distant, throwing up an orange haze she saw glowing in the rear-view mirror.

In the early morning she looked at the fuel gauge. 'Oh hell.'

'Know where we can get some.'
'Near?'
'Down there.'

Half a mile down a not very salubrious track, Tammy pointed her into what might have been described as a derelict yard surrounded by shabby concrete buildings. The lower storeys appeared to be garages or storehouses, the upper had rows of small windows, as if people lived over their businesses.

'Stop here.'

Miranda drew up.

'They'll sell it in cans.'

She fumbled in her bag for her card. 'Will they supply the cans? You get it, Tammy.' She waved the card. 'You'll want paypoints.'

The girl stared and laughed. 'Not here.'

'So how are you going to pay?'

Tammy bent down and reached under the seat. 'One of these.' She laid out objects on the table: a claw hammer, two speakies, an intelligence pad, a flowered cup and saucer, a talking-cam.

'Where did you get them, Tammy?' Miranda slowly took them in, looked up again at the girl, took in as she hadn't fully before, tense stance, pinched cheeks, knowing eyes. She turned away and gazed out of the window at grimy concrete streaked with long green stains, piles of rubble and tyres, some kind of industrial vehicle with shining wheels, broken tarmac, a line of grey roofs with wet cloud behind them. She took it all in, item after item. Then she turned back. 'OK, Boss.'

Tammy's hand hovered over the table. 'Didn't need them, those old horrors didn't.'

Miranda's lips tightened. She made the ghost of a shrug, 'Run along, Boss.' Sat till the girl returned weighed down by cans.

They filled the tank together pouring liquid hydrogen carefully through the feed-tube. When they were back inside Tammy held up a pair of filthy hands. 'Came off the cans.' She stood appraising the woman and came close. 'Ranna, you're far too clean for this place.'

Miranda felt hands on her face, firm but strangely gentle. She pushed her off. 'What you doing?'

'Making you dirty,' and as Miranda held her at arm's length, 'You don't know this place. Some of them they're –'

'Just leave me be.' She jerked round and in the mirror saw black streaks. 'You've done enough.'

'Get going then.'

Miranda stared.

'I said, get going. Don't you understand, you poltic?'

Miranda slowly climbed into the driving seat.

'Stop wasting time.' Her ferocity had a frantic edge.

They drove in silence till Tammy pointed to a turning on their right. 'Take that.'

Gradually a line of hills loomed up, the road began to twist up between them. Rock-faces drew in each side. Every so often a dark track wound through them away from the road, most likely the entrance to a quarry. The carriageway narrowed to a single track.

'You sure this is the way?'

'Bit longer but best.'

Miranda drove carefully.

'Didn't see, did you?' Tammy's voice was slower, more thoughtful. 'At that place – some of them was eyeing the van – could have followed – good van this, bit old but worth having – thought we'd better get out of the way – see?'

'You know this road?'

'Came this way once with Don. He'd fallen out with a bloke.'

'Ah.'

'Place up here for the day. No-one'll come.

A few miles further on when they turned onto an unmade track that led into a circle of hollowed rock. Several vans were parked there.

Miranda began turning the wheel but already a figure in knee-high red and green boots was striding towards them. In this place of all places he was wearing a mask. Ripped, of course. A frayed grey triangle flapped over his cheek. An eye shone cheekily through the hole.

He laid one hand on the door. 'Glasnost.'

Tammy leant across and raised her right fist. 'Down with the wall.'

'What you doing here?'

'Lost.'

'Who's she?'

'Friend.'

He gave Miranda a long look. 'Where you going?'

Tammy broke in, 'North.'

'Better not.' He shot her a sharp glance, 'Unless you're friends with the Frees.' His voice was ambiguous. 'Doesn't your friend have a voice?'

Tammy slipped down out of the van, gazed up at him, touched her mask-less cheek, pointed to the empty bracket at the front of the van. 'What you think?'

The eye ran over her. 'Frees is raiding tonight. Won't come up here – accidental landslip. Can't think how you got through.'

'Luck,' Tammy said airily.

'Some know how to organise it, don't they? Don't do to have too much that kind of luck.'

Tammy gave him a saucy look. Miranda squirmed

He leered, showed them where to park and left with a wave of the hand,

Miranda looked at Tammy, 'He'll be back, you know.'

'This van got good locks.'

Miranda looked to see what heavy objects were available to move against the door.

They woke to late afternoon light streaming in low, showing the scratches on the worktops, heated the last of the soup Ed had supplied. They drank slowly, elbows on the table between them.

'How'd they get that password?' Miranda asked dreamily.

'Film or something. There's always films.'

'You know what wall it's about?'

'Don't care.'

They lay about lethargically all the next day, glancing from time to time out of the window to see if anyone was approaching. They were still surprised when the van rocked in the late afternoon, they looked out and saw an old woman stood at the foot of the steps holding up steaming mugs.

Miranda opened the door a crack

A brown-cheeked face, smiled up. 'Do with some?'

'Thanks so much.' She opened a little wider, looked into dark eyes, took hold of herself, 'Do come up. Please.'

The woman passed up the mugs, grabbed the handles, pulled herself up more lightly than seemed possible for someone of her bulk.

Miranda waved her hand, 'Do sit.'

She spread her feet, planted her elbows on her knees and inspected their home. 'Nice van.'

She wore bright cloths twisted round her chest and hips and draped over her shoulders. Possibly the bottom layers might have been loose blouses or they could all have been pieces of material with invisible strings tying them in place. The top shawl was pinned in place by gold-coloured filigree brooch. The total effect was imposing – though a trifle grubby but Miranda stared at her ankles. At that level it was clear this woman was wearing a skirt. Miranda's yes kept straying back, eyeing those folds.

'Vanacar,' she said, 'old model now. ' She reached into a cupboard for the last of Ed's biscuits.

The old woman – if she was as old as she looked – received one and held it in her hand, gazing down with a kind of reverence before she raised it to her mouth and bit. Shrewd eyes were still roving round the interior of the van, rising to the roof to check the absence of red light, taking in bare benches, the holes in the carpet.

Miranda watched. Early in the morning she'd left Hayle she'd carried the computer into the room where Tammy had been sleeping, all the books, except Elizabeth's *Persuasion*, her Homer and the album that recorded them setting out in the New Dawn, all the bedclothes except one blanket each, the cushions – Tammy ripped them off the seats – 'Tammy,' she'd said, staring at bare wood but the girl had been stubborn – all the crockery except for two mugs, most of the cutlery.

She studied long lines in their visitor's face. 'Frees often raid?'

The old woman licked the last crumbs of biscuit off her mouth. 'Now and then.'

Miranda held out the plate. 'Take several. What they looking for?'

'Speedcars much as anything.' She wiped her hands on her skirts, picked several biscuits, laid all but one on the table-top, raised that one to her mouth, bit it into it delicately. 'Vans. Stuff. Whatever.' She leered. 'Everyone here's done something. Wouldn't be here yourself, would you, if you hadn't done something?' She picked up another biscuit.

Miranda began at the black nails, inspected fingers, raised veins, blotched skin, wrinkles, eyed tattered shawls, stained sleeves, long scar on the back of the right hand. Tammy had withdrawn into the shadow allowing curls as uncared for as this woman's to fall forward over a face that was similarly pinched.

'No,' she jerked out at last, 'no, I wouldn't.'

The woman gave a lop-sided grin. 'Not used to it yet, are you?'

She drew in a breath. 'No.'

She cackled. 'You'll learn.' She swallowed the last biscuit and rose. 'Bring those mugs when you're ready.' She paused, looked sideways, 'Long journey, eh?'

'Could say so.'

The woman waited a little then clambered laboriously down the steps and turned, looking up, her hand still clasping the rail. 'See you.'

Miranda found herself smiling. 'I'll bring them across soon.' She reached out and touched the back of the hand. This was someone's mother, not Tammy's, all the same surely a mother. 'Thanks. See you too one day, maybe.'

'You was right not to say where we was going,' Tammy emerged from the back of the van and stood closer. Miranda noticed a definite waist, hips that were beginning to spread, small, pointed breasts.

'She didn't ask. And she was friendly.'

'Just friendly, you thought?'

'For goodness sake, Tammy –' She stared out past the vans to rock walls. 'D'you think the Dreamies will be like this?'

'Hope not. How should I know?'

She touched the girl's arm, 'You can't.' Then as Tammy didn't shake her off, 'I'd like to wash and brush your hair.'

'Why?'

'Would look better.'

'Don't matter what it looks like.'

'Tammy,' she said, pulling the girl round to face her, 'you're growing up. You'd feel better if you looked nice.'

'Fill the water tank first.'

'Are we that low?'

'Yeah, fill it,' she repeated urgently.

Miranda sighed. 'OK, Boss.' She clambered into the driving seat.

'Stand-pipe – see just inside the gate.'

She saw it for the first time, swung back against the rock-face.

'OK.' Her hand rested on the switch, she took all the details of their hiding place – two or three large, bright-coloured vans each with its own space round it. Their visitor had come from one of these. A line of broken down vehicles was parked nose to tail round curve of the quarry furthest from the gate.

She got her van underway. The woman appeared on her vanstep. 'Where you going?'

She smiled at her friendliness. 'Fill our water tank.'

'There's the stand-pipe.' She pointed the opposite direction to the way Tammy had indicated.

Miranda felt the girl tauten, took a quick glance at the tap, listened to her own voice saying, 'Thanks – but it's too low. Our in-pipe's in the roof.' She felt Tammy relax.

The woman was still watching as she manoeuvred the van close to the tap, listened to water running.

The minute the tank was full Tammy hissed, 'Now, off, out the gate. Don't stop. And keep going. Fast.'

Miranda hesitated briefly then moved smartly down the track. 'This obedience is becoming a habit, Boss.'

'Don't laugh. Nothing funny. Turn left at the end here.'

'But –'

'Don't argue.'

After a mile or so of taking twists and turns rather too fast she slowed. 'Dodging that landslip, are we – the one meant to block the Frees?'

Tammy snorted. 'Seen any cherubs overhead, have you? Use them first, Frees would.'

The road narrowed, turned to a rough track climbing and twisting continually up into he hills. Miranda switched on the lights.

'Turn them off, you poltic.'

'Want us to go over the edge, do you?'

'Can see us for miles.'

'Who? The Frees?'

'Don't need to bother with them.'

'Can't see an inch.' Miranda slowed the van to a crawl. 'Who then?'

'That lot down there. Stop, can you?' She opened the passenger door. 'Getting out.' She jumped down, stood a few yards ahead of the van in the centre of the track, waved, began to walk.

Miranda eased in the clutch, let the wheels creep forward.

As the road climbed the edge of the hill gradually became distinct as a more solid form of darkness. It levelled, they seemed to have reached a summit and the van was tilting downwards. She needed to brake.

Hours passed slowly while she stared through the windscreen, back pressed hard against the seat, hands tight on the wheel, following a pale shape that gradually became more solid as dawn came.

At last Tammy held up her hand, Miranda drew up, the girl pointed, 'In there.' The van jolted over stones, branches scraped the roof, a space appeared beside a muddy pool, hidden from the road by low-hanging leaves. One of Don's little secrets, no doubt.

Soon they were devouring most of the remaining bread. It was going to be a long afternoon before they could be on the road again. When they'd finished Miranda stood up and returned to a subject that had been dogging her

'Come here,' she said and waited, a little tense.

Tammy came closer and stood an arms-distance away. Miranda breathed more easily, placed her hands on her shoulders and, meeting no resistance, turned her round and pushed her towards the bathroom. Didn't close the door.

She put the plug in the basin and ran a tap. They weren't going to need to rely on that tank much longer.

'Lean over and I'll wet it.'

The girl wriggled like a much smaller child, pulling away a little at first, but not totally, then relaxing, though still bent-legged, leaning onto the balls of her feet. After a minute her shoulders dropped, she lowered her head further, her right hand stole into the basin, began to join in, slopping water over the ends of her hair.

Miranda felt a surge of warmth. watching these timid, eager dabbings. She worked her fingers heavily backwards and forwards, shifting the scalp, massaging, feeling stringy curls soften and spread, watching the water blacken, pondering.

'My goodness, that's made a difference. Now stand up and I'll rub.'

Tammy bowed her head.

Miranda started combing, holding tresses close to the scalp while she teased out what seemed at first to be impenetrable tangles but slowly straightened and as she let go, fell into curls. She pulled them full length with the brush, lifted, patted so at last they made a soft cap round Tammy's head.

Miranda wiped the condensation off the mirror. 'Now look.'

She looked and said nothing. Miranda was disappointed, though also amazed at who she'd got here.

The new order showed that the ends were straggly. She must have hacked at them with scissors when she was preparing to be a boy. With scissors and hatred. Later she'd let them grow. Now she gave herself a brief, almost horrified, glance and turned from the mirror.

Miranda said nothing, hurried back to the sitting area, said nothing when Tammy seized a bucket and went out.

Later that afternoon she went to the small cupboard above her bed and took out Elizabeth's Homer, sat down on the blue duvet, opened the inside cover, read, 'the first day of the New Dawn,' Elizabeth's graceful, firm writing, felt under the brown paper cover, drew out an ancient photo, stared down a cool, sceptical eyes. Her face creased, she stood up, almost threw the book onto the bed, then stood, bent her elbows, stared down at the fore-arms right-angled forward, touched the freckled brown skin of the left one, pinched it, then harder, harder still, till her lips tightened, she almost stopped breathing, watching the white patch spread.

She let go, crossed to the window, gazed across the pond into the massed leaves. Her hands clenched, she raised her fists and laid them on the glass, pushing against it, leant her head forward, rested it on them, closed her eyes. Eventually threw back her shoulders, straightened, went to see what Tammy was up to.

She was washing the van, washing and polishing, buffing up handles, windscreen, lights. Took no notice of Miranda.

She retreated into the van, came out later as the light evening was drawing out. 'Leave that, Tammy, come on.' She fidgeted round. 'We have to be up before dawn.' She came closer. 'A long way yet.'

Tammy turned her back, mulish, obstinate.

Miranda gazed at it, then wandered off beside the pond. She considered the reflections, watched a water-boatman sculling on its back, turned away into a bramble-free space between the trees, continued till she came to a hillside with a rowan and an assembly of holes, a scrape worn on the steep bank beside them. She examined the ground, smiled, noticed a tree, touched a ring of gnawed bark, listened. Went on listening.

At last she turned back to find Tammy still bent over a wheel. She approached. 'That couldn't be more perfect. Come inside now.'

She got them warm drinks, sat cradling her mug. 'You know, Tammy, the drivers who live in the Breakers' yards are so lucky – to have all this to come up to.'

Tammy snorted. 'Don't ever – not if they don't have to.'

'Why ever not?'

'Don't like it.' A pair of sharp eyes glanced up. 'And what you doing up there? Decent sort don't go there, do they?'

'Don't talk like that.'

'O-o-oh? Why not?'

'Shut up.' She jerked to her feet. 'Give me that mug.'

The next morning shapes were detaching themselves from darkness when they came to the exit gate. She leant back against the seat and gazed through the bars at empty strands of motorway. Twenty miles – and then?

'Come on, Tammy. Do your stuff with the card. Had hoped we'd get here earlier.' The sky was rapidly lightening. Her fingers curled round the wheel. Mist hung over the road. 'Hurry, Hurry,' she called. The gates opened, the van jolted. Tammy had climbed in the back. Quickest thing perhaps.

Gantries sped past. A river. Shadowy hills rose. She fixed her eyes on the road.

Now they were closer, dawn was already defining their edges. There was an outline she recognised. She pressed on. Sunlight crept down the slopes.

Just as the first rays of the sun touched the ground, they came in sight of the guard post. Beyond it a mountain road wound up towards trees. She slowed and examined the bars. There was no electronic slot on the gate, nowhere to insert a card or token.

She slumped. They'd needed darkness to force a way through.

She felt breath over her ear, swung round, looked over her shoulder. Tammy leant through the space between the seats. She was robed in her golden dress with Elizabeth's amethyst scarf as a cummerbund.

'Horn. Sound the horn. And drive. Whatever you does, don't stop.'

The van rocked as the girl ran back inside, and then a second time. She must have opened the side-door.

'Drive, can't you. Horn. Sound the horn.'

Miranda let in the clutch. Leant on the *horn, honk*, honk. Then, suddenly enjoying this reckless absurdity, *honk, honk, honk*, imperious. A guard appeared rubbing his eyes and suddenly she knew what he must be seeing, a figure in a gold uniform standing on the step, demanding entry. *Honk, honk, honk*. Come on, man. Do what you're told.

He stumbled to the gate and swung it open.

Once they were out of sight she drew up under trees. A giggling Dawn Servant slipped into the seat beside her.

Part 8

On the track coming up through the hills from the Breakers Yards, invisibility had been the one great thing. Now it was speed. But some coldness in her chest or stomach or legs was making her flabby. She clutched the wheel. The familiar grip steadied her and as she settled into the van's rhythms, her eyes narrowed. She forced herself to relax – arms, chest, hips, left leg. Any tension could throw the van off-balance. She didn't dare grit her teeth. All the same the skin over her cheeks was taut as she swung the van downhill round hairpins.

Heather and rocks sped past. There was a jagged edge on the right, a glimpse of a cliff the other side of a narrow, stony valley. At last the road levelled beside a burn. Very little chance of coming face to face with another vehicle round here. She put her foot down for the last half mile.

Today again no-one was on duty at the castle. She slowed and looked round. Treetops met over the road. The tarmac was spotted with sunlight.

That cherub, months ago, had spotted the van under the oak.

'We won't rush things – hide the van and then have a day quietly here. Later on we'll go over the hill and introduce ourselves.'

'Won't want us.'

'They'll take us in.' She felt the body in the passenger seat slump lower and responded sharply. 'You heard what Ed said. We'll have to learn to fit in.'

She urged the van ahead as far as the right-angle bend in the road, drew up, checked the track that lay straight ahead. Hard, rough – so wheel prints wouldn't show.

She drove a hundred yards, rounded a corner, switched off, gazed at the undergrowth. 'We want no-one to find it for a long time.'

'Poltic at the gate'll think we went out another way.'

'OK – but –'

Suddenly Tammy opened her door, leapt out, left it swinging, ran round to the driver's door, treated it the same way, stood at the bottom of the steps in her golden dress, waving her hand imperiously. 'Get out, Ranna.'

This time she did grit her teeth. 'We don't want anyone coming across it – for years, if possible. You find the best place.'

And the girl did, a dip at the foot of over-leaning crags, buried behind hazel and brambles, far from the road. The van bumped over the uneven surface, slowed, stopped. Miranda switched off.

Tammy appeared again beside the window. 'Get out, Ranna.'

Miranda pushed her back into the seat, rested her arms on the wheel, looked down. 'Get that dress off.'

Tammy's face dropped. 'What yer mean?'

'Exactly what I said.' She turned her head and stared straight ahead at bramble clambering over rock.

'Don't you like it?' Her voice was rising.

Miranda took a deep breath. 'Don't throw a wobbly at me, young lady. Just do it.'

Tammy clenched her fists, stared into the woman's face, jerked her arms towards the ground. 'But why?' Her voice rose in a wail filled with blank despair.

Miranda set her teeth. 'A cherub could spot you from a mile off. Want that, do you?'

There was a long silence. Then Tammy looked at her sideways. 'No need to talk like that. I'm not stupid.' Her eyes glinted, 'What's the matter with you, Ranna?'

'Look –' The tiredness from which she spoke seemed bottomless, a great sea of it washing over her. 'I wouldn't be here –' She didn't care now if the truth she'd been hiding, trying to spare the child's feelings, came gushing out

– 'if it weren't for you. I'm doing all this for you, for your sake, d'you understand?'

Green eyes stared up. 'All what?'

Miranda pushed her spine back into the seat, then relaxed her hands on the wheel, watched the blood washing back into white knuckles. 'Gave up all I'd ever wanted – for your sake.'

'Didn't need to.' Tammy glared. 'Can look after myself.' She swung away, but remained where she was, three-quarters turned.

Miranda strained her ears. The burn wasn't far off. Apparently the undergrowth was too thick to let sound through. No blackbird rustled among the leaves, no chink of a wren, no woodpecker, jay, curlew. Nothing but this heavy silence.

'You came to me.'

'Plenty of others.' She turned back fiercely. 'Look, don't need no-one. None of them's any good.' She swung away, kicking the ground.

Miranda stared into air that was as heavy and blank as the silence. After a while her arms dropped. 'We're none of us much good, are we?' Did she imagine she heard a raven croaking? Bit too symbolic. 'Sorry, Tammy. I'll get out.'

The girl came closer, her hand slid up towards the handle. Miranda forced a smile. The door opened. Miranda laid her hands on her shoulders, slid down, continued holding her, gazing over her shoulder. Eventually she looked directly into her face. 'This morning, you know, dealing with that Free – you were wonderful.'

Radiance broke into the girl's face and suddenly they were dancing, leaning back on each other's arms, swinging, as the hill, crags, trees whirled round them, laughing, each of them simultaneously gasping, 'D'you remember – way that polite stood gawping?'

When they were out of breath they dropped hands. Grass, rocks, sky. Still no bird's cry or sound of water, the place seemed totally empty.

'This where we going to live?'

'That sleepy Free may have come to by now. There'll be cherubs out searching.' She rested her hand on the bonnet. 'Nothing for it, Tammy. I'm sorry. You'll have to change.' And stayed there leaning on her hand till the girl returned in a vansuit.

Tammy inspected the van. 'Dirty it, shall I?'

'Eh?'

'Harder to see.'

Miranda's fingers pressed against white paint. Then she nodded. 'Makes sense. But later? OK?'

Tammy's lips moved apart as if was about to say – 'cherub' – perhaps? What she did say was, 'Eat?'

They took their picnic down beside the burn, Breakers Yards bread, Hayle raspberry jam, the last of the Hayle eggs, hard-boiled. Peeling off the shells, breaking the rubbery white, coming to the yolk.

Hayle old curtains. Miranda's mind swung to her mother: taking them out of enormous plastic bags, spreading them across the dining-room table – 'Even on the gloomiest day they'll bring in the sun.' Her face turning towards them in the middle of a meal.

And then Tammy wearing them, bringing Mum and her sunshine back, clothing Tammy in Hayle.

Brown water tumbled past, shallower than the Amond, faster, more assertive, its weight continually increased by trickles running in over the banks, falling into pools that eddied and rippled, allowing no tranquil reflections of leaves, no views of golden pebbles.

Miranda watched for a long time. Then she spoke slowly. 'You couldn't ever have known the New Dawn, could you Tammy? It's hard for you to imagine what it was like for us who were there. You'll think it was daft maybe, way we threw ourselves in, chucked out all the clobber, lit bonfires and danced. But for us – '

'What's 'clobber'?'

'Everything that did damage. To save the environment we had to be ruthless.' Her fists pressed into the ground, her face turned fiercely onto the girl. 'Some of it was very hard –' she knew she wouldn't say what but had to look at it – 'We had no mercy on ourselves. That was how it had to be.'

'Kind of running away?'

'How can you be so –' She pulled herself up, 'Never been there, have you?' and spoke slowly, 'The New Dawn was the greatest thing that's ever happened.'

'Now?'

'What d'you mean, now? Nothing's changed.'

Tammy stared, dropped her eyes, shrugged.

'This a new start, Tammy. You need a fresh start.'

She shrugged again. 'Speak for yourself.'

'You said you wanted to come,' Miranda said quietly.

'Couldn't be worse than anything else, could it?'

She fidgetted all morning. Miranda suggested she should try paddling. She took off her vanshoes, rolled up the legs of her vansuit, put her feet in the water, screamed, fell in, demanded to be pulled out.

They found a few leftover biscuits at the bottom of a bag and consumed them. Afterwards Miranda lay back and closed her eyes, couldn't sleep. Tammy snuggled up close. Miranda shifted. The girl lay for a moment, stood, stumped off.

Shadows were lengthening over the burn when Miranda drew her legs under her and leant on a hand. 'D'you remember, when we last came the rowans were in flower? The berries are ripe now.' She fastened her eyes on them. There had been times when all she'd wanted then or for the rest of her life was to go on sitting and watch berries ripen.

After a minute she heaved herself off the ground, took one last look at the burn, all body now, doing what had to be done.

Back at the van she picked up the mask she'd left lying on the table, held it for a moment, threw it down, grabbed clothes, bundled them into her rucksack, stamped on the temptation to switch on the computer and contact Milla. Say good-bye.

She shoved her hand to the back of the cupboard, reached Elizabeth's *Odyssey*, slipped it into her bag. The yellow dress was lying screwed up on the floor. She glanced at Tammy's back, tightened her lips, bent and picked it up, stuffed it in her rucksack.

When she turned she saw Tammy had dragged back her hair and tied it behind her head with a scrap of dirty string. Her face looked sharper, slyer.

Miranda took it all in, swallowed, descended the steps, reached up, locked the door, kept the key in her hand all the time they were doing what had to be done to the van.

When it was finished she set off without a word, charging so fast uphill she was puffing by the very first bend. She let her pace drop, didn't bother to look back, didn't call. If that girl wanted to be a slut – but gradually, as short grass bounced underfoot, the reek of wet bracken crept into her lungs, wind touched her cheeks, she sank into a deep sadness – this was how Tammy felt she had to look, the way she felt safe to face the world. At the top of the pass it seemed right to look back.

She drew back her arm and flung the van keys high into the air, followed their line as they caught the sun and fell through the branches of a stunted rowan into a place she couldn't see. Tammy was still lagging behind.

She waited. The girl stopped altogether.

'Come on.'

She sat down.

'We've got to get there.' After several minutes gazing north to the higher hills, watching cloud pile up over them, tapping her foot, Miranda turned slowly back, sat on the ground beside her. Said nothing for some time.

Then, 'Thanks, for all your help.' She gazed into a silence that hung like fog between them. Eventually she asked, 'Tammy, what did the old woman in the quarry really want? Not just friendly, was she?'

The question produced a sight of an eye. 'You're so innocent, Ranna – though good thing you was. Said what was needed as if you believed it.'

'What exactly did she want?'

'Slavers aren't they? See all those shitty vans?'

'They'd have held us? So why they let us go?'

'You said the right thing so innocently she knew you didn't understand – expected us to go back and park in the same spot.'

'They didn't chase us?'

'Blokes were off somewhere.' She turned full face. 'And we weren't that useful. One thing she'd sussed out. Not strong enough for carrying things, not good-looking enough for anything else. Nothing much in the van worth having.'

'Oh.' And after she'd digested that, 'The Dreamies will be different.'

'Will they?' She hugged her knees. 'Not going.'

'Tammy, for goodness sake –'

She buried her head in her knees. Miranda stood up, bent over. 'We can't do anything else.'

She swung round, snarling. 'Speak for yourself. Got you here, didn't I? What more you want?'

Miranda's fists curled.

'Leave me, Ranna, leave me. Got it?'

Words poured out. 'Not after the way you forced yourself on me. I was managing on my own and you wouldn't let me – Boss – remember? Well, after that – your choice, not mine – you owe me something and that,' she said, throwing back her shoulders, 'is to stop all this moaning – you got plenty of guts. Well, use them, get going.'

Slowly, with her head turned away, Tammy dragged herself onto her feet.

They came to the summit and saw the houses they'd seen on their previous visit. Miranda's steps slowed. She stopped, turned her head right, left, back to the centre, went on looking.

A small man and a large dog rose from the heather – someone with a rucksack, a short grey beard, trousers and top of a material that wasn't fleece or cotton or terylene or – anything –

He held out his hand. 'Hark,' he said, watching them flinch from a direct gaze, 'that's what they call me.'

'Miranda –'

In a whoosh of air Tammy was hurtling downhill. Miranda spun round. A hand grasped her wrist. She tore it away.

She heard him pounding behind her over stones and tussocks of grass, both of them barely able to control the speed. She got her feet under her on the edge of a steep dip, stared at rocks and heather.

He came close. 'Leave her.'

'Can't – must find her – before –'

'Yes?'

'If she goes back to the van –' He was at her side, very quiet, not throwing his weight about. She was panting a little, gasping. 'It's what we did to it.'

'What did you do?'

She remembered sharp edges of stones digging into her knees as she crawled round letting down the tyres, Tammy standing over her. 'What you doing that for, Ranna?'

'So's anyone who finds it thinks it's been here for ages.'

'See to the windows, shall I?'

'Eh?'

'Smash them.'

She forced out an answer through stiff lips, 'If – you – if it's the best thing, yes.'

But now – long slivers of glass lying over the seats. Tammy could get in without the key.

She told him, but not the way the girl had gone at those windows. They went back. She wasn't there.

The burn kept running. A chaffinch examined them from a birch branch. After some time Hark slid her a sideways look. 'I don't think this is her agenda. Let's go back to the top. We'll be completely obvious there. If she wants to find us she'll see and come.'

'I daren't leave this – just in case –'

'No need to hurry.' He turned lightly. 'Good view of the place from here. That looks a good rock. Let's sit, shall we?' They settled their bottoms. The dog came and lay beside them. He opened his rucksack and pulled out a flask. 'Tea?'

It didn't taste like any tea she'd ever drunk

'Like it, do you?' From the corner of her eye she caught him examining her profile. 'We experiment,' he said, 'in every way possible. That's what this place is about.'

'Oh.'

'Pleased to meet you, by the way. They always send an escort so today they picked me.'

She smiled, still didn't look. They sat together, drinking the tea. The flask contained more than might have been expected. Her fingers kept twisting and plaiting knotted stalks of grass.

'This isn't her agenda,' he said again.

'What you mean? You don't know her.'

'She reacted just like a rabbit. In a human, that's panic. Sudden and complete panic.'

'What at?'

He leant towards her. 'I'd need to know her better. You tell me.'

She worked again at the grass. 'No idea.'

'New place? This landscape – big, you know.'

She shrugged, 'Been here before,' concentrating on turning the grass into a single string.

'Strange man?'

'You? Well – Ed told us to get out.' She paused. 'She didn't want to come here.'

'So why did she?'

'Twisted her arm, didn't I?'

He hesitated. 'Don't want to get personal – but she liked you enough to let you?'

'Spooked out by Hayle. And yes, I suppose, yes.' She risked a brief glance into his eyes. 'Could put it that way.'

'She'll come – and when she does the dog'll win her over, he always does, the great soft creature.'

Miranda considered a mass of hair. The animal turned its head. Its eyes were even more appealing than its master's.

He stood up. 'We'll go up to the summit. Be very obvious there.'

It was obvious he knew every step and stone on that path and had a gift for finding comfortable rocks.

He leant forward, rested his arms on his knees, began talking, suddenly flung out an arm. 'The Mains' we call it – Scots term for the Home Farm – though it's more than that – much more – but a good, plain name. Though actually most of the time we simply say 'The settlement.'

While he spoke, her eyes kept swinging sideways to examine a bare cheek, a nostril, grey hair curving over lips, a flappy ear. Outdoor life had covered his cheek with tiny broken blood vessels. There was a large mole high up on the cheekbone, greyish unlike the general brown of his skin.

'From here it's so steep down you get almost an aerial view, the angle I think that bit more acute than from an aircraft. A section's hidden by the curve of the hill.'

She blinked, forced herself to relax.

'There are precisely a hundred houses. You can't see some of them because of the contour line. Your arrival brings the total number of members up to five hundred and seven. That includes children, of course, of which we have thirty-six.'

'I see.'

'Statistics aren't everyone's passion. I love them.'

'Oh.'

'We're happy here,' he said suddenly.

'Compulsory, is it?'

His gaze roamed across the valley. 'Can take time.' He paused for a long breath. 'Took me – years perhaps. Figure I don't want to calculate, far too long.' He released his knees and twisted toward her. 'So much holds us to that madhouse out there.' Large grey eyes were searching for her.

She turned away.

He spoke softly. 'Takes time to see how unreal that world is. Like most of us you need a break to sort yourself out. No-one will mind.'

'Certainly Tammy needs help.'

'I asked to be the one to meet you,' he said, 'because you seemed to be victims of the New Dawn.'

'Not victims.'

'Sorry, sounds so helpless, doesn't it?' He gazed again at the valley. 'But of course you'll be more interested in where you're going. Let's get you orientated. This hill we're on is a spur of the Grandons, that range running there to our right. The atmospheric peak way over to the left with the sun dropping towards it, that's Erdonnell. I sometimes come up here in the evening just to see it framed against the sunset. Much lower of course than Ben Nevis or most of the Highlands. But why judge that way – if it makes you lift your eyes?' He was doing that now, with a kind of quiet rapture. 'The low range opposite slanting away towards it is another spur of the Grandons.'

His voice ran on, slow as the Amond, seeming to belong back in that lost world. He started pointing. 'Willow plantation beside the burn, byre, stable, pig house, fields –'

She followed his gaze to acres and acres of rectangles outlined by walls, making a pattern over whole floor of the valley and the lower slopes of the hills. Some were obviously stubble, others intended for grazing but – the rest. 'So much green at this time of year? Surely not autumn wheat so far north?'

He smiled. 'Field beans. Green manure. You're asking the right questions.'

'Country girl.'

'Ah – but to come back to the settlement. There's the main street, see?'

Again her eyes followed his finger. 'Aligned practically due east-west, ends in the main square, long roof beside it is the great hall – the central cell – where the buzz is. Always something to eat there if you want it. Most of the roofs round it are the houses we live in.'

'Suppose it's what you get used to – remember being on the Downs with my Dad. Ten I must have been, maybe eleven. He was pointing out the farm where he'd been born, the village where he'd taught, the house he and mum had lived in when they were first married – but this doesn't seem a very systematic layout.'

'Too much individual choice for that. As far as possible we 'Dreamies',' he caressed the word, laughing, 'allow people to choose the position and aspect of their home. Though even that brings order, unplanned but instinctive.' He turned two large brown eyes on her. 'I was surprised at first – how sensitive a human group can be – in the right circumstances. See those two terraces? They were what first placed the Main Street – then beyond it that more higgledy-piggledy arrangement – mostly on the eastern edge, d'you see? The romantics fancy that and then there's the hermits – I'm exaggerating of course – places for one or two of them out in on the hills. See that cottage, there tucked in under the birches? That's Tong's. Comes in most days, does his share of work, no problem but best going back to his own company in the evening. Great musician. Composer. We think he gets his inspiration from the winds.'

'Before the New Dawn there were composers who imitated the birds. Messiaien, remember?'

He nodded. 'Listened to the experts. It's very rarely silent here you know. If you listen there's always water, a bird or simply something falling. Effect of the wind or some little creature going about its business. So you're not alone either.'

Miranda sensed a movement in the air and swung round. 'Where the hell you been?'

Tammy gave the sweetest smile, sat down, glanced at Hark under her lashes.

He went on talking. 'Now for the practical end of the business. Windmills, you've seen, solar panels – on all the roofs, see? Archimedes screw in the burn, anaerobic digester – for slurry, our sewage etc. Nothing wasted.'

Miranda followed his line. 'A very natural way of life.' She kept glancing at Tammy, sitting there, demure as a little brown bird, continually tense under its feathers.

'In some ways. That double storey complex over to the left is the labs.'

'In this wilderness?'

He laughed. 'They call us "Dreamies" but actually the first founders were very practical people. They'd stockpiled solar panels and brought the lot. We've gone on from there developing resources of energy. Water, wind, methane, hydrogen. Though everything has its limitations of course. World Universities have assigned us the project to develop the most capacious battery possible. Computers are greedy things.'

'I'm not scientific. I can't do anything like this.'

'Perhaps Tammy will turn out to be interested?'

The angle of her nose suggested otherwise.

'Last but not least – the radio mast. That keeps us in touch.'

'With what?'

'Universities, mostly. There was a great exodus of academics at the New Dawn – which resulted in the outlandish fact that in this universe Cambridge, Mass. and Cambridge, England are only a few miles apart. Did you know that? We laugh about it sometimes. More seriously we access their data.'

His eyes were following a buzzard as it circled, slipped sideways, soared over the moor. 'That's what I like about this place. All our jobs are about the same thing. I was in the labs this morning. This afternoon Brindle and I came up to check the ewes. Then we met you.'

His eyes were still with the buzzard. 'Not as if it were an eagle – buzzards are no threat to lambs unless one's already weakened by something else. That's nature. The buzzard'll take mostly rabbits.'

'Yes.'

'That's what's so good about this place – that we aim to live out what we are, not to pretend we're the great kings or the great know-alls, just creatures who evolved on this planet along with all other forms of life.' His eyes opened as his voice swept along. 'We want to do as little damage as possible, not to dominate or exterminate – simply share the planet with its other inhabitants.'

Tammy squawked and slapped her right leg. Then the left. She leapt up clawing her hair. Miranda felt a ferocious jab on her cheek.

Hark and she pulled themselves up.

'Calm down, Tammy.'

'Can't stick this place.'

Hark looked full at her. 'Midges.'

She gazed back, probing. 'What's that?'

'Insects.' He stood quietly, accepting the insolence of her gaze and, apparently, stings that kept both of the others slapping. 'Should have thought, not kept you up here in the evening without suits. Let's go down quickly.'

He talked all the way, about a population of red squirrels, methods of applying methane, a culture in which new materials could be grown from cells, the medicinal uses of lichens, that two pairs of merlins had raised chicks, that he'd identified a range of different soil types within a mile's radius of the settlement.

Miranda struggled to concentrate, partly because the midges had taken a fancy to her blood, partly because she was noting stone walled fields where sheep, horses, cattle were grazing – what else had she expected? The radio mast, a cluster of other masts, the dark houses, the much larger two-storey building, the meshes of a new life drawing in.

She started to keep her eyes on the ground as if watching where to place her feet, as if, in a new place, mud might stick, drew apart from her companions, didn't allow herself to drop behind.

Hark slowed at the last corner above the village. 'They all tell me I talk too much. You'll get used to it.'

'Go on, Hark, just keep talking. It's interesting.' His sentences were curtains, shimmering in the gathering dusk.

They descended a long twisting path with a clear view down onto roofs where solar panels lay on top of heather, and as they came lower in among the houses their shoulders were level with the edge of the thatch, the ridge still high above.

'Like the traditional black houses,' she murmured while at the same time noting hawsers stretched from the eaves to the ground, holding roofs against winds.

And then it was the High Street. She couldn't keep her eyes off the little front gardens. Roses still in bloom – and hollyhocks, a few pink and cream flowers still standing tall in October against the rough darkness of dried heather.

A shaggy poncho was crossing the square as they came to it. He grinned and raised a hand. 'Hiya.'

She drew back, didn't look and then did, remembered from a long way back – a smile was expected.

'That beetle you discovered, Hark – Jay's done a thorough search of all the literature, been onto Cambridge, Beijing, Harvard. None of them know it. You've got a first there. Well done, boyo.'

Hark waved an airy hand. 'We met by accident – just being in the right place at the right time.'

He brought them to the hall door. Miranda looked it over – that weight of wood, plain but well shaped. Nice.

Part 9

She counted steps down – one, two, three, four, watching her feet – took a first rapid glance at a room that seemed all shadow.

Far off to her right was a group of occupied armchairs from the depths of which a shape unfolded onto its feet. A male voice was reassuring, 'Come and sit down. We're so glad to see you.' A hand summoned them forward.

Miranda tried to smile; her eyes, encountering theirs, slid to the ground. She advanced awkwardly, almost sideways. No-one seemed the least surprised.

'Miranda and Tammy? These two seats are for you. I'm Pete, this is Tilia – Frag – Doe.'

Tammy glared at the chair, dragged it round 180°, plonked herself down. No-one reacted.

Miranda concentrated on sitting neatly and crossing her legs. She pulled her lips into a smile. She could feel their eyes. Hers refused to leave the ground. The huge room was a blurred weight all round. As her gaze rose through the silence, four motionless figures slowly shaped up, four maskless faces; two men and two women wearing strange clothes. None of them with much to say apparently. If they didn't want to talk she was happy not to.

After a long pause the tallest one, the one who called himself Pete murmured, 'Glad you've made it here. Of course Hark will have given you tea on the hill but we've laid out a little something to welcome you.'

There was a small table beside him with cups and cakes. He poured and handed round with quiet, precise movements.

Tilia was almost opposite Miranda. Black hair rioted round her face. Her red cheeks were amazing.

Hands seemed safer to examine than faces, and Tilia's were remarkably beautiful, pale and soft with no signs of manual work – but Hark had said everyone did it.

Frag wore a dark poncho and had enormous hands, freckled, pudgy, with blunt fingertips. They looked good for grasping fence posts and hammers. Weeks later, when the community was building Arv's house, she'd watch his fingertips caress planed wood. Another day he'd bandage her wrist – the day she put her hand into dry grass and it turned out to be concealing a wild rose.

Doe was a full-breasted someone in a dark poncho, leaning back with clasped hands. Miranda didn't dare look up to discover whether she was considering their interweaving or examining the new arrivals.

From the corner of her eye she caught Tammy holding up a cup cake, rotating it, examining it from all sides. She glanced at their hosts. No-one said anything. Or even particularly looked. Ever since they'd arrived these people had reached out so little, no introductory explanations, no questions, no chit-chat. They'd sat there smiling, offering cake, waiting. Presumably thinking.

She leant back and began examining her surroundings: hatch at the far end with tables and chairs set out on a rug, long table pushed against one wall, bookshelves crammed with books, music centre, piano, row of blue cupboards, pelargoniums and begonias in pots ranged high up along the window sills. Nothing sinister. Which had to count for something.

Her eyes rested a long time on the walls. White plaster, not black like the exterior, the surface not undulating as if there were joins underneath but smooth. Gradually she became aware of a scent she'd spend time later trying to work out what it was, something that always scented the Home Room. Not thyme, nor roses, nor honey.

Four small legs crossed the outside of the window. She blinked, worked it out – cat, at street level, raised her head, saw Doe smiling. Relaxed her lips into a smile. This quiet had wrapped itself round her like silk, gathering her and the reception committee into one.

Eventually Doe stood up. 'I'll take you to your room.' She waited for the pair of them to move. 'We're sorry it's not a full home.'

Miranda's eyes widened.

'Arv and Solana are having a baby. Second.' She paused as if giving weight to what she'd said – or maybe examining it. 'We're at full stretch extending their house. Finish that, help you build yours.' Again that pause. 'No need to panic – about building – we're experts.'

She led them out again into the square and along the street, a large woman who put down her feet down lightly on the paving planks. Her hips swayed gently. In the last light of day her hair looked faintly red.

Miranda listened to the sound of feet on the wooden surface, a dull, firm plonk, more homely than the hollow drumming of the bridge over the Amond, a very sensible, sustainable way of covering damp ground.

Doe stopped outside another well-made door. 'Hope you feel comfortable with us. Things to explain – can wait.' She looked out across the moor. 'From here – no way back. Everyone has to fit in.'

She still didn't face them as she spoke and this made Miranda more aware of the soft blend of near black, indigo and madder in the darkness of a poncho resting over generous hips. Doe went on describing how everyone here allowed room to all the others; Miranda studied natural dyes.

'You'll have your own place. Soon as it's ready. One thing – a lot of people here have come loaded with a past.' She mentioned Hark, as someone still wrestling. She didn't say why, outlining his need for space. 'Like a number of others you'll get to know. If anyone needs time out – most of us from time to time – even the founders – pretty stable lot on the whole – but in a small community – in a remote place – give each other room.'

She flung open the door of no 6 and descended steps. 'First right. For time being. Hadn't banked on new members. Ed pressing. Very.'

It was a moderate size, white-washed like the Home Room, two windows at shoulder height, a red and blue carpet, two beds with woven bedspreads, two chairs, two small chests of drawers, a small table.

'Kitchen in your own place. Till then come to the Home Room. Always something available. Anyone not cooking is there in the evening. Take this cream.' She produced a brown jar from the folds of her poncho. 'To protect skin. Make sure your wear it – faces, hand, arms, anywhere exposed.' She flung out her hands. 'Hope – hope you'll be happy. We like newcomers. You'll hear the bell.'

She left. Miranda began slowly unpacking, laying clothes on the bed Tammy wasn't sitting on, stowing them in drawers. She didn't look at the girl.

When she'd finished she turn to look. Tammy was sitting with her feet on the bedspread, hiding her face against her knees.

'It's all right, Tammy. We'll manage.'

The reply was muttered into bony flesh. 'Do care, don' you, Ranna?'

'Suppose so.' Miranda stood tense, looking her up and down.

'Told you before, stupid to care.'

'I don't think so.'

'You need to learn.'

Lips tightened. 'Sit up and speak clearly.'

The voice became shrill. 'Don' get it, do you?'

Miranda went on looking, edged nearer. 'We're in a good place.'

'That's it, innit?' A grey face stared out. 'These are good people.' Tammy burst into tears.

Miranda laid her hands on her shoulders. They weren't shaken off. She moved them slowly round onto her back, pulled her in towards her, held her in silence.

The girl rested against her, passive but stiff, resisting a little. Then she pushed her violently away. 'Get off, Ranna. Think you know it all, don't you?'

Miranda reached for her jerko.

'Where you going?'

'Dining room.'

'Why can't we eat here?'

They'd been shouting for some time when Doe stood in the doorway. They turned to face her, suddenly silent. Miranda's eyes fell.

'We're waiting to start dinner.'

Next morning Pete organised Miranda into the party digging the foundations of Arv and Solana's extension.

'What about Tammy?' she asked, studying a sullen face.

Doe swooped down. 'Tammy, I'd like company whitewashing the byre. Think you could give a hand?'

The girl opened her mouth. Doe watched impassively, except that the ends of her lips twitched. 'Come on. Let's get going.'

Miranda hesitated, half raised a hand, jerked herself round, marched off with the work-party.

She took the spade someone handed her. It was good work, jab, heave, throw; steady, monotonous, absorbing. Pete trundled the barrow. They went at it until he called them for myrtle tea and they sat with their legs hanging over the edge of what was by now a sizeable hole, Miranda, Pete, Marlin, Fili, Brock. Solana was in the labs with an experiment.

'Arv's our top chef so we don't waste his talents digging holes. Well actually,' Brock added, 'only when it's all hands. Could be Solana will be available when we come to yours.'

By lunchtime her back was aching.

'Need practice, don't you?' Fili didn't seem to be criticising, more stating facts. 'World of cars out there gets you out of touch. You'll shape up eventually. Did well sticking it so long.'

Miranda shrugged and stroked the grass.

Fili narrowed her eyes and gazed. 'If you don't mind my saying – you're like Hark.'

Miranda shrugged again.

'When he first came here. Though you're not quite in the state he was. He was shattered, soggy like uncooked sourdough. That was one of the first things we did – taught him to make sourdough – didn't like that – the activity not intellectual enough, but when he tasted how good flatbread is hot off the girdle, pennies began to drop, he began to imagine it might be possible to make a new life.'

The sun was warm. Her back was aching.

She'd have liked to lie back, instead gestured towards a heap of black walling material. 'What's that stuff?'

'Watwill. Like to have a look?'

They wandered across. Fili handed her a strip. 'Feel it.'

Miranda frowned, bending it backwards a forwards. There was enough play for it to curve a very little and straighten. 'You know – when I saw the walls first – thought they were stone – what else would be black like that? Absurd, I know. Never been any industry for miles and here was I looking for soot. Then when we came indoors I saw the interior walls didn't – didn't show signs of courses of stone – so decided they must be hardened mud. Wattle and daub, is it? Something like that? But it's flat.'

'Made of specially treated willow wands.'

'Oh?'

Miranda listened as Fili's soft voice murmured a loving recital of processes: cut long wands, strip off the bark, crush and soak them, run a long comb through them to separate strips, weave them, put a roller over, lay them over a huge pit of boiling water, let the steam felt them. Her fingers moved, sliding to grip and pull.

The sun was still warm, a buzzard was wheeling overhead. Everything was quiet apart from Pete and Frag murmuring not far away,

'Think I might fancy a go at that.'

'Wait till you smell the retting pits. Could have a go at combing. Heavy work though.'

Miranda scrabbled round the edges with her fingers. 'Thin.'

'We use two layers, ten centimetres apart, fill the cavity with fleece or dry bracken –'

'That's it – of course.'

'Er?'

'Really is bracken – scent in the home-room, very faint – I did wonder, of course – a very faint whiff of dry bracken.' She pulled herself in. 'Sorry.'

'OK.' Fili produced a slow smile. 'Shall I continue? We cover the external wall with oily plaster. Same oil we use that in the clay that holds the base of the walls'

'Oil?'

'From the peat hag. You must have seen the oily sheen on pools between the heather?'

Miranda looked into a distance, tugged at grass. Her face clouded

'No oil source can be sustainable forever – we try not to use too much. Arv's immersed in experiments – to see if he can find something else. No luck so far.'

Then again all afternoon, jab, heave, throw; jab, heave, throw, workers falling into a shared rhythm. Sun on her back, wind in her hair, quiet hills, her back aching.

At last Pete straightened and waved a hand. 'Miranda, think you could you take those mugs back to the kitchen? Then that's it. Enough slog for a first day.'

When she got back to the room, Tammy wasn't there. She was alone in that calm, well-insulated room; the only sounds chickens clucking in Frag's garden, a slight rustle in the thatch that could have been a bird or a mouse or wind. She fell asleep.

'We was making the place nice for animals.' All Tammy could find to say about her day. She sounded dubious.

Miranda opened a reluctant eye.

Tammy splashed water over her chest and face, threw herself on her bed.

Miranda curled away. Later she heaved herself onto her feet, dressed, looked down. 'Supper, come on.'

She had her hand on the door when a voice materialised. 'Ranna, these people are creepy.'

'Creepy? You said yesterday they're good.'

No answer. She sighed and turned back. 'Was it Doe? What did you talk about?'

'Not much. With me and didn't talk.'

She thought back to her morning. Fili and she had sat with their feet hanging over the edge of a hole they'd dug, warm sunshine on their shoulders, rested, talked, then stopped, shared that quiet digging.

'They have this way of not talking,' she said firmly. 'Could be restful.'

'Not real. She's soft, like you. They're all soft.' She suddenly scowled. 'Don't know nothing about life.'

A week later Miranda stood in front of the mirror holding in her stomach, tight, tight, turning to view herself.

'Fancy yourself do you?'

'Our first Monthly Dinner.' Her voice rose harshly, 'Should be great, Tammy.' And as she listened to herself, she modulated into warmth. 'Why don't you run a comb through your hair? You'd look amazing – and you did so well working with Doe all day.'

She was the one met them at the door. 'I've put you next to me, Miranda.' She turned with a smile to someone behind her. 'Hark, here's Tammy. Take charge, will you?'

He held out a hand. The girl looked him up and down, shrugged, moved forward.

Almost as soon as they'd sat down at the long tables, Pete called them to their feet again for the toasts. Miranda looked along the line of people in thick clothes holding glasses. She picked up hers.

'We're trying our hands at myrtle wine.' Doe murmured.

'First to Hark's beetle.' he paused. 'I have to announce we received the confirmation today – it's been officially recognised as a new species.' He paused again looking around. 'Let's raise our glasses to *Scaraboides Harkensis*.'

Voices rang out in chorus, '*Scaraboides Harkensis*.'

Miranda glanced at Hark, a few places down on the opposite side. He was looking down, blinking.

'Secondly but no less important, the purpose we must never forget, 'The hope of lessening our impact.'

'Of lessening our impact.'

They sat. The cooks carried in huge, fragrant bowls. People passed them from one to another, helping themselves. The room became quiet. The air grew warm. Miranda bent over her plate.

Cutlery clattered. Gradually voices resumed and flowed up and down the long table. She ate slowly, investigating what vegetables were in the stew, keeping her eyes mostly down, though a flick upwards told her whatever it was the man sitting opposite was wearing it wasn't a jerko. She wriggled inside hers, glanced along the row at Tammy, who looked mildly sullen, nothing worse.

This man who didn't have a jerko was leaning towards her across the table. 'It's something very modest, really, we aim at. Just to reduce our impact on the planet.'

She jerked to attention. 'Yes. Of course.' She gazed at him, her face creasing.

'Ford,' he said. 'We haven't met before.'

'Ah – Miranda.'

'Welcome, Miranda.'

She tried to smile but her face, eyes, shoulders, body were heavy.

Doe nudged her gently. 'More potatoes, Miranda?'

She blinked, sat up, took the spoon she was offered. 'Potatoes,' she said, spreading out the word, tasting it. 'Those red vita – "carrots" – look wonderful too.'

Doe's lips were quivering. Miranda stared sideways. Their eyes met.

Doe pulled herself together. 'Sorry. Should know. New arrivals always like that. All were.'

'Like what?'

'Longing – for those words. "Beet – root", she said, dramatically stretching and projecting her lips.

Miranda collapsed.

After that they got on with the business of eating. By the time Miranda had said what gloriously old-fashioned things they ate here and demolished a plateful of apple pie and cream, she was looking round her more boldly.

She turned to Doe. 'Thanks for taking Tammy off my hands.'

'General policy. Hark will look after her.'

Doe watched her face. 'Lovely chap. Know why we call him Hark?'

'No.'

She laughed, that plump, rumbling laugh. '"Hark, hark, the lark", you know?'

'Oh – "at heaven's door doth sing"?'

'That's Hark – always endless praises for whatever it is. Not stupid, just excited – very observant – loves small creatures. Discovered that beetle. Meticulous notes. Show you sometimes. We use them as models.'

Miranda sat expressionless.

'Won't lay a finger on her – if that's what you're afraid of.'

'It was her more – doesn't get on with men.'

'Hark's gay,' she said softly.

'I see – well, yes, maybe.'

She waved Tammy off each morning, got on with whatever job was allocated, learnt some names and then more, came to understand the routine, didn't bother with conversations – everyone seemed friendly but nothing to do with her. In the evening she'd sit beside the bookshelves in the Home Room, slip away if talk threatened, go to bed, turn her back on the other bed, curl up facing the wall, sleep.

When she was free Doe would sometimes come, sit beside her in the Home Room, say nothing. The comfortable silence that seemed endemic to this place spread round them.

One evening Miranda broke it. 'I've never thanked you for interrupting our shouting match that first evening.' Her fingers twisted together. She looked down at them. 'Must have made a very bad impression. I'm really sorry you had to.'

'Pressed, weren't you?'

Miranda squirmed, then relaxed, nodded. 'Had enough.' She shot a hooded glance. 'Also – to tell the truth – I was as scared as she was.'

'Yes?'

She gazed into the shadows of the room, pulled back her shoulders. 'Having to share space – I didn't want her weighing in all the time, breathing down my neck, insisting on my attention. Even in the van there's been some little space I could call my own. And then – I wasn't used to other people.' Words were threatening to become a torrent. 'Those few days at Hayle I spoke to no-one, except Ed and I'd known him way back. Since then I'd had years on my own. Seems ridiculous really, to be terrified of you and Doe and Hark and Pete and all the others. But I was.' For the first time she looked Doe full in the face. 'During all the time I had been unpacking the terror had been rising. Somehow the fact that I'd seen some of the members made it worse. They'd been so real, there in front of me, barefaced – but I couldn't make them out. Can you imagine what it's like – naked faces after years of masks? I'd lost the knack of reading expressions.

'Didn't react there in front of you all, but when Tammy and I were alone in our room – began to feel cold – empty – as if I was nothing. Tried – swallowed down panic, threw back my shoulders, told myself it was idiotic, unworthy, all those things. Perhaps it would have been better if I could have been honest with Tammy. She probably smelt the fear and that increased her panic.' She relaxed into a shy smile. 'We were a pair, weren't we? I hid it from her, pretended to be in charge, when I knew I was completely at sea.'

After that they were often in the same work-group. And Doe told her about Hark.

That was after Tammy set fire to Miranda's bed.

Miranda came home from the moor, opened the door, smoke got her in the throat; she turned, hurtled up to the Home Room yelling. Pete emerged from somewhere. He rounded up a gang, they all came rushing with buckets.

Fumes were still pouring off when they allowed her back in. She stood in the centre of the room, choked, stared – ceiling and walls – grey smears, black streaks; charred scraps of sheets and duvet, mattress still smouldering, blackened springs poking through. Her bed grimy, but relatively intact.

Pete turned. 'How did it happen, Miranda?'

'Came back and found it.'

'Was Tammy here?'

'I've no idea.' She gazed heavily into his face and looked away. 'How could something like this happen?'

He looked round the room. A cupboard door was swinging. He jerked it full open. Nothing. Miranda stared inside. All her clothes had gone.

He opened Tammy's cupboard. Her things all there, including the yellow dress that Miranda had secretly brought from the van. There it was, hanging in front of everything the girl owned. Miranda's lips twisted; she looked away, sighed. Such a scanty collection, so little that was nice.

Pete looked at her. 'This couldn't just start on its own. Something – someone had to cause it.'

'Yes.'

'Where do you think she's gone?'

'Up the hill? Where else?'

They set about searching. Hark came into his own, a skilled shepherd accompanied by his dog. He came back gently driving her ahead of him like a sickly ewe. 'Found her shivering in a hole under those crags half way up Mangon.

Doe took them to her place. 'Empty nest. Needs filling.' Separate rooms for each.

As soon as the door closed Miranda sank onto the bed and closed her eyes.

Quiet gathered around her, became oppressive. She turned onto her other side, screwed her eyes tighter shut, curled in; couldn't sleep.

When she got up, a much less pale-faced Tammy was lounging in Doe's sitting room. When Miranda came in she looked up, grinned, went on grinning all through supper, chattered cheerfully.

Miranda was the one sank away into silence, stared occasionally at Tammy, didn't raise her eyes towards Doe; would have slunk back to her room if Doe hadn't stopped her.

*

From then on, in the daytime the community kept them apart. Doe brought hot food, myrtle wine, talked about this and that. She encouraged her to join work parties. Where everyone treated her without any special gentleness, as if nothing had happened.

She dug, painted walls, mended library books, washed up, anything she was asked to, sometimes as part of a group, sometimes with just one or two other members, sometimes on her own.

There were long hours in the Home Room – the Great Hall as she'd come to call it – gently taking down the books, opening them with the tips of her fingers, turning over pages to find which were loose, stroking crumbling, powdery paper, noting foxing and stains, wondering how many fingers had turned them over, how many minds had taken in what they had to say.

Pete brought Frag's paper, advancing towards the table where she'd spread the books, bearing this block like some great treasure. He put it down gently. 'Grass paper.'

The block shone with a faint green tinge.

'Frag made it before the New Dawn. His hobby was papermaking. Spent hours researching traditional methods. Can imagine him, can't you?'

She pictured that clumsy looking man with such powers of concentration, nodded.

'This is pretty well transparent.' He got out a penknife and inserted the tip gently under what she now saw as a top layer and lifted. 'Look.'

She saw the table through it.

'You'll need to cut it. There's fresh horn-glue in a jar in the cupboard.' He showed her how to use them both.

She was days at the job, cutting and glueing, placing, smoothing that cool pearl under her fingers, seeing it make a page firm, blend in, almost disappear. So many battered books. Still treasured. In a place where apparently no-one for ages and ages had used books. Every room had a computer. Every pocket contained a k-card. Fingers were always tapping screens. The library shelves were stacked with e-books. Yet here they were, piles of old print. She began to hum as she worked.

Then they sent her out to the byre to be with the cows. She'd go in early, find them sitting, they'd turn great sleepy heads, lumber to their feet and gather round, stretching out slobbery noses, huge blue eyes gazing up under pale, curly lashes. They get in her way as she pulled down hay and filled troughs, never trod on her feet or pushed her over, even while their belches and the grassy reek of their breath poured round her. Great, lumbering beasts, light on their toes as cats. And just as inquisitive.

She'd been beginning to sweat shovelling muck, taken off her jerko; turned round, a slimy nose was marking it up and down, then crossways. A long blue tongue appeared and began twisting. She jumped forward, grabbed.

'Must be dull for them,' she said to herself, 'shut in the byre all winter. But even in the field soon as something new appears they all have to see. An audience of large blue eyes.'

As December moved into January and the days lengthened into February Tammy was more often at meals at the same time as Miranda. They spoke in a civilised way under Doe's supervision.

Miranda put questions aside and went walking. There were some lovely days at the end of February and people were still being very kind. She couldn't figure out why.

After making herself useful mornings, she'd take herself off up the hills. Stones bit her boots, rock and the distant hills were reservoirs of calm, clouds re-shaped, their shadows moved on the grass, a free wind stung her cheeks, ravens croaked.

Just beyond the horizon vans were being electronically hooked into streams, masked drivers turning into the gates of overnights, finding allocated slots, locking themselves in.

A dead leaf was drifting about in a place – that wasn't strange – she'd been in places like this before the New Dawn – but undeserved, wrong – however much it might stretch out its hands.

She'd find energy sometimes in the byre, slapping the rump of a cow, 'Come one, girlie, get over,' and the animal would heave itself sideways, trying not to tangle its feet in hers, swing its head towards her and gaze, friendly and dumb.

Quiet was far from what Tammy was the evening she came bouncing in to show off her poncho.

'Where'd you get that, Tammy?'

'Solana helped me make it. Like it?' She folded it across her, coy and looked through her eyelashes.

'Don't do that.'

'Why not?' She glanced at Miranda under her lashes, lifted her arms and spun round on tiptoe. Waves of multi-coloured wool woven in an openwork pattern of shells shimmered around her. Her hair, which was long now and shiny, swung free. The air seemed to come alive.

Miranda's voice was cold. 'Very nice. Mind you look after it.'

The glow left Tammy's face. 'Ranna?'

'Said it was nice, didn't I?'

'Supper's ready.' Doe swept them to table.

Afterwards Miranda looked and said nothing when Solana collected Tammy for some activity or other. Doe and she washed up.

'You were a bit rough with Tammy.'

'Said I liked her poncho, didn't I?'

'You did. Rose-hip tea?'

She suppressed a sigh. 'Lovely.'

'Go and sit down. I'll bring it.'

She sank luxuriously into the cushions on Doe's sofa, spread herself over pinks and purples, splashes of orange, looked round the room, saw how their warmth infiltrated the cool of white walls. Her face softened. Though one foot was tensed against the floor.

Doe came swimming back with mugs. 'Here you are.' She sank down on a chair, facing her but at a distance, planted her legs, let her knees fall apart. 'End of the day.'

'Yes.'

'Wonderful place this, but hard work.'

Miranda looked her over, hesitated. 'You're a founder member?'

'One of those who won the right for this place to exist.'

'Can't imagine how you did it.'

'Pig-headedness. Tell you some time.'

The lamp that picked out foxy highlights in tumbling curls showed up the shadows under her eyes. Although she seemed relaxed there was a kind of watchfulness about her.

'Fine,' Miranda said.

At last Doe stirred, her eyes rose. 'Miranda, you need to come to terms with Tammy.'

'Nothing to come to terms about. I'm quite happy. So's she, having a wonderful time tripping round with Solana et al.'

'Hark, mostly.'

'OK, then, Hark.'

'She's fond of you, Miranda.' Firmness had slid into her voice.

Miranda launched a stare across the space between them. 'And I'm fond of her, of course.'

'After what she did? Be real, woman. You're furious.'

'No. Not worth getting bothered about.'

'Beneath you?'

Miranda drew in a breath. 'Not how I'd put it, just indifferent, really. Do we have to discuss this?'

Doe's jaw compressed. 'As you said – a founding member. This community – everything. Not going to have it come to grief – bad relationships – caused by new arrivals. Can't afford it. Too few of us.'

Miranda's eyes sank.

'Come on,' Doe said leaning forward, sliding a hand over the poncho resting on her thigh, 'give it a go.'

Miranda pushed her hands together. The warm colours all round seemed to be stifling consideration of her rights. Eventually she said, 'The day we arrived Tammy said "These are good people". Perhaps, Doe, I'm not up to it?'

She gave a harsh chuckle. 'Try another line.'

'What you want? What have I got to confess to? I'd like to pay for the restoration of that room –' that was a grand gesture 'if I could but there's no money here. I've taken my share of work. More or less. Could do more afternoons. Look,' she said sitting up, 'I'll put in full time every day. That enough?'

Doe sipped her tea. 'Nothing to do with it – and you know it, Miranda.'

It wasn't the spread of her shoulders or the way she'd planted her feet that got Miranda glaring but the way she dared to hold her head, the authority she allowed in her voice.

She went on the same way, 'We can see you're exhausted.'

The royal "We".

'We very much admire how you must have coped with Tammy on your own –'

What a lot of words – by her standards – she'd managed to pack into one breath, all blarney. 'We've had one or two little ups and downs with her –'

'Why didn't you tell me?'

'Thought you didn't want to be responsible,' she remarked blandly.

She sat up. 'I can take it.'

'And you have.' She leant forwards; Miranda shrank back.

'It's taken it out of you – when she set fire to your bed it was the last straw.'

'The last straw standing on end.' That was true. But what came to her just then was how that girl had turned her back on them all in the Home Room. A feral creature.

'If you can speak of it with that degree of humour – perhaps there's hope.' Doe's eyes were green like Elizabeth's. But contained brown flecks that gave them warmth. 'She's fond of you, you know.'

'You keep saying that. Funny way of showing it.'

'She appreciated your efforts. She likes you.' She paused, 'Loves you, I think I mean.'

'So why did she burn my bed?'

Silence. Then she said, 'I'll leave you to work that out.'

On the way to the building site next morning, she murmured. 'Find it helps newcomers – talk to Sal – very understanding – sometimes helps them record their story on disc – think over what brought them here – could fix it for you. Like that, Miranda?'

'Maybe.'

'OK – Easy time this morning. Be impressed.'

The machine looked like a line of scaffolding extended along the edges of the trenches into which the base of the wall would fit. A system of cables and pulleys gripped a wooden frame that held two layers of watwill with a couple of centimetres air-gap between them. Arv bent and pressed a switch. The first wall rose, shaking a little but silent. The bottom dropped into place, the top quivered and was still. Then a second, a third, a fourth. The rectangle was complete, windows and doors already cut.

Miranda showed nothing. 'Same principle as pre-made before the New Dawn.'

'Why not?'

She gave an elaborate shrug, turned away. And back. 'Out here?'

Doe smiled. 'Fastening them together. Watch.'

Arv stopped the machine and began to pull himself up foot-hold at one corner of the scaffolding. A rope attached to his belt shook as he climbed. When he reached the top he pulled a huge needle from his belt and began to thread rope through a series of holes running vertically down the two edges, lacing them together. Solana, Fili and Pete tackled the other three. They all reached the ground and stood looking up.

'OK, Arv.'

Wheels began to move again, an arm lowered grips holding huge cables onto hooks on the top of the walls.

'Oh – I thought they held the thatch in place.'

'Watwill – flaps in high wind. Might take off.'

Other cables were run across the interior at beam-height.

'Must be visible inside.'

'Painted to match roof. Any way – you don't look up.'

Miranda smiled ruefully. 'Probably not.' She went on staring at the scaffolding. 'Doe – that machine. Powered how?'

'Electricity. Generate it – solar, wind – must've seen? Not spotted the anaerobic digester? Behind the byre? Archimedes screw in the burn. Every way we can. Better batteries – hold bigger charge longer. Solana's pigeon.'

'Ah – only for some jobs?'

'Digging's good – contact with soil.' She swung to face her companion. 'We're too few. More manual work than we could do and get on with research – and gazing. Gazing's vital. Need machinery.' She let her gaze swing away over the hills. 'That's what we're about – living scientifically – as part of nature. Not dominating, you know?'

Miranda nodded. Then her face clouded. 'But anything we do is interference.'

'Can humans help that?'

Miranda curled away.

Some weeks later Solana arrived just as they were finishing cooking. 'Hark's taken Tammy up to the hall for the evening.'

Miranda looked up sharply. 'Everything OK?'

Solana spread her hands. 'So-so.'

'So what?' And as Solana hesitated. 'Did she go for you?'

'Why would she do that?'

It was Miranda's turn to hesitate.

'Sat down – that was all. We were clearing dead wood in the upper wood and she sat down.'

'Oh dear.'

'Nothing the matter. Said she didn't feel like it.'

Doe chuckled. 'Sounds like our young lady.'

'We left her to it. She tried to slope off when she thought no-one was looking but Pete wasn't having any. Then Hark came through. Said he'd take her up on the moor. She looked thunder – no intention of budging – but the dog got to her – hugging it then onto her feet. Very hard to resist that animal when it gets its eyes on you.'

'Like its owner,' Doe said.

Solana laughed. 'Anyway it or he'll've taken charge for the evening. A couple of other youngsters – Carex and Sal, I think, going to be up there. See if she can mix.' She turned. 'Must get back.'

'How old's Tammy?' Doe asked as they sat down to their meal.

'Eighteen, she told me.'

Doe gave a level glance.

Miranda met it. 'When she took me over she pretending to be about ten. A Devil Driver mask's much that age and she was small and skinny enough to get away with it. I'm beginning to put her at fourteen, fifteen maybe. We'll never know exactly, will we?'

'Understands too much,' Doe said slowly.

Miranda paused fork half way to her mouth. 'Does she?' Her eyes fell away, she filled her mouth, chewed, swallowed, looked up. 'Does she understand anything at all?' Her hands lowered towards the table as if she was going to lay down her knife and fork. Instead she speared a lump of potato, went on eating.

Later, over tea, Doe asked, 'She doesn't understand?'

'Swings. All over you one minute – next – setting fire to your bed.'

'Miranda –'

She hardened her face to it. 'All those moments – since we left Hayle – thought we were becoming happy together – must have been a complete illusion.'

'Perhaps she changes?'

'So volatile she can't ever be trusted? That what you mean? Or just shallow – can't make any relationship?'

'Can happen,' she said softly. 'Sorry, Miranda.'

'Doesn't matter. More fool me.'

Doe sat still. Then, 'Not necessarily so.'

'I know Tammy.'

Later, going to her room, she opened the door of Tammy's. It was a disgrace. She glanced over her shoulder, slid in, started picking things up, folding them, opened the cupboard, gazed a long time at the golden dress; searched in drawers, under the pillow, let herself breathe.

Another evening when the girl came bouncing in with a 'Hey what, Ranna?' she responded. 'What, Tammy?'

'Bet you don't know.' She danced off into the kitchen and came back with a mug.

Miranda breathed deeply and let herself say what she was thinking. 'You used to look horrible in the Devil Driver mask.' The girl was plumper now, her cheeks pink, her hair smooth, her figure forming.

She giggled and eyed the woman sideways. 'Wanna know?'

'Let me sit first.' She took her time. 'Go on.'

'Know Hark?'

'Have heard of him.'

'Know who he is?'

'A man who likes beetles,' her mind wandering years and years back to the yellow monster she and Elizabeth had watched, chewing up Trenchard's Field. 'Who said he's anyone?'

'Solana.' There was hint of smugness in her voice

'How does she know?'

'Know what? Haven't told you anything, have I?'

She paused, still loathing that monster. Then, 'Go on.'

'Dawn Prophet.'

'Don't talk nonsense.' Her voice rose. 'Gavin Claring?'

'That his name was it?'

'Yes.' Could have been a stage name, of course. 'Thought he'd died.' Ten years ago? Fifteen? Drivers had been talking in the overnights.

'Can't have.'

'Wouldn't be here. Not in this place.'

'Sol said so.'

'You got the wrong end of the stick.'

'Don't want to know, do you?'

Miranda looked away.

'True – no-one would want to pretend to be that man.'

'Don't look much.'

'Never did. It was the way he talked.' And his eyes. They hadn't changed.

'Why you listened to him? No sense, was there?'

'You were with us day we arrived. That first evening on the hillside, him showing us everything. Remember? You were listening just as much as I was. Couldn't help it.'

'Think so, do you?' She said and took herself off, cradling her mug.

*

While they stacked logs next morning Miranda checked the story with Doe, moulding backache into talk. 'Probably got the wrong end of the stick. Girl's got a gift for not listening.'

'Right this time.'

She straightened, holding a log in both hands. 'No business here.'

Doe started to roll another log towards the pile. 'Does what he's told. Good worker.' She looked up over her shoulder. 'When you've finished with that, take the other end of this, could you? Still loves to go off – to the hills to watch creatures.'

'Still takes photographs?'

'Sometimes. Gives a show sometimes.'

'Lovely,' Miranda kept her voice level.

'Can't stop himself talking of course. Born talking, never stopped – can sit – complete silence watching a spider – interested – but when he's excited – words in torrents – exhausting – but great – love him then.'

Miranda turned away. They'd moved all the biggest logs by now. Her face was heavy as they gathered the smaller pieces and placed them evenly so that the stack would be stable, bending and reaching up through an afternoon that turned increasingly weary.

As they took off their boots, Doe suddenly said, 'Don't condemn.' Then pulling on soft shoes. 'Knows now – damage he did.'

Miranda's lip curled. He'd been intoxicated then. With his own voice, his own power. Also intoxicating.

Some days later she was standing, looking across the table just before supper. Tammy was jiggling from one foot to the other. A request to stand still received a sideways glance. Miranda waited, forcing a smile, thinking. At last she came out with, 'Know what, Tammy?'

The jiggling was a little less.

'Hark must know about life.'

Tammy swung towards her, 'Crap.'

'He feels so bad about things he's done. And he knows that everyone here knows. Not easy, is it?' In spite of all her efforts a derisive edge slid into her voice.

'Knows they're soft.'

'None of us is an angel.' Specially not you, my lady. Specially not me.

Next monthly dinner Arv took her education in hand. 'How long is it you've been here? Three months, is it? Long enough to have grasped we don't go in for being starchy,' he began, capturing her gaze, 'but we feel a need to keep reminding ourselves.' He laid his hand palm down flat on the table and leant back. 'So easy to forget.'

'What?'

'Humans can't help being top predators.'

'Rather sweeping, isn't it?' For the first time she took in the lines that bit into the lean face of a quiet man.

'Our brains put us at the top of every food-chain.'

She shrugged – it was all too obvious and his eyes were boring into her head – nodded.

'That's why here we're not all vegetarians. A lot of us are of course – but many are not. They help us face facts. We have teeth and stomachs that allow us to digest meat. The majority of human beings like it. The Cave Men were hunters.'

She considered the knife lying beside her plate, stainless steel, perfectly adapted for its purpose.

'Just because we're civilised doesn't mean our underlying nature has changed. We need to remember that. So we're grateful to those of us who eat meat.' He glanced at her plate.

She smiled politely.

She got her chance with Hark at the end of the meal when he slid up beside her at the hatch. 'Have a good day?'

Her fingers tightened on the cup. 'Yes, thanks.' She began to move off, turned, stared into his face, 'When you were on TV did they paint out that mole?'

His eyes faltered. 'I'm afraid I let them.'

She couldn't stop. 'Did you admire the result?'

He paused then plunged. 'I think I may have.'

The thrill of the chase subsided. She took her tea to the library corner and found a quiet chair. When she'd finished drinking she began to pick books off the shelf beside her and sort them out for mending.

She'd noticed a tendency for most members of the community, if words such as 'community' or 'membership' could be applied to people who seemed so determined not to tie themselves down with labels, to drift through the Home Room some time in the evening. They might use it as a route to the labs, or to the 'tavern', or linger and exchange a few words with whoever happened to be there, settle to a board game, flop into a chair, talk softly or sit in the companionable silence that was part of life here.

She refused to smile when Tammy sidled up and plonked herself opposite.

It wasn't that she held hard feelings. The girl couldn't help being driven by devils – no – be fair – by life itself, all it had done to her. Still need to face facts – she'd stood by her long enough, covered up, not told Doe all she could have – far from it – that skill with knives – a girl who hated her so much she'd set fire to her bed; who now wouldn't leave her alone, sometimes came strolling up all airy as if she'd done nothing, sometimes slid alongside giving sly glances under her lashes or just came and stood near, obstinate and clinging; her presence so intrusive that in the mornings Miranda would stay in her room listening, only come out when the house was silent.

She picked a box off the top shelf and began examining it. When that wasn't enough, she turned and glared. 'Go away.' She opened the box and stared inside till the girl picked herself up and went.

She picked out the little machine, checked for a disc, adjusted the mike, pressed the playback button. A loud male voice. She switched off.

Weeks later there was a morning of blue light reflected off snow, which covered the tops but didn't yet reach down into the valley. Patches of bracken glowed reddish-brown, birches gleamed beside the burn. She and Doe sat on a sunny bench with their backs to a wall of watwill with paint-pots beside them.

'Emulsion – smells like honey.'

'Mmn, honeyish.'

They leant back in silence till Doe heaved herself onto her feet. 'Better get back.' She paused, half-straightened, twisting round. 'Some time – get me to tell you about gazing.'

About then Pete decided she should be full time on book mending so she spent hours alone in the Home Room. One morning she took down the box containing the recorder, took out the instrument, switched on. A voice she didn't recognise began to tell his story. For the next half-hour her fingers moved mechanically, cutting, smoothing, gluing while she took in how someone she'd never met – what had happened to him? Had he died? Was there somewhere she hadn't found – a graveyard? – took in how this man had struggled and suffered for the right to be here, how he'd loved living creatures, plants above all, how he'd brought vegetable seeds here and planted them, watched them grow, thought of ways to help them adapt to the wet and cold.

When he came to an end she switched off though it was clear there was space on the disc for more voices. She wanted time to think about this one.

The listening grew into a habit. She recognised some voices. There were a number she didn't. She'd stay on at the end of her work-stint sitting quietly, thinking. One day she hid the machine under her jerko and took it to her room – not that she needed to make a secret of it – no-one would have objected – more as if she wasn't letting her right hand know what her left was up to.

She'd been listening on the free afternoon when she wandered up to the Home Room and found nobody there. She began to pick up objects she'd not had time for and examine them, electronic book-stores, a print-out of an article on podsols, an array of devices for holding information, a pile of battered flat cardboard boxes pushed to the back of a cupboard. The top one contained a handful of wooden figures and a folded board, a bishop, a knight, a king, pieces familiar before the New Dawn, since then seen only on the screen. But to handle smooth objects with precise weights, place them in particular positions in real space where a pattern of shadow fell over them from sun that was actually slanting in, that now seemed something completely new and yet, at the same time, tremendously old. Who knew exactly what individuals had first taken each other on in mock battles and before them, who had first picked up pieces of bone or wood, arranged them in dents in the ground and started to move them in ways that would develop into a system of sophisticated rules and gambits?

'Want a game?' Doe stood beside her, gently gazing down.

Her full hips came between Miranda and the light. She moved her hands deprecatingly. 'Too tired, I think.' Not looking up.

Doe smiled. 'This place can be exhausting.' She swept a long skirt under her. 'Mind if I sit down?'

After a long silence she murmured, 'Everyone – needs their own time to settle – normally wouldn't rush. Bothered this time.'

It had to come. 'Is it Tammy?' Hasn't done anything more, has she?'

'No.' She let time pass, then, 'What exactly might she do? Very hard to get hold of, isn't she?'

She gazed at two regiments of shadowed chessmen, then back at Doe. 'She has problems.'

Doe's lips twitched. Miranda sat up. 'She's lovely,' – golden girl waving from the van step – 'really intelligent – quick to respond. And tough. Resourceful. I've been finding I can rely on her.' When that suited her agenda. Whatever that was. The more she thought about it, the less she knew. 'Nothing that's happened to her has been her fault. Don't imagine she's to blame. She didn't ask her Mum to dump her.'

Doe's face went soggy.

Miranda tried again. 'Can be violent.'

'Ed was guarded in what he said – but you may have noticed, we've never left her unsupervised.'

'Unspeakable I think what I suspect's happened to her.'

'All too likely. Meanwhile – you'll have to tell us, Miranda. We need to know.'

'Surely Ed told you?'

'Said a lot. Not everything.'

Miranda looked away, then back. 'Attacked a smaller kid. Had to pull her off.'

'Did she do much damage?'

'Fortunately not.' She curled back against the chair, studied her hands, raised her eyes. 'But she wanted to.'

'Any idea why?'

'Said the kid needed to learn.'

'Learn what? Just an excuse.'

Miranda studied he hands again, frowning. 'Wheera's mother – had visited and just left'

'And Tammy had no mother?'

'The child could have been crying – that's it, I think. Tammy told me when her mother upped she said, *Learn not to care.* So Tammy excused herself for taking it out on Wheera by saying it did her good – meaning – of course – she must learn not to care.'

They looked at the idea together. It had its points.

'That all?' Doe's eyes were searching.

Miranda's eyes widened, she still hesitated. Then, 'Keep knives away from her. She can be deadly accurate, I've seen her kill a small bird at several yards. And she's used one to get her own way. She attacked Ed – Ed of all people – and when she first came in on me – I thought she was a boy then but that's no excuse – so much smaller than me but I was scared, really terrified though I thought he was only ten years old but having seen what he could do with that knife – I let her keep me prisoner, just caved in – but – what else could I have done? On your own, aren't you? Have to be sensible?'

'You've survived.'

'There's – another fact – she's used one on herself.'

'We'll keep watch. Seems to have fallen under Hark's spell. Think – on the whole – that's OK? Don't you?'

Miranda shrugged. 'Even he'll have a hard time with her.'

She burst into laughter. 'What we all think. And she with him. Well – see – 'Her face fell serious, her gaze roved round the honeyed walls. Finally she spread her hands. 'Heavy stuff – not saying it doesn't matter – simply – don't let it become central – Tammy will find her way –' Her voice was becoming softer, diffident even.

Miranda leaned forward into the voice

Then Doe came out with it. 'I wonder if I could talk about gazing?'

'Later maybe?'

Doe turned her eyes onto the chessmen. 'So glad you got them out.' She picked one up, turned it over, rubbed it slowly. 'Your skills –' Her voice firmed up. 'If you don't take to planting or plumbing – set you to weaving or dyemaking – maybe knowledge gathering? You've some computer expertise. We'll see – your choice in the end –' She stood up abruptly. 'Going now.' The walls glowed softly in slanting sunlight. A faint scent that might or might not be honey had spread through the room. She flicked a few fingers and departed.

Miranda sat on in the quiet.

Some evenings later Tammy plonked herself opposite her again. Again she didn't look. Took refuge in the community silence.

She started scrolling through its contents of an e-book, was conscious of movement, observed Hark/Gavin lowering himself into a chair beside Tammy.

'Enjoy reading?' he asked, fixing her with his eyes.

Tammy looked him up and down, took a deep breath. 'It's OK.'

Miranda's mouth fell open.

'What books d'you like?'

Miranda jerked up. Her hand moved as if to touch Tammy, then stopped.

The girl inspected him again, interlocked and considered her fingers, looked up, glanced at her sideways and spoke with more than a hint of self-satisfaction. 'There was this one about rabbits.'

'About rabbits?'

Miranda considered Tammy's expression, smiled to herself.

'Had these burrows in a place they was going to build houses.'

'*Watership Down?*' he asked raising his eye-brows.

'Something like that, yeah – yeah, that's it.'

Miranda ignored Hark. 'How did you get it, Tammy?'

'My Mum left it.'

'Did she teach you to read?' This was the kid who'd carried a book by one page, flapping it about, demanding to know what it was?

'Course.' Head raised, slightly challenging look.

'An E-book? You read it a lot?'

'Don locked me in. Before I learnt how to get out. Yeah, used to like reading it.' She turned away from me addressing him. 'Friendly. Them rabbits was friendly.'

Hark glowed. 'How about next time Brindle and I go up to the ewes you come too and on the way down we'll stop and watch rabbits?'

She shrugged, 'Could do,' she said in a rising tone.

Miranda's gaze rested on her, moved to honey coloured walls and slowly back to Hark. 'Gavin –,' she watched him flinch, 'if it's OK, that is, if you don't mind, d'you think? Perhaps –'

'You want to know how I got here?' He tilted his head and eyed her through his lashes. 'Much rather tell you about my beetle.' A naughty smile lit his face.

She pinched her lips. 'You have to?'

'*Scaraboides harkensis*,' he said, tasting the words and, as a faint smile wobbled onto her face, 'Looks like a scarab –' He described its shape, head abdomen, elytra – 'wing-cases – sorry – used to specialist audience now. The jaws are made for tough work. You should see them – under the microscope, of course. And it digs. With the front pair of legs. The power in those limbs is quite extraordinary.' And of the eyes he was turning towards her. Without any possibility of doubt this was Gavin Claring,. 'No scarab does that. In its habits it's closer to the scorpion beetles. Lies in wait under a stone, when a centipede comes along, disables it with a swift bite, injects saliva, then – this is what makes it unique – uses leaves – tough ones like hazel and bramble – as neat wrappings round its prey, drags the parcel down the hole, stacks it, lays its eggs on top of the heap.'

'Why the parcel?'

'Still trying to work it out. Sealed with saliva – may be a preservative.'

'Oh,' she said, 'delightful.'

His gaze was level. 'That creature's life.'

She hardened hers. 'And yours?'

He, paused, smiled. 'You don't want the whole spiel? Just the part you're aware of?'

She shrugged.

'At the time you're thinking of, I meant every word.'. His voice had an unfamiliar seriousness.

Miranda held her face blank.

'I'd spent so much time watching, observing, knew so much, understood the needs of all these wonderful creatures, could see what we were doing to them – and I was young, very fervent. You're so fervent when you're young.'

Tammy jerked up, her mouth opened.

He got in first. 'Calm down as you get older – go dull – but then – All my life I'd spent as much time in the open as I possibly could. At first I just looked and tried t remember. Then I saw what I could do with a camera. That was the day that made me – caught a pair of woodpeckers one after another, head out, shoulders, wings flat against the body – heave, wriggle and out, one after another from the same hole. One seemed enough of a gift but when the second appeared – I was standing on the road only a few yards away and there they were, getting on with their lives. When I went home and saw what I'd got full screen – it was the birth of a passion.' He paused, inspecting his words. His mouth twisted. 'So I had to have my crusade. Of course, Tammy, you know who I was?'

'Dawn Prophet.'

'That is the name they gave me.'

Tammy wrinkled her nose. 'Never knew what it meant, not really,'

He jerked, staring. Miranda settled more comfortably.

'It means,' he said in an edgy voice, 'the New Dawn was my idea,' and then launching in, 'I conceived and planned it from start to finish.'

'The day of the great setting off must have given you quite a high.' Miranda smiled sweetly.

He gazed over her head. 'I must admit, it was wonderful. The fulfillment of my dreams and more. I'd bought a very modest van and that day of the launch-out I put on dark glasses and the kind of pollution mask people wore then and mixed with the crowds. Not a soul spotted who I was.'

She turned to Tammy. 'Ever heard of the Caliph of Baghdad? Great king who used to wander round the city at night in disguise. He'd be kind to people secretly – next morning reveal himself and everyone cheered.'

'Ranna – why you being like this?'

Miranda let acid flow out. 'That mole on your cheek –' she felt the weight of Tammy's eyes 'did they cover it up on telly?'

His eyes became heavy. 'They always do, you know. I told you before. But I let them, I admit it now, I let them.' He saw her watching. 'I deluded myself.'

'You – deluded us all.'

'Should have seen much earlier – soon as it was obvious the Dawn Servants hadn't weren't going to let themselves be uncomfortable, not the least little bit – and we had to fence off the countryside and I went to them and said we were going wrong and they laughed and said who did I think I was?'

Miranda smiled again.

'They'd access to all the media and I had none – they saw to that. And,' he said with a deep breath, 'I missed the wild creatures more than I'd ever imagined. I'd sit in my van and watch videos I'd made, tell myself this was how it had to be, it was a great thing, but the security screens started going up, everyone put on masks, became numbers, people became hard, no-one talked to anyone else –'

Tammy leant forward. 'No friends?'

'I'd always preferred wildlife.'

'The sparrows still investigated the van of course, rooks, starlings, crows, flies, creatures that have learnt to exploit humans – fleas – came across one or two of those – bedbug once. There was a robin but of course you're not allowed to stay to make friends.'

'Yeah,' she said, 'yeah.'

Miranda took him on. 'You sound very sorry for yourself. Didn't you ever think what you were doing to the rest of us? Have you no idea how we suffered, how millions out there are still suffering because of your cock-eyed ideas? You were lonely. What d'you think they are? Have you taken on board the crime, the violence the evil you've let loose? You silly little man –'

'Shut up, Ranna.'

'He caused so much misery – people are still out there going round and round day after day pounding along, locking themselves in, never seeing a plant –'

'Leave him go, Ranna.'

Miranda glared. 'He needs to hear exactly the truth. He set himself up as a great man, he had this vision and we all fell for it. We gave up everything because of him. Universes slid apart because of him. Because of him we can't ever go back. There are people we'll never see again. Not ever. We're stuck in this wilderness.'

'Didn't have to believe him.'

Miranda stood up. 'I don't want to hear any more of this' and left her gazing at him. She closed the door quietly but firmly behind her, headed for her lodgings.

Doe gave her a quick look. 'Tea?'

'Thanks.'

While Doe was busy Miranda looked round a room that never stopped amazing her. Oranges and pinks that at first sight had seemed startling – though not outrageous – they'd always somehow blended in – now showed themselves as glints in purple, deep plum red, a green just to the yellow side of moss, the pattern vaguely reminiscent of flowers but not so clear as to block the imagination. It felt rich – richness you could sink into and it would hold you. She held herself upright, careful.

The tables and chairs were obviously made on the spot, not crudely – they were beautifully jointed and polished but they weren't the kind of thing we'd had before the New Dawn. Then we'd never kept all these little mats lying about. Maybe here they didn't have the protective surfaces to apply.

She put the tea in Miranda's hand. Her fingers brushed the skin.

Miranda cradled the cup, thinking about the van. 'Doe,' she said, 'did you bring these curtains with you?'

Doe sank back against her cushions. Earlier that day she'd lifted a five-foot fence-post as easily as a man, lowered it into a hole, banged it in.

'Didn't you want that old life entirely behind you?'

'Maybe – never great hopes – not like – you seem to have had.'

'Surely –'

'This place – cold decision. Old universe headed for disaster – and – apologies to Hark – his idea a load of old codswallop. Be up against it – had to do it – not hatred for the old life – good things there – but for the joy – of being close to living things – exploring how to fit in with them. The choice was cold – because of the consequences – taken in warmth. That make sense?'

'The consequences ?'

'Rough time – they'd hoped we'd be trapped in the old universe – but our minds were free and we came across –

so what then? Enemies of the New Dawn, they said – instead of destroying our houses shut us in them – isolated among ruins – starve us till we agreed to go with them. We hung banners out of the windows – everyone in vans could see we weren't being allowed to leave – against the spirit of the time. Pete and his family were beaten up – locked into a quarry – won't go into that – very hard time. Gill and I got away with it – more or less. Managed to negotiate – promised never to import anything, live entirely off what we could make – special dispensation for lab supplies. Scurried round, collected up everything we could – their big mistake not destroying our houses – we'd stored away a lot of stuff – like Frag's paper and those rainproofs I gave you. Glad of them, weren't you? Vans get you out of touch – don't they?'

Miranda's lips fell into a huge smile.

'So Gill was?'

'My partner. Lot older.'

Miranda gazed round the room. Which of the things here had been hers?

'You said you'd tell me about gazing.'

Doe sank deeper into her cushions. Then she said, 'Gazing's –' Her voice slowed, '– something we all do here – no rules or rotas, no expectations – what you or anyone else might achieve – all have to be here, no choice – though came by different routes – all want to slot into the place – what love is, isn't it, slotting in?'

Miranda frowned. 'Lunch-break other day I saw these ants. Army of them. Ugly little creatures, hard black bodies sparkling, all dashing around – doing whatever it is those frantically conformist insects have given their lives to. To be honest, the afternoon seemed hard after that.'

Doe was silent. Then she laughed. 'Time off – allowed here.' She fell back into silence, considering her hands. Then she raised heavy lids. 'Our life here – not guaranteed to last – too special –' Her voice was full of sadness. 'Can only exist for a small group.' She looked at me straight. 'Face facts. But we might learn something – that would help. That we could bring – the world out there – at present – unreal.'

'Almost spooky, those drivers just shadows of themselves.' Suddenly, perhaps for the first time for years, as Miranda pressed her feet into the floor she felt them really on the ground. 'When I look back I feel I'd become a robot.'

'Small group – nothing but Dreamies,' Doe said quietly. 'Funny thing – we need them – to make us real. One day we'll come together.'

'You think?' Miranda said, frowning.

'Contact with universities – keeps us going. Use their computers. They share data with us. Knowledge goes forward.'

'Uhuhn.'

'U.S. Australia – so much space. Universities could migrate and set up. But glad of what we tell them – how to live at close quarters – equal but more responsible. Understand?'

'Sort of.'

'So – gazing. Something we all do, regularly, several times a week. Probably a good many every day – we don't ask – for many of us it's part of our work. All it is – stop, watch some small creature or plant – try to enter its life. Hark for instance,' Miranda tensed, 'will be going back to his beetle – getting to know more and more how it moves, where it lives, what it eats, what its enemies are, when it mates, where it leaves its eggs, what sounds it reacts to, how it learns about its environment, coming to respect it, discovering one way we'd never previously imagined of relating to this countryside. Answers to problems – like midge suits – techniques for coping with hard weather.'

When she got going she could be almost fluent. 'Hark makes notes. Specially interested in the way his insect digs.

Shape of its shoulders. Does it turn round or back out? Information may never be useful, just a way of coming close. Some people draw – we greatly prize drawings, show someone has watched and watched – others sit and look. Tong's music comes from listening.'

Her words seemed to float in the air. Apparently Gavin – Hark – whatever – wasn't the only one in this place who could carry you along.

'Makes sense.'

'So we're not isolated. Pioneers – in communicating without moving from the spot. Share anything new with thousands of scientists, engineers, writers, religious teachers – all studying how to live on this globe without damage – how to find fulfilment in getting the most use from one drop of oil – you might say. We also study how to remain in one place.' She smiled ruefully. 'A big topic – it it's to be of any use to millions – but perhaps, if we can learn to be fascinated by our immediate surroundings, they can too. Some of the urge to be continually dashing around will abate.'

Miranda sat staring, frowning, studying her hands.

Noah's ark, till the waters abated.

Doe started to push herself out of the chair. 'Great ideas, aren't they, all these? Life has to be lived – look as if you wouldn't mind a good night. Me too.'

She was on her feet now. 'Manual labour – tough at first. Get used. Most – come to like it.'

She cornered Gavin again a few days later in the sitting room. 'Didn't have time to hear all your story.' Opening her eyes wide, receiving a long, deep smile from a very ordinary little man – hardly taller than she was – whose only assets were melting eyes and a liquid tongue.

He eagerly offered, 'Tell you the place I came to?'

'What I was wondering.'

He swept blandly on. 'It was the Riddle-me-Ree. That construction was universally acknowledged to be the greatest achievement of the New Dawn. But one day I drew up underneath, saw all those soaring, twisting arms and saw, not beauty but insolence: *Look on my works ye mighty and despair.* Understand?'

She shrugged but her eyes had brightened.

'Yet it was beautiful, it was splendid, every line said, *Look how we defy nature*. It was full of cars screeching, drivers pitting themselves against gravity, asserting mastery.' His pause gave her the impression of someone looking at this concept, hearing his own words. 'I knew then that was the last thing I'd ever wanted. I'd longed to work with nature – not against it – and my efforts had come to this.' He dropped his voice. 'I'd seen the misery of the overnights, but this was when it came home to me – the damage I'd done. Brooded on it before – you do, don't you, alone in your van at night, hear things, know what's going on, can't do anything, Dawn Servants don't care. And for me, I had to ask myself who gave them their power? Who put them in that position? Can't go along knocking on van doors, *Sorry, sorry, never meant this*. Got to face up to it: this is what you did, all these people affected but you can't go back. You go over and over and it's useless; you see what a pathetic little creature you are.'

She chewed it over, watching him struggle with an apparently unaccustomed block in his fluency. His eyes swung full on her. 'Actually I was working out which of those fly-roads would do. Needed to work out whether it would be better to tip over near the sea or crash down from a height. Settled that and was counting which number turning I'd use.'

'Tip over? You mean – down among the fishes?' Tammy had arrived.

He glared, sat for a moment with his mouth open, pulled himself in. 'Close to my right ear it was, this rap on the window. And this shadow looking in. Free making a nuisance of himself, I thought. He rapped again. Didn't want to look. No choice. First sight of Ed. '

Now a full smile lit his face. 'No need to explain what he's like. Once his mind is made up you haven't a hope. Upshot was I was at his place for some time and then – no idea how – if they'd known who I was Dawn Servants would never have let me go – he got me here. Said I was some sort of maladjusted non-driver most likely. So I arrived all dazed and they took me in. Not easy at first but people here don't hold the past against you. They praise me, you know,' he said almost naively, 'because I've discovered a beetle.' He raised his head. 'You'll be all right.'

Miranda felt sick. 'Come on Tammy. We'll go back to Doe's.'

Naturally, the girl took no notice.

She struck out towards Doe's but when she reached it, instead of going in, followed the burn uphill. A few hundred yards from the settlement and she couldn't see her feet. After several months she was still amazed by the darkness. And that there was space inside it. Judas went out into the dark, the story said. As if that blackness was evil. This night poured itself round her, gave her room, hid her. Thanks to its friendship she could scream, weep, stamp, throw herself on the ground and no-one would know.

She strode out, partly guided by the sound of tumbling water, partly putting her feet down at random as fury directed.

Gradually the effort of climbing a rough path she could barely see brought her to a standstill. A small wind made her hug her arms round her chest.

She felt cheated. Surely her rage should have been enough to keep her warm. She began muttering, as if the movement of her lips would stimulate the circulation. Felt sorry, had he, for all those people? Sorry for himself more like. Sitting in the driver's seat indulging this fantasy of drowning, that great heroic moment when this kamikaze would turn the van's nose towards the crash barrier and go through? So meanwhile he sat. Till Ed turned up.

The burn went on tumbling past, something rustled in long grass, an owl cried that she'd wasted her life, and repeated the message, piercing and eerie. She hugged herself tighter, resolving to go back and deal with the sod who'd led a universe to disaster.

The owl cried again. Tawny, she thought, yes that's a tawny. They nested round Hayle. Still did. Hayle was still there. And all this moorland, all this windy expanse, peat hag fringed by sundew, hiding place for centipedes, ants – yes – Hark's beetle he was so pleased about – that everyone was so pleased about –

All round in the grass unknown thousands – millions – of mice, foxes, ants, worms, seeing, smelling, hearing her better than she could perceive any of them. They'd stop perhaps for a moment, track down where she was, what she was doing, then get back to work – searching, digging, feeding families, avoiding other creatures' teeth and claws, not caring about her. She was so unimportant at night in that place. And there were such huge numbers of them.

On that scale, how important was Gavin? She'd have liked to sit to think that out but the ground was too wet. She began to stumble down over the rough path, stopped to control her feet. No point in breaking an ankle for the sake of that little fake. Not exactly a fake, that wasn't fair – just a little man with one gift that made him fatal. But no match for the Dawns.

Going downhill she was facing west towards the Maldons. They were darker than the sky, which towards the south was faintly tinged with orange from the lights of overnights and motorways. She ran her eyes along the line of jagged peaks. She could name one or two now. She repeated them to herself. This place was becoming home.

*

When she got back to Doe's, Tammy was stretched at full length on the sitting-room sofa. She rolled over and sprawled at length, presenting her with eyes like boiled sweets.

Miranda inspected her, then asked, 'Whatever got into you, saying that about the fishes? Hark knew you were laughing at him.'

'Wasn't. Came to me, that's all.'

'But why? Something must have made it.'

'Remembered.'

She looked at her carefully. 'Remembered what?'

'Don. Took me there once. Said you were up in the clouds or down next the fishes.'

'Did you have a good day?'

'Liked to hear me screaming, Don did. I was small then.' She paused and smirked. 'Didn't scream when you went fast, did I?'

'Naturally. You were making me do it.'

'Was I?' She studied the ceiling, then she muttered. 'Said he loved me. His little girl. What he made me do.' Her eyes swung briefly towards the woman. 'I hate love.'

Miranda absorbed it slowly. 'You're right to hate what Don wanted.'

'Am I?'

'Absolutely no doubt about it.'

She sat up and started removing a sock. It was the pair with the green and blue stripes. She rolled it down very slowly over the ankle, eased it over the heel, pulled it off by the toes. When she'd finished she sat holding it.

Miranda watched, mesmerised. At last she said, 'You know, Tammy, it's usual to take one's socks off in the bedroom.'

'Is it?' she said dreamily and sat staring. After a while she said, 'Hark hate himself, you think?'

Miranda gazed at her back. 'Yes and no – probably.'

Suddenly she straightened. 'Upped, didn't I?'

'That's right. So – ?'

'Never thought of it before. I upped.'

'What did you think you were doing?'

'Running away, weren't I?'

'If you were running away you were right. You chose to go. You upped.'

She sat down, slowly took off the other shoe and sock, stretched her feet in front of her, admired them, rolled the socks together into a striped ball. 'Match those roll-shoes, ones with the wings.'

'The ones we bought together?'

'That's right.'

In her room later she took down Elizabeth's Homer and sat on the edge of her bed turning over the pages, not reading but thinking. The day they'd left the flat. The day they'd looked over it before they took it – 'Look, Elizabeth, the view from this window' – snap – and getting their armchairs up the stairs – 'For god's sake, Mira, stop laughing.' It was Elizabeth photographed that blockage, Miranda leaning against the wall, the chair arm resting on her chest before they discovered to turn the chair on its side – the photo a little blurred because even she couldn't control her laughter – Elizabeth in the passenger seat of the Fly, parked under the cedar at Hayle. First time she came there. 'It's lovely, Mira. You know, there are so many places I'd love to see.' They'd made lists – the Rockies, – Ayers Rock, Darwin, St Petersburg, Rio, the Gobi, the Great Wall, a coral reef, Timbuktu, wherever, the whole world – nowhere they didn't consider – if conditions allowed, if she began to get better.

Miranda stroked the pages, raised the book to her nose and smelt the faint, musty scent. Something rustled in the thatch, there was a sleepy squawk. Jackdaws. Which could be a pest, but could also be gazed at.

The next evening Doe and she watched live-clips for a couple of hours. Finally Doe switched off. 'Gather you had a chat with Hark.'

'Yeah.'

'Feel better now? Things off your chest?'

Miranda stared at a cushion, then raised her head. 'Fine.'

'Fine? What way?'

'No need to bother. Nothing to him, is there?'

'Tough chap, Hark.'

'Oh –'

Doe smiled. 'Some of us – Pete and Frag – gave him a hard time when he came here.'

'Quite right too.'

'Ed said – see if he means it – make sure. And they did.'

Miranda gazed again at a cushion where orange and pink streaks shone out among moss green and purple. 'Ed seems to be at the bottom of a lot of things.' Again she raised her eyes and sought Doe's. 'Those wildlife programmes of his – did you seem them? Absolutely riveting. Year I was doing Middle Baccalaureate. Never missed one. Broke off revising. Perhaps you did the same? Remember how you saw through his eyes, his voice told you how much he loved those creatures?' She hesitated. 'Seems silly – but – you know his lens seemed almost to – caress things – hair and feathers, beaks, muscles under the skin, fish eyes and insect eyes – showed how strange they are and then –' she was sitting up now, glowing, 'those extraordinary moments when some animal behaved out of character, like when, you know, this golden eagle tore a rabbit in pieces, then pushed lumps of raw meat gently, gently into the beaks of its nestlings.'

'I was at uni by then. Saw them, yes. Terrrific.'

Miranda sank back. 'You don't really sound all that thrilled.'

'Well –' Doe took refuge in staring at her hands. 'Well, ' she told them, 'unfortunately he had this gift – of inspiring his viewers with the same love.'

Miranda looked at her sharply. 'Unfortunately?'

'Gift of the gab – could happen to anyone.'

'Not everyone would get himself up as the Dawn Prophet. How come such an ordinary little man had got such an inflated idea of himself?' She paused. 'Or was he completely in the hands of producers?'

'Surprised him at first, perhaps – all those millions – listening to him – his words – able to hold them – began to think up more – ideas. Disciples – out there – panting to hear them.'

'You weren't one?'

'Came here – didn't I? Learnt something. Still learning. Fascinated by that beetle.'

'Learning to gaze?'

'Live alongside – yes.'

Miranda rested a moment, gazing back over the years into eyes gazing out of a screen. They had been true doorways. He hadn't been cynical, just listened to himself too much, becoming more and more convinced by the sound of his own voice.

'We felt that was our voice, saying things we couldn't find words for. We mouthed his utterances as if they were divine truths, stupidly hung on every scrap he uttered.' She frowned, wrestling, then looked up with a shine in her eyes. 'Perhaps in the end we created him, we became – sort of – a wave – that crashed into a new universe carrying him on its crest. And there, we were one heart beating out the rhythm of a new life.' She was silent a moment. Then stated her thoughts. 'It was all delusion and fell to pieces.' And, forcing herself further, ' As it had to.'

She lapsed back into silence, frowning, pushing her hands together. 'How much does he count in the community? Really?' Then, as Doe said nothing, 'People let him ramble on – seem amused as much as anything, seem to like him on the whole.'

Doe heaved herself to her feet. 'More to him than that. Try again. Bed now.'

She turned at the door, 'Really should talk to Sal, Miranda. Get it sorted.'

'Don't like thinking about that life.' The end of one lip curled slyly up.

Doe watched carefully. 'Find some way of keeping it at arm's length but do it.'

There was no reply.

Part 10

I love the way light's slanting in this morning, April sun with a glint of ice in it, softened by creamy walls, filling the rest of the room with shadow.

That's it now. First time I've heard that disc all way through, listened to myself talking about myself as if it was someone else – that young woman – girl really – when it all started she was so young – twenty-seven, I suppose, twenty-eight but young for her age and so fired up, so convinced, throwing her whole life into the project; so changed now, having turned her back on all she'd stood for. They say you change your whole skin every seven years. This requires more. It's not just skin, it's far deeper. How come – to become another person?

I've listened to those others on disc – Arv, Solana, Tilia. Frag was good – straightforward, honest – Pete OK too – not a trace of self-justification, no excuses, no sly puffing himself up. Hark wasn't on it. Another tape perhaps.

With him – always a feeling of professional penitent – as if he'd schooled himself. Even after one hearing I can tell mine's OK, clinical, clean. And severe, I hope.

It's likely I'll go on listening. Maybe I'll find myself changing details, but only because I see more, understand better.

No-one need know. It will stay private.

Meanwhile I'll indulge myself with something that's pure fiction, but enticing. A conversation that might happen yet. Though I shan't force it, will try not to dodge if it does come.

It'll be Doe.

Maybe Tammy'll have done something,

Doe will report 'Thrown a wobbly.'

I'll sigh, spread my hands, say feebly, 'Quite a time since she's done that.'

'Getting better.'

'Why we came here. Knew this place would do her good.'

'You too.' She'll look me through and through. 'You were glad to come here.'

Hope I don't shout, 'I gave up everything for her sake.'

Even then she might have the patience to continue, 'You've been unhappy a long time. You wanted to come.'

I hope I'll have the decency to look her full in the face, say, 'Yes, Doe. You're right.'

Apart from that which hasn't happened yet, there's yesterday evening. I'm going to record that it in my own voice. Open at last. Living through it again.

There'll still be that element of fiction. Even at this closeness – can't get exactly what anyone said.

Elizabeth would've loved those conversations I've come up with – and Gavin's broadcasts – as if I'd remembered every word, her eyebrows so delicately raised, lips pursed.

'One of your Ancient Greeks,' I'd say. 'You told me.'

'Oh?'

'Historian with no idea what anyone said on any particular occasion. Made up what seemed suitable.' Now I can remember what it felt like and looking back, can see better what was going on.

I'll switch on the machine again, press "Record", murmur this new memory that has a strange glow in it:

Late July, Saturday evening. Doe enters our room with creamy brown garments hanging over her arm.

'What are they?'

Doe shakes one out. It's folds fall with the elegance of a burka but it's clear it would stand away from the body more like a beekeeper's outfit. It's unlike either because the fabric's not net, but see-though in an uneven, wispy kind of way. 'Midge suit.'

'What's it made from?'

'Wool. It's a very thin felt bound with a special glue. The wispy ends make it difficult for our winged friends to get through.'

She sizes up Tammy. 'These will fit – don't necessarily have to have full length. Depends on your trousers – if they're firm and grip the ankles they'll do. Up to you. Can have them gathered into the waist – or with a drawstring round the hips.'

Her gaze swings to me. I stand there, feel her eyes roam across my body, smile back. Tonight we're going out onto the hillside to watch stars.

When she's invited, Tammy gives the habitual shrug but I think I detect a brief spark in her eyes.

Two hundred or so shrouded figures are standing about in the square when we get there, feeling most peculiar enveloped in these garments. I consider heights and bulks, ways of holding oneself. I can recognise people – Frag, Solana, nearly everyone, and when they come close I can make out faces through the meshes.

A light figure comes drifting across.

'Hiya, Hark.'

'We're going to major on Saturn,' he says. His smile is criss-crossed by wisps of wool. When someone's wearing a mask what you search for is the eyes. It's not like that with a midge suit. I found myself concentrating on his voice and when you do that, like with an audio tape, you hear things you normally miss.

He stands awkwardly lowering his head a little, turning sideways. 'Miranda –' he says.

'Yes, Hark?'

'You were right to be angry.'

I pause. 'Maybe.'

He doesn't seem to notice my hesitation. 'I was too full of myself. I've known that for a long time.'

What I want is there in his voice. Did I miss it before? 'You said what we wanted to hear – and perhaps, Hark, d'you think, possibly, that was an experiment we had to make?'

'Some people are still making it. And dreadful lives they've got. I keep thinking.'

'Doe thinks in the end, when we've learnt enough, both lots will move on into another universe.'

His voice warms. 'It's a wonderful thought.'

We stand quietly side-by-side, then I say, 'What's this then about Saturn?'

'Good time of year. Not often so clearly visible from here.' He focuses on Tammy and I don't mind. 'Know about Saturn?'

She doesn't reply.

'Or Mars, Venus?'

'Them? Planets of course. Where aliens come from.'

He chuckles.

'Stories, you think,' she growls. 'I've seen them.'

'Where?' He sounds genuinely curious.

'Spook bins.' She scrabbles the point of her shoe on the ground, turns fully towards him. 'And on my own, you know, outside, night, dark, I'd look up. All those sparks up there – what was they? Really?'

Is she perhaps catching some fluency from him?

'Stars,' he says, 'and planets. This earth is a planet.'

'We're not aliens.'

'No. We belong here.'

We all begin to drift uphill towards the knoll where a telescope has been angled towards the right part of the sky. The three of us climb together with him still talking, explaining about other suns and their satellites.

He says, 'The Greeks called them planets because in their language planet meant wanderer…'

My mind runs back to Ed, how I argued with him in those early days when the overnights opened onto the wild, how I met him later, settled; and now I think what a long way I've come since then, remember that Doe said even this place was somewhere to move on from.

I turn to him. 'You remember, Hark, you said humans were all nomads?'

He laughs.

'Planets wander then?' With a swish of her midge-suit Tammy comes closer.

He laughs again. 'An illusion. If you think our earth's the centre that's what it looks like.'

'Our earth wanders too?'

'Perhaps it would look like that from somewhere out there.'

'Drivers – people – wander?'

'I like that,' he says raising his arms as if to place them on her shoulders, dropping them. 'All of us, creatures of our planet.'

Now we're all settling down and Pete's taken his stand beside the telescope. He begins talking and pointing. I see Tammy leaning back on both arms, hands flat behind her on the grass, head tilted back, gazing.

Life, which took Elizabeth away, seems to have landed me with something uncommonly like a daughter.

And Doe – Doe?